THE BABY THE BILLIONAIRE DEMANDS

JENNIE LUCAS

To my wonderful editor, Nicola Caws.
I never could have written this trilogy without you.

USA TODAY bestselling author **Jennie Lucas**'s parents owned a bookstore, so she grew up surrounded by books, dreaming about faraway lands. A fourth-generation Westerner, she went East at sixteen to boarding school on a scholarship, wandered the world, got married, then finally worked her way through college before happily returning to her hometown. A 2010 RITA® Award finalist and 2005 Golden Heart® Award winner, she lives in Idaho with her husband and children.

Tara Pammi can't remember a moment when she wasn't lost in a book—especially a romance, which was much more exciting than a mathematics textbook at school. Years later, Tara's wild imagination and love for the written word revealed what she really wanted to do. Now she pairs alpha males who think they know everything with strong women who knock that theory *and* them off their feet!

THE BABY THE BILLIONAIRE DEMANDS

JENNIE LUCAS

SICILIAN'S BRIDE FOR A PRICE

TARA PAMMI

MILLS & BOON

First Published in Great Britain 2018
by Mills & Boon, an imprint of HarperCollins*Publishers*
1 London Bridge Street, London, SE1 9GF

The Baby the Billionaire Demands © 2018 by Jennie Lucas

Sicilian's Bride For a Price © 2018 by Tara Pammi

ISBN: 978-0-263-93556-1

MIX
Paper from
responsible sources
FSC® C007454

This book is produced from independently certified FSC™ paper
to ensure responsible forest management.
For more information visit www.harpercollins.co.uk/green.

Printed and bound in Spain
by CPI, Barcelona

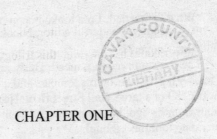

CHAPTER ONE

MONEY MEANT EVERYTHING to Lola Price.

Money was the difference between happiness and grief. Between joy and tragedy. She'd learned it at five years old, and every day since.

Growing up in a trailer on the edge of the California desert, in a dusty town where jobs were scarce, she'd seen her mother's daily struggles to pay the bills after Lola's father died. Her mother eventually remarried, but it only made things worse.

By the time she was eighteen, Lola had learned that there was only one way to protect the people you loved. One way to keep them safe and close—and alive.

You had to be rich.

So she'd dropped out of high school and moved to Los Angeles. Desperate to save what was left of her family—and without any talent or even a high school diploma—she'd hoped to instantly become a movie star, but her acting career never got off the ground. Without money, she'd lost everything.

Now she had a four-month-old son. And nearly a million dollars. Lola took a deep breath. No one would ever take her family from her again.

Sergei Morozov's booming voice brought her back to the charity ball, where he'd been swaying with her on the dance floor. "Can I kiss you, *Lolitchka*?"

"What?" Startled, Lola looked up at him. "Kiss me?"

"Yes. When?"

"Um…never?"

The Russian tycoon winced. Burly and in his mid-fifties, with gray hair on his temples and a strong accent, he was CEO of a large Wall Street firm. He'd also been, until four months ago, her employer. "When you agreed to be my date tonight, I thought…"

"I'm sorry. I don't feel that way about you." Around them, couples danced in the gilded hotel ballroom to the orchestra's elegant music. The children's charity ball was the social occasion of November in New York. She was just surprised her two best friends, Hallie and Tess, both newly married to billionaires, weren't here. They loved fancy events like this.

But Lola didn't see them. As she danced with her former boss—keeping an old-fashioned, almost Victorian distance between them—she saw dark-haired men everywhere in sleek, sophisticated tuxedos who reminded her of another previous boss, Rodrigo Cabrera. The Spanish media tycoon who'd coldly given her a million-dollar check, then tossed her out of his beach house, secretly pregnant and brokenhearted.

Sergei cleared his throat. "If you just need a little more time…"

"That's not it." She looked down at the marble ballroom floor. She never should have agreed to a date, she thought. She'd been swayed by her neighbor, a widow who occasionally babysat her son, who'd told Lola she 'needed to get out and live.' That, plus the weddings of Lola's two best friends in rapid succession, had made her feel her own loneliness. When Sergei Morozov had invited her out, she'd convinced herself it might be a healthy step forward, after a hard, lonely year.

Now she wished she'd just stayed at home.

"Some man broke your heart," he growled. "He abandoned you and your son."

Lola looked up in astonishment. She'd never spoken about Rodrigo to anyone, not even her best friends. "I never said he abandoned me—"

"You had pregnancy alone. Had birth alone. No man." His big hands tightened against her back. "Forget the idea of a date. Maybe I just marry you, eh?"

She sucked in her breath. "Marry?"

The burly man looked down at her. "I have wanted you for a long time, Lola," he said softly. "If marriage is your price, I am willing to pay."

Lola stared up at him in shock.

Marry him?

Her stomach looped like a roller-coaster.

Sergei Morozov wasn't a bad man. She'd worked as his secretary throughout her pregnancy. He was rich, arrogant, but not cruel. When she was eighteen, she would have jumped at the chance to marry a man like that.

Too bad for him that Lola was now twenty-five, with a pocketful of money and a scarred, bitter heart.

"I'm flattered, truly," she said awkwardly, "but—"

"Marry me, *zvezda moya*. I will cover you with jewels. I will—"

"I'd like to cut in."

Lola's heart dropped as she heard another man's voice, low and dangerous behind her. A voice she knew, though she hadn't heard it in over a year. A voice she'd never forget.

Slowly, she turned.

Rodrigo Cabrera stood beside her on the dance floor, wearing a sleek tuxedo over his muscular, powerful body.

Dark-haired, dark-eyed, with chiseled cheekbones and a five o'clock shadow along the hard, sharp edge of his jaw, he was even more handsome than she remembered.

Power, dark and dangerous and sexy, echoed off him like shock waves.

"Rodrigo?" she breathed.

"Lola." His cruel, sensual lips curved as he looked down at her. "It's been a long time."

Unwilling images went through her of the days and nights of their brief affair. The pleasure. The joy. The laughter. The certainty in Lola that for the first time since she could remember, she was no longer alone...

Now, pain twisted through her, pain she was careful not to reveal on her face. "What are you doing here?"

"Cutting in." He moved between her and Sergei with almost feline grace. He glanced at the Russian tycoon with casual amusement. "If you don't mind."

Sergei scowled. "Of course I mind—"

"It's all right, Sergei." Lola put her hand unsteadily on his arm. "I'll see you shortly."

Sergei set his jaw. "Once the dance is done, I'll be back."

Rodrigo's eyes flicked to her. "As the lady pleases."

After Sergei's grudging departure, the two of them looked at each other.

"So you're living in New York now," Rodrigo said coldly. "Are you here on business?"

He bared his teeth into a smile. "Is there any other reason?"

In spite of everything, Lola's heart was in her throat as she looked up at him. All the other people in the ballroom, all the laughter and music, faded away.

Slowly, Rodrigo pulled her into his arms. She breathed in his scent, of woodsy musk and soap and something uniquely him. She tried to tell herself she felt nothing, but her knees trembled, and she was glad he was supporting her in the dance.

He glanced back at Sergei, now glowering at them from the edge of the dance floor. "So he wants to marry you."

"Not everyone hates marriage like you do," she said unwillingly.

His lips quirked. "Another millionaire falls at your feet."

"Not everyone hates *me* like you do."

"I don't hate you, Lola." His voice was low.

She tilted her head back to look at him beneath her lashes. "You don't?"

"I despise you. That's different." His dark eyes gleamed. "You must have spent the million dollars I gave you if you're looking for a new sugar daddy. Do you intend to say yes? Are congratulations in order?"

Lola narrowed her eyes. She wondered what Rodrigo would say if he knew the real reason she'd taken his payoff money: because she'd found out she was pregnant.

Money meant more to her than pride. It meant safety. Her baby must never know, as Lola once had, how it felt to go hungry. He must never see his mother cry when she couldn't pay the bills, or be mocked for wearing clothes to school that were too small, or harassed by teachers for falling asleep in class, because he'd spent another night taking care of younger siblings when his mother had the night shift.

And most of all: Jett must never know how it felt to lose his family.

Taking Rodrigo's money meant no one would be able to take her baby away from her.

No one, that was, except Rodrigo.

She swallowed, her hands tightening on the shoulders of his tuxedo jacket as they danced. A father had rights. And although she still had most of the million dollars that he'd given her, she knew he had billions more. Enough to take whatever he wanted. Even Jett. And that made her afraid.

Because she'd been his secretary once. For over two years before they'd become lovers. She knew how ruthless the Spanish media mogul could be. How he could turn on people savagely if they failed him.

Rodrigo had good reason to believe the worst of her. Why wouldn't he, after what he'd learned about her past?

But he was in New York on business. He often came here. He even owned a house in SoHo. But they traveled in different circles now. He couldn't know about Jett.

If he did…

No. He must never know.

Rodrigo's expression hardened. "Well? Do you intend to marry him?"

"I haven't decided," she mumbled.

His arms tightened around her waist. "Is that a lie?"

Lola had no intention of going on another date with Sergei, let alone marrying him. But she wasn't going to tell him that. She looked up. "Why do you care?"

His dark eyes glinted. "I don't. I'm just wondering if I should warn him about the kind of woman you really are."

She stiffened. "What kind is that?"

"You're very beautiful, Lola." Rodrigo's hot gaze traced slowly over her modest, long-sleeved black knit dress. As they danced to the music, he cupped her cheek. *"Very."*

Electricity ripped through her body from where he'd touched her. Sparks raced down her spine, shouting, *Yes, yes*. This was her man, and she'd missed him, oh, how she'd missed him. She'd dreamed of him unwillingly every night from the moment he'd taken her virginity and made her feel—

Rodrigo dropped his hand. "But you're ugly on the inside. You'll do anything for money. Anything? *Anyone.*"

His cruel words were like a blow.

With a deep breath, she cut off the connection between her heart and her brain. She didn't care if he insulted her, she told herself. She just had to get through this song. Then he'd leave. And she'd make sure she never saw Rodrigo Cabrera again, or put Jett at risk of being taken from her.

Lola tilted her head, looking at him sardonically. "Ah. There's your famous charm. If you think I'm so horrible, why don't you go dance with someone else?"

"Why? Are you so eager to be back in your lover's arms?"

As if she'd ever let Sergei caress her! As the song finally drew to a close, she stopped dancing, nearly trembling with relief. "Okay, song's over. Not that this wasn't fun, but— well, it wasn't. Go find some other woman to torture."

Rodrigo stopped, looking down at her on the dance floor.

"And that's all you have to say to me?" he said softly. "After a year?"

Their eyes locked, and for a moment, in spite of her over-whelming fear, the truth rose guiltily to her throat. Once, they'd been so close; once, she'd told him everything.

No. She hadn't told him everything. And that had been what had destroyed them.

A hulking shadow appeared beside her. "Song is over," Sergei said sullenly. "I'm taking her back."

Lola looked at the Russian with gratitude, then glanced one last time at the Spaniard she'd once loved with all her heart. "I guess this is goodbye."

"I guess so," Rodrigo said, his dark eyes unreadable. He turned away.

The orchestra started a new song, and couples resumed swirling around them on the dance floor. Lola turned to Sergei. "I'm tired," she choked out. "Will you please take me home?"

"Konyechna." Sergei's voice was soothing. "I'm sure you miss your baby."

Lola sucked in her breath, praying Rodrigo hadn't heard. No such luck. As if in slow motion, he turned back to her.

"Baby?"

"Nothing to do with you." But her voice was strained, even to her own ears. She had to get out of here—fast. Tossing her blond hair as if she didn't have a care in the world, she turned back to Sergei. "Let's go…"

But Rodrigo blocked her path. "How old is the baby?"

"None of your business."

As she tried to walk past him, Rodrigo grabbed her wrist. His black eyes glittered. "How old, damn you?"

"It doesn't matter!" She struggled, desperately trying to hide her fear. "He's not yours!"

But as Lola croaked out the lie, her cheeks went red-hot. There was a reason she'd been such a washout as an actress. She was the worst liar in the world.

Searching her gaze, Rodrigo's eyes suddenly widened. Dropping her wrist, he staggered back.

He knew. She hadn't told him, but he still knew.

The ballroom started spinning around her. She tried to think of some way to get out of this. But her brain was frozen.

"The baby's mine," Rodrigo said in a low voice. "Isn't it?"

"Don't be ridiculous," she snapped. She pointed at Sergei. "He's the father."

She desperately hoped the Russian tycoon would play along. But Sergei just looked bewildered.

Rodrigo swept him with a dismissive glance, then faced Lola. His cold expression turned to fire as his dark eyes glittered in the light of the ballroom.

"Tell me the truth," he said in a low, dangerous voice. He gripped her shoulder. "I want to hear you say it."

"Let me go," she whispered, her throat closing.

All her fears were crashing around her like bricks. Lola tried to lift her chin, to glare at him, to defy him. Most of all, she tried to think of a good lie.

But looking up at Rodrigo's hard, handsome face, she

knew it would be no good. When it came to him, her lies always betrayed her.

"Tell me, Lola," he demanded mercilessly.

Heart pounding, she whispered, "Yes. You're the father."

A baby.

Rodrigo staggered back.

She'd had his baby.

The shock of that idea swirled in his brain, leaving him staring down at Lola in confusion.

From the moment Rodrigo had arrived tonight at the charity ball, coming alone as he couldn't be bothered to choose a date, he'd been the center of attention on the red carpet, not just from paparazzi, but from the other guests. As a wealthy, powerful billionaire, he could build anyone's movie career instantly across his entertainment empire. Rodrigo was eagerly greeted by famous actors and directors and beautiful women who all wanted a piece of him.

He barely paid attention. He was used to it; bored by it. He didn't fool himself that these women were after anything but his body, his money or his power. They weren't interested in him personally.

As a younger man, he'd relished the notice he received from beautiful women. But he'd been desperate then to find love, to get married, to have a home. How else to explain why he'd proposed to three different women in his younger years?

Remembering that disgusted him now. Humiliated him.

Love was for the naive. Only fools believed in a communion of souls. Men, as a rule, weren't supposed to yearn for such things.

But he once had. Stupidly.

Rodrigo was monogamous by nature. That was his darkest secret. He'd been the only child of wealthy, neglectful parents. Growing up, he'd dreamed of having a loving family and home. Even after he'd first taken over his father's small film studio in Madrid, he'd wanted some version of the fairy tales he manufactured for a living.

Ridiculous to think of it now. Because he'd swiftly learned his lesson. All three fiancées had cheated on him before the wedding date.

He'd never proposed to Lola Price, of course. He'd never even let himself love her during their brief affair. He was no longer that stupid, or that young, to believe in dreams of love and forever.

But he'd known her. Trusted her. She'd been his assistant for years before she'd been his lover. Working together, day in and day out, he'd been impressed by her determination, intelligence and drive. He'd respected her. Admired her.

But he hadn't touched her, in spite of her incredible beauty. He'd valued her far too much as his assistant to wreck everything for a brief affair, which was all it could surely be.

Until, one night in Mexico City, after they'd closed a deal, they'd celebrated with too much tequila at a famous restaurant. Then Lola had suddenly leaned over the table and kissed him.

It had been a revelation. An explosion.

They'd had a few incredible months, working together by day, making love by night. It had been—perfect.

Then Rodrigo had learned who Lola really was, deep down. What she'd done when she was eighteen. And that she'd been playing him all along. She'd claimed to love him. But all she'd ever wanted was his money.

He'd been stupidly blind. That was what hurt his pride the most. He'd let himself believe she actually cared. He would never forgive her for that. Or himself…

For the last year, he'd avoided thinking about her. He'd tried to forget. He'd told himself that he had.

Then he'd seen her on the dance floor tonight, in the arms of another man.

Lola.

She'd looked even more dazzling than he remembered, her hazel eyes huge in her beautiful face, her hips swaying in a slinky dress that fit her slender, curvaceous body like a glove. For a moment, when he first saw her, Rodrigo's heart had twisted.

Then he'd remembered how she'd deceived him, and taken the million-dollar check he'd thrown in her face in his fury. Cold rage had filled every space in his heart, leaving no room for any other emotion.

Lola Price had no shame. She was a liar, a deceitful gold digger. But he'd never imagined that even she could try something like hiding a pregnancy. Stealing his child away.

Rodrigo's arms tightened as he looked down at her.

She'd lost the tan she'd had in California. Her skin was pale, and she was dressed in head-to-toe black, like a true New Yorker. The knit dress had long sleeves, a high neckline and a hem to the floor. The only skin showing was her face and her hands.

It shouldn't have been sexy, but it was.

Everywhere he looked, Rodrigo saw something to tempt him, from the shocking beauty of her perfect face, with her high cheekbones, changeable hazel eyes and bee-stung lips, to her long, elegant throat. Even her hands drew him, with their graceful tapering fingers.

As his assistant, Lola had always been well-groomed and professional, as befitted the powerful executive assistant of an entertainment mogul. Now, he saw her beauty and wondered if she was trying to lure the burly, gray-haired Russian scowling beside her. Who was he? Her lover? Her soon-to-be husband?

The thought made him sick.

As the CEO of Cabrera Media Group, an international

entertainment conglomerate, Rodrigo was surrounded by beautiful women on a regular basis. His companies produced films and TV series around the world. He owned studios and networks and was about to launch a new streaming media company in South America. He should have been immune to Lola Price's charms.

But he wasn't. He still wanted her. Now more than ever. Maybe that was why, for the last year, he hadn't been able to touch another woman.

After a year of hot, frustrated need, no wonder his whole body felt the effect of being close to Lola now. Even as he learned of her latest betrayal.

Damn her.

"You were pregnant when you left California," he said in a low, dangerous voice. "And you never told me."

The sparkling lights of the chandeliers, soaring high above in the hotel ballroom, seemed to leave shadows across her beautiful face as couples continued to move around them on the dance floor.

Only the three of them did not move. The burly Russian turned to Lola in shock. "This is your baby's father? This man?"

She looked pale. "I think you should go, Sergei."

The man glanced uncomfortably toward Rodrigo. "If you would like me to stay, *Lolitchka*, if you need help—"

"No, thank you," she whispered. "It's better I do this alone."

"You heard what she said," Rodrigo bit out. "Get the hell away from her."

The older man's eyes narrowed, but he just turned to kiss Lola's cheek. "If you need me, I am always here."

The grateful look she threw Sergei made Rodrigo suddenly want to bash his face in. His hands tightened into fists at his sides until the other man left.

Taking Lola's hand, Rodrigo grimly pulled her away

from the crowds. He tried not to notice how soft her palm felt against his. He tried not to feel the electricity that pulsed through his body at that innocent touch.

In a darkened, empty corner of the ballroom, he turned to face her accusingly. "How could you not tell me?"

Lola wouldn't meet his eyes. "Because I don't need anything from you. I don't want anything."

I want you, Rodrigo. The memory went through him of the trembling ecstasy of her voice, long ago. *And I... I love you.*

As he looked down at her beautiful face, shadowed by the chandelier's light, he felt a rush of unwilling emotion as he remembered when she'd first spoken those words.

Two months into their affair, after closing a big business deal in Los Angeles, they'd returned to his beach house in triumph. Drinking wine, they'd lingered at midnight alone on his private beach, around a small bonfire he'd built from driftwood as the moonlight floated down. He could still smell the salt of the sea and vanilla fragrance of her hair as the hot Santa Ana winds blew against their overheated skin. He could hear the crackling of the fire and the roar of the waves when Lola had told him, her voice breathless and trembling, that she loved him.

For an answer, he'd kissed her, drawing her down against the soft blanket on the sand. In that moment, he'd been half out of his mind. In that moment, he'd almost wanted to love her back—

But Rodrigo didn't want to think of that, or the intensity of the grief and betrayal he'd felt a month later, when he'd learned the truth about her past from Marnie, his longest-serving, most loyal employee.

Sir, Marnie had said sadly. *Sir, there's something you should know about Lola Price—*

New anger went through him, pouring over his grief

and regret. But even that could not block out his biggest emotion.

Desire.

Even now, with his heart pounding with rage, he wanted her. His hands shook with the effort of not grabbing her and wrenching her into his arms for a kiss. His blood was boiling with the need to take her. To push her against the wall—to kiss her—to make her want him as badly as he wanted her, and make her regret—

Taking a deep breath, Rodrigo narrowed his eyes. "How could you keep my child secret? I never thought even you could sink so low."

Lola's cheeks turned white, then red. "I was going to tell you I was pregnant the night you threw me out. But you stopped me—remember?"

Rodrigo did remember that awful night, how she'd shown up at his beach house with joy in her eyes.

I have something to tell you—

Me first, he'd said flatly. *I saw the pictures. I know what you did.* He'd looked over her scornfully. *I know who you are.*

Lola's beautiful face had fallen, her expression suddenly tortured and guilty. Uncharacteristically for her, she hadn't tried to argue or fight. She'd just accepted his accusations with slumped shoulders. Until, finally, trying to get a re-action out of her, he'd written out the million-dollar check and tossed it in her face.

That's what you've wanted, isn't it? You were tired of being my assistant and hoped to upgrade your position to be my mistress or, better yet, wife! If money is what you want, here—take it!

Rodrigo had waited, heart pounding, for her to explain. He'd waited for her to throw the check back in his face. He could have forgiven her past. No one was perfect. Certainly he was not. What he couldn't forgive was her deliberately playing him for a fool, convincing him that she loved him, when all along she'd only had her eye on his wallet.

With a bowed head, she'd looked down at the million-dollar check. Then she'd crushed it in her hand, and left the beach house without a word. And he'd known his worst fears about her were true.

"You lied to me," Rodrigo said coldly now. "You moved three thousand miles away to keep your pregnancy a secret."

"You clearly didn't care about me." Her hazel eyes glittered. "So why would I think you'd care about our child?"

"It wasn't for the baby's sake. You did it to punish me."

Lola lifted her chin. The cold rage in her expression matched his own.

"You fired me. Tossed me out of your house. Told me you never wanted to see me again. You called me names and threw a check in my face. Why would I ever tell you I was pregnant?"

"So you stole my child away from me. Like a thief in the night."

She lifted her eyes furiously. "You made it clear you hated me. Why would I want to give you rights over my baby?"

Rodrigo refused to concede her the slightest bit of sympathy. Lola was a greedy, coldhearted gold digger. Hadn't she proved that, when she'd taken the check?

But she'd taken the check to provide for their child.

Suddenly, he sucked in his breath.

She'd known she was pregnant when she left. If she'd really been a gold digger, she wouldn't have simply taken his money and disappeared from California. No.

She would have told him about the pregnancy immediately, knowing that, as mother to Rodrigo's only child, she could have gotten far, far more than a mere million dollars.

But she hadn't.

Had he been…wrong about her?

He pushed down the emotion rising in his heart. No. He couldn't believe that. He clenched his jaw.

"So you moved to New York and replaced me with another rich man."

Lola shook her head. "Sergei was just my boss. I worked for him during my pregnancy, until the baby was born."

He frowned. "You worked?"

"As his secretary."

He wasn't surprised Lola had easily found a new job. She'd been a stellar assistant, and after their breakup, when he'd fired her, he'd still directed his HR staff to give her the glowing reference her work deserved. But, he didn't understand. "Why would you work? You had my check."

She lifted her chin. "I've kept that money in reserve to provide for the baby. I got us a nice apartment, and have stayed home since he was born, to take care of him. And—" she mumbled, looking away "—I studied for my GED."

Rodrigo stared at her in shock. "Your what?"

Lola looked at him. "It means General Equivalency Diploma—"

"I know what it means," he snapped at her. "But why would you need one?"

"Employers expect at least a high school diploma these days, if not a college degree. I was tired of feeling bad about it. So I studied for the test." She bit her lip. "I took it last week. I haven't heard yet if I passed."

"You're worrying about your résumé?" Jealousy pulsed through him, unwelcome and unreasonable. "That Russian was offering to marry you and cover you with diamonds."

Lola's lips lifted bitterly. "I loved one rich man, once." Her voice was acid. "That experience was enough for a lifetime. My son and I are better off alone."

Rodrigo's world was spinning. "Son? What's his name?"

"Jett. Jett Price."

He blinked. "You called him what?"

"What's wrong with it?" she said defensively.

"It sounds like something that might get mentioned in a stock report from Boeing or Airbus. Jet price?"

"No one will think of it that way!"

"His surname should be Cabrera."

She lifted her chin defiantly. "He's fine as he is."

"I want a paternity test. And then—"

"Then what?"

"Then we'll see," he said softly.

Lola looked at him for a long moment. Most of the people in his world feared him, and with good reason. He'd built his media empire by being ruthless and unpredictable. Looking down at her, he half expected to see fear. He should have known better.

"We're better off without you." Her eyes were defiant. "I won't let you take my child from me, Rodrigo."

"And you think you can fight me?" he said softly. "You know what I'm capable of."

"Yes." Lola lifted her chin. "And you know me."

"What does that mean?"

"If you try to take my son from me, you'll regret it."

He looked at her incredulously. "You're threatening me?"

She lifted an eyebrow. "It's a promise."

"And how would you fight me?"

"I've made some powerful friends."

Her eyes were cold. Rodrigo thought of her date. Sergei was obviously wealthy, and he'd proposed marriage. Was that the powerful friend she meant?

She'd said she was his secretary. That she'd refused his proposal. But for all he knew, they were lovers. The image came to him of her naked in the man's arms. The thought made him sick.

Rodrigo had been Lola's first lover. Of that, there could be no doubt. When they'd first made love, and he'd discovered her virginity, he'd been shocked, exhilarated, intoxicated with pride. Lola, so beautiful and desirable, had somehow still been a virgin at twenty-four.

But she might well have taken lovers since then. Any man would want her. While Rodrigo had been celibate as a monk.

"You and that Russian," he said with deliberate carelessness, "you are lovers, of course."

Her lips twisted. "I've never even let him kiss me."

He stared at her. No. It couldn't be true. Blinking hard, Rodrigo regained his reason. All the time she'd worked for him, he'd thought she was a terrible liar. But he must have been mistaken. Of course she was sleeping with the other man. Why else would he propose? What a little actress she was. Really, he should hire her for his next prestige film. "Liar."

"I'm not," she bit out, her eyes flashing. "I've only kissed one person in my whole life—"

She cut off her words, but it was too late. He stared at her, his heart twisting violently in his chest.

"You've never kissed another man? Even now?" He came closer. "Even after all this time?"

She looked up at him, her eyes shooting sparks. "I loved you, Rodrigo. Do you even know what that means? No. You don't. How could you, when you felt nothing?"

A razorblade lifted to his throat. He tried to keep his grip on reason. He ground out his words. "Why would the man propose, if he's never even slept with you?"

Her hazel eyes were luminous in the shadows of the ballroom. "Because he thinks it's the only way he can have me."

For a moment, Rodrigo couldn't breathe. Suddenly, it was as if a veil had been lifted from his eyes. He'd been right all those years he'd thought she wasn't a good liar. She wasn't. He could always tell on those rare occasions when she tried to lie. Her voice got strangled, her face turned red. He knew when she was speaking the truth.

And he could hear the truth in her voice when she said she'd loved him.

Had he been wrong about her all this time?

He wasn't wrong about one thing, at least, he told himself fiercely. He wasn't wrong about her stealing his child away.

"I want to see the baby," he said tightly.

"Now?"

"Now."

"Fine," Lola said coldly. "I'll get my coat. You can meet him. But that's it."

As he followed her out of the hotel ballroom, Rodrigo's gaze slowly traced down her body. Her generous breasts were even fuller than he remembered, emphasizing her hourglass curves, her tiny waist and perfect hips. She wore no jewelry. She didn't need jewels. Not when her eyes sparkled in her beautiful face. Not when she had that body. No man in the room could take his eyes off her—and Rodrigo was no exception.

Damn her.

His jaw tensed as he remembered the angry tremble of her voice. *We're better off without you.*

It wasn't true, he thought. He stiffened, remembering his own father. He was nothing like that bastard.

Maybe he didn't know much about fatherhood or parenting or happy families, but he could at least give his son a name. A stable home. A good childhood.

He could give him everything he himself had never had.

His eyes fell on Lola. Whether she liked it or not, Rodrigo was the one in control now. His eyes traced the full curve of her backside, the span of her tiny waist.

And he intended to have his way. At any cost.

CHAPTER TWO

Lola was in shock.

Gripping her arm, Rodrigo led her out of the ballroom and helped her collect her coat—a black faux fur—then led her out of the grand hotel. He handed his ticket to the valet, who brought his Ferrari around, gleaming sleekly in the night.

Now, it was just the two of them, alone in his car.

Lola tapped her high heel nervously in the passenger seat as he drove. She glanced at him out of the corner of her eye.

Maybe it was all for the best that he'd found out, she tried to convince herself. She hated lying, mostly because she was so bad at it. At least now it was all in the open.

She hadn't lied when she'd said she had powerful friends who would help her. Her two best friends were both married to billionaires, Hallie Moretti to the owner of the luxury Campania hotels, and Princess Tess Zacco di Gioreale to a Sicilian prince. Tess was also now a fashion designer in her own right. Lola had had to sneak out of Tess's first fashion show last week in order to secretly take the evening GED test. She didn't want her friends to know about it. Not until she knew she'd passed.

Lola hated admitting weakness of any kind. Which was why she'd never told her best friends anything about Jett's father.

But if Rodrigo tried to take custody, she knew her

friends would do anything for her—and their ruthless, adoring husbands would do anything for *them*.

She wouldn't let anyone take Jett from her.

Lola exhaled, tightening her hands in her lap as she looked out at the passing lights of the city, traveling east through Manhattan. He hadn't spoken once since she'd given him the address for her apartment in Murray Hill.

She pointed toward the nondescript apartment building. "That's it."

"Is there an attached garage?"

"Garage?" Her lips quirked. "There's not even a doorman."

With a sigh, he drove ahead until he found a parking spot on the street. Lola looked at the small parking space dubiously, but Rodrigo swerved the sports car into it with practiced ease. Opening her car door, he held out his hand.

Nervously, Lola took it. As he helped her out of the car, she tried not to notice how it felt to have his larger, stronger hand around her own.

He dropped her hand quickly and she shivered in her coat as they walked past trees with rattling brown leaves, in the heart of chilly November. She'd lived here for almost a year and liked it. It was a safe, comfortable neighborhood, not flashy but good for families, within walking distance of Grand Central Terminal. Her building was full of nice people, such as the kindly widow who occasionally watched Jett, as she was tonight.

Punching in her code to get in the door, she led him to the elevator, and then pressed the button for the fifth floor. At every moment, she was aware of him standing close beside her. They were alone, just the two of them, in this enclosed space.

She was relieved when they reached her floor. She hurried out of the elevator, then down the nondescript hallway.

Unlocking her door, she went inside. Rodrigo followed her closely, not touching, like a dark shadow.

Inside, her apartment was quiet, with only a single lamp on in the main room. The furniture had all come with the apartment and, though old, was comfortable enough.

A white-haired lady sat in an overstuffed chair next to the lamp. She looked up with a smile on her lips, knitting in her hands. "Lola, you're back early—"

The widow's eyes went wide when she saw Rodrigo, and no wonder. For the year Lola had lived here, she'd never invited any man to this apartment. Now, in the space of a single night, there'd been two different ones: Lola had left for the charity ball with Sergei and returned with Rodrigo.

When the kindly widow had told her she needed to get out and live a little, this probably wasn't what she'd had in mind.

"Hi, Mildred," Lola said. "Yes, I was feeling tired."

"Did you have a nice time?" the elderly woman said stiffly, looking at Rodrigo.

Lola never liked giving too much away. But she didn't want her neighbor to get the wrong idea. "This is Jett's father."

"Oh?" Her eyes went wide. She said with a big smile, *"Oh."*

"How was Jett tonight?" Lola said quickly, changing the subject.

"He was an angel. I gave him his bottle and bath. He's been asleep for about an hour." Gathering up her knitting, she rose to her feet, a grin on her wrinkled face as she looked between Lola and Rodrigo. "I'm sure you two have things to talk about."

Uh-oh. Now Mildred *was* getting the wrong idea. "There's no need to rush off—"

"Thank you for watching him," Rodrigo said gravely,

holding out a wad of hundred-dollar bills. The widow waved off the money.

"I'm happy to help. Jett's a little darling. I'm just glad you're finally here, after all this time," she added pointedly. "A baby needs a father. Just as a woman needs a husband."

With those firm words, the widow left.

"I definitely don't need a husband," Lola said, her cheeks burning.

"She thinks I abandoned you?" Rodrigo said, looking irritated.

She shrugged. "I've never spoken of you to anyone. Even my best friends don't know who Jett's father is." Her lips quirked at the corners. "I think they're under the impression that you're either married, abusive or a total alcoholic."

He glowered at her silently, his jaw tight.

Lola cleared her throat. "But you wanted to see Jett."

Hanging up her coat, she walked into the small apartment's only bedroom, motioning for him to follow.

A beam of moonlight pooled from the bedroom window to a spot between the bed and the crib wedged against the wall. Going to the crib, Lola looked down at her precious son. The four-month-old was sleeping peacefully, his chubby arms flung up over his head. A swell of love went through her.

"This is Jett," she whispered.

Rodrigo came up beside her, resting his powerful hands on the edge of the crib. He looked down at their sleeping baby. Lola's heart lifted to her throat as she looked between them.

Jett looked exactly like his father. She'd never realized it before, because she hadn't wanted to see it. But they had the same slight curl in their dark hair, the same black Spanish eyes. The baby yawned, showing a single dimple just like his father's. His dark lashes blinked sleepily.

The powerful media tycoon said in wonder, "He's so tiny."

"For now." A smile lifted her lips as she looked at him. "Someday he'll be as big as you."

For a long moment, they stood together, looking down at their son. She was aware of Rodrigo's hand just inches from hers. She could almost feel the warmth from his skin.

Suddenly, she yearned to tell him everything. To share things she'd never told even Hallie and Tess. Her friends thought Lola was so tough, but the truth was, she'd been scared, coming to New York alone after their breakup. She'd chosen it as her new home in a desperate, hopeless yearning to be closer to her little sisters, the only family she had left. Then she'd been too scared to contact them.

She'd thought of Rodrigo so many times during her pregnancy. When she'd gotten her first ultrasound. When she'd learned she was having a boy. When she'd gone into labor. And every day before, and since.

But she hadn't contacted him. Because she'd known the man she wanted—the man she'd loved—didn't exist. And in his place, with the same gorgeous, devastating body and heartbreaking dark eyes, was a man who could destroy her.

Now, Rodrigo lifted his gaze to hers. For a moment, she held her breath. Then his expression shuttered, his face turning cold.

"You should have told me."

"I couldn't," she whispered.

"I'm his father."

The baby stirred at Rodrigo's low, harsh voice. Alarmed, she put her finger to her lips and drew him out of the bedroom. Closing the bedroom door softly behind her, she whirled, glaring at him.

"You want to be a father? Then you should know the first rule of parenting is *Don't wake the baby!*"

He looked around the modest apartment. "I thought you said you got him a nice apartment."

"It's a wonderful place, you jerk!"

"You could have asked to stay at my loft in SoHo. I'm hardly ever there."

It was so pointlessly cruel, Lola sucked in her breath.

"You tossed me out of your house. You said I disgusted you and you never wanted to see me again! You think I would ever ask you for help after that? I'd die first!"

Her eyes were stinging. She blinked hard and fast. She wouldn't let herself cry. Only weak people, or children, cried in public and she hadn't been either for a long time.

Rodrigo's expression changed. He took a step toward her in the small apartment, his face half hidden by shadow.

"You don't need to ask for my help, or anyone else's, ever again." His voice was low. "Because if the paternity test proves he's my son, I'm going to marry you."

A rush went through her. A thrill of terror—or was it joy?

"What?" she whispered numbly.

"For his sake." His dark eyes burned through her. "You will be mine."

Lola's hazel eyes were astonished. As well they should be.

After three broken engagements, Rodrigo had never planned to propose again to anyone. For any reason. His youthful dreams of love and family and home were just that—dreams.

But looking at his sleeping son, he'd felt a hard shift in his soul that shocked him. Looking down at the baby's face, so much like his own, he'd remembered his own lonely childhood. And he'd vowed, to the depths of his soul, that his son would never feel like Rodrigo had once felt.

Jett would never believe his father didn't love him. He'd never feel like a burden, unwanted and unloved, as his parents left him in the care of nannies and neglected him for their own selfish romantic pursuits. His son would have a stable home. His parents would raise him together. There would be no instability in their family life, no revolving door of new lovers and spouses. They would be a family. With the same last name.

Lola might hate Rodrigo now, but she loved their son. That was clear in everything she'd done, even taking the million-dollar check that must have hurt her pride. But she'd done it, because she'd feared Rodrigo might try to take the baby from her.

She'd chosen custody of their son over the vast fortune Rodrigo could have offered her.

She'd made a mistake, taking the child from him. But he'd also made a mistake, believing the very worst of her.

For Jett's sake, he would try to forgive. They would start fresh. He would accept his responsibility to his son. Lola would do the same.

Or would she?

"Marry you?" She breathed, her eyes wide. "You're crazy."

"Our son deserves a stable home. Surely you can see that."

Lola's forehead furrowed. "He has one! With me!"

He said stiffly, "I'm willing to forgive you for stealing him from me—"

"I didn't steal him! I was protecting him!"

"But you have to realize that everything has changed now."

Her beautiful face looked numb. "It doesn't mean we have to marry. I know how you feel about marriage." She took a deep breath. "After all your fiancées cheated on you…"

Rodrigo stiffened, wondering how she'd heard. He certainly hadn't spoken about it over the years. But some people did know. His exes. Marnie. And gossip had a way of spreading, especially in his industry.

"This is different," he said coldly. "We're not in love."

She didn't look encouraged by this statement. Shaking her head, she lifted her chin stubbornly. "We can set up some kind of visitation schedule."

"Are you serious?" He raised his eyebrows. "Shuttling our baby from place to place, coast to coast? Always separated from one parent? Never really sure of where his home is? No."

"It doesn't have to be like that. Lots of healthy, happy children have parents who aren't married—"

"Not my son."

She glared at him. "Why marriage?"

Rodrigo couldn't explain to her what his childhood had been like. He'd never fully told anyone, not even the three women he'd claimed to love during his brief engagements long ago. He said shortly, "Is it so strange? I want us both to be there for our son. Every day. And for him to feel safe and loved."

"And you think he doesn't feel loved now?" she said indignantly.

"I know you love him, Lola. I can see it in everything you've done." She relaxed slightly, until he added, "Which is the reason you'll marry me."

She scowled. "I'm not marrying someone I don't love."

Rodrigo drew closer, looking down at her in the small apartment. "You used to love me. Once."

"I learned my lesson, didn't I?"

"Fine. You don't need to love me." His lips curled. "In fact, I'd prefer it if you don't. It keeps things simpler. But you will marry me, Lola. Soon." Straightening the cuffs of his tuxedo jacket, he said, "Sleep on it. Once you've calmed down, you'll see I'm right."

"I won't!"

Rodrigo looked down at her in the soft glow of the lamp-light. His voice was low. "This is a dangerous world. Much can happen. Accidents. Illness. People can die."

"Are you threatening me?" She gasped.

"What? No!" Jolted, he clawed his hand roughly through his dark hair. "I'm saying a child needs as much protection, as much security and love, as he can get. My parents died, Lola. One, then the other. What happened to yours?"

The blood drained from her face. She'd always refused to speak of her past, but now he knew his suspicions were right.

"You're an orphan," he guessed. Biting her lip, she looked away. "So our child already has a mark against him, with no grandparents to love him." He set his jaw. "I'm an only child. So no uncles or aunts."

Looking away, she muttered, "I have two sisters."

His eyebrows raised in surprise. "You do?"

Lola stared at the floor. "I haven't seen them for a long time."

Rodrigo sensed some pain there, but he didn't want to ask. He just pressed his advantage. "So already, our baby is more vulnerable, with no extended family. Don't you want him to have a father? Think of what I can give him. What I can give both of you."

She stiffened. "I don't need more money—"

"Not just money. My name. My time. My protection. My love."

She froze. "Your *love*."

"Yes. A father's love." He set his jaw. "Jett needs me as much as he needs you, Lola. I want to be there for him, to help raise him, to teach him how to be a man. Together, you and I can give him a better childhood than we had. Either of us."

He saw by her expression that his shot hit home. She

suddenly looked uncertain, her eyes luminous in the shadowy light.

Turning away, Rodrigo stopped at the door.

"My son will have my name, Lola. And so will you. This marriage will happen. Accept it." He gave her a hard smile. "Sleep well tonight. Because tomorrow, you're both coming home with me."

Rodrigo arrived the next day, as promised, bright and early. But his men came much sooner than that.

Lola peeked out the window again. Eight stories below, she still saw the black SUV parked across the street. It had arrived last night, thirty minutes after Rodrigo had left.

For all his fine words about marriage and family and love, she thought bitterly, he didn't trust her. He'd sent his henchmen to watch her apartment building to make sure she didn't try to flee with the baby.

They weren't even married yet, but he was already treating her like a prisoner.

But could she totally blame him? a small voice said inside her. She'd left California and kept their baby a secret for a year.

Shut up, she told that voice angrily.

But she'd finally come to the reluctant conclusion that Rodrigo was right. Their baby needed two parents, his whole family. Lola's own father had died when she was five, and she'd always felt that loss, somewhere in the back of her mind. In some ways, losing her father was the start of losing everything, because that was when her mom had had to go back to work. She'd earned only a fraction of what her father had, so they'd had to move out of their sunny three-bedroom house and into the trailer.

Now, Lola looked back at her small furnished apartment. She'd packed their meager possessions into three suitcases, leaving the dishware and odds and ends for the next tenant. She and Jett had been happy here, she thought wistfully.

Then she shook her head with a snort, remembering all the nights she'd cried herself to sleep over the last year. It was why she hadn't invited Hallie to stay here, when her friend had briefly needed a place to stay last summer. Lola couldn't bear to let anyone see her cry. Well, except Jett, but only because he'd cried even more.

Lola was supposed to be the strong one, the one her friends came to for advice and support, not the one who needed help. She'd pushed Hallie and Tess to get the financial support their babies deserved. She'd pushed them to get their lives together. And look at those two now—happy, in love, joyful. She'd helped them get there. *Speaking the brutal truth with love*, Lola called it, though her friends sometimes grumbled that her words could be more brutal than loving.

But they didn't know how scared Lola felt on the inside. She'd worked through her pregnancy because she was afraid to spend the money Rodrigo had thrown at her. Afraid that bad things could happen. And even after a year, she hadn't been brave enough to contact her baby sisters. Guilt still hung heavily over her at how she'd failed them at eighteen.

A child needs as much protection, as much security and love, as he can get. My parents died, Lola. One, then the other. What happened to yours?

She looked at Jett, now stretched out happily on a soft blanket over the rug. Rodrigo was right. As much as she hated to admit it. Jett deserved as much security and love as she could possibly give.

Because parents could die. They could get sick or go to jail. And even if Lola was ever brave enough to contact her sisters, they were still so young, Kelsey fifteen, Johanna only twelve. Whether they now hated her, or they'd forgotten her completely, the truth was, her sisters had a new family now. They'd been lost to her long ago.

Jett was all that mattered. She wanted him to be safe and loved. And from the moment Rodrigo had seen their baby, he'd seemed to feel the same.

Already our baby is more vulnerable, with no extended family. Don't you want him to have a father? Think of what I can give him... My name. My time. My protection. My love.

She'd barely slept that night, tossing and turning. Sometime around 3:00 a.m., she'd come to a decision.

She didn't love Rodrigo, and he didn't love her. But she would marry him. Their baby deserved that sacrifice.

Yet it wasn't easy. With a sinking heart, Lola looked back out the window and saw another car had arrived. She recognized, even at this distance, the gorgeous, arrogant man getting out of it. She swallowed hard. Then her jaw set.

Fine, they would marry. But it would be on her terms.

She heard the intercom buzz, and his husky voice demanding entrance. She pressed the button to let him in downstairs. Putting on her coat, Lola picked up her baby. Tucking his blanket into her diaper bag, she waited with a sense of dread.

A few minutes later, she heard heavy steps in the hallway. A hard knock sounded at her door. With a deep breath, she opened it.

Rodrigo's dark eyes burned through her. "You are ready?"

So much was encompassed in that simple question.

"Yes," she said.

"Good." Relaxing slightly, he strode into the apartment, looking so handsome she almost couldn't bear it. He wore a long, open black cashmere coat that revealed the shape of his broad shoulders and biceps, with a well-cut black shirt and trousers beneath. He was followed inside by his driver and bodyguard, both of whom she knew slightly from the old days.

"Have a long night, did you, boys?" she said to them dryly. As they gathered the suitcases, they glanced at each other. Rodrigo's smile widened.

"You knew they were watching?"

"Of course I knew," she snapped at him. "You're not very trusting."

"I'm glad you didn't try to run."

She pressed her lips together. "There was no point. You convinced me that you're right."

"I'm always right." But even as he spoke the arrogant words, his dark eyes looked her over appreciatively. As befitted the cold November weather, she wore a form-fitting black puffy coat, with a faux-fur-edged hood, and a hem that stretched down over her hips. Her legs were covered with black leggings and her black boots matched her hood, edged with faux fur.

Against her will, she blushed beneath his glance. It enraged her. Why did he still have that effect on her? It didn't seem fair!

"Is this all, Miss Price?" asked the bodyguard.

"And the stroller by the door."

As his two henchmen left the apartment with the suitcases and stroller, Rodrigo held out his arm. "Come."

"Wait."

At the breathless sound of her voice, Rodrigo looked down at her questioningly.

"Like I said. I realized you're right. Jett needs a stable home, and a father to raise him. We should marry. Even though we don't love each other." Her voice trembled a little. "It's best for Jett." She paused. "But—"

"But?" His voice was low and dangerous.

She lifted her gaze. "I just want to make sure we understand each other. This marriage is for duty. For convenience."

"Convenience?" he repeated.

How could he not know what she meant?

"In…in name only," she whispered, her teeth suddenly chattering.

He gave a low, hard laugh, his dark eyes glittering in the morning light. "Is that what you think?"

"I mean it, Rodrigo—"

"No." He cupped her cheek. "You don't."

His eyes burned through her, and he slowly lowered his head toward hers.

She sucked in her breath as, against her will, a fire of desire swept through her body that she was helpless to deny. Her toes curled in anticipation, and she closed her eyes, holding her breath, waiting for him to kiss her.

At the last moment before his lips would have touched hers, he stopped. Confused, she opened her eyes.

His face was cruel as he looked down at her with a cold, mocking smile. "In name only, *querida*?"

Her cheeks suddenly burned. "You arrogant bastard—"

"Come. We have a busy day planned."

His eyes softened as they rested on the dark-haired baby against her hip. He caressed the baby tenderly on the head. "We will be a family soon, *pequeño*." Then he gave Lola a smile that didn't meet his eyes. "No more talk of *convenient* marriages. You will be conveniently in my bed. And soon."

"In your dreams," she retorted. For answer, he gave her a sensual smile.

"Yes. I have dreamed of it, Lola," he said huskily. "And soon those dreams will be reality."

Her eyes widened at his admission, and her mouth snapped shut as she recalled all the hot nights when she, too, had dreamed of him. Fuming, she followed him out of the apartment.

When they reached the street, she saw one of his men placing the suitcases in the back of the black SUV, as the other put the stroller in the back of Rodrigo's sleek luxury sedan.

Lola frowned. "Where are we going?"

Rodrigo opened the sedan door. "A few places."

Seeing a brand-new baby seat latched securely into the sedan's back seat, she wondered if his longtime executive assistant, Marnie, had arranged it. She'd always hated that smug busybody, now more than ever. "Where?"

"You'll see."

As the SUV turned south, Rodrigo drove Lola and the baby north, to a cutting-edge private clinic on the Upper East Side. As far as she could tell, it had opened up on Sunday, bringing in a full staff, just for their paternity test. Within two hours, they had the results. Jett was Rodrigo's son.

"I knew it," Rodrigo said quietly when he got the results.

Lola looked at him irritably. "Then why did you insist on a test?"

"There's knowing, and there's knowing."

"That makes no sense. You could have just trusted me."

"I needed proof." He didn't explain further. When it came to asking for help or showing weakness, Rodrigo was even worse than Lola.

After the clinic, the next stop that morning turned out to be the prestigious white-shoe Manhattan law firm of Crosby, Flores and Jackson, where, amid the hushed elegance of a private office, Lola was presented with a fifty-page legal contract of a prenuptial agreement.

Sitting at the gleaming mahogany desk, she read through it slowly, to the obvious surprise of the lawyers, marking up any clause she didn't like with a red pen.

Lola had made below average grades in school, but she'd always been good at debate. It was why, when she was twelve, her mother had handed Lola the phone if she needed to convince the electric company to turn the lights back on, or deal with a debt collector. It was also how, after Lola's failed attempt at a "quick and easy" movie star career, she'd eventually become executive assistant to a powerful tycoon. Lola knew how to absorb and how to deflect. She knew when to pay attention and how.

In short, she knew how to argue.

Even opaque legal language couldn't confuse her. It was like following a shell game. You just never took your eyes off the ball.

Finally, she set down the papers.

"I have some changes," she said coolly.

"Do you?" Rodrigo's voice was amused.

"Yes. Starting with this clause in paragraph Four C…"

In the end, Lola got what she wanted. She negotiated away one financial item after another—the amount of money set aside for alimony, child support, housing and staff levels in case of a divorce—in order to keep the one thing she actually cared about, which was primary custody of Jett. That was the one thing she was never, ever willing to lose.

She marveled that Rodrigo seemed focused on something else entirely: making sure Lola would be punished if she were ever unfaithful during their marriage.

She was amazed he'd be worried about that. As she'd told him, she'd never kissed another man in her whole life. But as she'd heard from a gossipy production assistant, he'd had three fiancées cheat on him. So maybe she could understand, after all.

Whatever the reason, Lola gladly used it to her advantage. The prenuptial agreement was altered. In case of divorce, no matter which of them was at fault, Lola would get custody of Jett. But if she ever cheated on Rodrigo, even after thirty years of marriage, she wouldn't get a penny. No alimony. No marital property. Nothing but the three suitcases she'd arrived with.

But since she obviously wouldn't cheat, she'd won. She smiled as they left the law office.

"You never thought of becoming a lawyer?" Rodrigo murmured, his dark eyes gleaming as they pushed the baby's stroller out of the wood-paneled private office.

"Lawyer?" Lola snorted. "Me?"

"You think like one."

She shook her head. "I'm not even sure if I passed my GED test."

They left the law office and got back into the car. As Rodrigo drove her and the baby south toward his SoHo loft, he suddenly asked, "Why did you drop out of high school?"

She looked at him guardedly. "What do you mean?"

"You're smart, Lola. A fighter." He shook his head wryly. "Something I've sometimes learned the hard way. Why didn't you go to college? Why did you drop out of high school and go to LA and do—" he hesitated "—what you did?"

Her cheeks suddenly burned. "I had my reasons."

She couldn't explain why, at eighteen, she'd been so desperate to earn money, so stupid and naive, that she'd done things she wasn't proud of. Things that had caused Rodrigo to call her ugly names, six years later. She hadn't done everything Marnie had accused her of—not even close—but what she'd done was bad enough. And she'd still failed to save her sisters.

But she wasn't going to explain and let Rodrigo think she was a weakling and a failure, in addition to being a— well, he'd never actually called her a whore. But that was how he'd made her feel.

Wrapping her arms around herself, she looked stonily

out the window. Silence fell in the luxury sedan as he drove south through Manhattan, the only sound the yawns of their baby in his car seat behind them.

"You've always been quick," he said, his hands tightening on the steering wheel. "If you'd stayed in school—"

"I don't want to talk about it."

"You could have gone far. You could be a big-time lawyer or CEO of a major corporation by now. Why didn't anyone convince you to even try?"

She didn't look at him. A lump lifted to her throat.

She had been good in school once. When she was seven, she'd loved to puzzle over math and read. But after her father's death, her mother had been too busy and exhausted to help with school. Later, she'd remarried. After Lola's two half-siblings were born—and especially after her new stepfather was injured on the job—school had become a luxury. It just wasn't important anymore, not like making sure there was food in the fridge, and caring for her sisters when her stepfather was passed out drunk, and their mother working the overnight shift.

When Lola was fifteen, her mother had died. Bonnie had been feeling bad for months, but put off seeing the doctor, insisting she didn't have money or time. By the time she'd finally gotten her diagnosis, the cancer was terminal. She'd lived only a few months after that. Her stepfather, trying to cope with the grief and his family's sudden lack of income, ended up going to prison for dealing drugs. There had been nothing left to hold their family together.

Staring hard out the window of the luxury sedan, Lola wiped her eyes fiercely. She hadn't even told Hallie and Tess that. Just as she'd never told them anything about her baby's father, not even Rodrigo Cabrera's name.

It was the only way Lola knew how to deal with that kind of radioactive pain. To pretend it didn't exist.

"I didn't care, all right?" she said numbly, staring hard out the window. "I never cared about college."

"What do you care about, then?"

Lola thought of her family. Everyone she'd lost. Everyone she'd loved but been unable to save.

Setting her jaw, she whispered, "Protecting what's mine."

CHAPTER THREE

THE EARLY NOVEMBER morning was cold and gray as Rodrigo turned the car down Prince Street, turning on Mercer.

Lola rolled down the window, breathing the cool air, relishing the feel against her hot skin. The air made her shiver. Or maybe it was the thought that she'd soon be Rodrigo's wife. She looked up at the lowering sky. She wondered what Hallie and Tess would say when they were invited to Lola's wedding out of the blue.

Her lips quirked. They would be surprised, to say the least.

She'd met Hallie Hatfield and Tess Foster last year at a New York single moms' support group. They'd been the only ones who were pregnant, and they'd soon realized that none of them had told the fathers about the babies.

Her friends were both now happily married. While Lola just prayed she wasn't making a horrible mistake.

Rodrigo pulled his sedan to the front of a fashionable prewar building in SoHo, where a doorman took his keys.

"Good morning, Mr. Cabrera. In the garage like always?"

"Thank you, Andrews," Rodrigo said, walking around the car to get the stroller from the trunk. The doorman's eyes widened when he saw it, and even more when he saw Lola get out and take their baby in her arms.

Tucking sleepy Jett into the stroller, Lola followed Rodrigo into the lobby of the luxurious building, and into an elevator that he accessed with a fingerprint.

On the top floor, the elevator opened directly onto a private foyer. And Lola entered the penthouse loft she hadn't visited in over a year.

Shivering, she looked around the large, bohemian penthouse loft. Colorful furniture filled the enormous space, and huge windows showed an expansive, unrestricted southern view of the city, to the skyscrapers of Lower Manhattan. She could dimly see the steel and glass building where she'd once worked for Sergei Morozov. Strange to think that Rodrigo could have been unknowingly looking at her, whenever he'd visited New York. So close, but so far apart.

The bare brick walls were decorated with old original movie posters, along with old neon signs, which were no doubt originals, too. Rodrigo had occasionally seen neon signs he liked as he traveled to his movie sets around the world, from Tokyo to Sydney to Berlin. She'd watched in awe as he'd casually bought entire businesses, simply to acquire the signs.

That was Rodrigo, Lola thought, a little bitterly. He'd rip out someone's beating heart just to tap his toe to the rhythm.

She blinked hard, to make sure no trace of emotion was on her face. She might become his wife, but he'd never possess her. She'd never let herself love him, ever again.

"Miss Price!" The New York housekeeper, Mrs. Farrow, came in from the next room of the loft. The woman's plump face broke into a big smile. "I'm so glad you're back. And how exciting, you're going to be married?"

"Strange, huh?" Lola said, feeling awkward. Especially when the woman was followed by a white-haired, distinguished-looking man Lola didn't know.

"Not strange. Lovely." Mrs. Farrow knelt before the stroller, smiling at Jett. "And this is your baby?"

"Yes... Jett."

The older woman beamed. "He's adorable."

Pulling off her black gloves, one by one, Lola stuck them in her pockets. "Thank you."

The white-haired man smiled at her, his eyes twinkling beneath bushy white brows. "So should we get this show on the road?"

Lola frowned at Rodrigo. "What's he talking about?"

"This is the judge," he said. "He's going to marry us."

"What? When?"

"Today." Rodrigo's lips curved. "Now."

Lola stared at him in shock.

"We can't," she stammered. "We need a marriage license."

"Occasionally, when there's a good reason, the rules can be bent."

"What's the good reason?"

His black eyes gleamed. "It's Sunday. And I wish to marry you today. Not wait to get the license from City Hall tomorrow and then wait another twenty-four hours after that." He turned to the judge. "Shall we begin, your honor?"

"Now?" Lola's head was spinning. "No! I want a real ceremony! With my friends!"

Rodrigo's sensual lips curved sardonically. "Sorry to crush all your romantic dreams," he said, as if he was sure she didn't actually have any. "You'll have to settle—" he reached into his pocket "—for this."

Holding up a small black velvet box, he opened it to reveal an engagement ring. Her eyes went wide. The diamond was as huge as a robin's egg.

"We have everything else we need. Witnesses." He looked at Mrs. Farrow, and Tobias, the bodyguard who'd just come in through the front door. "A judge." Tilting his head, he said courteously to the white-haired man, "I hope your daughter is doing well."

"Yes, and I'll never forget how you helped her," the judge said warmly. "My four grandchildren still have a mother today thanks to you."

Rodrigo acknowledged his praise with a slight nod. "I was glad to pay for the experimental treatment. I'm pleased it worked. And grateful for your help."

"What, marrying you two?" The judge's voice was genial. "Marrying folks is my favorite part of the job! I'll make sure the paperwork's all handled right." Then, looking at Lola, he faltered. "Of course, only if the lady is willing."

"I'm not," she said flatly.

"Excuse us for a moment." Grabbing her arm, Rodrigo pulled her back to the foyer. "What do you think you're doing?"

Lifting her snoozing, limp baby from the stroller, she glared at him fiercely. "I'm not getting married without my friends!"

"Which friends are you hoping to see?" Rodrigo's voice was dangerous and low. "A certain lovelorn Russian, to try to make me jealous?"

Lola looked at him in shock, then burst into a laugh. "Sergei? You can't be serious!"

"I don't intend to wait." His expression hardened. "We're getting married. Right now."

"Or else what?"

"Do not defy me."

"Is that a threat?"

His voice changed. "Marrying me today will benefit you as well."

"How?"

"It goes both ways. Perhaps if we wait—" he tilted his head thoughtfully "—I'll get cold feet and decide to call it all off."

"Fine with me—"

"Perhaps I'll decide I'd rather sue for full custody, and

take my chances in the courts. I can wait out a long trial. Can you?"

She glared at him.

He smiled.

Lola looked down at her baby's fuzzy jacket, breathing in his sweet baby scent. "I don't appreciate ham-fisted threats."

He shrugged. "I despise long engagements—"

"*Long!*"

"I want to get this done." His gaze hardened. "Is there any reason to delay?"

Her friends, she thought desperately. She wanted Tess and Hallie here for emotional support. And what about her little sisters? She hadn't seen them for seven years, but it felt wrong not to have her only family here.

But she couldn't be vulnerable enough to show weakness. Especially not with Rodrigo.

Instead, she indicated her black puffy jacket and leggings. "Does this look like a wedding dress to you?"

Taking off his cashmere coat, he glanced down at his own black shirt and trousers and gave a sardonic smile. "We are both wearing black, which seems appropriate for the occasion."

"Meaning what? This is like a funeral for you?" Hurt rushed through her, followed by anger. "If you're having second thoughts about marriage…"

His dark eyes turned hard. "I'm not. And neither are you." He looked down at her. "It happens now."

Her heart sank. So there would be no pleasant pre-wedding afternoon at the day spa with Tess and Hallie. No deep intense conversations over champagne as they helped her get ready to be a bride. They wouldn't be here to support her as she pledged her life to the man who'd broken her heart. The man who'd judged her past mistakes and made it clear he didn't think she was good enough. The man who'd tossed her love back in her face, and would never, ever, have wanted to marry her if not for Jett.

Lola would face it alone. Dressed for a funeral.

She took a deep breath.

"Fine," she said coldly. "Let's get it over with."

They returned to the main room of the loft.

"We're ready," Rodrigo told the judge.

"There's no rush, you know." The white-haired man suddenly looked nervous, glancing between them as if wondering what he'd gotten himself into, and how he could get himself out of it. "Marriage is, after all, a solemn occasion. Now that I think about it, there's a reason why the State of New York, in its infinite wisdom, instituted a twenty-four-hour waiting period—"

"Just do it," Rodrigo said harshly. His hand gripped her shoulder.

"Please," whispered Lola, ignoring the lump in her throat.

The judge hesitated. Then the baby gave a sudden sleepy whimper in Lola's arms, and she and Rodrigo both turned to comfort him. Watching them caring together for their son, tucking the baby back into the stroller for his nap, the judge seemed reassured. He gave a decisive nod when they returned.

"Very well. Ladies and gentlemen," he intoned. "We are gathered here today, in the presence of witnesses, to unite this man and this woman in the bonds of matrimony..."

The short ceremony passed quickly. As if in a dream, Lola heard herself speak the words that bound her to Rodrigo for life.

But the awful truth was, she'd bound herself to him long ago, from the night she'd become pregnant with his child.

And now, from this moment on, forever.

Rodrigo's dark eyes gleamed down at her as the ceremony drew to a close. He seemed almost surprised. Why?

Had he thought for some reason that something would prevent it?

Their eyes locked as he slid that obscenely huge diamond on her finger. Funny. Once, she would have dreamed of a moment like this. At fourteen, she dreamed of love, and a handsome prince. At eighteen, she would have just been keen to hock the ring.

And now, at twenty-five, how different this moment felt from anything she'd imagined!

"...I now pronounce you husband and wife." The judge looked between them with a wink. "You may now kiss the bride."

Kiss?

Lola looked up at the man who was now her husband. *I feel nothing*, she told herself desperately. *Nothing.*

As Rodrigo lowered his head toward hers, she put her hand up to stop him. His chest felt so powerful, so muscular, that in spite of herself, she shivered. "What about your wedding band?" His left hand was still bare. "Don't you need a ring, too?"

"I'm a man. I don't need jewelry to feel married."

She stiffened at his sexist remark. But before she could protest, he took her roughly into his arms.

"Mrs. Cabrera," he whispered.

Her lips parted in shock as she heard him speak her new name. Ruthlessly, he lowered his mouth to hers.

His lips were hot and sweet, tasting of spice and fire. As he kissed her, the world started to spin. Feeling the strength and power of his body against her own, she gripped his shoulders for balance. She forgot everything in her own aching need. She'd wanted him for so long. A sigh rose from deep inside her, the recognition that this man was hers, hers alone, as she had always been his...

The judge, housekeeper and bodyguard watching them

applauded, and Lola suddenly remembered they had an audience.

Pulling away, Rodrigo looked down at her with gleaming eyes.

Pleasure was still spiraling through her as her lips tingled from his bruising kiss. When his mouth had claimed hers, all the distance between them, all the coldness and anger, had exploded into fire, like two storms colliding. But now the distance was back.

She tried to read his expression, to see if the kiss had affected him like it had her. But his face gave nothing away. "Thank you," he said to the judge, then turned to the bodyguard, Tobias. "Everything is ready for our departure?"

"Already packed, Mr. Cabrera."

"Packed?" Lola frowned at her brand-new husband. "Are you going somewhere?"

"Not me. *We*." Rodrigo gave her a smile that didn't meet his eyes. "My jet is waiting to take us to Los Angeles."

It was like a splash of ice water, jolting her awake. "But New York is my home now. My sisters—all my friends—"

His lips twisted. "Friends like Morozov?"

"He was never my friend!"

He snorted. "Exactly."

Lola ground her teeth. "Why are you being so unreasonable!"

"You just agreed to be my wife, Lola. To honor and obey." Rodrigo gave her a cruel smile. Cupping her cheek, he looked down at her as he said softly, "Now you will."

Rodrigo could hardly believe it.

After all his engagements that had never made it to the altar, this one actually had. They were married. He was almost in shock.

Perhaps it was true he'd rushed their vows that morning. But once he'd made up his mind to marry her, he couldn't give Lola a chance to betray him like the rest. He couldn't take any chances with fate, or whatever else had cursed his life.

This marriage would work. It had to work. They had a child.

Now, as Rodrigo drove his red convertible north, traveling from the private airport outside Los Angeles to his beach house near Malibu, Rodrigo glanced at the rearview mirror. He saw his baby's pudgy hand waving from the rear-facing baby seat. Jett was making cooing noises, and seemed delighted to be in California, beneath the palm trees and warm blue skies.

It was strange to think he had a child. Even stranger for Rodrigo to think he was a father. What did he know about fatherhood?

His own parents had left him in the care of nannies. His mother, an American actress, had traveled the world enjoying her love affairs, as the man who'd supposedly been his father, Francisco Cabrera, had tortured himself with jealousy pursuing the unfaithful wife he adored.

It wasn't until Francisco's funeral, when Rodrigo was twenty-one, that his mother told him the reason the man always seemed to despise him. Rodrigo's real father had been the chauffeur.

"He was very handsome, and I was bored, what can I say?" Elizabeth Cabrera had told him, putting her finger to her cheek thoughtfully. "It was just a one-night indiscretion. Francisco wanted me to get rid of you. Perhaps I should have. My figure was never quite the same after."

Now, Rodrigo glanced in the rearview mirror of the convertible, toward his son. Jett was such a sweet little boy, with big black eyes and chubby cheeks. He'd been obviously well fed and well cared for. Obviously loved. Beneath Lola's ferocity, there was utter devotion for their son.

He appreciated that about her, at least.

In some ways, their new relationship was simple: they were a family. But between Rodrigo and Lola, now husband and wife, it was a little more complicated.

His gaze now shifted to his wife, sitting beside him in the convertible. Her arms were folded, and she was seething silently at the wide Pacific Ocean as they drove up the coastal highway. He smiled grimly.

He hadn't lied when he'd said she was smart and a fighter. She'd been the best personal assistant he'd ever had, even better than Marnie, his longest-serving secretary. He'd relied on Lola's intelligence, on her strength. She'd been a miracle worker as an employee, always able to achieve the impossible, willing to work any hour of the day or night, even on Christmas Day.

For two years, he'd wanted her. But he hadn't let himself even flirt. Then, after Lola had kissed him in Mexico City, he'd taken her to bed, and discovered she was a virgin. From that moment, they'd been intoxicated, drunk on passion and pleasure. When she'd told him she loved him, in spite of everything, his heart had expanded in his chest.

Then Marnie had given him those awful photographs of Lola half-naked in that chair, looking seductively into the camera. And there was more.

Sir, there's something you should know about Lola Price.
Rodrigo still felt sick thinking about it.

But why had Lola ever done those sordid things at eighteen? The thought jolted him. Because she clearly wasn't the coldhearted gold digger he'd once believed her to be. If she'd cared only about money, she would have demanded a huge payout from Rodrigo the moment she'd discovered she was pregnant.

So why had Lola posed for those provocative photographs? Why had she done even worse? Just youthful stupidity? He ground his teeth. He'd had his share of that himself, with his own three broken engagements. But was there more to it? Had she just been desperate to be a movie star? Or had something forced her into it?

Rodrigo looked at Lola out of the corner of his eye. The warm wind was tossing her blond hair in the sun. But her jaw was tight, and she was tapping her fingertips on the convertible's armrest in repressed fury.

No point in asking her, he knew. She guarded the darkest secrets of her soul with grim determination. In that, she and Rodrigo were the same.

During the flight from New York on his private jet, they'd sat at opposite ends of the cabin, ignoring each other. She'd accused him of bossing her around, being a tyrant. Not a great start. But it wouldn't go on for long.

His gaze traced down the curve of her cheek, to her swanlike throat and full breasts. He'd promised to honor and cherish her, forsaking all others. She didn't realize that he'd already done that for the last year. He was hungry for her. Starving.

He wanted her in his bed. Tonight.

But first, he needed her to actually look at him. He grudgingly extended an olive branch.

"Are you really so upset about leaving New York?"

"You had no right," Lola said, turning to him with her eyes blazing. "Just because I'm your wife doesn't mean I'm your slave. I wanted to stay in New York, but you didn't care! Just like you didn't care you frog-marched me through our wedding!"

"You wanted Morozov there?"

She let loose a curse that would have made a sailor blush.

"Not Morozov, then," he said, amused. "Then who?"

"My friends. Hallie. Tess." She looked disconsolately out at the hills. "My sisters."

"You said you haven't seen your sisters in years."

"I haven't," she whispered.

"Then I don't see why it matters that they weren't there today."

Lola took a deep breath. "They're a lot younger than me. Still just kids. My mother died when they were just five and eight. They were sent to foster care, then adopted." Her jaw tightened. "When I left California last year, I went to New York. I intended to finally ask them to forgive me. For not keeping my promise to get custody back." She looked down at her hands, twisting in her lap. "But I never had the guts."

Admitting failure was so unlike Lola that he glanced at her in surprise. He switched gears, stepping hard on the gas as they drove up the highway. "You'll think of some way to smooth things over. You always do."

Lola looked at him hopefully out of the corner of her eye. "You think so?"

He snorted. "You never had trouble arranging people when you were my assistant. You always managed to get me appointments with anyone from feared dictators to beloved religious leaders."

"Because you're you."

"And you're you," he said firmly. "You know how to argue people into things. When you're ready to see your sisters, you'll figure out how."

Lola bit her lip thoughtfully. He could almost see the wheels start to turn in her mind. "I could send them some amazing present. Just to break the ice. Then they'd have to contact me to say thanks."

"That could work," he said, smiling. He was glad to see some of the dark cloud lift from her shoulders—and glad to distract her from being angry at him for rushing her into marriage and back to California.

"It could." She smiled back, and it was warmer and brighter than the California sun.

Then her lips twisted mischievously. "I'm warning you. The gift will probably be expensive."

Rodrigo shrugged. "Spend whatever you like. What's mine is yours."

"Do you mean that?"

"I already know you didn't marry me for my money, Lola."

"No." Her expression darkened. She turned away, her arm resting on the edge of the convertible as she looked out at the ocean. "I married you because you blackmailed me."

The brief moment of camaraderie, of shared sunshine, abruptly disappeared.

Rodrigo turned the convertible off the highway, traveling down a private lane to the edge of tall stone walls that blocked off his compound. He punched in the security code, and the gate slid open. He drove the convertible inside the courtyard, followed closely by his longtime bodyguard, Tobias Watson, in the SUV with all the luggage.

"Back to home sweet home," he murmured.

"Yes," Lola said, looking up at the beach house.

Getting out of the convertible, he reached in the back seat of the convertible to unbuckle their baby.

"I can do that," she said, alarmed.

"It's done." Gently, he lifted their baby from the car seat and held him in his arms. Lola looked panicked, and then, looking closer, confused.

"You're holding him correctly," she said, clearly shocked. She looked at his face. "How did you learn to hold a baby?"

"You think I'm completely incompetent?" Rodrigo drawled.

"You've never held a baby in your life."

"Then I must be a natural." He didn't bother to explain that while she'd been studiously ignoring him on the flight, when he'd been working on his laptop, he'd actually been reading articles about the proper care and handling of infants. He wasn't going to let Lola lord her greater knowledge over him, or be forced to ask her for the favor of teaching him what to do.

Once, he would have asked her, without thought, and been willing to humble himself for her. But not anymore. Their relationship was still on too shaky a footing for that. It probably hadn't helped that he'd bullied her into marriage and returning to California. But he had no regrets. It was the most efficient means of getting what he wanted.

As they walked toward his sprawling, luxurious beach house, the front door opened. His executive assistant, Marnie McAdam, appeared in the doorway, her eyes eager behind her thick glasses. "You're back—" Her expression changed when she saw Lola and the baby. "What…what's she doing here?"

For an answer, Lola lifted her left hand in a movement so violent it was almost an obscene gesture, to show her the huge diamond ring.

Marnie's eyes went wide as she looked between them. "You're married?"

"Isn't it wonderful news?" Lola said.

His assistant looked pale. A year older than Rodrigo, Marnie McAdam had been a college graduate traveling in Madrid when he'd hired her as his first employee at his new company, Cabrera Media Group, after he'd taken over his father's small studio. Over the last fifteen years, Rodrigo had come to depend on Marnie for her dedication and loyalty. Before Lola had arrived, she'd been his top assistant.

No wonder the two women hadn't liked each other. Marnie was the one who'd told Rodrigo about Lola's past, telling him all the awful facts as she'd put the photographs in his hands.

And Lola knew it. She gave the older woman a hard smile.

He had the sudden alarming image of the two women

coming to blows. He was fairly sure Lola, with her hard-edged fearlessness, would emerge the victor. He had no desire to see Marnie in the hospital, so he stepped abruptly between them.

"That'll be all for today, Marnie. You can head home."

"Whose baby?" She breathed unsteadily, looking at Jett in his arms.

"Mine," he said.

"You didn't know?" said Lola sweetly. "I thought you might have arranged things for us in New York."

"No," Rodrigo said. "She didn't." He looked at Marnie. "We might need some additional baby furniture, though. I'll contact you later."

"Of course, Mr. Cabrera." Turning to Lola, she said, "Congratulations."

Lola glared at her. "You heard what he said. Get going."

Biting her lip, Marnie looked at Rodrigo.

"Thank you, Marnie," he said, more kindly.

With a nod, she turned and hurried to her car. As the older woman drove out of the gate, Rodrigo turned on Lola coldly. "Was that really necessary?"

His wife didn't answer. Taking the yawning baby from his arms, she strode ahead of him into the beach house, proud and scornful as a queen.

Irritated, he followed her into the house's enormous great room, with its wall of windows overlooking the beach and bright blue ocean.

"You can't hate Marnie for telling me the truth about your past."

"The truth?" Lola looked at him incredulously. "Is that what you think?"

"Are you saying you didn't pose for those pictures? You didn't let that man—" But he couldn't go on. Just remembering the rest of Marnie's report still made his blood boil with unwilling jealousy and rage.

Lola's lovely face was pale as she turned away. "I need to put Jett to bed."

"Wait. I'm talking to you—"

"Not now." Behind them, two bodyguards were bringing in suitcases from the SUV. Lola pointed at her suitcases. "Can you please take those to the baby's room?"

"Baby's room?" Tobias Watson asked, frowning.

Glancing at Rodrigo, she said coolly, "I assume there is one."

"I told Mrs. Lee to arrange the best guest room," he said grudgingly.

As the bodyguard nodded and started down the hall, Lola said without looking at Rodrigo, "I'll be sleeping in there, too."

Without another word, she collected the diaper bag and swept down the hallway, leaving Rodrigo alone in the great room with the amazing view of the Pacific.

He ground his teeth.

But he could understand why Lola was already so defensive and irritable. Part of him felt the same. Having her back here, in this house where they'd once been lovers, gave him a sense of vertigo, like an earthquake beneath his feet. Wistful memories of their love affair still lingered in every room.

Looking slowly around, Rodrigo gave an involuntary shiver. *There* he'd made love to her against the wall. *There* they'd lazed Sunday mornings on the sofa. He looked out through the double-story windows. Closing his eyes, he felt the sun burning hot and bright against his face, without the gentle mercy of clouds.

And *there*, on that white sand beach, one moonlit night beside the bonfire as the Santa Ana winds blew, Lola had told him she loved him. For answer, Rodrigo had taken her in his arms and kissed her hungrily, as she'd clung to him as if her life depended on it. The explosive heat of that sensual night! He shivered at the memory. They'd always been scrupulously careful about protection, but that one time, they'd been carried away by passion. Which was another way of saying they lost their minds. It was almost certainly the night she'd conceived their baby.

Turning away, he went to the wet bar and poured himself a drink. A few minutes later, when Lola returned from the baby's nursery, he saw her before she saw him. She'd long since taken off her coat, but she still wore the same black shirt, leggings and boots she'd been married in. He suddenly yearned to take those off, too. To feel the warmth of her naked skin.

A flash of heat went through him.

He gulped the last of his Scotch, letting it burn his throat as he set down the glass with a bang. "You're not sleeping in the nursery, Lola. I thought I made myself clear. You're sleeping in the bedroom. With me."

She whirled to face him, her beautiful face wild. "Forget it."

Rodrigo took an unwilling step toward her.

"I can't," he whispered. "I can't forget."

The memory of all the times he'd kissed her in this house, all the nights he'd made love to her, all their moments of laughter and lazy sensuality and joy burned through him. He had to clench his hands at his sides to keep himself from pulling her roughly into his arms.

"You forgot me long ago." Lola looked at him in the warm pink and gold light of the late afternoon sun, her eyes bright. "I'm sure you've had lovers here by the score since you tossed me out."

"Wrong," he said.

He heard her intake of breath. "What?"

Coming forward, Rodrigo cupped her cheek.

"I've had no other woman here. None," he whispered. Slowly, he ran his thumb along her tender bottom lip. "Not here, nor anywhere else. For the last year, I've hungered for you, Lola. Only for you."

"I…" She breathed, trembling beneath his touch. "I can't believe it…"

"All this time, I've wanted you." Pulling her body against his own, he whispered, "And now you're mine, I'm never going to let you go…"

His lips lowered to hers in a hard, passionate kiss. He held her body fast against his own, giving her no chance to resist. But she didn't even try. With a soft sigh, she reached her arms up to twist around his shoulders, pulling him down against her with the same hunger.

And in that moment, the kiss that had started as a mark of possession began to explode in pure light.

Lola hadn't realized it would be so hard to be back in this California beach house. The short months of their affair had been the happiest of her life.

Until her past had caught up with her. The most humiliating mistakes of her life. And when he'd discovered them, he'd tossed her aside as if she meant nothing.

Because she hadn't. Rodrigo had never loved her. Not even a little.

But Lola had still been stupid enough to love him.

Returning to this house today, she'd felt memories burn through her like acid. As she'd tucked their baby into the crib of his lavish new nursery, Lola looked at the little sofa nearby and vowed to herself that she'd sleep there alone every night. But she hadn't quite believed it, even then. Not when her traitorous body was yearning to be back in Rodrigo's bed.

Now, as her husband kissed her, his lips seemed pure fire.

His powerful arms tightened around her in the sunlit great room of the beach house, with the wide view of the white sand and blue Pacific. His mouth was hot and rough against hers. And the thought of any path that didn't end with them falling into bed was impossible.

So what? she thought suddenly. Sex didn't have to mean anything. It didn't mean love. It could be just a benefit of marriage, like filing jointly for taxes.

Lola closed her eyes in ecstasy as he pressed her against the wall, kissing slowly down her throat. She felt the heat of his lips against her skin. His hands gripped her wrists, as if to prevent her from running away.

As if she could, when this was all she wanted.

Her eyes fluttered open as he picked her up in his arms, as if she weighed nothing at all. His footsteps echoed against the red tile floors, his dark gaze unreadable as he carried her down the hallway to the enormous master bedroom.

White stucco walls surrounded the enormous bed, with its four large posters of black twisting wood, and a magnificent view.

Held in his arms, Lola looked back up at his face. The last time he'd brought her here, it had all been joy and laughter and passion. Because she'd loved him, even if he hadn't loved her back.

Now, everything they'd once had was lost.

Or was it?

No other woman. She still couldn't believe it. Even hating her, he had been faithful to her? That didn't make sense. Why would he be faithful?

The hazy golden light of late afternoon poured in from the west-facing windows as he set her on the bed, in a pool of warm sunlight. His eyes were dark as he stood above her, beside the bed. Never taking his eyes off her, he loosened the cuffs of his black shirt, then the buttons.

Her heart was in her throat as she looked up at him. The golden light caressed the hard planes and curves of his powerful, muscular chest, laced with dark hair. He was even more hard-bodied than the last time they'd been lovers, making her wonder if he'd spent the past year in the gym, or perhaps a dojo or boxing ring, getting out his frustrations in that most traditionally masculine of exercise: controlled violence.

Watching him now, Lola held her breath. Then he reached for her. Slowly, he pulled off her knee-high black boots, one after the other, tossing them to the floor with a noisy skitter of leather against tile.

Climbing beside her on the bed, he leaned forward to kiss her. She wrapped her arms around the warmth of his skin, feeling the hard muscles of his back.

He lifted her arms over her head and pulled off her shirt, revealing the black lace bra that barely contained her full breasts.

His expression was savage. Lowering his head, he kissed her lips hungrily. As his mouth moved slowly down her throat, she gripped his bare shoulders, closing her eyes, letting her head fall back against the pillow. He kissed her collarbone, and then lower, as his hands cupped her breasts over the black lace. He slowly caressed down her body, to her waist, to her belly and the edge of her black leggings.

He pulled the fabric slowly down her legs. She felt the butterfly-soft stroke of his fingertips move over her thighs, to her knees and calves, all the way to the hollows of her feet. He tossed the leggings aside, leaving her spread on the bed in only her bra and panties.

He looked at her, his expression dark.

"You're mine now, Lola," he said in a low voice. "To do with as I please."

She leaned up to cup his rough, angular cheek. "And you're mine…"

Reaching up, she kissed him, softly, seductively, swirling her tongue against his. She heard his soft groan.

With a low growl, he pushed her back against the bed, covering her body with his own. Reaching behind her, he unhooked her bra with a flick of his thumb, dropping the flimsy lace to the floor.

A choking sound came from the back of his throat when he saw her full, naked breasts. He gently cupped each one in awe, before kissing the valley between them to the soft slope of her belly, flicking her belly button gently with his tongue. His hands gripped her hips as his head moved lower.

She closed her eyes, her breath coming in ragged gasps as he kissed her skin along the top edge of her black lace panties, then, soft and slow, he pulled the lace down her hips, down her thighs, and took them off entirely.

She was naked in his bed, in a golden glow of light, with the windows open and the warm salt air breezes blowing in from the ocean.

Slowly, he spread her legs apart, kneeling between them. As he lowered his head, she felt the heat of his breath between her thighs. His fingertips slowly stroked up her hips, reaching around to grasp her backside.

Closing her eyes, she held her breath as he bent to taste her.

He slowly, ruthlessly, possessed her with his lips and tongue. She gasped with the intensity of pleasure as he splayed her wide with his hands, first lapping her, then moving the tip of his tongue around her taut nub in a sensual swirl that sent her higher and higher, until her whole body panted for release, and her hips started to lift off the bed.

When he lifted his head, she looked at him, and saw his black eyes glittering with feral need. In a single movement, he pulled off his trousers and black silk boxers.

She reached up her arms to him in silent demand. He moved up, and she felt his hard shaft between her thighs.

Then, as their eyes locked, he slowly pushed himself inside her.

She gasped as he filled her, inch by delicious inch. She gripped his shoulders, feeling him deep inside her, and hard, so hard. Slowly, he pulled back to thrust again, even deeper this time. She started to tremble as pleasure drew her back in a wave so high it threatened to drown her.

He rode her harder, faster. She held her breath, feeling dizzy as joy lifted her higher and higher still. Until suddenly, as he filled her to the hilt, pleasure exploded inside her, flinging her past the sky, into the stars.

CHAPTER FOUR

RODRIGO LOOKED DOWN at Lola as she cried out with pleasure, her face incandescent with joy. He gripped her shoulders, barely keeping himself from exploding into her.

He'd thought he could keep his distance, to make this about their bodies, only about sex. He was wrong. It wasn't just her body.

It was her face. Her voice. It was her.

Lola.

The only one he'd wanted. The one he'd dreamed about for the last year, in hot, unwilling dreams. Every morning, he'd woken up, still aching for her.

Now, at last, she was his. Forever.

And you're mine, she'd said.

Her claim washed through his soul. He trembled. He gloried in his possession of her.

But he could not surrender in his turn. Could not give himself fully. Not to Lola, or any woman.

But his hands were shaking as he gripped her. When he saw her burst with pleasure, a rush went through his body, through his soul, with a pounding roar.

Cupping her face in his hands, he said urgently, "You're mine forever. You'll never betray me. Say it."

"I'll never betray you," she said breathlessly, her beautiful face rosy with passion, her half-lidded eyes bright with ecstasy. And he believed her.

Lowering his lips against hers, he felt a searing joy—almost like pain—as his heart cracked inside him, like steel in sparks of flame. He wanted to trust her. He wanted to. She was his wife now. His—

And in that moment, for the first time in his life, Rodrigo lost control.

Gripping her hips, he gave in to the pleasure punching through him with violent force, knocking out his breath. A low growl built into a roar as he shattered, shuddering as he poured himself inside her.

And he collapsed.

When Rodrigo finally came back to awareness, it could have been minutes or hours later. He found himself tenderly holding her body against his own. Their bodies were intertwined, and he saw the warm, fading glow of twilight.

As he held Lola in his arms, joy went through him. It was as if the last miserable year had just been a bad dream.

Then he saw the motes of dust moving lazily in the light, like flickers of gold floating softly to the floor. And he remembered—everything.

Remembered why he could never trust any woman.

Especially now. They were married. They had a child. There was too much at stake.

He couldn't let down his guard. Because every time he did...

Pain cut through him, even more overwhelming than the pleasure had been. Suddenly shaking, he withdrew his hands from where they'd rested so cozily, so tenderly, on her body.

Rodrigo had thought he could have sex with a cold heart. But the joke was on him. He'd thought he could take her like a conqueror. Instead, after a year of mutual hunger, she'd matched his fire, and they'd burned together like a phoenix rising to the sun. It hadn't just been physical, but almost holy.

Far from conquering her, he'd wanted to give her—everything.

Slowly getting out of bed, he silently backed away. But as he picked up his trousers and boxers from the tile floor, he heard her lilting, husky voice.

"Where are you going now?"

His spine snapped straight. He turned to face her.

"Out. I'm going out."

Frowning at his tone, she slowly sat up in bed. "Where?"

His gaze traced unwillingly on her soft skin, the smooth curves of her body now a soft pink in the fading sunlight. He kept his face expressionless, careful to give nothing away. He'd learned, while building his media empire, that any emotional weakness only invited destruction.

But he hadn't just learned it in business. He'd learned it long before. From every single woman he'd known.

He said shortly, "Where I go is none of your concern."

Her lips twisted. "Of course it is. I'm your wife."

"I have business."

"Where?"

He thought fast. "South America."

"What?" Lola sat up straight, her expression incredulous. "You can't be serious. You just dragged me to California!"

"My business cannot wait," he said, but the truth was, *he* couldn't wait. To be as far away from her as possible.

"We'll come with you, then." She lifted her chin. "You married me so we could be a family. So you could help raise our son. Our place is at your side."

He had said that, Rodrigo realized. Did she see what had changed? Could she see the sudden weakness in his soul? Ice filled his heart.

"Your place is where I say it is," he said harshly. "I won't have you dragging Jett around the world for no reason."

She drew her knees up against her chest. She looked

suddenly young and forlorn. "Then why did you bring us here? Just to leave us?"

Rodrigo stared down at her, his heart pounding. But he couldn't let himself bend. If he did, he might break. Making love to her had left him strangely vulnerable. The walls around his soul, normally impregnable, felt as brittle as untempered steel.

"I will return soon. In the meantime, Mrs. Lee can help with the baby. Tobias and Lester will guard the door and drive you anywhere you require."

"Don't go," she whispered, her hazel eyes luminous.

"You'll be fine." Looking into her beautiful face, all shadows and rosy light, Rodrigo came closer. He lowered his head to briefly kiss her lips. She was soft and warm in his arms. He felt his body start to respond.

Ripping away, he choked out, "I'll leave my credit cards. My checkbook. Buy anything you desire."

And he left, without looking back.

Lola didn't expect to miss him, but she did.

Over the next week, she tried to distract herself from his absence by busily settling in to the beach house and caring for their baby. She bought new clothes for both her and Jett, suitable for the warm California weather and sunny days on the beach or by the pool. She found a new pediatrician, and a wonderful baby boutique in Santa Monica. Rodrigo had told her to use his credit cards, so she'd done her best.

But her heart wasn't in it. Shopping felt lonely. Strange, since she was never alone. Rodrigo's bodyguards, Tobias and Lester, insisted on driving Lola wherever she needed to go, and accompanied her and the baby whenever they left the compound. Even back at the beach house, kindly, warm Mrs. Lee was there all day, keeping the house in order and puttering in the kitchen, always offering to help or chat.

But Lola wasn't feeling chatty. The enormous, luxurious beach house had lost its shine. She felt Rodrigo's absence every day.

And every night.

Lola wasn't a romantic like her friend Tess. She had no dreams of hearts and flowers. But having her husband disappear after one day of marriage was beneath even her low expectations.

The big diamond ring weighed heavily on her left hand. Whenever she looked at it, it seemed to glitter back at her hollowly.

What kind of stupid marriage was this?

Lola tried to tell herself she didn't care. After all, she wasn't the one who'd demanded marriage. She and Jett had done fine without Rodrigo before. They could again.

She just wished if he'd changed his mind about their marriage that fast, he would tell her, so she and Jett could go back to New York, where they belonged. Where she had friends, people who would at least answer when she called!

Rodrigo only ignored her. Just that morning, Lola had gotten the thrilling news that she'd passed her GED, forwarded to California from her address in New York. Rodrigo had been the first one she'd wanted to tell. After all, he'd encouraged her, telling her she should have gone to college or even law school. Almost bouncing with excitement, she'd dialed his number.

But he didn't pick up his phone. Even after she called him multiple times. Finally, disconsolately, she texted him the news. He hadn't responded to that either.

Of course he hadn't. He'd given her the silent treatment all week, ignoring her calls, and even simple messages like her asking where things were in the house or if he'd already arranged a doctor for the baby. Even the message she'd sent him yesterday, informing him of the six-figure gift she planned for her baby sisters, had gotten no answer.

It was enough to make her hate this beautiful beach

house, where they'd once been so happy. And yearn to be somewhere else. Anywhere. But especially New York.

Wrapping her arms around herself, drawing her cashmere cardigan closer, Lola looked out the wall of windows overlooking the pool and, beyond that, the ocean and sky.

The sun was golden and warm, just like it had been the day Rodrigo brought her back here as his bride. He'd looked at her with so much emotion in his dark eyes before he'd kissed her. He'd made love to her with such fire and heat, such explosive pleasure, even more spectacular than she'd felt during their affair. She'd looked up into his handsome face as his body covered hers, and for one moment, she'd imagined their marriage could be about more than duty.

But obviously, she'd thought wrong. Because when Rodrigo had gotten up from the bed, he'd looked at her as if he hated the sight of her. And ever since, he'd ignored her, as if she were Typhoid Mary and he was afraid he might contract her disease from wherever he was in South America. If he really was in South America.

What had she done, to make him suddenly want to not only leave the bed but leave the continent?

Tess and Hallie would know, she thought suddenly. Hallie was always so sensible and practical, while Tess was idealistic with those rose-colored glasses. Missing them, she felt a lump in her throat. She'd sent them messages about her GED, and unlike her husband they'd immediately called, to cheer for her.

"Lola, you're so sneaky!" Hallie had said. "You never even told us you dropped out of high school when you were a kid!"

"You should have told us you were working for your GED," Tess chided. "I could have baked you cookies to help you study!"

Lola smiled now, thinking about them. Then her smile faded. What would Tess and Hallie say when they learned she'd left New York without telling them, and now lived in California? What would they say when they learned the identity of Jett's father, and that Lola had married him without inviting them to the wedding?

She should have told them, when they were congratulating her for passing her GED. She'd tried to. But the words had stuck in her throat. She wasn't like her friends, wanting to talk and talk about their unsolved problems.

Lola solved her own problems. *Then* she'd talk about them.

And the problem of her marriage felt very much unsolved. How could she explain why she'd married Rodrigo and moved to California at his demand, only for him to promptly dump her and Jett here and disappear?

Suddenly, Lola narrowed her eyes. She'd tried to be patient. But she'd had enough of waiting and wondering.

Any action was better than this.

He'd told her to spend his money? Fine. She would.

Going into Rodrigo's home office, she found his checkbook and wrote out a six-figure check, which she signed with a flourish. Anger made her fearless. Getting an envelope and paper, she wrote a letter to her sisters, the first time she'd written them in seven years.

Seven. She'd never meant to fall out of her sisters' lives so completely. But the days had passed so fast. Already, Johanna was twelve, and Kelsey was fifteen. *Fifteen.* The same age Lola had been when her mother died. When she'd decided to make it her life's mission to save her family.

She'd failed then. But maybe, if her little sisters knew how hard she'd tried, they would forgive her. And this check couldn't hurt, either.

With a deep breath, Lola signed the letter and tucked it into the envelope with the check. Sealing it, she wrote the address she'd long ago memorized by heart.

Her hand shook as she left the home office. Collecting

Jett from his playpen in the sunny main room, where he'd been happily chewing on toys, she felt so elated at what she'd done, she sang him a song she used to sing to her sisters. The baby giggled and cooed as she danced with him, pausing to look out through the windows at the bright blue ocean and sky.

Then she stopped. What if it didn't work? What if her sisters ignored her, just like Rodrigo?

Squaring her shoulders, Lola forced herself to go into the enormous, gleaming kitchen, where she found the housekeeper taking bread out of the oven. It smelled delicious.

"I made your favorite, Mrs. Cabrera," Mrs. Lee said, smiling. "I know how much you love it."

"You're too good to me. I was, um, wondering…" Lola nervously held up the envelope. "Is there any way you could take this to the post office? I'd do it myself but…" *But I'm scared I'll chicken out.*

"I'd be happy to." Wiping her hands on her apron, the older woman took the envelope with a smile. "I have a bunch of errands to run this morning anyway. Shall I do it now?"

"Yes, please, if you don't mind. And please get a tracking number and receipt."

"Oh, my." Mrs. Lee tilted her head. "It sounds important."

"It is. It's a present. For my…my sisters." Lola's heart was beating fast. She knew the girls were happy in their adoptive family. She'd long ago given up thoughts of custody. All she wanted now was for her sisters to remember her. And maybe, if she was very lucky, to forgive her. "Thank you, Mrs. Lee."

After the housekeeper was gone, Lola changed into a modest swimsuit and cover-up, put a swimsuit on the baby and slathered him with sunscreen, and put hats on them both to block out the hot California sun. Carrying Jett with one arm, and a large wicker basket full of toys with the other, she struggled out onto the white sand. Stretching out a beach blanket, she set up her baby comfortably, then sat down beside him.

With a deep breath, Lola stared out at the wide blue ocean stretching out to the west, all the way to Hawaii and Japan. She wanted to call back Mrs. Lee, and tell her not to send the letter. She felt scared and alone. Would her sisters ever forgive her?

But as she reached for her phone to call back Mrs. Lee, she heard Rodrigo's firm words.

You know how to argue people into things. When you're ready to see your sisters, you'll figure out how.

With a deep breath, she put down her phone. She'd try to be strong.

She wondered where Rodrigo was at this moment.

Staring out at the horizon, she saw something out of the corner of her eye. Turning, she saw a man coming toward her on the beach. For a moment, she thought it was Rodrigo. But it was a stranger. It was so unexpected, she sat up straight on the beach blanket, blinking in surprise.

A stranger? On this beach?

All of California's beaches were public, at least in theory, but this beach was virtually private, as it was on an isolated inlet surrounded by cliffs to the north and south.

The man looked like a surfer, wearing board shorts, flip-flops and an unbuttoned shirt that showed off his hard-muscled chest. He had blond hair, a deep tan and a toothy smile.

"Hello," she said, frowning.

"Hello," he said, smiling down at her. "Are you all alone? You're too beautiful to be lonely. Would you like some company? You and your charming baby?"

Lola's mouth dropped. Was this stranger hitting on her?

She wasn't wearing a bikini but a modest cover-up. But

he was looking at her as if he were a cat and she was a fish. For the first time, she wished the bodyguards were around.

"No, thanks." Picking up Jett from the blanket, she quickly packed up her things in the wicker basket. "I was just leaving."

"You were?" he said, his tanned face disappointed.

"Sorry." Straightening her big sun hat, she carried the baby and wicker basket back to the house, walking swiftly. Once she reached the safety of the terrace, she turned to look back. The beach was empty. The stranger was gone.

Of course he was. Lola exhaled. Obviously, she'd been alone in this house too long, to get so weirded out just by someone being friendly. Or maybe she'd finally become a true New Yorker. Strangers talking to her made her suspicious and alarmed.

But still, she couldn't shake the uneasy feeling.

Inside the beach house, she went to find the bodyguards. Lester was nowhere to be found, but she discovered Tobias pacing angrily in the courtyard, speaking into his cell phone.

"Chelsea, what are you talking about?" He gripped his phone. "You know I'm supposed to have him. This is the third time you've brushed me off." He listened, then an expletive escaped his lips. "That's a lie and you know it. He doesn't have homework. He's five! I deserve to see my son. And he deserves it, too. I pay child support. I've tried to be patient, but we both know the real reason..."

Tobias saw Lola, and his face went pale. "I have to call you back," he said, then scowled, "No, Chelsea, *tonight*. And if you even think you..."

Coming forward, Lola calmly plucked the phone out of his hand. "Hello, this is Mrs. Cabrera. Tobias's employer."

"So?" the woman's voice was sour, ready for battle. Good, because that was exactly Lola's mood.

"If you don't let him see his son, which is apparently

his legal right, we're going to have to either let him go, which means you'll be getting no more child support, or else we'll consider sending a full team of LA's best lawyers to ask the judge to reopen the case and pursue full custody on his behalf."

"What do you care?" the woman bit out.

"I don't," Lola said coolly. "But he's supposed to be protecting us, and it's obvious he can't do that when he's so distressed. Why won't you allow him to see his son?"

"None of your business!"

"But it is, as I just explained. So what's it to be? No more money? Or back to court?"

Silence fell on the other end.

"My new boyfriend doesn't like Tobias coming around."

"I understand," Lola said, relaxing. "But your son is the most important thing. Right? And your son needs his father. Doesn't he?"

There was a grudging sigh. "Yes," the woman said finally. She paused. "Fine. I'll deal with my boyfriend. Mason misses his father, too. He's been complaining about it. Put Tobias back on."

Lola handed the phone to Tobias. "Here."

Satisfaction flashed through her as she headed back into the house, carrying her baby on her hip. At least she hadn't lost all her skills. After unpacking her beach bag, she gave Jett a bath to wash off all the sunscreen. She toweled him off, changed him into fresh clothes and then held him close, relishing the clean baby smell.

Afterward, she carried him back toward the kitchen, intending to make herself a comforting cup of tea. Tobias was waiting for her in the great room.

"I get to see my son tonight after work," he said. "My ex is even going to give me extra time, to make up for the days I missed." He shook his head. "How did you talk her into it?"

She shrugged. "It wasn't hard."

"I guess the real question," he said slowly, "is why did you get involved?"

"As I said, I wanted your full attention—"

"Mrs. Cabrera." Shaking his head, he gave her a grin. "How dumb do you think I am?"

She stared at him, unblinking. Then she said slowly, "My father died when I was five, the same age as your son. I have almost no memories of him." She looked away. "I hate it when families are separated."

"I see," Tobias said quietly. He paused. "Was there some reason you came looking for me earlier?"

Sitting here, in this elegant, luxurious beach house, her earlier fears about the stranger on the beach seemed paranoid. "I just wondered if you'd heard from my husband since he left. Because…because I haven't. He hasn't answered any of my calls." At his astonished expression, she said quickly, "I just want to know Rodrigo is okay."

Tobias stared at her, then held out his phone. "Try calling him with this."

Lola's eyes went wide. She looked up at him. "Are you sure?"

He shrugged.

"He might fire you," she said.

"He can try." Tobias gave a crooked grin. "But I'm backing you, Mrs. Cabrera."

"Thank you," she whispered.

He turned away. Lola stared down at the bodyguard's phone in her hand. Slowly, she typed in Rodrigo's name. His number came up.

Taking a deep breath, she hit the dial button.

An hour after Rodrigo's private jet landed in Los Angeles, he walked into his office building downtown, feeling exhausted in a way that had nothing to do with his hectic business travel to his bustling film studio in Mexico City or his newly acquired television network in Buenos Aires.

For the last week, he'd barely slept. Even when he had, peace had evaded him. And he knew why.

Because of *her*.

He'd taken Lola as his wife. Taken her to his bed. He now had her securely under his control, and at a distance. He hadn't answered any of her messages or calls. He got reports on her welfare, and that of his son, from his bodyguards. He'd thought that would create the emotional distance he needed.

So why did Rodrigo still feel so vulnerable?

Why did he dream of Lola every night, in sensual dreams that were even worse than before?

Why did he wake up gasping for her like a suffocating man struggling desperately for breath?

He didn't have control of her, damn it. He didn't even have control of himself. It was why he'd left. Why he hadn't wanted to let himself be near her. Why he couldn't bear to look at her or hear her voice.

Lola made him want. She made him *feel*.

And feeling anything for a woman always led to loss. Women were liars. Deceivers. They couldn't be trusted, except to cause pain.

Keeping his distance was the only way this marriage would work. The only way to give his child a stable family and home.

But even being thousands of miles away hadn't created the distance he'd wanted. He had to find another solution. Because Lola was right. He hadn't dragged her to the altar just to abandon her and neglect his child.

Being away from his tiny son for a week had been intolerable. And Rodrigo knew Lola. She wouldn't put up with this silent treatment forever. Honestly, he was surprised she hadn't already tried to revolt.

Setting his jaw, he strode into his private office and tossed his briefcase carelessly on his gleaming dark wood desk. Turning, he looked out the windows overlooking the skyscrapers and haze of downtown Los Angeles.

Sleeping with Lola hadn't gotten her out of his system. For the last week, as he'd made deals, the image of her soft and rosy in bed, the memory of her body against his own, had fogged his brain in a hum of desire. He wanted her. In bed. On his desk. Against the wall. He wanted to possess her until they were both utterly satiated, however long that took. Even if it took forever.

But how could he make love to her, without being tempted to care?

"You're back!" Turning, he saw his executive assistant, Marnie McAdam, standing in the doorway. "Here are your messages, Mr. Cabrera." Setting down a small pile on his desk, she cleared her throat. "The International Studio Guild wants to know if you're bringing your wife to Madrid."

Rodrigo had the sudden vision of appearing with Lola on his arm, in all her rapturous beauty, when he accepted the award in Madrid next week for CEO of the Year. He'd be envied for his wife, even more than the prestigious award. And afterward, he'd take her to his bed and...

He shivered inside.

"I haven't thought about it," he said shortly.

"You need a date. It's a social event." Marnie tilted her head, looking at him owlishly through her glasses. "If she can't come, I could do it. Not as a date or anything," she added hastily, "but, you know, just to help out."

Rodrigo frowned at his assistant. Bring her to the ceremony? What was Marnie talking about?

Then he saw her pale, determined expression and relaxed. Marnie wasn't flirting with him, *gracias a Dios*. She was merely trying to solve a logistical problem on his behalf, like any good secretary would. "Thank you," he said smoothly, "but such a sacrifice on your part won't be necessary."

"It would be no problem, truly—"

"I know you don't care to travel. I'll deal with it."

Yes, by bringing Lola to Madrid, his body suggested slyly.

Perhaps he was taking it all too seriously, Rodrigo thought suddenly. Perhaps the emotional reaction he'd had last week had been a one-time thing, caused by his year of wanting her.

He blinked.

Sí, it was possible. In which case, the only way to prevent it from happening again was to take Lola to bed and binge on her until he was cured, like someone who, after drinking whiskey until he's sick, can never bear to taste it again.

Yes. The more that he thought of this—

His phone rang from his pocket. Looking down, he saw the call was from one of his bodyguards, Tobias.

"That'll be all for now, Marnie." He nodded at her. As she closed the door behind her, he answered his phone. "Is my wife becoming a problem?"

"I'm your problem now."

Her low voice made electricity skitter through his body, even as his spine snapped straight.

"Lola." He breathed deeply. "How did you get this phone?"

"I had no choice, did I? You're clearly not interested in taking my calls."

Rodrigo exhaled, and kept his voice a cold, deliberate drawl. "I've been traveling for business—"

"When I married you, Rodrigo, I meant it to be forever. But forever's not going to be like this."

And the phone went dead in his hands.

CHAPTER FIVE

WHEN RODRIGO ARRIVED at the beach house, Lola was ready for a fight.

She'd already packed her clothes and the baby's. Because she knew an ultimatum always came at a price—of possibly being forced to go through with the threat.

But she hadn't married him to be abandoned. If Rodrigo didn't intend to actually fulfill his promise to be a good father to their baby, then Lola was taking Jett back to New York, to be around people who actually cared about them. Marriage required two people, not just one.

When Rodrigo burst through the door, he strode into the great room, darkly handsome and a little terrifying. Lola faced him defiantly, holding their baby in her arms.

As usual, he was dressed entirely in black, even in sunny California. Unlike Lola, who now wore a T-shirt and shorts suitable for the weather, Rodrigo never changed, no matter where he was or what country he was in. He expected the world to conform to him, not the other way around.

Sometimes she'd liked that about him, that he was steadfast and strong, like an oak in a world full of weeds. Today wasn't one of those times.

"Nice of you to visit," Lola said coldly. "I thought maybe you'd forgotten you were married. Maybe you do need a ring."

He dropped his briefcase with a bang on the floor, causing their baby to jump with surprise in her arms. "I was *traveling*. For *business*."

She juggled Jett on her hip. "You got here fast, at least."

"I arrived in LA this morning. I was at the office when you called."

It surprised her how much that hurt. "You went there first? Instead of home?"

"Business comes first. You know that."

"Over family?"

"You were fine. You had Tobias and Lester and Mrs. Lee."

Lola glared at him. "You're seriously not this stupid."

He looked at her incredulously. "Stupid?"

"Is this your idea of marriage, of family, to just dump us and disappear? Because it's not what I signed up for."

Rodrigo looked irritated. "It's only been a week."

"Our first week. Our *honeymoon*."

"Don't be ridiculous, Lola." His dark eyes glittered. "We're not in love. Our marriage isn't based on romance."

"It should at least be based on respect. We have to look out for each other." She lifted her chin. "Otherwise, what's the point?"

Rodrigo scowled, then turned away, staring out the wide windows toward the infinite blue water of the Pacific.

Lola took a deep breath. "Look, if you want out of this marriage—"

"I don't," he said, cutting her off.

"Are you sure?" She set her jaw. "Because I've packed my bags. If you're just going to ignore me, I'm taking Jett back to New York. To be with friends."

Rodrigo slowly reached out to stroke Jett's hair. Then his dark eyes met hers. "You're right. I never should have left."

She sucked in her breath. She hadn't realized until that moment how tense she'd been. She hadn't expected Rodrigo to admit fault. He never had before.

"I'll never abandon you like that again, Lola," he said quietly. "I give you my word."

Lola felt a strange sensation in her chest. She'd been so ready for the worst. She cleared her throat. "Oh. Well, good." Her voice was a little hoarse. "We're supposed to be a family."

"I want that, too."

They stared at each other for a long moment. Then she turned away.

"Jett's started to get a tooth, did you see?" Lola pointed at his mouth. The baby, now four and a half months old, was cuddled against her hip, babbling happily to himself as he tried to chew on his pudgy hand. "That's why he's drooling. Yesterday, he rolled over for the first time. And he's gained another pound. His pediatrician says he's doing great."

"Look at you, *pequeño*," Rodrigo said, putting his hand on the baby's back. As he moved, his fingertips briefly brushed the bare skin of Lola's arm. Electricity went through her.

"You missed so much," she whispered. "I wrote to my sisters."

"Yes. You sent the gift?"

"Yes."

"You said how much it cost," he said dryly. "You didn't say what it was. A new house?"

The corners of her lips lifted. "I promised to pay for the entirety of their college educations. Medical school, law school, anything they want, at any university in the world."

His eyes widened. Then he smiled. "Very nice."

"And I passed my GED." In spite of her best efforts, hurt filled her voice. "I sent you a message. I wanted you to be proud of me."

"I was proud. I knew you could do it."

"But you ignored me!"

"I told Marnie to arrange flowers. Didn't she send them?"

Her eyes narrowed. "No. She didn't."

His jaw, dark with a five o'clock shadow, tightened. "You need to get over your irrational hatred for her, Lola."

Her eyes went wide. "Irrational!"

"She thought I had the right to know about your past. Both as your employer and as your lover."

"She's a smug know-it-all!" Lola thought of all the times Marnie had put her down for her lack of education, implying she wasn't smart enough for her job. "She wasn't doing it for your sake. She was trying to get rid of me!"

His expression shuttered. "Stop blaming her for your own bad choices. She's not the one with half-naked pictures, or who tried to sell herself at eighteen to be a star."

"I never tried to sell myself!" Lola cried, her hands tightening on her baby, who was fidgeting in her arms.

Rodrigo looked at her incredulously. "I saw the pictures. Why won't you admit the rest?"

Pain burst through her. She turned away, trembling. Carefully, she set Jett down in his baby play gym, leaving him to batt happily at colorful dangling toys. Taking a deep breath, she counted to ten. Then she faced Rodrigo.

"I didn't try to sell myself to be a star," she said in a low voice. "I was just desperate for money."

He snorted. "If you think that sounds better—"

"Just shut up a minute, will you!"

He fell silent. Her hands clenched at her sides.

"I told you my sisters and I were split up into foster care..." Her voice trailed off as she remembered how, at fifteen, with her mother dead and her stepfather gone, the social workers had pulled her from her half sisters, then only five and three. The little girls had cried and screamed, clinging to Lola, begging her not to let them go. Their screams haunted Lola for the next three years.

"Yes?" he said.

She shook her head. "I promised I'd get them back as soon as I could, so we could be a family again. The day I turned eighteen, I dropped out of high school and moved to LA hoping to make enough money. My plan was to be a movie star. I failed."

"Most actors do fail," he said matter-of-factly.

"I know that now." She flashed him a tremulous smile. "Plus, you know what a bad liar I am. I couldn't act my way out of a paper bag. I'd always been told I was pretty, but Los Angeles is full of pretty girls. Then I met a man who said he was an agent, and could make me a star. I let him take pictures of me in lingerie. He said they were test shots."

Folding his arms, Rodrigo was silent, watching her. Not meeting his eyes, Lola forced herself to continue.

"He sent me to a hotel suite, supposedly to meet with a producer. But the man didn't even bother letting me read for the part." Her cheeks went hot. "He tried to rip off my clothes and hold me down on the bed."

Rodrigo growled. Looking up, she saw waves of fury visible around him, from his tight shoulders and hard eyes.

"I kicked him in the groin and ran from the hotel room. He shouted after me that I'd never work in Hollywood again." She looked down at the floor. "And I didn't."

Rodrigo came toward her. "I'm sorry."

She swallowed hard, imagining she saw pity in his eyes. "Marnie must have spoken with my old agent to get the photographs. But she got the story wrong. I never tried to seduce anyone for a role." She gave a low laugh, wiping her eyes. "In fact, the whole experience was so awful I avoided being alone with men for years. Until—" She lifted her gaze.

His dark eyes burned through her. "Until me?"

She lowered her head. "Later, I almost wished I'd just

given the man what he wanted. Because by the time I earned enough as a secretary, it was too late."

"Too late?"

Lola turned away, toward the great room's windows. For a moment, she stared out past the terrace and slender palm trees toward the white sand and blue ocean. "Too late to get my family back."

Her heart hurt as she remembered how, after she'd finally earned enough to get her own apartment without roommates, she'd rushed to visit her sisters, to tell them they could all finally be together. She'd been nearly weeping with joy and relief.

But she found Kelsey and Johanna, now nine and six, pedaling gleaming new bikes on a perfect street in front of a new two-story house in the LA suburbs, as their golden retriever bounded in the sunshine.

"What happened?" Rodrigo said.

"They didn't remember me," Lola said in a low voice. "When I told them I'd be taking them to come live with me, they started crying and clung to their foster mother. The woman started yelling at me. And I found out—"

"Found out?"

"My stepfather had already relinquished his parental rights from prison." Her shoulders sagged. "They'd just been permanently adopted by their foster family." She took a deep breath. "I started yelling and crying. The parents were so scared of me, they moved away. To New York."

"Lola," he said softly.

Suddenly, she couldn't hold back her tears.

"I lost my family, Rodrigo," she choked out. "I failed."

For the first time in her adult life, she let someone see her cry, not a pretty cry either, but ugly and raw. Without a word, Rodrigo pulled her into his strong arms. For long moments, he just held her, stroking her hair as she wept against his shirt.

Finally, her sobs faded. Silence fell. With her cheek pressed against his chest, she could feel the steady, comforting beat of his heart.

"You didn't fail them, Lola," he said in a low voice. "You tried your best, when you were barely more than a kid yourself. You need to stop blaming yourself." He gently kissed the top of her head. "You'll hear from them soon."

Drawing back, she said breathlessly, "You think so?"

"Definitely." He gave her a crooked grin. "After the present you gave them, I don't see how they could resist."

Wiping her eyes, she gave a small laugh, like a sob.

Reaching out, he cupped her cheek. "And you have a new family now," he whispered. "Jett." His eyes met hers. "Me."

Their eyes locked. "You're my family?"

"I want to be," he said quietly, then shook his head. "Obviously I'm not very good at it. But I've never had one before."

"What are you talking about? You had parents. You were rich. You inherited a fortune—"

A flash of emotion crossed his hard, handsome face, but was quickly veiled. "Being wealthy isn't always what it's cracked up to be."

Rodrigo had been hurt, too, she realized. Somehow, in his childhood, he'd been hurt. Her arms tightened protectively around him in turn.

"We have to look out for each other," she said. "Watch each other's backs. Just like we used to, when we worked together. Do you remember?"

"You and me against the world?" She nodded, and his dark eyes flickered. "Remember what you said the first day you came to work for me?"

A whisper of a smile traced her lips. "I said you were a disaster and you'd hired me just in the nick of time."

"It was true. Since you left, my company hasn't done nearly as well. Neither have I."

"You have Marnie," she said, striving to keep the bitterness from her voice.

He shook his head. "She's had to hire two extra assistants just to keep up with what you did on your own. She's loyal and tries hard, but she doesn't have your skill. People still ask for you. You always remembered everything." Looking down at her, he said softly, "I miss you. I achieved more with you at my side."

"I'm back at your side now."

"You're right," he said slowly. He took a deep breath, then said humbly, "I have a business trip next week to Madrid. Would you come with me? You and Jett?"

Lola put down her arms, looking uncertain. "Madrid?"

Rodrigo tried to look modest. "I'm getting the award for CEO of the Year from the International Studio Guild."

It was an incredibly prestigious award. She sucked in her breath in delight. "You are?"

Reaching out, he tucked a tendril of blond hair behind her ear. "You're a big reason for it."

She tried not to tremble at his touch. "Me?"

Rodrigo gave a nod. "You helped me organize and acquire a television network that now stretches around the Pacific Rim, from Tierra del Fuego to Alaska to Manila. You're the one who convinced me to produce a film no one else wanted, which cost almost nothing to make but has now made almost half a billion dollars worldwide."

Her eyes were big. *"The Sapphire Sea?"*

"Turns out that romance is back in style."

Her lips lifted. "Who knew?"

"So will you be my date?"

Lola paused. "Sure."

"Good," he said quietly. Hearing a loud, noisy yawn, he looked at their baby in his baby play gym. Then he looked back at Lola, and they both laughed.

"It's time for his nap," she said.

"Let me do it."

She hesitated, then nodded. Reaching down, he lifted the baby gently into his powerful arms.

"You missed your *papá* this week, didn't you, *pequeñito*?" he said tenderly, looking down at Jett.

Seeing the two of them together, the tiny baby held against Rodrigo's powerful chest, caused Lola's heart to twist. She quickly turned away before he could see new tears in her eyes. Really, all this crying was getting out of hand. What was wrong with her? Had she gone completely soft?

"Here's his blanket," she said, pulling it from her nearby diaper bag. "There's a bottle already in the fridge. I usually rock him to sleep—"

"We'll be fine," he said, still smiling down at the baby. But as he carried Jett toward the hallway, he stopped and looked back at her in the beach house's great room. "And, Lola?"

"Yes?"

"Thank you for trusting me." For a moment, his dark eyes glowed at her, tender and warm, then he turned back to the baby in his arms, and disappeared down the hall.

Standing in the shadows, Lola stood still. She felt her heart thudding painfully in her chest. Her cheeks were hot. She felt vulnerable, exposed. She'd never shared the story of her past before, with anyone. But then, Rodrigo wasn't just anyone. Not anymore.

Then, slowly, a smile lifted to her face.

They were a *family*.

A week later, Rodrigo smiled at his wife in the back seat of the Rolls-Royce as their Spanish chauffeur and bodyguard drove them through the streets of Madrid.

Her beautiful face lit up with pleasure as she pointed out the sights to their baby in the car seat between them, while their chauffeur drove them down the wide Calle de Alcalá. Lola had always loved Madrid when she'd come here as his assistant. Now, as he looked at her joyful face, everything felt new. For both of them,

He'd been wrong about so much. When he thought of the way he'd tossed her out of his life so ruthlessly last year, he felt almost ashamed. He should have asked Lola for an explanation, rather than just believing the worst of Marnie's report.

Trust didn't come easy for him, it was true. Mostly because every single time he'd trusted someone, they'd betrayed him.

But this was different. He'd known Lola for years. He should have given her the benefit of the doubt.

He'd make it up to her, Rodrigo told himself now. He'd watch out for her and give her the life she deserved. The life they both deserved.

A shudder went through him at the memory of the pleasures they'd shared over the past week. Their relationship had only intensified after Lola—tough, fearless Lola—had cried in his arms.

From that moment, all he'd known was that he had to protect her. She was a part of him now, and he never wanted to let her go.

He'd had her story checked out, of course. Trust, but verify. It was the best he could do. Women had lied to him too often, and though he'd believed her, he'd needed proof. There was knowing, and knowing.

But if anything, his investigator had told him, she'd downplayed the poverty and tragedy of her childhood. She'd left out the fact that her stepfather had gone to prison, then died there a few years later. She'd left out the fact that the illness of her mother could have been cured, if only she'd had money and time to see a specialist earlier.

And while the investigator was at it, Rodrigo had had

him check to see if Lola had had contact with any other men, especially Sergei Morozov. She hadn't.

Rodrigo could trust her. Really trust her.

It was a shock to his system. He couldn't remember the last time he'd really trusted anyone.

But it had turned out, though his wife had grown up in poverty in the California desert, and Rodrigo had grown up in luxury in Madrid, they weren't so different after all. They'd both been hurt.

But never again.

Rodrigo's eyes caressed his wife's beautiful face as she happily pointed out sights to their baby through the streets of Madrid.

They were a family.

The Rolls-Royce pulled to the curb in front of an elegant nineteenth-century building in the exclusive Salamanca district, on a wide, tree-lined avenue overlooking the vast green expanse of the Parque del Buen Retiro. As the driver opened the passenger door, Lola unbuckled their baby from the car seat. Getting out of the vehicle, she looked up in awe.

"It's actually finished?" she breathed.

"*Sí.* Finally." For most of his adult life, he'd avoided this building, preferring to stay at a luxury hotel like the Campania Madrid, rather than face his childhood home. It was Lola who'd convinced him, two years before, to remodel the place and make it his own. She'd been aghast at the thought that he'd allowed a nineteenth-century penthouse on the Calle de Alcalá, overlooking the famous park, to dilapidate into dust.

"I can't wait to finally see inside," Lola said now, her eyes sparkling. "You never let me see it before."

Rodrigo looked up at the building as memories floated back to him of his childhood. He'd been lonely here, with his parents often gone. And when they were home, the house was filled with their screaming fights, slamming doors, his mother's taunts, his father's broken bottles smashed against the walls and the sour smell of expensive, wasted wine.

"Rodrigo? Is something wrong?"

Coming back to himself, he shook his head. "There wasn't much to see, after twenty years of neglect. Broken-down walls. Dust."

"I can imagine," she said quietly, looking at him.

A twinge went through him at the sympathy of her gaze. It was too close to pity, which implied weakness.

Lola reached for his hand, her eyes glowing and warm. "But everything is different now."

For a moment, Rodrigo was lost in her eyes. Then he pulled his hand away.

"Yes." He turned on the Madrid sidewalk. "Come see."

As the chauffeur and bodyguard lingered outside, getting their bags from the car, Rodrigo led her into the lobby. Hiding a smile, he turned to see her reaction.

Holding their baby, Lola looked with awe at the grandeur of the seven-story atrium, with the large oval staircase climbing all the way up, around each floor. Her steps slowed, then stopped, as she tilted her head back to look up at the stained-glass cupola crowning the top ceiling, beaming warm patterns of colored light against the marble floor.

"Wow," she breathed. "You paid for the lobby to be remodeled, as well?"

"I bought the whole building. I remodeled all the other apartments and sold them at a fat profit."

She glanced at him sideways. "Nice."

"This way."

Rodrigo led her to the new large elevator that had replaced the rickety birdcage elevator he remembered as a child. His nanny had often taken him to play in Retiro Park, when his parents' screaming became too loud. But usually the screaming was still going on when they returned, even hours later. They could always hear it before they even reached the top floor. So his nanny, looking stressed and sorry for him, would invent games allowing them to linger in the elevator.

Now, the gleaming silver door slid open silently, and they rode it to the top floor. There, they had a view of the entire atrium, stretching seven stories below. At the penthouse door, Rodrigo paused for a moment. He realized he was listening. But the apartment was silent now. No one was screaming or smashing glass.

His proud, aristocratic Spanish father—or at least, the man he'd believed to be his father—had been wealthy from birth, and bought a small Spanish movie studio, which was where he'd met Rodrigo's mother, a spoiled, much younger American actress. He'd loved her—been obsessed with her—but she'd never loved him, only his money. She'd enjoyed taunting him with her affairs. His father's rage had finally gotten the better of him, and he'd died of a stroke when Rodrigo was twenty-one. His mother had died a few years later, from a bad reaction to anesthesia during plastic surgery.

He'd never met the chauffeur who had supposedly sired him. The man had died when Rodrigo was just a child.

So many lies. So much deceit and rage. Rodrigo took a deep breath, closing his eyes.

"What's wrong?" Lola said cheerfully, coming up to the door. "Did you lose the key?"

He looked back at her. Jett's childhood would be so different. He was beginning to trust his wife as no one else. They had the same goals. They respected each other. And there was no messy emotion like love or jealousy to cloud anyone's judgment.

But he knew he'd never tell her about his childhood. There was no point. He wanted neither her sympathy nor her inevitable attempt at psychological analysis. There were some things a man dealt with better on his own.

And his past was in the past. Over. Forgotten.

"Don't worry." Reaching into his pocket, he held up the key. "I have it."

Pushing open the door to the penthouse apartment, he let Lola enter first, with the baby. As she passed him, Rodrigo's gaze traced hungrily over the lush curves of his wife's body.

Her eyes were wide as she looked around the elegant, minimalist apartment with its large windows and view of the park and much of Madrid, beneath the Spanish sky. "This was your childhood home?"

He remembered the screaming, the expensive clutter, the broken glass. "It didn't always look like this."

"But still." The edges of her lips lifted as she turned back to him. "You should have seen the place I grew up."

"A trailer," he said. "On the edge of the California desert."

Lola's hazel eyes went wide. Her beautiful face turned pale as she breathed, "How do you know that?"

He came closer. "I had to find out what was true."

"You had me investigated?" He heard cold anger beneath her voice. He shrugged.

"I had to know if I could trust you."

"And now?"

Reaching out, he pulled her into his arms.

"Now I do," he whispered, and he lowered his mouth ruthlessly to hers.

CHAPTER SIX

SINCE THEY WERE in Madrid the day before the awards ceremony, Rodrigo decided to visit the set of his company's new prestige film, a historical drama-romance of the Spanish Civil War currently being shot near the Plaza de Canalejas.

But even there, as he discussed the production's progress with the film's director, his eyes rarely strayed from his wife.

He couldn't look away from her. The way her beautiful face lit up as she chatted with the cast and crew. The warmth of her hazel eyes. The joy of her smile.

Lola was more beautiful than the star of any movie, he thought. Her long, highlighted hair swayed over her shoulders, caressing the tops of her breasts. She was dressed modestly, in her black coat and jeans that showed off her shape. As she pushed the baby stroller, she seemed utterly unaware of the fact that wherever she went, Rodrigo's eyes followed her.

Every other man's, too.

As she walked, her curvy body moved so gracefully and sensually, she seemed to be dancing to unheard music. Rodrigo frowned when he saw her speaking earnestly to the star of the film, a famous Spanish actress whom Rodrigo had once known well. *Very* well.

Ten years before, when Rodrigo was just twenty-seven—in the first flush of success, having expanded the derelict

Madrid studio he'd inherited from his father to twenty employees, including Marnie McAdam—he'd been briefly engaged to Pia Ramirez.

He'd fallen in love with Pia before they'd even met, while watching her onscreen, where she'd played a poignant heroine who sacrificed everything for love before she died, nobly and beautifully, at the end of the film. Five years older than Rodrigo, she'd seemed equally lovestruck after their first date. Within two weeks, he'd proposed marriage, and she'd accepted.

A month later, he'd been anonymously sent photos of Pia naked in bed with a man he didn't recognize. Young and naive as he'd been then, it had nearly killed him.

Little had Rodrigo known that this pattern would be repeated twice more, with two other women. A quick engagement, followed by an equally swift betrayal. With photographs.

But a few months earlier, when the director had wanted to hire Pia for this film, Rodrigo hadn't tried to stop him. Pia was talented and, at forty-two, still a major draw at the international box office. His other two ex-fiancées also still worked in the movie industry, and he'd never tried to hurt their careers. If you blacklisted everyone who betrayed you in Hollywood, you'd have no one left to work with.

But now, as the director continued to talk anxiously about the film's dailies and bloating budget, Rodrigo barely listened. His eyes kept falling on his wife talking to his former fiancée. He wondered what the two women could be talking about so intently. Him? No, surely not. Why would they?

Rodrigo's gaze dropped to Lola's backside, her hips. The gentle curve of her waist. She drew him like honey. He could hardly wait to take her home and—

He watched Lola take her phone out of her coat pocket. Looking down at it, she read something and smiled. A warm, intimate smile. As if she had a wicked secret. Still smiling, she tucked the phone back in her pocket.

What message could make her smile like that?

Who had sent it?

A memory of her voice came back to him. *If you're just going to ignore me, I'm taking Jett back to New York. To be with friends.*

Friends? A trickle of ice went down his spine. Friends like Sergei Morozov?

Why would the man propose if he's never even slept with you? His question echoed in his memory, along with her answer.

Because he thinks it's the only way he can have me.

It's nothing, Rodrigo told himself firmly. *She hasn't been in contact with Morozov. I know she hasn't.*

So why did he feel so suddenly on edge?

He interrupted the director in the middle of the man's sentence. "Excuse me."

"Of course." The director looked shocked, as if no one had dared to be rude to him for a long time. Leaving without a glance, Rodrigo strode past the side lights and cameras to the edge of the set.

"Hello," he said shortly to Pia Ramirez, who had been married to another man for eight years now. They had three children, none of whom he'd met, but he knew about them, in the way that everyone knew everything in the insular world of television and film production.

The Spanish actress sobered. "Hello." She smiled at Lola. "I just met your new wife."

"I see that." He looked at Lola. "What have you been talking about?"

Her lovely face was blank. "Nothing in particular."

But Rodrigo thought Lola had a guilty expression. What was she hiding? He didn't like it.

He ground his teeth into a smile. "I'm done here. Shall we go?"

"Sure." Her voice was overly casual as she turned to tuck a blanket around their baby in the stroller. "Jett is hungry, anyhow."

"So am I," he said.

She fed the baby in their waiting Rolls-Royce, then they decided to have lunch at his favorite tapas bar in Salamanca, on the Calle de Serrano. Afterward, sending away the Rolls-Royce and driver, they walked home down the lovely, boutique-lined street, pushing the sleeping baby in his stroller on the beautiful, though chilly, November day.

As they walked, they spoke of inconsequential things, such as the recent nominees for Best Picture and Best Director, and the speech Rodrigo intended to make during tomorrow night's International Studio Guild awards ceremony. But as he tried to tell himself he was being paranoid, because he'd already decided he could trust her, he found himself growing increasingly on edge as he heard pings from her coat pocket, indicating she was getting more messages on her phone.

Messages she studiously ignored.

Messages she obviously did not want to read in front of him.

Trying to reason away his sudden irrational fear, he reminded himself about the prenuptial agreement. Lola would never cheat on him. She'd lose everything.

But the more pings he heard from her pocket, the more his nerves felt scraped raw.

At Rodrigo's suggestion, they stopped in a designer boutique so Lola could find a new dress for the awards ceremony. As she went to the private dressing room with an armful of gowns, he waited in a private sitting area, next to their sleeping baby, calming his nerves with a glass of good champagne given to him by the solicitous salesgirl. He was already anticipating seeing Lola in the gowns.

Then he heard the noises from her nearby dressing room.

The pings coming fast and furious from behind the curtain.

And he realized, with a sickening lurch, that Lola was secretly, frantically sending messages back to the person who'd made her smile.

Rising from the comfortable white leather sofa, he crossed four steps to her dressing room. Scowling, he yanked open the velvet curtain.

Turning, Lola gasped, instinctively covering her half-naked body with her arms. He had a swift glimpse of her full breasts barely covered by a lacy black bra, and flimsy black panties. Instantly his breathing was hard, and so was everything else.

Then he saw the phone in her hand.

His body went cold, his breathing steadied, and everything became clear again. Looking down at her, Rodrigo said, his voice like ice, "Who are you talking to on your phone?"

Lola suddenly seemed to forget she was naked. She straightened, dropping her arms. Clutching her phone behind her back, she lifted her chin. "None of your business."

It was like waving a red flag in front of a bull.

"None of my business?" His voice was dangerously quiet now. "You're my wife."

"Your wife." Her eyes glittered. "Not your prisoner."

"Give me your phone."

"No!"

Reaching around her with his powerful arms, he felt her soft, half-naked body brush his own. As her plump breasts were crushed against his chest, his gaze fell to her full, raspberry-red lips.

He heard her intake of breath. Watched as the tip of her

pink tongue nervously licked the corners of her mouth, before her white teeth tugged into the tender flesh of her lower lip. For a moment, he felt lost, dizzy with need.

Grimly, he shook off the blinding haze of desire and reached around her to snatch her phone from her hand.

"You are such a jerk!" she cried.

He expected the phone to be locked, and for him to have to demand her password. But to his surprise, it wasn't protected. He touched the screen, and instantly saw whom she'd been talking to.

Rodrigo's eyes widened. She hadn't been exchanging messages with Sergei Morozov, or any other man.

She'd been chatting with two women. One called Tess, the other Hallie.

He looked swiftly through the messages, then looked up, dumbfounded. "These are just your friends."

"Of course," Lola said angrily, snatching the phone back. "Who else would I be talking to?"

"Why did you try to hide the messages from me?"

"Because they're private. They're my friends, not yours!"

"No." Did she think he was that stupid? He glared down at her. "There's a reason."

She narrowed her eyes, then said resentfully, "Fine. I wanted to ask you later tonight. After I had the chance to butter you up. Fat chance of that now!"

"You can't butter me up," he said arrogantly. She snorted, then shook her head.

"My friends were worried, since they hadn't seen me around for a while. They went to my apartment and Mildred told them I went away with some man."

"Not just a man. Your husband."

She sighed. "I didn't share that part yet. They were shocked enough as it was. I just said you were an ex who'd come back into my life." She bit her lip. "They're dying to know more. Tess invited us to Thanksgiving dinner next Thursday. I want to go. And tell them everything in person."

Rodrigo looked at her blankly.

"You know Thanksgiving, right?" she said, with exaggerated patience.

"Of course," he said. "It's one of the most profitable film weekends of the year in the US."

She rolled her eyes. "It's also a time to be with friends. Family. Turkey and mashed potatoes. Football on TV? Does that ring any bells?"

"I know Thanksgiving," he said, annoyed. "My mother was American."

Her eyes lit up. "So you know how important it is to spend the day with the people you love."

"It's not that big a deal. My parents usually were away that day. With…friends." His mother typically went jet-setting with her current lover, while his father either lost himself in work or pursued her in a rage, depending on his mood. Pushing the memory aside, he said, "But my mother always told our cook to bake me something like turkey. Often it was Spanish chicken with saffron rice."

"You're kidding." Shock flashed through Lola's eyes. "Your parents left you alone on Thanksgiving?"

"Somehow I survived," he said dryly.

She shook her head decisively. "You deserve a real holiday."

"So you're offering to visit your friends in New York for my sake? Noble."

"All right, you got me. I want to see them. Selfishly." Lola put her hand on his shoulder. "I couldn't invite them to our wedding. I wanted so badly for them to be there. But now Tess and Stefano are hosting Thanksgiving at their new home. I want to spend the day in New York. Either with you—" she lifted her chin "—or without you."

For a moment, Rodrigo was distracted by her soft touch

against his arm, and the full view of her breasts as she looked up at him with defiant hazel eyes. His blood quickened. "You're not taking my son away from me on Thanksgiving."

Her lips quirked. "So now it's suddenly a super-important family holiday?"

Staring at her full, wet lips, he murmured, "It's growing on me." Then he looked up. "Tess and Stefano? You don't mean Prince Stefano Zacco, the fashion billionaire?"

"That's him."

"You're best friends with Zacco's wife?" His eyes narrowed. "And what about the other one… Hallie? Do I know her?"

Lola gave him a cheeky grin. "You often stay at her husband's hotels."

His eyes widened. "She's married to Cristiano Moretti? Your best friends are both married to billionaires?"

"So?"

"Were they the ones who were going to help you fight for custody?"

She nodded. "We look out for each other."

So she'd never been plotting with Sergei Morozov behind his back. All his irrational fears had been just that—*irrational*. As she set down her phone, he said quietly, "I'm sorry I doubted you."

"Yeah. You should stop it." Putting a hand on her hip, she gave him a tilted glance beneath her dark lashes. "Get this through your head. I'll never betray you, Rodrigo. Ever."

Hearing Lola speak those words caused a strange rush through his heart. His gaze fell to her full, lush breasts in the bra, traveling down her nearly naked body, to her tiny bare waist, expanding to the curve of her hips, with the little flimsy black lace panties. Behind her in the mirror, he could see most of her backside, with only the tiny strip between.

"Show me," he whispered.

Pulling her into his arms, he lowered his mouth to hers. Pushing her against the wall of the changing room, he gloried in the feel of the soft curves of her body pressed against his own. He felt the tremble of her lips. Felt her hesitate.

He lured her, tempted her. He gripped her wrists to the wall, ruthlessly kissing her until her lips began to move against his, slowly at first, then hungrily, as her fire matched his own.

Pulling her wrists from his grip, she wrapped her arms around his shoulders, drawing him down harder against her.

Outside their small changing room, in the exclusive, private waiting area, their baby was still noisily snoring in the stroller, parked beside the white leather sofa and three-way mirror. For now, they were alone, but at any moment, Rodrigo knew they could be interrupted. Perhaps the boutique's salesgirls would come in to offer him more champagne, or bring more ball gowns for his wife to try on. He glanced back at the waiting area. For all he knew, there were security cameras.

He should take her back to his apartment, he knew, where they could be assured of privacy. But it would take too long. It would be twenty minutes. Thirty.

He needed her *now*.

Jerking the velvet curtain closed over the changing room doorway, Rodrigo kissed her passionately, cradling her face in his hands.

She was so sweet. So indescribably sweet. His earlier suspicions had melted away, and his heart was full of an emotion he didn't want to identify.

I'll never betray you, Rodrigo. Ever.

Lola belonged to him, him alone, now and forever.

Her long blond hair tumbled down her back as he slowly kissed down her throat. Her skin smelled of vanilla and summer, soft, warm and sweet. He felt her tremble as he caressed her bare arms, to her naked waist, his hands running over the hot skin of her back. He unhooked her bra, letting it drop to the parquet floor.

He cupped her full, magnificent breasts, and heard her intake of breath. Lowering his head, he kissed her creamy skin, all the while running his hands over her hips, her back, her delectable backside.

He was hard. Aching. It felt like he'd been hard for days, wanting her. It was some kind of strange magic: no matter how many times he possessed her, he hungered for more.

Her initial hesitation had disappeared, replaced by fierce, undisguised desire. It was something he'd always loved about Lola. She never tried to hide her desire for him, which only made him want her more, making the fire inside him burn hotter still. Holding her in his arms, in this small enclosed space, he felt a sense of urgency, knowing they could be discovered at any moment.

He stroked the edge of her black lace panties, letting his fingertips trail over her skin, from her hip around the curve of her leg to her thighs. He lightly grazed his hand over the lace, then moved the fabric aside to slowly stroke her beneath it.

She was wet. Hot and wet. He felt her tremble, heard her sharp intake of breath, and he wanted more. He wanted to hear her gasp and feel her shake as she shattered beneath his touch.

Kneeling, he peeled off the panties. Lifting her leg over his shoulder, he paused between her legs. For a moment, he inhaled the scent of her, letting her feel the warmth of his breath, teasing her. And when he felt her shiver, he pressed his mouth against her skin and tasted her.

She gasped, one of her hands pressing against the wall, the other gripping his shoulder with increasing intensity as he worked her with his tongue, one moment swirling the taut wet nub, then lapping her with the full width of his tongue.

She gave a sudden muffled cry, biting her lip to choke back the noise. But he felt the full force of her explosion by her fingernails gripping into his skin, deep enough to draw blood.

He'd given her pleasure, but it wasn't enough. He wanted to give her more. Much more.

His wife was naked, but he was still fully clothed.

Rising unsteadily to his feet, he unzipped his fly. Lifting her against the wall, he wrapped her naked legs around his hips. In a single thrust, he buried his shaft, thick and hard, deep inside her.

So sweet. So hot. So tight. Holding her backside with the width of his hands, he felt a wave of pleasure as he filled her. He groaned in ecstasy.

She gasped, her hips moving against him, her legs tightening around him as he pushed inside her, riding her against the wall. Then he made the mistake of looking at her face.

Lola's eyes were shut, her beautiful face glowing with sensual, almost sacred joy.

Seeing that, he lost control. With a low growl, he thrust deep inside her, hard and fast. This time, she screamed with pleasure, uncaring of who might hear them. And at that, he exploded, spilling himself inside her with a low, ragged roar.

They barely had a moment to catch their breath, when, in the private waiting room beyond the velvet curtain, they heard a surprised snuffle, followed by a plaintive wail.

"Now you did it." With her legs still wrapped around his hips, Lola gave him a heavy-lidded grin. "You woke the baby."

"I did?" He returned her grin. "You were louder."

"Your fault," she said loftily.

For a moment, they just smiled at each other tenderly, their bodies still entwined. He felt that strange burst of happiness, coming from the vicinity of his heart.

His heart.

A chill went through him. Abruptly, he released her, letting her feet slide to the floor. Not looking at her, he zipped up his fly.

"I'll go take care of Jett," he mumbled, and left her, closing the velvet curtain abruptly behind him.

As he took their baby out of the stroller, comforting Jett after the noise had woken him from his cozy nap, Rodrigo pulled a bottle from the bag tucked in the bottom of the stroller. He tried to tell himself he hadn't felt what he'd felt. It was good sex. That was all. Just sex.

"Everything is all right, *señor*?" An alarmed salesgirl looked in on the private waiting area. "We heard a noise. It sounded like a scream."

Rodrigo gave her his coldest, most supercilious stare. "My son woke up from his nap. Surely that's not a problem. If it is, we can shop elsewhere."

"No, no, of course not, *señor*." The salesgirl backed away. "Let us know if your lovely wife needs anything more."

He stared after her.

His lovely wife already had everything she needed. His fortune. His name. His body. She needed no more.

She'd loved him once. She wouldn't make that mistake again.

And neither would he. Every time he'd loved a woman, she betrayed him. Was every woman faithless? Or was there something about Rodrigo that made them so, from the moment he loved them?

He didn't know, but it had happened not just once, not twice, but three times. He wouldn't make it four.

These feelings he felt for Lola were sexual, nothing more. And that was all they could ever be.

CHAPTER SEVEN

THE NEXT NIGHT, as they walked into the large, elegant ball-room of a grand hotel on the Gran Vía, Lola kept sneaking glances at her husband on her arm.

Over the last twenty-four hours, they'd made love six times. Before she'd even stopped blushing from the shocking sexual encounter in the luxury clothing boutique they'd barely gotten home when Rodrigo had started kissing her again. In the great room with its view of the autumn colors of Retiro Park, Rodrigo had pulled her onto the sofa, and made love to her, this time taking off his own clothes, with gentle, seductive urgency.

Later that night, once their baby was properly asleep in his crib and they had hours to call their own, Rodrigo had made love to her again, slowly, lingeringly caressing every inch of her. As if they had the rest of their lives to enjoy each other.

Which they did.

Lola didn't understand how any woman could ever be unfaithful to Rodrigo. And she wasn't the only one, apparently. Even his ex that she'd spoken with on set yesterday, the famous actress Pia Ramirez, had seemed bewildered by it.

"So you're Rodrigo's new wife," the older actress had said. "I'd started to think he would never marry."

"And you're the one who cheated on him," Lola had

replied bluntly. The other woman's eyebrows raised, as if she were trying to decide whether to be offended; then she'd sighed.

"I loved Rodrigo, with the impetuous love of the young. He was working, chasing his empire. While he was gone—" she'd lifted her hands helplessly "—a handsome actor started paying attention to me every day. He said he was desperately in love, that he would die for me. But after he got me into bed, somehow, pictures were sent of us to Rodrigo." She'd looked away. "I'm happy now, married with a family. But I still wonder sometimes who sent those photos. And who that man was. I never saw him again. But he destroyed everything."

"You destroyed it," Lola said coldly. Then her phone buzzed, and she'd been distracted by funny messages from Tess and Hallie in New York, begging her to come for Thanksgiving.

But the more Lola thought about it, the more confused she was by the whole thing. She looked up at him now, in the gilded ballroom of the grand nineteenth-century hotel. How could anyone betray Rodrigo?

He looked impossibly attractive, dressed in a sleek tuxedo that accentuated the hard, powerful shape of his muscular body. Even now, while he was surrounded by people congratulating him on getting his award, his dark eyes lingered on Lola in the slinky, low-cut red dress she'd chosen from the boutique.

He'd helped her put it on tonight in their bedroom. Then, after taking one look at her, he'd helped her swiftly take it off again. Which is why they'd arrived twenty minutes late. Her cheeks went hot, remembering.

It wasn't like her to blush. But her husband did that to her. He peeled away her defenses, leaving her trembling and gasping and hot. Just as he'd peeled away her lingerie in that shop.

As they walked through the crowded ballroom, as they ate dinner at the head table, as she saw her husband honored by his peers, Lola basked in the glory of being his wife. Especially since he made it clear to everyone that it wasn't just his glory, but hers. Whenever anyone congratulated Rodrigo, he said: "It was entirely my wife's idea. She should be getting this award with me." His dark, sensual gaze simmered through hers. "I'll thank you later, believe me."

She shivered. She didn't think she'd ever get enough of him *thanking* her.

Her heart was bursting with pride as she watched him go up to the podium, to thunderous applause. But as he started his speech on stage, someone plopped beside her at the table in the darkened audience, into his empty chair.

Looking in surprise, she saw Ulrika Lund, the well-known director, whom Rodrigo had briefly been engaged to after Pia Ramirez, some eight years before.

"So you're the wife." Ulrika said without preamble. She was very thin, with muscular arms, and dressed in severe black.

"Do you mind?" Lola said, annoyed. "I'm trying to hear his speech."

"I'm sure you are, because he's praising you. He praised me once, too. For about a day." Her jaw tightened. "But as soon as I agreed to marry him, he was suddenly too busy to see me."

"Is that your excuse for cheating on him?" Lola said coldly, looking up at her handsome husband on the stage, wishing the woman would go away.

Ulrika leaned forward, drumming her fingers impatiently. "I met another man while Rodrigo was gone. A man who hung on my every word. Eventually I gave in. Then someone sent Rodrigo photographs of our night together. That gave him a convenient excuse to end our engagement." She paused. "I never saw the other man again.

Even when I tried to find him. I discovered he'd given me a fictitious name."

A warning buzz went off in the back of Lola's mind. It sounded almost exactly like the story that Pia Ramirez had told. *Coincidence*, she told herself firmly. Pushing the disquieting thought aside, she said, "And this affects me how?"

"I think Rodrigo was behind it."

"Don't be ridiculous," Lola bit out. As her husband continued to speak on stage, other people at the table looked in irritation at their whispers.

"It took me a while to figure it out," Ulrika said with a hard stare. "But every time Rodrigo gets close to a woman, he sabotages it. I used to blame myself, but not anymore. Not after it happened in all three of his engagements." She looked at Lola. "He actually married you. So the devastation will be twice as crushing when it comes."

"It won't—because I'd never cheat on him!"

"Don't get comfortable. That's what I came to tell you. Because you won't be with him for long." The woman glanced up at the stage, her lips twisting bitterly. "He'll see to that."

And she left.

Lola felt dizzy as she tried to focus back on stage. Her husband was smiling, gripping the edges of the podium, looking out of his spotlight toward the thousand film industry people sitting at tables in the ballroom.

"And most of all, I'd like to thank my former assistant, now my wife, for being the reason I'm here tonight, accepting this award. And more importantly, for giving me the greatest gift of all—our baby son."

There was a low *awwww* from the crowd, and then applause, scattered at first, then building to a roar, as he smiled for the crowd and, gripping his gold statuette high, left the stage.

But Lola only dimly heard his words or the crowd's

adoring response. All she could suddenly think about was the stranger who'd shown up in California, when Rodrigo was in South America. The stranger who'd come out of nowhere to chat with her on the beach.

Are you all alone? You're too beautiful to be lonely. Would you like some company? You and your charming baby?

He'd made her nervous, but she'd told herself it was just typical California friendliness. And as for the man's uncanny good looks, well, half of Los Angeles were out-of-work actors. Good-looking people were the norm, not the exception.

But now the whole thing had a surreal, almost sinister aspect.

Every time Rodrigo gets close to a woman, he sabotages it. I used to blame myself, but not anymore. Not after it happened in all three of his engagements.

No. Lola took a deep breath. It couldn't be true. He wouldn't sabotage his own engagements. Why would he?

She had the sudden memory of his face when they'd returned to the apartment in Madrid. He'd looked almost— haunted.

And yet she knew he'd grown up surrounded by wealth, with both parents. She'd always assumed he'd had a happy childhood, growing up in privilege. But now, not for the first time, she wondered about the dark shadows she'd seen in his eyes. Not just in Madrid, but from the day they'd met. That edge of cold ruthlessness in him, beneath his civilized veneer.

Together, you and I can give him a better childhood than we had. Either of us.

She'd never seen a picture of his parents or even of Rodrigo as a child, she suddenly realized. No family pictures, not in his beach house or anywhere else. And the story he'd told of his parents abandoning him on Thanksgiving, leaving him with the cook. Who did that?

What didn't she know about his past?

A trickle of ice went down her spine. Could Ulrika Lund's suspicions have a shred of truth?

I still wonder sometimes who sent those photos. Pia Ramirez had sounded bewildered. *And who that man was. I never saw him again. But he destroyed everything.*

Was it remotely possible that Rodrigo could have hired those men himself to try to seduce them, as a test of his fiancées' loyalty?

Or, worse, as Ulrika had suggested, because Rodrigo just wanted a good excuse to end those engagements?

No, Lola thought desperately. *Rodrigo's not like that. He wouldn't do that.*

But she knew he had a cold, ruthless streak. She thought of the way he'd cut her so abruptly out of his life because he'd seen a few lingerie photos and heard a vicious, untrue rumor.

Right after she'd dared to say she loved him.

"Well?" Rodrigo sat down beside her, putting the gold statuette on the table with a grin. "How did I do?"

"It was very good," she said, wishing she'd been able to actually listen to his speech, rather than the unsettling ideas that Ulrika had put in her head.

"I meant it." His dark eyes focused on her intently. "Every word."

"Oh. Um." She bit her lip, lowering her gaze, feeling the smiling gaze of others around them at the table. "Good."

Lola wondered what he'd say if she told him about Ulrika's accusation. Surely, Rodrigo would laugh. Yes. He'd laugh. Then they'd both laugh together.

And yet, she couldn't force the words out. Because she was scared of what would happen. Scared of what he'd say.

Lola remembered again that man on the beach. Walking

alone, without any apparent reason to be there. Or any way of getting there, unless he'd climbed over the cliffs jutting out into the ocean. Why would anyone do that?

Unless he was paid.

Unless it was his job.

How easy would it be to hire an actor willing to do underhanded work for exceptionally high pay? Especially for a billionaire who happened to own an international conglomerate of television networks and film studios?

"Lola? Did you hear me?"

She blinked up at Rodrigo, sitting beside her in the hotel's grand ballroom in the center of Madrid. "Yes, I mean, no. What did you say?"

He looked at her like she was crazy. "I've decided I'll go with you and the baby to New York for Thanksgiving."

An unexpected smile lifted her lips. "You will?"

"If nothing else, I can use the time to negotiate with Cristiano Moretti for a deal with his hotels." He grinned. "Though I know what you're thinking."

"I doubt that," she said faintly.

"You're going to tell me that I work too much. That Thanksgiving is a time for friends and family."

"Yes. Exactly." She turned away, reaching for her tiny handbag so he couldn't see her expression. "I'll let Tess know to expect us."

As she sent a message on her phone, the ballroom lights suddenly became brighter, as guests began to take their leave. With a deep breath, she looked up at her devastatingly handsome husband, sitting beside her, barely acknowledging people's congratulations as they passed by. His dark gaze was focused only on her.

"Shall we take advantage of the housekeeper watching Jett tonight, and go to the after-party?" Leaning forward to tuck hair behind her ear, he whispered huskily, "Or would you rather go home?"

Lola tried to pull away. To keep her body from responding to his touch. To be guarded and cold. To protect herself, just in case her worst fears were true.

But she couldn't.

"Home," she breathed, searching his gaze.

"Good." Her husband cupped her cheek, his dark eyes lazy as he gave her a sensual smile. Exactly, Lola thought with a shiver, like a cat would look at the mouse in its claws.

"You're sure this is it?" Lola said nervously, juggling their whining baby in her arms.

Rodrigo stopped ahead of her down the hall, pushing the empty stroller. Double-checking the number, he looked back at her.

"There are only two on the penthouse level," he said, waiting for her to catch up. "This is it."

Lola saw the number clearly on the door, and felt foolish. But then, she'd felt foolish a lot today.

After their five-day trip to Madrid, they'd left for New York later than planned yesterday. Jett had been fussy on the plane. He was teething, which made the baby irritable and unable to sleep, which made him miserable. Which made his parents miserable, too.

They'd woken up exhausted that morning in Rodrigo's luxurious SoHo loft, cranky and tired from a transatlantic flight followed by a sleepless night. Her husband had suggested they let the baby sleep in that morning, and the two of them enjoy the time in bed.

But Lola had dreamed of seeing the New York Thanksgiving Day parade since she'd watched it on television with her mother, long ago, and then later, when her mother worked on that day, with her little sisters. She was determined that their baby's first holiday season would be magical, starting with this Thanksgiving weekend in New York.

So she'd insisted on waking Jett up, getting everyone

dressed and out early into the cold, icy morning to wait on snow-covered streets. They'd watched the parade from Rodrigo's specially arranged VIP seats, and at first, it hadn't gone too badly. Holding their bundled-up baby in her lap, as they waited for the parade to begin, Lola had felt excitement that exceeded the cold nip of the air. This was exactly the life she'd yearned for when she was younger. This moment. Being a family. Having enough money to be safe and secure. Jett was having the childhood she'd only dreamed of as a girl.

Reaching for Rodrigo's gloved hand, she'd whispered, "Thank you."

He looked surprised, then his dark eyes gleamed. "All this for some seats at a parade?"

"You don't understand." She blinked hard in the cold air. "My whole childhood, I dreamed of this. The life only rich people could have. To be in New York for the Thanksgiving parade, and see real snow, and eat a pretzel on the street and spend New Year's Eve in Times Square…"

"You know that you don't have to be rich for any of that, don't you?"

"And a big expensive Christmas tree. And a mansion in Beverly Hills."

"Beverly Hills? Malibu isn't good enough?"

"I know. That part was silly." She looked down. "But my first Christmas in LA, when I was still trying to be an actress, I delivered flowers for a shop in Beverly Hills. I saw all these gorgeous mansions decorated for Christmas, and sometimes I'd see the people who lived there. There was one house in particular, once owned by silent film stars. El Corazón, I think it was called. One Christmas Eve I saw the family who lived in it and I dreamed…"

"Dreamed of what?"

Catching herself, she flashed a crooked grin. "Dreamed of their mountains of presents around the tree."

"Ah." His voice was amused. "Mountains of presents in a Beverly Hills mansion. That does take money."

As he took her hand in his own, Lola wouldn't meet his eyes. Her dream hadn't been mountains of presents, but something less tangible. She'd seen just a brief flash of the wealthy, perfect family, the handsome husband playing with his children as his wife answered the door in an apron, obviously just come from baking some kind of holiday treats. All of them glowing with health, happiness and love. To Lola, heartbroken over her baby sisters, with just five dollars to her name, that life had seemed as perfect and untouchable as their magnificent manicured gardens beyond the walls.

Lifting a dark eyebrow, Rodrigo said wickedly, his fingers tightening over hers, "But you're getting ahead of yourself, *querida*. Santa brings mountains of presents only to those who are good, not naughty like you."

"Oh, but I've been good," Lola whispered, leaning toward him on the VIP bench as they waited for the parade to begin. Reaching out with her glove, she'd cupped his cheek, still dark with five o'clock shadow as they'd rushed out that morning early with no time for him to shave. "I've been very, very good. But maybe I can be even better..."

Rodrigo's black eyes had gleamed as he leaned down to kiss her.

Then their tired, irritable baby burst into a plaintive cry in Lola's arms.

She spent the next hour juggling him, with a pacifier and a teething toy. She was so frantic, bouncing him in her lap to keep him from crying, that she barely noticed the enormous balloon floats finally fly past or the marching bands pass by. As Jett continued to fuss, she imagined people around them judging her harshly for bringing a five-month-old baby to sit outside in the freezing cold morning for a parade that took hours. She glared at someone who dared to look at her. She would have yelled something rude, but Rodrigo suddenly took the baby from her.

"Relax," he told Lola firmly. Then he looked down at the baby in his lap. "Don't keep your mother from enjoying her parade, *mi pequeñito*."

The baby looked up at his father, tears still staining his plump face, his lips parted. But something about the low rumble of Rodrigo's chest seemed to calm the baby. Frowning, Jett waved a chubby arm in his father's direction, then chomped quietly on his chew toy, staring up at the big cartoon balloons in the sky.

Lola just stared at them together, tears burning behind her eyes.

After all her years of dreaming about seeing the parade in New York, she barely remembered it afterward. What she remembered was the way Rodrigo had comforted their baby.

After they left, they'd visited an expensive toy store, where Rodrigo ordered thousands of dollars of toys for Jett without once looking at a price. Since Jett wasn't fussing, it was all enjoyable. Until Lola suggested having the toys delivered to their SoHo loft.

"It'll be delivered to California," he said firmly. "That's our home."

Lola felt deflated. "I know. But it's so nice being back in New York. That's where my friends live. My sisters."

"My accountant said your sisters still haven't cashed the check you sent them for college. Did the girls ever contact you?"

"Um… No. Not yet." Her heart tightened. She was trying not to think about that, or what it might mean. She rushed to say, "Maybe they've been busy. You know how teenagers can be…"

"They might be thoughtless, but what about their parents?"

Lola thought of the one and only time she'd spoken to her sisters' adoptive parents, when she'd showed up unannounced at their suburban home seven years before. When, while the girls had clung to their new mother, their father had told Lola to get the hell out before he called the police.

Lola pushed the painful memory away. A lot had changed since then. Surely they would realize they had nothing to fear from her now, and they'd accept her gift? And, you know, send a thank-you note or something?

But they hadn't. Even that big check hadn't made them want to talk to her.

Lola's heart twisted, but she turned away with a shrug. "It doesn't matter. Eventually I'll get through to them." Biting her lip, she looked up. "Though it would be easier if we lived here in New York instead of California…"

His face shuttered. "No."

Tilting her head, Lola said thoughtfully, "Did you know that as the film industry is increasingly a worldwide market, New York has become a hotbed of media companies that will dominate the future of the entertainment business?"

Rodrigo looked as if he were fighting a smile. "You just made that up."

Her lips quirked. "It could be true."

Rodrigo snorted, shaking his head. Then, as they'd left the toy store, he'd said quietly, "I'm sorry, *querida*, but we live in California. Enjoy your time here while it lasts."

Now, as they stood in the hallway of Tess's new co-op building, Lola looked at her husband, her heart in her throat.

Enjoy your time while it lasts.

Would their marriage last? Or would that, too, soon end?

Every time Rodrigo gets close to a woman, he sabotages it… He actually married you. So the devastation will be twice as crushing when it comes.

"Well?" he said sharply, standing in front of the penthouse door. "You were so worried about getting here on time. What are you waiting for?"

"Nothing." But as Lola lifted her hand to knock, she heard people laughing inside the apartment, and hesitated.

Looking at the huge diamond ring on her left hand, she suddenly wished she'd told Tess and Hallie the news of her marriage over the phone. Earlier, she'd grinned at the thought of seeing the shock on their faces, that Lola, the one who'd bossed the other two girls into telling their ex-lovers about their babies, had suddenly—without warning—married her own baby's father.

Because, unlike her friends, Lola had always refused to reveal the identity of her baby's father. Hallie and Tess had crazy theories about who Jett's father might be—that the man was married or some kind of criminal. Tess was especially good at coming up with eye-popping theories.

She hadn't wanted to tell them the simple truth, that Jett's father was Lola's old boss. She'd been trying to forget his existence, and thought if she didn't say Rodrigo's name, she wouldn't think about him, either.

But now, she felt like she was springing the news on her friends out of nowhere. *Hey, you know how I stubbornly refused to tell you anything about Jett's father? Well, here he is! And he's a Spanish billionaire! Ha-ha! And guess what? We're married!*

Well, Lola consoled herself wryly, at least the two women wouldn't be able to complain about having yet another bridesmaid's dress gathering dust in their closets for eternity.

Squaring her shoulders, she knocked hard on the door.

A moment later, it opened, and she saw Tess's beaming, pink-cheeked face, her red hair tumbling over her shoulders.

"Lola!" she squealed. She turned to call over her shoulder, "Hallie! Lola's here!"

The brunette came quickly, almost at a run. Lola came

inside carrying Jett, Rodrigo following a moment behind her, pushing the empty stroller. Helping her and the baby off with their winter coats, he disappeared behind the closet door. Tess's eyes went wide, and she looked at Lola, her eyes full of questions.

"I like your new place, Tess," Lola said evasively, looking around the gorgeous penthouse, with two-story windows overlooking most of snowy Central Park. "But where's your furniture?"

"It hasn't arrived from Italy yet. We've only just got the keys." She glanced back at her husband, who'd come up behind her. "Stefano wanted to wait and host New Year's Eve instead—"

"But Tess insisted on Thanksgiving," the Sicilian prince said, wrapping his arms around his wife's waist, who giggled.

"I'll host New Year's Eve," Hallie's husband, Cristiano, yelled from the next room.

"Anyway." Rolling her eyes, Tess turned to Lola. "We had to have the meal catered, but I knew you and Hallie wouldn't care if we sat on folding chairs. Love is what matters, right?"

"I couldn't agree more," Stefano said, nuzzling his wife. Then he seemed to remember they were surrounded by people, and straightened. His eyes focused on Rodrigo, who'd just closed the closet door. "Cabrera? What the hell are you doing here?"

"Rodrigo Cabrera!" Tess exclaimed, clapping her hands together. "I knew I recognized you!"

"Hey, Zacco." Looking at Tess, he said politely, "Thank you for the invitation to Thanksgiving."

Tess looked utterly bewildered.

"Who's he?" Hallie demanded, her face puzzled as she stared at Rodrigo. "Why is he pushing Jett's stroller?"

Behind her, Cristiano wandered in carrying an empty

tray. "Table's all set," he said with pride, then stopped when he saw Rodrigo. "Who are you?"

Lola took a deep breath.

This was it. The moment of her big announcement. She thought she'd feel smug and cheeky. Instead, she just felt awkward.

"This is Rodrigo Cabrera," she began. "I used to work for him in California. He's…um…" She looked at him, then mumbled, "Well, he's the father of my baby."

"What?" Tess said.

"No, seriously?" Hallie said.

"That's not my only news." Adjusting her baby against her hip, Lola lifted her left hand, letting the huge diamond engagement ring glitter in the light.

Her friends gasped.

"I can't believe it," Hallie said, grabbing her hand to look closer at the ring.

"And we're not just engaged. We're…we're married."

"Married!"

"I knew it!" Tess cried, practically bouncing with joy. Reaching out, she stroked Jett's soft, downy hair. "I knew you wouldn't love someone who was no good!"

At the word *love*, Lola's cheeks went hot, and she glanced back self-consciously at Rodrigo. But he'd been drawn across the room to accept the raucous, teasing congratulations of the two other men.

"Why didn't you tell us?" Hallie said softly, her soft brown eyes accusing. "We imagined your baby's father must be a total disaster, since you refused to tell us his name." She eyed Rodrigo. "He doesn't seem so bad."

Lola looked at her husband. "He's not." Her voice trembled a little. "He's not bad at all."

The two women stared at her.

"Oh, man," Tess said. "You've got it bad."

Oh, no! The last thing Lola wanted was for that rumor

to go around, especially when Rodrigo was only ten feet away! Lola turned on the redhead with a growl.

"Don't be ridiculous. We only got married for the baby's sake. To be practical."

"So you're not having sex?" Hallie said.

Lola's cheeks went hot. "It doesn't mean anything. It's just a benefit of being married." Her voice turned husky as her eyes unwillingly returned to her handsome husband. "He's my baby's father, and I respect him, and like him so much…"

Hallie followed her gaze, then the usually sensible brunette said, almost in awe, "Tess is right. You love him like crazy." She slowly looked over Lola's black cashmere sweater and leggings and knee-high boots. "It's written all over you."

"Hush!" Lola angrily grabbed Hallie's arm. "He'll hear you."

The brunette looked bewildered. "And that would be a bad thing?"

"Yes," said Tess, looking at Lola's face. Taking Jett from her arms, the redhead waved for them to follow. "Come in here." Turning toward the men, she said loudly, "We'll be in the kitchen."

Prince Stefano called, "Need help?"

"No, we, um, Lola wants a good recipe for pie and she was wondering whether to use butter or shortening for crust."

"Oh," said Stefano, his eyes glazing over.

"Let's go watch the game," Cristiano said heartily. "My father's already in there, keeping an eye on Esme and Jack. You coming, Cabrera?"

"What game?" Rodrigo said.

The other two men laughed. "It's Thanksgiving, isn't it? The Cowboys. Come on."

"Men and sports," Hallie sighed with a fond smile, shaking her head as the men disappeared.

"This way." Still holding Lola's baby, Tess led them down the hall to a gorgeous kitchen which looked completely untouched.

"We're still waiting for our pots and pans," she said apologetically. "Stefano offered to buy everything new and have it delivered yesterday, but I just want our old things from Sicily. I didn't think you'd mind eating off the caterer's plates." She bit her lip, suddenly looking worried. "You don't mind, do you? Is it tacky?"

"Not at all," Hallie said soothingly.

Looking around, Lola said in sudden worry, "But we're having a real dinner, right?" She added apologetically, "It's just that it's Rodrigo's first real Thanksgiving—"

"Don't worry." Tess's round face broke into a big smile. "Dinner's being catered from one of the best restaurants in the city. Well, except for the rolls and pies. Those are being brought by my cousins. Did you hear? They're running the family bakery now."

"Your cousins!" Lola was astounded. "But they're so young!"

"Just a few years younger than we are. Old enough to know what they want in life." Tess's smile lifted to a grin. "But obviously still learning the business. They called to say they're running a little late."

"But I'm sure Tess didn't really drag us into the kitchen to talk about pie." Hallie leaned back against the spotless marble counter, her dark eyes piercing. "What's going on with you and your new husband, Lola?"

"And how could you have a wedding without us?" Tess looked suddenly hurt. "We should have been bridesmaids. Just like you were for us."

Lola's first instinct was to refuse to explain, to make an excuse, to grab her babbling baby out of Tess's arms and wander into the front room to join the men watching football.

But suddenly, her heart was in her throat. Tears lifted to her eyes.

"Lola?" Hallie said.

"Lola, are you all right?" Tess said.

Her friends looked shocked. They had never seen her vulnerable before. Lola had always prided herself on being the strong one. She was the bossy one giving them advice, not the other way around.

"I'm sorry," Lola whispered, wiping her eyes. "I didn't sleep well last night."

"Do you want a cupcake?" asked Tess anxiously.

"A glass of wine?" asked Hallie.

It was so typical, Lola unwillingly laughed through her tears.

Then, with an intake of breath, she told them everything.

Her poverty and helplessness as a child, seeing her mother work herself to death, seeing her stepfather injured, disabled and finally sent to prison for trying to sell drugs. How Lola had felt, being responsible for her baby sisters when she was still a child herself. How, after their mother's untimely death, the girls had been dragged away from her, their screams still ringing in her ears. How she'd felt at eighteen, seeing them happy in another family, having forgotten her completely.

"I decided that money was the only thing that mattered," she whispered. She looked down. "I did some things I'm not proud of."

Hallie patted her shoulder. "We all have. It's part of being human."

"Oh, Lola." Tess looked heartbroken. "I never imagined. You always seemed so tough."

"Like nothing could hurt you," said Hallie.

Lola choked out a laugh, then wiped her eyes. "I pushed you guys so hard, while I was a coward in my own life."

"No, never," Tess said loyally.

"You helped us," Hallie said.

"So now let us help you," the redhead said. "Do you love him?"

"No, I—" But Lola's words caught in her throat. Memories flooded through her of Rodrigo tenderly taking care of their baby. Of him caring for her. Of all their days talking, and the hot nights when he'd made love to her again and again. Looking at her friends, she couldn't lie to them.

With a shuddering breath, she whispered, "I don't know."

Hallie and Tess looked at each other.

"You don't know?" Hallie said gently.

"I can't love him." Lola wiped her eyes. "I did once, last year, before I knew I was pregnant. But when I told him my feelings, he found an excuse to break up with me, and practically tossed me out of California. He doesn't believe in love. He thinks it only brings pain." She hesitated, then said quietly, "He was engaged three times before he met me."

Idealistic Tess looked shocked. *"Three times?"*

"And they all cheated on him before the wedding."

"*All* of them?" Hallie said faintly.

"I'm sorry I didn't invite you to the wedding. But as soon as Rodrigo found out about the baby, he insisted we get married at once. A judge was waiting at his loft to marry us right after the paternity test. With his housekeeper and bodyguard as witnesses."

"You didn't even get to plan your own wedding?" Tess said indignantly.

Lola looked down.

"It wasn't so bad," she said in a small voice.

"And whoever heard of a man engaged so many times?" Hallie said wonderingly.

"It happens," Lola said, a hard edge coming into her voice. She felt suddenly protective of him.

Tess's plump face was bewildered. "And all three women cheated on him before the wedding?"

Lola took a deep breath, wondering if she should tell them the worst, the fear she could barely even admit to herself—that he'd arranged those betrayals himself, either to test their loyalty or have an excuse to end the relationships.

He's not like that, Lola told herself desperately. *He wouldn't do something so underhanded.*

The house phone rang on the kitchen counter. Tess picked it up. "Hello?" Her face lit up. "Yes, of course. Send them all up!" Hanging up, she said happily, "That was the doorman. My cousins are here, and so are the caterers!" Moving to the wide, open doorway, she called, "Boys! The food's here!"

There was a loud yell of glee, and the trampling of heavy male feet.

"Will you be all right, Lola?"

Hallie's voice was quiet behind her. Lola turned to see the brunette's worried eyes.

With a deep breath, she lifted her chin. "Don't worry about me. I'm just being silly." Wiping the last of the tears from her eyes, she took Jett back into her arms with a smile. "Rodrigo and I are happy. We have a baby together. We're married. Friends." She gave a crooked smile. "And the sex is fantastic."

Gentle, romantic Tess looked at her. "But without love, how can it last?"

Don't get comfortable, Ulrika Lund had said. *You won't be with him for long. He'll see to that.*

As Lola looked between the worried faces of her best friends, a trickle of fear went down her spine.

I have to understand what happened, she thought suddenly. Had her husband really been behind all those betrayals and broken engagements? Or was it just a wild coincidence?

She'd spoken to his first two fiancées, but not the third, Elise Patel, a world-famous composer who now lived in Los Angeles. Perhaps her story would turn out to be completely different.

Lola's eyes narrowed. One way or the other, she would find out the truth.

CHAPTER EIGHT

IT WAS STRANGE, Rodrigo thought, to have one's first Thanksgiving at the age of thirty-seven. But no stranger than the rest of it, he supposed.

He looked down the long table, surrounded by mismatched folding chairs, in this magnificent, half-empty Manhattan penthouse overlooking Central Park. It was strange to be eating a traditional Thanksgiving dinner off the caterer's rented china, surrounded mostly by strangers.

Rodrigo knew Prince Stefano Zacco, the luxury fashion mogul, only slightly. His only acquaintance with Cristiano Moretti was that he'd often stayed in the man's hotels.

Rodrigo had no memory whatsoever of when Stefano's wife, Tess, had apparently worked as a waitress at one of his cocktail parties. He'd never met Hallie before, nor Cristiano's father who'd just come from Italy, nor Tess's two young cousins, who looked barely old enough to be out of high school, but who apparently now ran the family bakery and, he had to admit, certainly knew how to bake.

This Thanksgiving was strange, for sure.

But in some ways, it wasn't strange at all. It was exactly how Rodrigo had imagined it might be, when he was a child left on his own in Madrid to eat *arroz con pollo* with the nanny and the cook, as his mother flew off to ski in Aspen with her latest lover, and his cold, distant father disappeared to quietly rage at a film set.

Now, as Rodrigo sat at the table, listening to all of the people around him laugh and joke and tease each other, he felt like he was on a film set himself. A scene for a Thanksgiving movie, or an advertisement for any holiday that brought family and friends together for a meal. He ate the butter-basted turkey and cornbread stuffing, the mashed potatoes and gravy and fresh cranberry sauce, and it was all so delicious. After eating a huge plateful of food, he'd gone back for a second—having been told it was tradition to eat until one was utterly stuffed—and afterward, he found himself relaxing into warmth and pleasure, smiling as Lola and her friends good-naturedly fought over who got the wishbone.

"It's mine," Lola said ferociously, holding one side of the wishbone.

"No way, mine," Hallie retorted, gripping the other.

"Let Lola have it," Tess whispered to Hallie. "She needs it."

The brunette instantly released it. "You win."

Rodrigo looked between them in confusion. "Why does Lola need it?"

His wife flashed him a look he couldn't read. Fear? Regret? Hope? But before he could analyze it, it was gone. She shrugged. "It's good luck, that's all."

"But why do you need luck more than anyone else?" he persisted.

She gave him a crooked smile. "I'm married to you, aren't I?"

"And I'm married to you," he pointed out, returning her grin.

"So maybe you're the one who needs it, then." She held out the wishbone. "We're supposed to wait until it dries, but I'm not that patient. Grab a side, make a wish and pull."

As ordered, he grabbed the other side of the wishbone

and pulled it, hard and fast, at the same time she did. There was a loud crack.

Rodrigo lifted his bigger piece of the wishbone. "What does this mean?"

Lola looked disconsolately at her smaller piece, then sighed. "It means you win." She gave him a strange look. "What did you wish for?"

"I didn't wish for anything," he said honestly. He looked around them. "I have everything any man could want."

Applause and approval went around the table. But he again saw that flash of emotion cross his wife's face. An emotion that he didn't understand. Emotion that was quickly veiled as she turned away. "It's time for dessert."

She was hiding something.

The insidious thought went through him like a hissing snake, twisting and curling from the base of his skull down the length of his spine.

His wife had a secret. Something she didn't want him to know.

What?

Lola, Tess and Hallie returned from the kitchen with six pies—two each of pumpkin, pecan and apple. With a flourish, Lola cut him a slice of each kind, covered them with whipped cream and slid the plate in front of him.

"Three slices?" he said, bemused.

"Try them all, then decide which one you like best." Kissing his temple, she said, "I want your first Thanksgiving to be perfect."

Rodrigo lifted his fork, to do as commanded. But as he tasted each slice of pie, all the buttery, sweet, creamy, crunchy goodness he'd anticipated tasted like ash in his mouth. As he looked at her veiled eyes, a panicked, animal suspicion skittered down his spine.

What was she hiding?

Against his will, he was flooded by memories of those

other women who'd hidden secrets. Secrets that inevitably ended with Rodrigo looking at pictures of them naked in bed with other men.

He still wondered who'd sent the photographs. One of his rivals? One of his friends? Whoever it was, they'd hovered in the shadows for a decade, looking out for him. He was grateful to them.

But he also hated them.

"So which one do you like best?" said one of Tess's cousins anxiously.

"Yes, which?" said the other.

Standing beside him at the table, Lola looked down at Rodrigo with inscrutable hazel eyes.

There was no question which woman he liked best.

His wife.

He could not bear to lose Lola. Not at any price. They were married now. A family—

Stop, Rodrigo told himself angrily. He was no longer a weak boy, lonely and desperate to be loved. He'd realized the truth long ago. Anyone he loved, he lost. That was the reality, or at least his reality.

But he didn't love Lola. Therefore, he told himself firmly, he had nothing to worry about. His investigator had already assured him she wasn't in contact with Sergei Morozov, or any other man. And having a home and financial security for Jett meant too much to her. She'd never cheat, not when it would leave her without a penny.

His shoulders slowly relaxed.

"Well?" Lola said softly, "What is your answer?"

"Kiss me," he said huskily, "and I'll tell you my favorite."

Putting her hand gently on his cheek, Lola lowered her head to his, and softly kissed him, in front of everyone. Her lips were tender and burned through his body. Through his soul. Finally, she pulled away.

"Pecan," he said, because it was closest.

"I knew it." One of Tess's cousins looked at the other triumphantly. "I told you it was the best, Natalie."

But Rodrigo wasn't thinking about pie. He looked up at his wife.

No other woman had ever been so important to him before. His life had become better from the moment Lola had come into it. He had the sudden disquieting thought that she could destroy that happiness, if she chose.

No, he told himself fiercely. *She doesn't own me. As long as I don't love her, I can trust her.*

But he saw the evasion of Lola's gaze, the wistfulness of her smile. And all the warmth and happiness of the day melted away.

Rodrigo suddenly knew one thing. He had to find out her secret. Before it was too late.

Before he got another anonymous photograph in the mail.

"Thank you for meeting me, Ms. Patel." In California a few weeks later, Lola rose from the table in the outdoor patio of the beach café, holding out her hand. "It's an honor."

"The honor is mine," said the other woman, shaking her hand. Lifting her designer sunglasses to her black, shiny hair, Elise Patel looked around them, blinking in the bright sunshine. "Honestly, it's the first time I've left my studio in weeks."

"Composing a new score?"

"Not just composing. Producing, too." Dropping her expensive designer handbag carelessly to the rough wood patio floor, she got the waiter's attention with a snap. "Triple espresso, please."

"Triple?" Tucking Jett's blanket around him in the nearby stroller, Lola said with a laugh, "If I drank that, I'd be awake for weeks."

She snorted. "I wish. I'm still trying to wake up, after three hours' sleep. I only have ten minutes before I need to get back to work." With a slight smile, she shook her head. "Honestly, I do not have time for this."

The famous composer did indeed look a little tired, with dark circles beneath her eyes, wearing oversized jeans and a plain black sweatshirt, though she'd driven up in a two-hundred-thousand-dollar SUV.

Lola leaned back in her chair. "So why did you agree to meet me?"

Elise Patel's lips curved at the edges. "I was curious to meet the woman who actually managed to marry Rodrigo Cabrera."

All around them, beautiful people were chatting, sipping their lattes at this trendy beachside café not too far from Malibu. The sun was bright in the California sky, and though it was now mid-December, the air was warm enough that, in the stroller, Jett was wearing just a T-shirt and shorts over his fat baby legs, and Lola wore a simple cotton sundress and sandals, her long blond hair in a ponytail.

"I wanted to meet you too," Lola said, sipping her cappuccino. "I've already met the other two women who cheated on him, but not you."

The composer's eyes flashed in irritation, then she gave a grudging smile. "You're direct. I like that. Saves time." She looked up at the waiter who'd arrived with her espresso. "Thank you." Taking a sip, she sat back, then sighed with pleasure. "Delicious." Elise lifted a dark eyebrow. "So did you just invite me here to insult me, or were you curious about me as well?"

"Curious about one thing." Lola leaned forward. "Why did you do it?"

"Why what? Why did I cheat on him?" The other woman rolled her eyes. "That's a rude question. There's no reason for me to answer it. Unless you're afraid you might do the same?"

"Of course not!" Lola said.

"It all seems so long ago."

"Not even five years." She knew Rodrigo had ended his engagement to Elise a year before Lola started working for him.

"Yes, five years. An eternity." Blowing the steam off her espresso, the composer shook her head good-naturedly. "Do you know how many film scores I've written since then? How many awards I've won?"

"Yes, I know you're very busy and very famous," Lola said. "Is that why you cheated on Rodrigo? For the attention?"

"I loved him, I think. But I never saw him." She took another sip of espresso. "After he proposed to me, he suddenly got very busy with work and disappeared for months. Then a gorgeous production assistant suddenly was bringing me flowers. Asking me about my work. Singing my praises. Offering me foot rubs." She shrugged. "It happened. It's not something I'm proud of."

"And you ended up falling in love with the other man?"

"Love? It was just one night." She snorted. "And the sex wasn't even good. I regretted it instantly. I might have tried to work it out with Rodrigo, but someone sent him photographs. It was all very strange. If it was meant to be a blackmail attempt, the man never asked for money. He just disappeared."

"Disappeared…" Prickles lifted on the back of Lola's neck. She looked down at Jett, burbling happily in his stroller. The story was too much a duplicate of the other women's to be a coincidence.

"Honestly, looking back I'm almost relieved it happened," the composer said. "Since he dumped me, I've devoted myself to work, and it's all paid off. Tell Rodrigo that when you see him. Tell him thanks."

"Um…all right," she said, a little surprised.

Tilting her head, Elise murmured, "I think I can see why he married you."

Lola was flattered in spite of herself. "What do you mean?"

"I heard you were his assistant. You quit your job for him. So you have nothing else going on. You can just follow him around. You're his trophy. His pet." Her lips creased. "I think that's what he actually wanted in a woman all along. So maybe your marriage will survive." She finished the espresso at a gulp, then tossed a twenty-dollar bill on the table. "Thanks for the coffee."

And the other woman left, getting into her expensive SUV and driving fast down the coastal highway.

Lola stared after her in shock.

You quit your job for him. So you have nothing else going on. You can just follow him around. You're his trophy. His pet. I think that's what he actually wanted in a woman all along. So maybe your marriage will survive.

She tapped her fingertips angrily on the table. His trophy, was she? His pet? As she signaled for the bill, her heart thrummed with anger. Lola was his wife! The mother of a tiny infant! She had *plenty* going on!

But the insult burned through her.

For most of her life, Lola had prided herself on working longer and harder than anyone else. Just as her mother once had. Being an assistant to a powerful tycoon was long, difficult work, and she'd done well. She'd thrived. And being the logistics and operations manager of their household was no joke. She—

A man walking through the restaurant patio paused as he went past her table. "Oh. Hello again."

Still lost in her indignant thoughts, Lola looked up.

For a moment, she struggled to recognize him. Tall and blond, wearing a tight T-shirt and board shorts over his muscled body, he was handsome, tanned with a white, gleaming smile.

A chill went down her spine.

"Don't you remember me?" the man said, drawing closer to her table. His eyes seemed to caress her, and so did his smile. "We met by chance a few weeks ago? On the beach?"

Lola rose up, trembling.

"Who sent you?" Her voice hardened. "Who hired you?"

The young man went pale beneath his tan. "What? Nobody!"

"Tell me!" she demanded, pounding the table.

"You're crazy," he said, backing away nervously. He looked around the patio with its view of the ocean across the street. "She's crazy!"

Turning, he practically ran from the café.

"Don't ever harass me again!" Lola yelled after him.

After the man was gone, it took some moments for her to calm down. Blood pounded through her body, making her shake. Ignoring all the open stares, she knelt before the stroller to comfort the baby, who'd started to cry. Trying to comfort herself.

"Is everything all right, Mrs. Cabrera? What did that man do?"

Looking up, she saw one of their bodyguards, whom she'd purposefully left behind at the beach house today. And not even her favorite one, Tobias. "What are you doing here, Lester?"

"Boss told me to keep an eye on you."

"To spy on me?"

The man looked uncomfortable. "He just wanted—"

"I don't care what he wanted," she snapped. "Stop following me." Tossing money on the table for her cappuccino and croissant, she tucked her bag into the stroller and stomped away from the bodyguard, to her husband's Mercedes SUV parked behind the café.

She felt sick.

Could Rodrigo have hired the handsome stranger, who looked like a cross between a surfer and out-of-work soap opera actor, to try to seduce her?

Was that why Lester was there—to follow and get pictures?

No, she told herself fiercely. But her hands shook as she buckled her baby into the SUV and tossed the stroller into the back. Taking calming breaths, she reminded herself that Rodrigo was in San Francisco on business today. He couldn't know Lola would be at this café with his ex.

The thought reassured her as she started the engine. Then she stopped, staring out at the blue ocean.

Elise Patel's phone number was unlisted. Lola had gotten it from Marnie yesterday. Rodrigo could have easily found out where she planned to be. He could have sent the stranger, either as some kind of loyalty test, or something more malicious.

Was it possible that Rodrigo was trying to get rid of her, just like the rest? Trying to end this marriage as cheaply and easily as he could, by luring her into an affair—or even just the appearance of one?

Fear went through her, followed by rage. She gripped the steering wheel.

Enough of this. She would ask him directly when he got home tonight.

No. She couldn't. If Rodrigo was innocent, if this was all just a wild coincidence, he would think she was crazy, for getting so upset over two chance encounters with a man who had been, after all, merely friendly.

After she got back to the beach house, she spent hours pacing back and forth, unable to decide. She felt like she was losing her mind.

The truth seemed to be screaming in her face.

But she didn't want it to be true. She wanted to be blind, to take whatever comfort she could, for as long as she could, while denying the evidence that was piling up all around her.

"Mrs. Cabrera?" The housekeeper looked in on her.

"What?" Lola snapped, turning on her mid-pace. At the other woman's expression, she instantly felt bad. "I'm sorry, Mrs. Lee. Did you need something?"

"You received a letter. I'll just leave it here." Leaving an envelope on the gleaming wood sideboard, the housekeeper backed away.

"A letter?" Frowning, Lola came forward. Then she saw the return address. A suburban town in New York.

Her sisters.

Heart pounding, she ripped it open.

The money she'd sent for her sisters' college fund, the six-figure check she'd sent them as an olive branch, floated gently to the floor.

They'd returned it. Uncashed.

Lola's heart lifted to her throat, choking her. Her sisters weren't interested in forgiving her. They still hated her...

But there was a note. Desperately, she clutched at it. The childish uneven handwriting looped in pencil.

Dear Lola,
Thank you for sending us this college money. Our parents said we can't accept it. We have enough and we don't need charity.
But they said we should invite you for Christmas. And I think that's a good idea because we could use a big sister. Not me, cause I have one, but Kelsey could. I'm sick of her always bragging about her memories of you and I'd like some, too.

I'm sorry I was scared last time. I'm not scared anymore. Please say you'll come.
Yours truly,
Johanna Sandford

Tears rushed to Lola's eyes as she crushed the note to her chest. A torrent of conflicting emotions rushed through her.

The last day Lola saw Johanna, she was just six, riding her bike happily with her older sister on the shaded street in front of their two-story white house with green shutters. When Lola had told the girls she was going to take them away, she'd expected them to cry with joy. Instead, they'd clung to their mother and the family's golden retriever. Johanna's face had been terrified. After that, Lola had never been able to face either of her sisters again.

Now, pain lifted in Lola's throat, sharp as a razor blade. She blinked fast, looking out through the beach house's windows. Jett was sleeping in the nursery. The room was shadowy and silent. In the distance, she could see the pink and orange sunset over the black ocean.

All these years, she'd been too scared to face them. She'd told herself that they'd either forgotten her, or hated her.

Only the money—and Rodrigo—had given her the courage to finally contact them, hoping they could forgive her, and let her back in their lives.

But they'd sent back the money. They didn't want it.

They just wanted her to come for Christmas.

She closed her eyes, holding her baby sister's note like it was a precious gift. Raw emotions were pouring through her like torrential rain.

I'm sorry I was scared last time. I'm not scared anymore.

Then she opened her eyes, as everything became suddenly very clear.

Later that night, when Rodrigo came home from his trip, she turned on the light where she'd been sitting on the sofa, waiting for him.

"Lola." He looked surprised. "I thought you'd be asleep. What are you doing, sitting in the dark?"

Gripping her hands at her sides, she rose to her feet. "We need to talk."

Rodrigo's black eyes gleamed. "I'm glad you're awake. I've missed you, *querida*." He gave her a sensual smile. "I can hardly wait to—"

"A handsome stranger flirted with me today."

He froze, staring at her. "What?"

She shrugged. "He was just being friendly. It would be no big deal, except it's the second time he's tried. And—" she paused "—it's exactly the same thing that happened to all your other fiancées."

His expression changed. "I heard how you spent the morning. Having coffee with Elise Patel."

"Did Marnie tell you that?"

"She mentioned in passing you asked for Elise's phone number. What I don't understand is why."

"Ulrika Lund came up to me at the awards ceremony in Madrid, while you were giving your speech." Lola met his eyes evenly. "She had an interesting theory about why all your engagements ended."

"Because they were unfaithful," he said flatly.

"Yes, but why?"

He stiffened. "What kind of question is that?"

"Did you hire men to deliberately seduce them?"

Rodrigo dropped his suitcase with a loud bang against the floor. He gave a harsh laugh. "Is that some kind of joke?"

"Maybe you were just testing their loyalty. Or maybe…"

Speaking her deepest fear, she whispered, "Maybe you were afraid of loving them, and wanted to get rid of them before they got too close."

His black eyes glinted sparks in the small halo of lamplight as he came forward. "You're insane."

Lola set her jaw, trying desperately to appear strong, but her voice wobbled as she said, "Did you send that man to flirt with me today? Are you trying to get rid of me?"

"How can you even think such a thing?" he said in a low, dangerous voice, looking down at her. "After I decide to trust you—"

"*Trust* me! Is that what you call it, when you have Lester follow me?"

"That was for your own protection!"

"No!" she cried. Her chest rose and fell in quick, angry breaths. "It was for yours!"

The two of them glared at each other with matching ferocity.

Behind him, she could see the sweep of silver moonlight through the windows. He towered over her, powerful and fierce in the shadowy great room.

Reaching out, Rodrigo gripped her shoulders, searching her gaze. "Tell me this is a joke. You know I would not do such a despicable thing."

"Tell me why, every time anyone gets close to you and starts to care, you push them away."

"If you know about my exes, you know my reason—"

"No," she said steadily. "It started before that. Because every time you got engaged, you disappeared. For weeks or months. And you did the same thing after you married me."

His expression changed. Releasing her, he turned away. Going to the wet bar, he poured himself a short glass of forty-year-old Scotch. He took a drink, then finally turned to face her. "You're right. I learned not to trust anyone long ago. When I was a boy."

"Your parents," she whispered, looking at him.

Rodrigo took another gulp of Scotch. The moonlight caressed the hard edges of his face. "My father wasn't my father."

"What?" She gasped.

"My whole childhood, I always felt like my father despised me. He never hugged me. He barely looked at me." He looked away. "At his funeral, my mother told me why. He'd known all along I wasn't his son." A sardonic smile traced his sensual lips. "She'd had a brief affair with the chauffeur. Just one of many. She enjoyed throwing his love for her back in his face."

"So that's why you wanted the paternity test," Lola said slowly. "And why you insisted on marrying me."

"I didn't want my child to ever feel like I felt that day," he said in a low voice. "Or any other days."

Lola no longer wondered why he had trust issues. Indeed, now she could only wonder that he was able to trust anyone at all.

Rodrigo stared out the window bleakly, toward the dark, moonlit beach. "Growing up, I could hardly wait to get married. I wanted a real family, a real home. But it was never real." He gave her a crooked smile. "With Pia, I fell in love with the role she played in a movie, not her. Ulrika and I just argued all the time. Elise—well, we both loved our careers more than each other."

"She said to tell you thanks, by the way. For breaking up with her. Giving her more time to work."

"That sounds like her. And I felt the same." Looking back out the window, he said softly, "Maybe you were right. Maybe I always knew they were wrong for me. And I was glad for the excuse to leave."

Lola swallowed. "But you didn't—"

"Didn't set them up to cheat on me?" He shook his head, his dark eyes luminous in the shadows. "No."

Looking at his face, she believed him.

"Now I have a question for you." Gulping down the last of the Scotch, he set the glass down on the end table. "Is there something you're keeping from me? Some secret?"

"Secret?" She frowned. "I just wanted to know what happened to your engagements. If you were behind the betrayals."

His dark gaze cut into her soul. "Why?"

"Because—" she took a deep breath "—I had to know if you were going to do the same to me."

Rodrigo stared at her. Then he pulled her into his strong arms.

"I will never betray you, Lola." He looked down at her fiercely. "Not in that way, nor any other. When I spoke those vows to you, I meant them." He cupped her cheek. "To love and cherish. For the rest of our lives."

As she stared up at him, feeling the gentle touch of his powerful hand, a rush of relief went through her so great, she almost cried. She hadn't realized until this moment how tense she'd been. How afraid.

"I believe you," she said.

His dark eyes turned warm. "You do?"

"Yes."

His hand moved softly down her neck, through her blond hair, hanging down her shoulders. "I bought you a Christmas present."

"You did?" Just knowing that he hadn't sabotaged his past engagements, and wasn't trying to secretly end their marriage, was all the gift she needed. But he was looking at her so expectantly, she said, "What is it?"

He gave her a wicked smile. "You'll have to wait and see."

"I heard from my sisters today," she blurted out.

He pulled back to look at her, his dark face unreadable. "You did?"

"Well, technically, it was just my youngest sister, Johanna. They sent back the college money, can you believe it? They didn't even want it!" Picking up the check from the floor, she showed him. "They just want us to come for Christmas!"

"Christmas?" he said slowly. "In New York?"

She nodded happily. "Think of it, Rodrigo. Christmas with my sisters, then New Year's Eve with our friends. Cristiano's hosting a party at his new property in Times Square… What do you say?" she rushed out.

Rodrigo stared down at her, his handsome face expressionless. "It's our first Christmas as a family. I thought we'd spend it here. I've made plans…"

"Please." Her voice caught. "You don't know what it means to me that they want to see me."

He looked down at her in the dark, shadowed beach house. "It means so much, *querida*?"

"So much," she whispered.

Rodrigo took a deep breath.

"Then of course we must go."

Joy filled her. With a cry, Lola threw her arms around him, standing on her tiptoes to cover his face with kisses. "You won't regret it!"

Smiling, he murmured, his voice muffled by her kisses, "I'm glad already."

Drawing back, Lola looked up at her husband. The moon's silver light grazed the hard edges of one side, with the lamplight's golden glow on the other. Her heart felt bigger than the world.

And that was when she knew, she really knew, that she loved him.

CHAPTER NINE

IT WAS THE day before Christmas Eve, and the weather had grown cooler, even in Los Angeles. Lola had to wear a soft cotton sweater and jeans instead of a sundress and sandals. But amid the palm trees and California sunshine, as she listened to Christmas songs on the radio about snow and family, all she could think about was their upcoming trip to New York.

Everything was planned. Tomorrow, they'd leave for New York on Rodrigo's private jet, and not return until New Year's Day.

Lola tapped her feet excitedly. Just one more day until she'd finally see her sisters after all these years. She'd done a video chat with them last week, and she could hardly believe how shockingly grown up they looked now. She'd even spoken briefly with their parents. Lola remembered the older couple as guarded, but they seemed warmer now and friendlier.

Perhaps because they weren't scared of her anymore, either. They knew she wasn't a threat to them. She'd never try to fight them for custody or add stress to their lives. How could she? She was grateful to them, for taking the girls into their home as foster kids, then adopting them and giving them such happy lives. When Lola had first seen Johanna and Kelsey's parents seven years ago, she'd been so jealous, she'd hated them, picturing them as entitled and rich.

She knew now that they were just regular people. The father was an engineer. The mother was a school secretary.

Lola had loved seeing pictures of the girls' tidy little house in their picturesque little town, an hour outside New York. Lola had introduced them to Jett in the video chat and shown them pictures of Rodrigo and their beach house in California. Since that time, Johanna kept sending Lola funny pictures of their dog, Peaches, telling her firmly that she "had" to get a dog for Jett, too.

He's not even six months old, Lola had texted back, amused to see her own bossiness manifest in her baby sister.

Jett's my nephew and he needs a dog, Johanna had replied firmly.

Jett had aunts now. More family to love him. And Lola was so grateful.

She'd already wrapped their Christmas presents. The gifts weren't flashy like the college money, expensive and designed to impress, but simple and from the heart. A crystal unicorn for Johanna, who loved anything that was pink and pretty, and an original-press, rare vinyl ABBA album for Kelsey, who was way too young to be a fan, but there you had it. For their parents, she'd bought a pizza stone and accessories, after hearing about their Thursday pizza nights. Even the family dog, Harley, would receive a basket of top-of-the-line homemade dog treats and chew toys.

Lola smiled, just thinking about it.

Jett's Christmas gifts had already been sorted at Thanksgiving, from her and Rodrigo's spree in New York. But she'd spent time writing heartfelt thank-you cards to the housekeepers and bodyguards, to go with their holiday bonuses.

Leaving only one person to shop for. One impossibly difficult person. She'd racked her brain, all the way until today, when it was almost too late.

Until finally, while shopping with the baby today, Lola had had an idea.

Now, as Tobias drove her and Jett back to the beach house in the luxury SUV, Lola leaned back against the soft leather, peeking down at the glossy blue bag in satisfaction. Inside it, she saw a small blue box that held an engraved gold ring.

Finally, her husband would have a wedding band. And when he saw what she'd had engraved inside it…

She shivered. Could she be brave enough?

As the Escalade pulled into the gated courtyard of the beach house, Lola was pulled out of her reverie when she heard Tobias's voice from the front seat. "Mr. Cabrera just sent a message that he's expecting you, ma'am."

"Thank you, Tobias."

She smiled, her heart quickening just at the sound of her husband's name. Since their last argument, the night he'd returned from San Francisco, Rodrigo had taken no more trips away from the family, not even short ones. He'd drastically cut back his hours at work, in a way she'd never seen before. The reason was clear. He wanted to spend time with Jett.

He wanted to spend time with her.

Every morning, he'd stayed late to have breakfast with them, served on the terrace next to the pool. And nearly every evening, he'd been home in time to join them for dinner, then help with the baby's bath. On weekends, they'd gone on family excursions, Disneyland, hiking trails in the nearby hills, visiting art museums and the zoo and the farmer's market, even boating to Catalina Island. All normal things that any family might do. Well, except for the fact that Rodrigo owned the yacht that took them to Catalina.

But tonight, he'd hinted, before they left for New York, he had something extra special planned.

"Not just for Christmas," he'd told her that morning,

nuzzling her in bed. He'd drawn back to give her a serious look as he said huskily, "For always."

All day, Lola had tried not to think of what it could mean. So of course it was all she could think about.

Now, as Tobias parked the car, she asked suddenly, "How's your son doing?"

"Great." The bodyguard grinned. "Both of us are great, Mrs. Cabrera. Thanks to you."

"Good." As he got out to open her car door, Lola lingered over the seat belt of her baby's car seat.

Please. She fervently closed her eyes. *Please let Rodrigo's surprise be him telling me he loves me.*

Because she loved him. It was always on the tip of her tongue now. Every time she watched him tenderly hold their baby. Every evening they spent together on the poolside terrace at sunset, drinking a glass of wine after Jett was asleep. Every night he took Lola to bed and moved his hot, sensual body against hers until he set her world on fire.

She loved him. She wanted to scream it to the world. She wanted to look into his rugged features and speak the words, again and again, like a sacred incantation.

Then she wanted him to say the words back to her.

Please, she thought. She didn't want any expensive gifts for Christmas. She didn't want anything but this: for her husband to love her.

"Mrs. Cabrera?"

Pasting a smile on her face, Lola lifted her baby out of the car seat. Walking to the front door of the sprawling beach house, she looked up at the tall, slender palm trees, swaying in the wind, silhouetted purple against the lowering sun in the orange and red horizon.

Squaring her shoulders, she carried the baby to the front door, her footsteps echoing against the flagstones. She opened the door.

And gasped.

The great room of the beach house, with its luxurious furniture and double-story window views of the Pacific, had been filled with roses of every color, hundreds of them, pink and red and yellow and white. But that wasn't even the most amazing part.

Rodrigo stood beside the doorway, devastatingly attractive in a tuxedo, holding out a long-stemmed pink rose.

Lola's heart slammed against her ribs. Her hand shook as she took the rose. "What's this?"

He gave her a wicked smile. "Christmas."

"It's not even Christmas Eve yet."

"Tomorrow's for family." His dark eyes gleamed down at her. "Tonight's for us."

"For us?" A flash of heat went through her, and her cheeks burned. "I thought we'd be getting a Christmas tree tonight."

"We are. In a way." He allowed himself a smug smile, then glanced behind him. "Mrs. Lee will be watching Jett."

The housekeeper came forward, smiling as she took the baby from Lola's arms. "Have a nice evening, Mrs. Cabrera."

"But—where are we going?"

"Go to our bedroom," Rodrigo said, his dark eyes burning through her.

"Now?"

"Right now."

Going down the hall to the palatial master bedroom, Lola dropped her shopping bag in shock when she saw a famous personal stylist waiting for her, with two makeup and hair stylists.

"Hello." The personal stylist, who dressed movie stars for worldwide events, gave Lola a cheeky smile. "I'm here for you, my dear. To make you even more impossibly beautiful than you already are." He motioned toward a rack of ball gowns and brand-new designer shoes. "Choose your favorite. They're all in your size." He held up a sleek, well-used sewing kit and double-sided tape. "I can make any gown fit."

Thirty minutes later, Lola felt so ridiculously like a princess, she was sure even Johanna would approve. Looking in the full-length mirror, Lola hardly recognized herself.

Her long, highlighted blond hair was sleek and perfect, falling nearly to her waist. Her strapless pink chiffon gown fit her perfectly, showing off her curves. Black kohl and fake eyelashes lined her eyes, making the hazel color pop dramatically, and her lips were pink.

Standing in the sparkling six-inch designer heels, Lola breathed, "I don't even need jewelry."

The stylist gave her a wicked grin. "You sparkle enough on your own."

"I feel like Cinderella," she said.

"You look like her, too." He tilted his head. "You married the most powerful man in showbiz, girl. This city, this world, is yours to command."

Lola felt like she was in a dream as she walked back down the hall in the strapless pink chiffon gown. Even the six-inch heels felt fantastic on her feet, as if she were floating on air. She'd never had a problem with designer heels making her feet hurt. They were too beautiful—too expensive—to hurt.

But what were they doing tonight?

Lola looked down at the glamorous pink gown. Obviously, not going Christmas tree shopping.

When she returned to the great room, the housekeeper and Jett were gone. Rodrigo stood alone amid the roses.

His eyes widened when he saw her.

"Querida," he whispered. "You take my breath away."

"Thanks." Coming forward shyly, she reached up to straighten his black tie. "You don't clean up so badly yourself."

"I bought you some Christmas decorations."

"Mistletoe?" she guessed.

"I should have thought of that. But no." Pulling a black, flat velvet box from his tuxedo jacket pocket, he held it out. Lola sucked in her breath when she saw a magnificent diamond necklace, sparkling in the twilight, amid all the sweet-scented roses.

"Oh," she whispered.

"Hold up your hair," he said huskily.

She did as he commanded. Dropping the black velvet box on an antique side table, he placed the diamonds around her neck, attaching the clasp behind her.

The necklace felt cold and heavy against Lola's skin. But the feather-light brush of his fingertips as he hooked the clasp sent a flash of fire through her body.

"There." Turning her to face him, he stroked her cheek, tilting her head upward. "*Now* you are ready."

Lola looked up at him, her heart thudding in her chest. *I love you, Rodrigo.* The words lifted to her throat. Her lips parted—

"Don't look at me like that, *querida.*" He gave a low, rueful laugh. "If you do, I'll cancel our plans tonight, and spend the next twelve hours with you in bed."

"Would that be so horrible?"

"No…and yes." He gave her a wicked grin. "Because I have something very special planned for you."

"Are we exchanging our Christmas gifts tonight?"

"Maybe," he said huskily. "Except my gift to you can't be wrapped. Something I know—" his eyes met hers "—is your heart's desire."

Joy pounded through her, making her dizzy. *He was going to tell her he loved her.* Tonight. She blurted, "I have something for you, too."

Turning, she raced back to the master bedroom, where the stylists were packing up clothes and beauty supplies.

Finding her bag from the jewelry store, she pulled out the gold wedding band she'd bought as his Christmas gift. She glanced at its inscription: *I love you now and always*.

But where could she hide it until the right moment? Biting her lip, she looked around desperately. "Is there a handbag to match my dress?"

"There's always a bag," the stylist said lazily. He narrowed his eyes, then gave a satisfied nod and handed her an adorable pink minaudière laced with pink crystals. Hastily, she tucked her phone, ID, a lipstick and a bit of cash inside. She felt bright with happiness. "Wait," the stylist said, wrapping a pink stole around her shoulders. "Take this. It's cold out."

When she returned to the great room, Rodrigo came closer, dark-haired and devastating in his sleek tuxedo. Lifting her hand to his lips, he kissed it, causing her to shiver as ripples of electricity and heat whipped through her body.

"Tonight, I want to fulfill all your dreams," he said seriously, wrapping her hand over his arm.

Lola's heart was pounding as he led her outside, where she saw his red two-seater Ferrari waiting. She tried to tell herself to calm down but couldn't. She felt like she was in a dream as he helped her into the passenger seat.

After starting the engine, Rodrigo drove past the beach house's gate and onto the coastal highway, heading east, into the sprawl of Los Angeles.

When they reached the outskirts of Beverly Hills, traveling a winding road past all the hidden mansions with their gates and fortress-like hedges, a sudden suspicion began to grow inside her.

"Where are we going?" she asked.

Rodrigo shook his head, a smile quirking his sensual lips. Then he turned into a driveway blocked by an elaborate wrought iron gate. Words were worked into the top of the tall gate: La Casa del Corazón.

"What are we doing here?" She turned to her husband, eyes wide. "Is there a party?"

"You might say that." Reaching out of his window, Rodrigo punched in a code on the security keypad, causing the electronic gate to smoothly slide open. The car continued up the sweeping driveway. To her surprise, Lola saw cars parked along the short private road, all the way to the massive circular driveway around a Spanish-style stone fountain. Parking directly in front of the lavish mansion, he turned off the engine.

He turned to face her, his dark eyes shining.

"The house of your dreams." Taking her hand, he put a key into her palm. "It's yours."

She blinked. "What?"

"It wasn't on the market." He gave her a quietly proud smile. "But you told me you wanted it, so I made the owners an offer they couldn't refuse."

Lola looked up at the stunning 1920s-era Spanish Mediterranean mansion. Built by silent film stars a hundred years before, this home was a rare beauty, an architectural landmark. Tears lifted to her eyes.

It wasn't that he'd bought her a mansion. They already had one of those, a nice one on the beach.

It was that Rodrigo had listened. When she'd told him her youthful dreams, he hadn't mocked them. He hadn't forgotten. He'd tried to make them come true.

"But why are we dressed up like this?" she said, blinking fast. "And why are there so many cars? I don't understand."

His smile widened. "There's more."

"More?"

Searching his gaze, she caught her breath. He'd brought her family and friends here, she thought suddenly. Since they hadn't been at the wedding. He was going to tell her he loved her tonight, in front of everyone she cared about, in front of Hallie and Tess and their families. In front of her sisters. The certainty, the overwhelming romance of the moment filled her.

And suddenly, she couldn't wait. Fear disappeared, along with pride.

Lola let him see her heart. She didn't even try to hide the joyful tears suddenly falling down her cheeks.

Looking up at him as he sat beside her in the Ferrari, she whispered, "I love you, Rodrigo."

He blinked. He said slowly, "You love the house—"

"No. You." She lifted her hand to his rough cheek. "Not your money. Not these diamonds—" she glanced down at her necklace "—not even this beautiful house. I love you," she said fiercely. Shaking her head, she smiled through her tears. "I don't think I've ever stopped loving you. From the night we first kissed. All this time. Even when there was no hope."

His gaze shuttered. "Lola—"

"I told you I was only marrying you for Jett's sake. But it was a lie. I was scared to admit the truth, even to myself. But I can't deny it any longer." Taking a deep breath, she whispered, "I love you. Only you. And I'll love you forever."

She couldn't mean it.

Lola…loved him?

A horrifying flash of memories raced through Rodrigo of three other women speaking those exact same words, with the same apparent sincerity—right before they slept with another, with his engagement ring still on their fingers.

Only fools put faith in love. Fools and masochists. If he let himself love her, he knew how this would end.

And yet… His heart cried out for her.

He wanted to believe. His long-ago engagements felt like nothing—just the hasty, shallow infatuations of a young man—compared to what he felt for her now.

The thought shocked him.

Rodrigo's gaze fell to the diamond engagement ring gleaming on Lola's left hand. He couldn't let himself love her. What if she betrayed him?

No. He took a shuddering breath. He couldn't live through it. It would destroy him.

Rodrigo forced himself to give her a casual, crooked smile. "Lola, you don't need to say you love me. I've already bought you the house. You can relax."

Lola's beautiful face, which had been hopeful and bright, closed up instantly. He felt an answering wrench in his chest that almost made him sick.

He knew she wasn't pretending or buttering him up. She actually believed she loved him.

But he also knew it wouldn't—couldn't—last. He could not take the chance of loving her. They were married. They had a child. There was too much at stake to risk it on something so deceitful and destructive as love.

His jaw tightened. "We have guests. We should go inside."

"Guests?" she said, with a tiny sliver of hope in her voice. "What guests?"

"It's part of your surprise. A housewarming party."

"Who did you invite?"

"Everyone."

Her eyes lit up. "My sisters? My friends?"

Rodrigo suddenly wished he had. He should have invited the Morettis and Zaccos and those sisters of hers. It hadn't even occurred to him.

"No," he said quietly. "Industry people."

The light in her eyes faded. "Oh."

Looking down at her, he felt it again, that punch in the gut. And all of his Christmas plans he'd been arranging for weeks with Marnie, the mansion he'd been so excited to give his wife tonight as a surprise, suddenly seemed meaningless and cheap.

His shoulders tightened in his tuxedo jacket. Getting heavily out of the car, he opened her door. Holding out his hand, he said, "Come."

Her hand shook as she placed it in his. She wouldn't meet his eyes. As they entered the house's glittering foyer, beneath the wrought iron Spanish chandelier high above, he felt a ragged blade in his throat.

"Mr. Cabrera!" Marnie McAdam strode toward them in black stilettos, her skinny frame swathed in a black sheath dress. "You're here!" She looked at him happily, then glanced at Lola. "Mrs. Cabrera, I hope you like your party."

There was a strange note of satisfaction in Marnie's voice that Rodrigo didn't understand.

She's just being a good assistant, he told himself. Marnie cared so much about her job, of course she wanted to make sure his wife has a good time. And yet it struck Rodrigo as odd.

Then he looked around them.

The enormous grand foyer, framed by a sweeping wrought iron staircase on each side, was filled with the most powerful people in the entertainment and media worlds: studio heads, directors and movie stars. He'd invited them because he wanted to properly introduce Lola, not as his assistant, but as his wife—to gain their respect for her as a power in her own right.

But now, as he glanced at Lola on his arm, Rodrigo realized his mistake.

The Spanish-style mansion was decorated in glamorous Christmas finery, with holly and ivy draped along the wrought iron handrails of the dual staircases. In the center of the enormous foyer, a twenty-foot Christmas tree was decorated with sparkling ornaments and lights glittering like stars. Beneath the tree was a veritable Himalayan mountain range of gifts, all for Lola and the baby, elegantly wrapped in red, as the decorator had arranged for maximum effect.

For weeks now, Rodrigo had imagined Lola's face when she saw this. He'd been determined to give her everything she'd once dreamed of when she'd come to this city at eighteen, broke and alone.

But now, Lola's beautiful face was sad. Her big hazel eyes looked heartbroken and numb. He'd never seen her look so vulnerable. Her lovely face still was tracked with dried tears, from when she'd told him she loved him just moments before, when she'd been crying with joy.

And now, of all times, he was forcing her to face judgmental strangers, his business partners and rivals. Now, at the very moment he'd hurt her so badly.

Rodrigo suddenly hated this stupid party. And this stupid house. He wished he'd never thought of this gift. He would have given anything to have the two of them back at the beach house. Alone.

All the people in formal gowns and tuxedos, drinking expensive champagne, turned toward them with a cheer.

"To Mr. and Mrs. Cabrera!" someone cried from the back, and everyone held up champagne flutes.

"Congratulations!" The shout rang across the enormous foyer.

"You did it, old man!" laughed a hot young filmmaker, barely out of USC film school, holding up his flute.

"And Merry Christmas!" cried someone else. "Wishing us all fat profits in this happy season!"

Lola suddenly burst into tears.

"Excuse me," she choked out, covering her face.

"Lola, wait," Rodrigo said desperately, but she ran out of the foyer. He tried to follow but found his passage blocked by ten different people, all of them coming forward to congratulate him—that was to say, determined to network with the powerful Spanish film mogul in hopes of getting their various projects made.

"Don't worry, sir." Standing beside him, Marnie flashed a sympathetic look. "I'll go check on her."

He tossed her a glance. "No, wait—"

But his assistant was already gone.

Five minutes, he told himself grimly. He'd let Lola have five minutes to gather herself. He'd never seen her sob like that before. He knew her pride. She wouldn't want him to see.

But he'd already seen the tears overflowing her lashes. Just as he'd already seen her vulnerable heart.

I love you, she'd whispered. *Only you. And I'll love you forever.*

"And in the spirit of Christmas, Cabrera—" a Hollywood power agent was saying eagerly, pumping his hand "—I'll let you read my client's screenplay. You're a lucky bastard, because it's truly spectacular—"

Screw five minutes, Rodrigo thought. He couldn't wait. He couldn't know Lola was somewhere, crying alone, while he did nothing to comfort her. It was unbearable. He had to protect her. Comfort her. He had to make it right.

"Excuse me," he said to the agent as he droned about his client's high-concept plot. "I have to find my wife."

Without waiting for a response, he turned and pushed his way through the crowds of glamorous, wealthy guests, in the direction Lola had disappeared. Suddenly, Marnie blocked his path. Her thin face was anxious and worried.

"There's an uninvited guest."

"Take care of it," he told her harshly. "I need to find Lola."

But as he impatiently started to pass her, his assistant stopped him with a tug at his arm. "It's Sergei Morozov."

His wife's old boss from New York? The Russian tycoon

who'd wanted to marry her? That grabbed Rodrigo's attention. He scowled at Marnie. "He wasn't on the guest list."

"No. Somehow he snuck in."

Rodrigo took a deep breath, trying to shake off the sudden tension in his shoulders. What could Morozov be doing here, three thousand miles from New York? Old fears started to creep in. Could Lola have…?

No. He thought of the emotion shining in his wife's hazel eyes when she told him she loved him. Lola would never cheat on him. He trusted her, as he trusted no one else.

"Let the man stay. I don't care," he said suddenly. He turned away. "I need to find my wife—"

"That's just it, sir." Marnie stopped him with her solemn, owl-like gaze. "I'm trying to tell you. Mr. Morozov is here. He's with Mrs. Cabrera." She hesitated, then said, "They're *together.*"

Rodrigo frowned, unable to make sense of his assistant's words. "Together?"

She bit her lip. "In the back garden. I saw them. Kissing—"

Marnie kept talking, but suddenly Rodrigo couldn't hear her.

As he looked around the foyer, all the people talking and laughing and drinking champagne suddenly seemed like mere noise to Rodrigo, just smudges of color.

He had no memory of how he walked through the crowds to the French doors overlooking the terrace. He'd only remember the feeling of wading through air like water, feeling like he couldn't breathe.

Outside in the cold air, he heard his assistant behind him as he walked across the Spanish terrace, looking out into the manicured tropical gardens, lush beneath the moonlight.

But he saw nothing. No one.

Waves of relief went over him. There was no one here.

Reason returned to his brain and he started to turn back to Marnie. "You were mistaken—"

Then he saw a gleam of pink chiffon from the corner of his eye. A flash of Lola's long blond hair.

And Rodrigo saw, in the shadows on the other side of the terrace, the sickening sight of another man embracing his wife.

"Do not worry, *zvezda moya*," he heard the Russian croon, holding Lola tenderly in his arms. "You are safe now. With me."

CHAPTER TEN

Shocked, Lola struggled in her old boss's arms.

A moment before, she'd run out on the dark, empty terrace to sob alone, when a man had suddenly appeared from the shadows. At first, she'd thought it was Rodrigo, and unwilling hope had risen in her heart. Then she'd recognized her old boss, Sergei Morozov.

"Sergei? What are you doing here?" she'd said in surprise, choking back her tears.

"What has he done to you, *Lolitchka*?" he'd said indignantly. "Look at you. Crying. He did this?"

She'd shaken her head vehemently. "No, he—" Then she'd stopped. Because Rodrigo was exactly the reason why she was out here crying alone.

No. That wasn't fair. He'd told her all along not to love him. Just like he had during the months of their first affair. And just like she had then, she'd let herself care for him anyway.

Only this was so much worse. Because she truly loved him. And she didn't know how she'd ever be able to face him again, knowing all he felt for her in return was pity.

She'd done this to herself.

Wiping her eyes, she'd said to Sergei, "Did Rodrigo invite you here? Are you friends now?"

"Friends?" Sergei's eyes had flashed. "No. This man you married, he sent me a message. Inviting me to take you."

Lola had frowned. There must be something lost in translation. "Take me? Take me where?"

"Away from him." He'd snorted. "I do not understand how he could so easily tire of you. Now I, I would not so quickly tire. But I do not question. I am here. I gladly take."

"Take?" she'd said, backing away until her heels hit the mansion's stucco wall, trapping her.

"Da," he'd said huskily. "His email said we must be seen together. Then he pays nothing to end the marriage."

"What?" she'd gasped in shock, staring at him. "He would never say that!"

She'd heard a French door open, as someone came out on the moonswept terrace. Grateful to have someone else there, to stop her old boss's apparent madness, she turned to see who it was—

"Do not worry, *zvezda moya*." His eyes gleamed. Grabbing her suddenly with his big arms, he yanked her hard against him. "You are safe now. With me."

"What? Stop!" Lola struggled in his arms, breaking away just in time to see who'd come out on the terrace.

Rodrigo.

His handsome face looked pale beneath his tanned, olive-toned skin, his dark eyes black as death as he stared at her. In another man's arms.

"No." Lola breathed, realizing what it must look like, after all the times he'd been betrayed. "No, Rodrigo, wait! It's not what you think!"

But her husband didn't wait. Without a word, he turned on his heel and went back inside the house.

Lingering behind him on the terrace, Lola saw his assistant, Marnie, staring at her smugly. Then she, too, turned and left.

"Sergei," Lola gasped, shoving him away. "Why did you do that?"

He frowned. "You do not like?"

"Of course I don't! What gave you the impression that I would?"

"But I thought you were a gold digger. Why not me instead of him?" He pounded his chest. "When I grow tired of you, I will openly give you a divorce! With money!"

Gripping her pink-crystal minaudière, Lola shook her head tearfully. "I love my husband. I would never, ever betray him!"

The man's expression changed. "I am sorry. I did not know." He looked after Rodrigo. "Sadly, he does not feel the same."

With a tearful glance, she rushed to follow her husband into the Beverly Hills mansion. She pushed through the crowds, desperate to find him, but she could not.

Finally, she ran out into the front courtyard, by the burbling stone fountain. She came out just in time to see Rodrigo driving away.

Desperately, she ran out in front of him, blocking the Ferrari's path. "Stop!"

Rodrigo's black eyes pierced through her, filled with anger. "Get out of my way, Lola."

"Not until you let me in this car!"

His voice was cold. "Your funeral."

Lola half expected him to drive off and leave her as soon as she was no longer blocking his path. But he let her climb into the passenger seat beside him. Without looking at her, he stomped on the gas.

They drove away from their own party, from their new Beverly Hills mansion, from all the guests and gifts and everything else.

She stared at her husband in the moonlight. His eyes remained stubbornly on the road, as if she weren't there. But she saw the way his jaw twitched, saw how tightly his hands gripped the steering wheel.

Lola took a deep breath.

"Please," she whispered. "You can't think—"

"Can't think what?" he bit out, his voice dangerously low. "Can't think the woman who claimed to love me betrayed me for another?"

"I know that it might have looked like that, but I never—"

He gave a low bitter laugh. "I know what I saw."

"You don't!"

He flashed her a glance, his dark eyes like ice. "Then what did I see?"

"Sergei said someone sent him an email, pretending to be you. Inviting him to take me. Practically begging him to."

"What do you mean, *take you*?"

"But I know it wasn't you," she whispered. "I know you wouldn't do something so underhanded and dishonorable."

"No. *I* wouldn't." He turned right, taking the corner too fast.

"Neither would I. Because I love you—"

"Stop it." His eyes narrowed as he stared at the road. "You invited him to the party tonight. Admit it."

"How could I? I didn't know about it!"

"You must have found out somehow," he muttered. Looking at his tight posture, at the way he stared so fiercely at the road, she felt the waves of misery coming off his body, and her heart broke for him.

Lola thought rapidly. If she hadn't invited Sergei, and Rodrigo hadn't either, then who? Who would have anything to gain by wrecking their marriage?

Every time Rodrigo gets close to a woman, he sabotages it. I used to blame myself, but not anymore. Not after it happened in all three of his engagements.

If Rodrigo hadn't sabotaged all his relationships, then who had? Who had the ability, and the reason?

Lola sucked in her breath.

Suddenly, she knew.

"It was Marnie," she choked out. "She did it. All of it."

Rodrigo scowled as he drove. "What are you talking about?"

Lola stared at him. In the window behind him, she could see tall palm trees turn silver in the moonlight. "Marnie invited Sergei tonight."

"Now you're blaming my assistant for your own unfaithfulness?" He gave a bitter laugh. "You must be truly desperate."

"It's the only thing that makes sense!"

He glanced at her coldly. "And why would she?"

She thought fast. "Marnie wanted you for herself," she said slowly. "So she's systematically rid herself of any rival who crossed her path."

"That's ridiculous. I've known her for over a decade."

"Exactly."

He gave a harsh laugh. "*Marnie* forced all my fiancées to cheat?"

"She's your assistant. She has access to everything. Your email. Your bank accounts. She could hire actors and pay them directly. She could even arrange for pictures to be sent to you as evidence."

"Because she's wildly in love with me." His tone dripped sarcasm.

She glared at him. "Don't you think it's a strange coincidence that you happened to come out on the terrace the *exact moment* Sergei grabbed me?"

For a moment, Rodrigo looked at her blankly. Then he narrowed his eyes. "Stop it."

"It's the only explanation!"

"Marnie McAdam had been loyal to me for years. I won't let you insult her." His voice was low, savage. "Not to assuage your own guilt."

"But—"

"Not another word. I mean it."

His body was vibrating with repressed fury. He didn't believe her.

With an angry breath, Lola turned away, looking out at the moonswept night as they drove past a charming commercial street. The palm trees were decked with white lights, the elegant restaurants and boutiques draped in artificial snow. It all felt so fake. Her heart hurt.

Living in the high desert as a child, there'd been no palm trees, just sagebrush and scrubby Joshua trees, and dirt yards instead of manicured green lawns. But at least that had been real. She would have preferred that, she thought with a lump in her throat, to this.

"Please, Rodrigo," she whispered, trying one last time. "Think about it. She had to have arranged it—"

Pulling the Ferrari abruptly to the curb, Rodrigo turned to her, his black eyes hard. "Get out."

"What?" She breathed in shock. She looked at his taut shoulders, his cold features. Shivering, she looked out at the trendy neighborhood, at the sleek, expensive apartment buildings on one side, and the luxury car dealership on the other. "You can't mean it."

"You lied to me." His dark eyes were like ice. Like an enemy staring at her over the barrel of a gun. "I want you out of my life. For good."

"You're not seriously going to leave me here?"

His low, hateful voice cut through her. "Get. Out."

With her heart bleeding inside her, Lola clung to her pride. It was all she had left. Slowly, she opened the car door. Gripping her pink-crystal clutch, she turned back to him, hating the begging in her voice but unable to stop herself. "Please, Rodrigo, please, if you'll only listen—"

But he didn't even look at her. The open door slipped out of her hands as he pressed hard on the gas, driving away from her without another word, or another look.

Lola watched the car drive away from her, leaving her abandoned on a corner of Santa Monica Boulevard, the old Route 66. She couldn't believe he'd left. Despair filled her as she clutched her pink stole over her shoulders, shivering in the cooling air. Fighting tears, she reached into her bag for her phone.

Then she saw it. The gold wedding band she'd planned to give him tonight. With the inscription *I love you now and always.*

Her eyes widened, and she fell to pieces. A sob racked through her, and she covered her face with her hands.

Her husband was gone. Everything was gone.

No. Not everything.

Lola looked up from her hands with an intake of breath. *Her baby.*

Fighting down emotion, she wiped her eyes hard. Finding her phone, she dialed with shaking hands. She waited as the line rang and rang. When the other person finally picked up, she nearly cried with relief.

"Please," she whispered. "Please help me."

Rodrigo felt nothing as he drove away. He felt numb, from the inside out.

As he drove up the coast, his phone rang repeatedly. Sure that it was Lola, he ignored it. Let her find her own way home. She had a phone. She had credit cards. Let her get a taxi. Or, hell, he'd abandoned her in front of a car dealership—let her buy herself one and drive herself home.

He wouldn't be at the beach house when she got there.

A woman had cheated on him. *Again.* And not just a fiancée this time.

He'd been betrayed by his wife. His partner. The mother of his child. The woman he—

Rodrigo's stomach twisted. He glanced out at the sweep of moonlight against the black ocean. He should have known better than to trust her. He should have known better than to care.

Stopping at a traffic light, he cursed loudly, punching the dashboard. As he clawed back his hair, he saw the people in the next car staring at him in alarm. As soon as the light turned green, they drove away in a terrified puff of smoke.

No wonder they were afraid. He probably looked like a madman. But the truth was worse.

He was cursed. Cursed from childhood.

His own mother hadn't loved him, his biological father hadn't claimed him, and the man who'd given him the Cabrera name had despised him. Rodrigo had been desperate from childhood to find someone to love.

But he hadn't.

And he wouldn't.

He would never love anyone. Or be loved in return.

A chill went through him, like the sudden frigid calm that came over someone sinking into icy waters for the last time.

Whatever. He set his jaw. He didn't need it. He didn't need Lola, either. He'd forget her, just like all the rest.

Except she wasn't like the rest.

Their relationship hadn't begun with flowers and fancy televised awards shows, or amid the fantasy of a big screen dream, but quietly, slowly over time. He and Lola had been partners first, then friends, and finally lovers.

He knew her. He trusted her.

Or at least he *had*.

That was what made her betrayal the worst of all.

Swallowing against the lump in his throat, he tightened his grip on the steering wheel. He'd make her regret it. He'd fight for custody of Jett. Whatever the prenuptial agreement had promised, Lola didn't deserve custody of their son. She was corrupt, deceitful, a horrible excuse for a human being. She was no fit mother—

Memories of all her hours caring for their baby, so lovingly and so well, ripped through him. All her time and care had gone to their son, while his own hours had often been spent building his business empire.

Would he really hurt Jett, by taking him from the care of a loving mother, to leave him instead with paid nannies, as Rodrigo had once been? Could he be so determined to punish his wife that he'd hurt his son as collateral damage?

Furiously, he set his jaw. Fine. He'd let Lola keep custody. But he'd take everything else. The prenuptial agreement was watertight. If she cheated, she ended up with nothing. She should enjoy buying that car from the dealership tonight. She wouldn't have it long.

When he finally pulled past the gate into the courtyard of his beach house, he parked haphazardly. He had to take a deep breath before he picked up his phone. But to his shock, he saw it hadn't been Lola calling, but Marnie. She'd left several messages.

She was probably worried, after he'd abandoned his own party without an explanation. But Marnie had seen what happened on the terrace. She didn't need one.

Rodrigo stared up blankly at his beach house.

How could Lola have betrayed him? How?

Had she lied when she told him she loved him?

I love you. He heard the echo of her tender whisper. *Only you. And I'll love you forever.*

He felt sick, remembering. If she loved him, how could she have immediately betrayed him?

Had she been so crushed by Rodrigo's rejection of her love that she'd immediately jumped into the arms of another man? And she'd somehow invited Sergei Morozov to the party beforehand?

But that didn't make sense. He remembered Lola's shock when she'd first seen the magnificent Spanish-style mansion. She hadn't known about the party.

Then who?

Marnie wanted you for herself. So she's systematically rid herself of any rival who crossed her path.

No. He shook his head angrily. Sweet, loyal Marnie, who'd devoted nearly fifteen years to his service? No, impossible. He wasn't going to listen to Lola's excuses or impossible story.

Perhaps Morozov had been stalking Lola all this time. Perhaps the investigator had been wrong, and the two of them had continued to secretly be in contact after her marriage. And tonight, when her pride was wounded, she'd immediately phoned the other man, telling him she wanted him—

It didn't matter. Going inside the beach house, Rodrigo slammed the door behind him. He would send for his lawyers at once. But first, he had to see his son. Right now. He had to feel like there was still one thing on earth he could depend on. One person he could love, who loved him back.

But the house was dark and empty. Feeling cold, Rodrigo walked through it, calling the housekeeper's name. But the kitchen was dark.

So was the nursery. The crib was empty.

His son.

Snatching up his phone, he frantically dialed his housekeeper's number, then his bodyguard's. If Tobias didn't pick up, he'd call the police—

He nearly gasped with relief when the line was answered.

"Jett's fine, Mr. Cabrera," Tobias replied calmly. "He's safe here in the car. With his mother."

Rodrigo's jaw dropped. "Lola is with you?"

"Yes. I'm driving Mrs. Cabrera to the airport now. She's taking the first flight back to New York."

To New York.

Gripping his phone, Rodrigo looked slowly around the

shadowy beach house. Outside, the silvery moonlight on the vast, black Pacific seemed hollow and gray.

"She called me after you abandoned her on the side of the road." His bodyguard's voice was reproachful. "That was cold, Mr. Cabrera. God knows I hate my ex, but even I wouldn't do that."

Let me talk to her, Rodrigo wanted to say. Then he remembered how he'd told her he wanted her out of his life for good. How he'd left her standing on the sidewalk in Santa Monica. Lola would never forgive him for that. Ever. Even if he'd wanted her to.

"You don't have to fire me for it, either," Tobias said. "Because I qu—"

"You're not fired," Rodrigo said heavily.

The man paused. "I'm not?"

"You're right," he said flatly. "My son should be with his mother. Lola knows how to love him. I don't. Take them to the airport. And leave me the hell alone."

Rodrigo hung up. Grabbing a bottle of whiskey—not tequila, never tequila, it would only remind him of Mexico City—he drank it straight from the bottle.

He drank through Christmas Eve, until Christmas finally came, bright and fine. The sun sparkled in the blue sky, shimmering against the wide ocean, which stretched out forever.

Just like his empty beach house. Once, Rodrigo had thought this house was the perfect size. Perfect for dating, perfect for entertaining and impressing others.

Now, it stretched with the vast emptiness of space, lacking oxygen, leaving him to float, with nothing to cling to. Especially after Mrs. Lee arrived to pack up all of Lola and Jett's things and mail them to Hallie Moretti's house in the West Village.

The day after Christmas, Rodrigo put the whiskey away. He forced himself to get up. To shave. To shower. To run ten miles along the beach, then visit a boxing gym, where he punched the hell out of everything.

For the rest of the week, he focused on work, ordering his whole team to come back into the office early, in order to greenlight production of as many new films as possible. If anyone on his staff dared voice a single regret at giving up their holidays with their families, Rodrigo verbally ripped them apart. He didn't need a family. Why should they?

He was better off alone. They would be, too.

By midafternoon on New Year's Eve, Rodrigo was holed up in his luxurious private office in the Cabrera Media Group headquarters in downtown Los Angeles, staring at his computer, manically reading script after script. He'd been there all night, sleeping fitfully on the sofa in his office. He planned to do the same tonight for New Year's Eve. As long as he kept working, there'd be no need for him to return to the beach house. Ever.

Or think about the divorce papers his lawyers had prepared for him, already waiting at his house for his signature.

Marnie, who all week had seemed as nervous of him as a caged tiger, peeked into his office. "Mr. Cabrera?"

Impatiently, Rodrigo waved her in. "You have my clothes?"

"Yes, sir." She handed him the duffel bag of clean clothes she'd brought from his beach house.

Grabbing it, he turned away. "Thanks."

"Are you doing all right, sir?"

"Of course I'm all right." He glared at her. "I'm not like my board, whining about their families and the holiday season. They have no work ethic." He took a deep breath, controlling his tone. "But you do, Marnie. You haven't complained once. Thank you for that."

"I'm glad to be here, sir." She set down a stack of papers on his large dark wood desk. "Ned Stone sent over a script. He says it's a four-quadrant film."

Ned Stone was the biggest agent in Hollywood, and a four-quadrant film was the holy grail of the film industry: a movie that would appeal to both men and women, young and old.

But looking at it, Rodrigo didn't feel elated. He just felt tired. So tired, in fact, the room seemed to swim in front of his eyes.

"Take it back," he whispered, not moving. "I don't want it."

Marnie stared at him, her eyebrows lifted in shock. "You don't care about a four-quadrant film?"

"No," he said slowly. "I don't."

Since Lola had left, he'd tried to lose himself in work. He'd committed hundreds of millions of dollars to projects he couldn't even remember now. Half his board was threatening to quit and muttering dark suspicions about his mental health. But for all that, he felt exhausted and numb. Hollow.

He'd tried to run away from his feelings. He'd tried not to think of Lola. But he'd failed. She was all he could think about. He hated work. He hated home. Most of all, he hated himself.

Because without his wife, nothing else mattered. Not success, not fame or fortune. Not even a four-quadrant film.

Because he loved her.

Rodrigo felt a *whoosh* go through his body, like vertigo. He staggered back beneath the weight of the realization. The duffel bag slid from his hands to the hardwood floor.

Oh, my God. *He loved her.*

All this time, he'd tried to keep his heart cold. But he'd been lying to himself. The truth was, in the depths of his heart, he'd known it was already too late. He'd loved her from the moment she'd kissed him in Mexico City. Perhaps even before.

That was why he'd never slept with another woman. His body had known what his mind and heart refused to admit. He'd been too afraid to admit it, even to himself, after all the times he'd been hurt by the women he'd loved.

Except he hadn't loved his first three fiancées, he now realized. How could he? He'd barely known them. As a young man, he'd been so desperate for love, to have a real family, that he'd proposed marriage within weeks.

Then he'd promptly come up with a reason to leave. Because he hadn't loved those three women, any more than they'd loved him. If they had, they wouldn't have been so easily lured away.

But he loved Lola. It had terrified him. Seeing her in Morozov's arms had been all the excuse he needed to end their relationship. He'd almost been relieved to accept the worst rather than let himself be vulnerable, and love her.

But Lola, who'd also known pain and loss, hadn't given in to fear. She'd been brave. She'd been loyal. She'd had his back, all along.

Get this through your head, she'd said. *I'll never betray you, Rodrigo. Ever.*

And she hadn't.

Rodrigo was the one who'd betrayed her.

"Are you all right, sir?" Marnie frowned, coming closer in the downtown office. "You don't look well."

His jaw clenched. He'd betrayed Lola by not trusting her, when she'd been the best friend he'd ever had. He'd betrayed her by not being brave enough to give his heart.

"Sir?"

He slowly looked at his assistant.

And he'd betrayed his wife by not believing her, when she was the smartest person he knew.

Marnie wanted you for herself. So she's systematically rid herself of any rival who crossed her path. She's your assistant. She has access to everything.

"Marnie," he said quietly. "I know what you did."

His assistant's eyes widened beneath her thick glasses. Then, slowly, she smiled. "I've just acted as any good secretary would. And kept my boss out of trouble."

Ice went down his spine. Lola had been right about everything. "You sabotaged my engagements."

Marnie's eyes turned bright, eager. "It wasn't even hard. They all fell for it so easily. They cheated. They proved they weren't worthy of you."

He felt sick.

"But Lola didn't."

She scowled. "I sent the best porn actor from the agency. But she blew him off. I had to be more creative."

"So you sent the message to Morozov, pretending to be me."

"I knew you couldn't actually want to be married to her." Her expression darkened. "She doesn't love you. Not like I do."

I love you. The memory of Lola's beautiful face, her luminous hazel eyes in the moonlit night, came back to him. *Only you. And I'll love you forever.*

"I did it all for you." Marnie's thin face was triumphant. "Lived only for you. Sacrificed my life for you. You need me, Rodrigo. I'm the only one who can protect you from everything. From pain. From loss."

Rodrigo lifted his head.

"I don't want to be protected. Not anymore. I never wanted you to do any of this," he said in a low voice. "I'm sorry, Marnie. It's time for you to go."

She looked flummoxed. "Go!"

"I'm in love with my wife. Because of you..."

Because of you, I've betrayed her, he almost said. But

that wasn't fair. It hadn't just been Marnie's lies that kept him from loving Lola. He'd been scared. Scared of losing control. Scared of abandonment and pain. Taking a deep breath, he said quietly, "It's time for you to find another job and a different man to love."

His assistant's face crumpled. "No!" she cried. "I don't know how to do anything else." She gave a sob, wrapping her arms around herself. "I don't know how to change."

He hadn't either, Rodrigo realized. He might have spent the rest of his life focusing only on wealth and power, unloved and dead inside, as lonely as a mummy in a tomb full of cold treasures.

If not for Lola's warmth. Her bravery. Her love.

Because of her, he had the chance to be better. To make better choices. To be brave enough to change.

"I'm sorry," Rodrigo said, looking down at his assistant. He lifted the duffel bag with the change of clothes back to his shoulder. "You'll get severance for your years of service. But I love my wife. You have to know you can't work for me anymore."

Marnie wiped her eyes. "Then what will I do?"

"I don't know." Turning away, he paused to look back at the door. "I hear Sergei Morozov is moving back to Moscow and looking for a new assistant."

She blinked at him, looking like a mole who's just seen the sun.

"Good luck," he said.

Turning away, Rodrigo strode through his office, yelling right and left for everyone to go home, to spend the holiday with their families and friends. His employees' eyes lit up with delight. But he couldn't wait. He nearly ran out of the walnut-paneled lobby, holding his phone to his ear, telling his pilot to get the plane ready.

He had to see Lola. Tonight. Before the New Year began. He'd be brave enough to tell her he loved her.

But as he jumped into his car and stomped down hard on the gas, driving down the sunlit highway toward the airport, Rodrigo wondered if he'd be too late.

CHAPTER ELEVEN

WHY, OH, WHY had Lola ever let her friends talk her into this?

"It's almost time!" Hallie crowed, kissing her husband passionately in the crowded rooftop restaurant. "Just ten minutes left!"

All around Lola, happy couples were counting down the minutes until the start of a new year. Nearby, she saw Stefano kissing Tess under the mistletoe.

They were also celebrating Cristiano Moretti's new acquisition of this building, an old, rundown chain hotel with a location overlooking Times Square. He'd closed on the hotel yesterday. Tomorrow, the vast remodeling project would begin, to bring the property into line with the high standards of his luxury Campania hotel brand.

Only the rooftop restaurant was still open, with its Art Deco–style bar and enormous windows and terrace overlooking Times Square; and it was only open to Cristiano's closest family and friends, for his glamorous black tie New Year's Eve party. Everyone was drinking champagne and ogling the bright lights and electronic billboards of Times Square, shining brightly and shimmering in the cold winter's night below, as they, and about a million people on the streets, waited for the magical moment when the ball would drop, and a new year would begin.

But Lola just felt sad.

She shivered in the silvery, sparkly dress she'd borrowed from Hallie. Her friends were worried about her. Since she and Jett had arrived from Los Angeles last week, they'd complained that Lola didn't seem like her old self. She didn't brashly give her opinion. She didn't boss anyone around. Even spending Christmas Day with her little sisters and their parents, as wonderful as they'd been, hadn't healed her broken heart. Though Kelsey and Johanna would always be her sisters, she missed Rodrigo. She missed her husband. She wanted him.

Her heart felt broken.

Lola looked down at her palm. She held the plain gold wedding band she'd had engraved for him. The ring she'd meant to give him for Christmas. She'd brought it with her tonight, telling herself that she'd toss it away at midnight and start the new year fresh.

But feeling it in her hand, she couldn't let it go.

Oh, if he had only loved her!

Wiping a tear savagely before anyone could see it, she left the bar and went out onto the rooftop terrace. It was very cold, but the frigid, numbing air was a relief against her hot skin. It was also a relief to get away from her friends.

Hallie and Tess kept giving her worried looks, trying to tempt her to eat from the appetizer trays. They'd bullied her into coming tonight. Even the fact that she'd given in—meekly, without a fight—had seemed to worry them. She could still see them peeking at her through the windows, even as they danced in the arms of their adoring husbands.

Lola felt hollowed out.

She was glad for Tess and Hallie. She truly was. But they'd risked everything for love, and won.

Lola had risked everything, and lost.

A lump rose in her throat. *Stop it*, she told herself furiously, hating her self-pity. She was lucky. Her son was healthy and well. She had custody. Her baby sisters were back in her life. She had good friends. She had a place to live, at the Morettis' large, comfortable home in the West Village, where Jett was now being watched by their long-time nanny, along with Hallie's baby, Jack.

She'd even been offered two different jobs, one in Cristiano's hotel business, the other in Tess's growing fashion company.

Lola had refused both. She'd told her friends she intended to go to community college, and maybe even law school. They'd loved that idea. So did she. It was Rodrigo who'd given it to her. In that sense, he'd believed in her, in a way no one else ever had.

But for now, she couldn't think of the future. She still had money saved. She'd think of it all later.

She looked down at the diamond Rodrigo had given her, sparkling on her left hand. She should send it back, she knew, like she'd sent back the necklace. But as heavy and cold as the ring was, she hadn't been able to take it off.

Their divorce would be simple, at least. All the details had been arranged in the prenup. Any day now, she expected to get the paperwork from Rodrigo's lawyers. Lola looked out at Times Square gleaming around her. She was lucky, she thought dully. It all would be easy. Happy New Year.

Enough, she told herself savagely. *Go back to the party. Pretend you're having a good time, for your friends' sake, if not your own.*

Wiping her eyes one last time, she forced her face into a smile and turned around. Then she stopped with an intake of breath.

There, standing in front of her, was Rodrigo.

Lola's legs went weak.

"What are you doing here?" she whispered, wondering if he was a dream wrought by her feverish heart.

Rodrigo's chiseled face was darkly handsome beneath

the bright lights of Times Square as he came toward Lola on the rooftop terrace. He was dressed in a black shirt and trousers beneath a black overcoat. His jawline was dark with a five o'clock shadow. His voice was low and deep. "I came for you."

He was real. He had to be. She could see the white cloud of his breath in the cold air. And she'd never seen anything so beautiful in her life.

Shaking, Lola took a step forward. Reaching up, she put her hand against his rough cheek. She felt him tremble beneath her touch. Just like she was trembling.

There were shadows beneath his eyes. As if he hadn't slept all week, any more than she had. "For me?"

Rodrigo put his hand over her own. "I came to tell you that you were right."

Lola's hopes, which had been rising as high as the Empire State Building, crashed to the ground.

"You mean about Marnie. I was right about her."

"Not just her." His dark eyes searched hers. "About everything."

"What are you saying?" she asked breathlessly.

Slowly, Rodrigo pulled her into his arms. His body felt so powerful. So solid. So strong. And so were his black eyes as he looked down at her.

"I'm in love with you, Lola."

Her heart stopped in her chest. "What?"

"I've always loved you." Gently, he moved his hands down her hair, against the bare skin of her shoulders above her party dress. "I loved you so much, it scared the hell out of me. Because I knew I'd someday lose you, just like I lost the others." He paused. "But now…"

"Now?" she choked out, searching his gaze.

"I'm not scared anymore." Rodrigo looked down at her, giving her a smile that seemed lit up from within. "After you left, everything fell apart. And I realized nothing else matters. You're all I want. All I need. You're everything. Because I love you."

As she stared at him, her heart twisted in her chest.

"And I was a fool." Rodrigo searched her gaze fiercely. "Marnie might have sabotaged those other relationships, but so did I."

"You?"

"The moment they agreed to marry me, I became restless, wanting to be away from them. But with you, it was different. With you... I admire you. Respect you. You're not just my lover. You're my friend. My partner."

As if from a million miles away, she heard noise from the party, as someone shouted, "The countdown has begun!"

"All I want is to be with you," he whispered. "Forever and always." His hand tightened against her shoulder. "You're my soul mate."

"Twenty..."

"And I know I ruined everything," Rodrigo said. "Leaving you like that, kicking you out of my car just for telling me the truth..." He shuddered. "You don't know how much I wish I could go back. But all I can do is go forward. And hope you'll forgive me. Tell me," he whispered, running his hands through her hair. "How I can win you back..."

"Ten..."

Lola stared at him, too overcome with emotion to speak.

His expression fell. Then his jaw set as his eyes narrowed with determination. "I'll do whatever it takes to win you back, Lola. Anything. Even if it takes everything I possess. Even if it takes the rest of my life—"

"Stop." Trembling, she reached her finger to his lips. They felt soft and sensual, warm to the touch. A shiver of desire went through her.

"Five..."

Opening her hand, she held out the golden wedding band on her palm. "This is my answer."

Emotion was raw on his face as he took the ring. Then he saw the inscription: *I love you now and always*.

Rodrigo looked up with an intake of breath.

"One! Happy New Year!"

A growl came from the back of his throat, and he pulled her into his powerful arms, wrapping her tight. And lowering his head, he kissed Lola as she'd never been kissed before: with pure, heartfelt love, holding nothing back. She returned his kiss, with the same promise and need.

They were fated. Bound. Married.

Soul mates.

A cheer rose up behind them, yanking Lola out of her spell. Pressing her cheek against his chest, she saw the Morettis and Zaccos and all the rest of the party pressed against the restaurant's double-height windows, grinning and applauding. Hallie and Tess were giving her beaming smiles and holding up champagne glasses, as if they'd always known love would win.

And it was true, Lola thought with tears in her eyes. Love won. No matter how difficult and awful life could be, no matter how much grief and pain a person endured, love could always win.

"Let's live in New York," he murmured suddenly.

She looked up at him joyfully. "Are you serious?"

"Why not?" He gave her a sudden wicked grin. "I hear it's 'a hotbed of media companies that will dominate the future of the entertainment business.'"

She giggled. "Not to mention it's near all our family and friends."

"Yes. Not to mention that." Rodrigo's face grew serious. "I've realized whatever makes you happy, makes me happy, too." Sliding the golden band on his left ring finger, he cupped her face in his hands. "I've spent my whole life looking for you, *querida*," he said huskily, looking down at her with tears shining in his black eyes. "And now I've found you, I'm never going to let you go."

"I love you," Lola whispered, smiling through her own tears.

"I love you. Now and forever." And as Rodrigo lowered his lips to hers, they started the new year, their new lives, with a kiss she'd never forget.

Summer had come to New York at last. The trees were green, the sun was shining and the tourists were in full bloom, returning to the city with the faithful constancy of the swallows of San Juan Capistrano.

Three friends were giggling together in the spacious, flower-filled backyard of a West Village mansion, watching as their three billionaire husbands argued loudly about the best method of barbecuing steaks.

"They'll get it eventually," Hallie said, smiling as she gave her fifteen-month-old baby, Jack, his favorite toy shovel before he toddled off to dig in the sunny garden.

"Oh, yes," agreed Tess, playing patty-cake with sixteen-month-old Esme, before the baby toddled unsteadily after Jack.

Looking at her friends in disbelief, Lola cuddled the youngest baby, eleven-month-old Jett, who was sleeping in her arms. "We might have to order pizza."

The three women giggled, then hid their smiles as the men looked over with a suspicious glare.

Taking a sip of sparkling water, Hallie sobered as she tilted her head back to look over her magnificent private garden, rare for Manhattan, and the four-story brick townhouse, at her toddler digging up flowers and her husband practically getting into a fistfight with his best friends over the best use of marinade.

"Can you believe how much has changed since we all first met at the single moms' group?" she said. Tilting her head, she said softly, "This time last year, I was desperate and alone."

"We all were," said Lola.

"I thought I'd never have what I wanted most." Tears rose to Hallie's eyes. "A family. A home."

"And I wanted love," Tess said, a dreamy smile tracing her lips. "Love that would last forever."

"I was the only one who was practical," Lola grumbled. "Unlike you two numbskulls, I knew money made the world go 'round."

The other two stared at her, then burst into a laugh.

"What?" Lola said, looking between them indignantly.

"You can't fool us," chided Tess, still snickering.

"Yeah, Lola. The jig is up."

"What are you talking about?"

"You never wanted money, you old softie." Hallie grinned. "You wanted family and home and love, like the rest of us."

"Don't worry," Tess said, patting her hand. "Your secret's safe with us."

For a moment, Lola looked disgruntled. Then she sighed, leaning back in the comfortable patio chair, as she reached for her own glass of sparkling water with lemon. "All right," she said softly. She smiled at them. "You got me. That was what I really wanted, all along."

Tess squeezed her hand, and then all three women leaned back in their chairs, relishing the warmth of the June afternoon, sipping identical drinks, as they watched their husbands argue over the best way to barbecue and their babies play in the sunshine.

Flashing the husbands a guilty glance, Hallie whispered, "Can you keep a secret?"

"We have no secrets now," said Lola, waving her glass airily.

"Tell us," Tess begged.

Hallie blushed, then she looked up with a smile so bright, her brown eyes glowed. "There's a reason I'm drinking sparkling water tonight, instead of sangria."

"Me, too," breathed Tess.

Lola sat up straight in her chair. "Me, too."

The three women stared at each other, wide-eyed.

"All of us together—"

"Pregnant again—"

"Friends forever—"

And in a loud burst of noise, they all hugged each other in a raucous cacophony of laughter and tears.

On the other side of the garden, the three men frowned, looking across the yard at their wives.

"I wonder what that's all about," said Cristiano.

"Could they be talking about us?" wondered Prince Stefano.

"Doubtful," said Rodrigo. While the other two men were distracted, he took the opportunity to commandeer the grill. Let the Italians stick to pasta, he thought. Only Spaniards knew *parrillada*. And he knew Lola liked her steaks spicy, like her man. Like her life.

"What could make them cheer like that?" Cristiano pondered.

"Yes, what?" Stefano frowned.

Rodrigo looked back over his shoulder, at the sunlit garden, their happy children, their mysterious, powerful, beautiful wives. And he flashed a grin back at the other men. "Something tells me we'll soon find out."

* * * * *

SICILIAN'S BRIDE
FOR A PRICE

TARA PAMMI

For my very own hero, my husband, Raghu.

Twenty is nothing—
I could write a hundred heroes inspired by you.

CHAPTER ONE

Dante Vittori stared at the legal document that had been delivered an hour ago. The floor-to-ceiling glass windows that made up three whole sides of his office on the forty-sixth floor of Matta Towers in Central London cast the luxurious space in an orange glow, thanks to the setting sun behind him.

Vikram Matta—his mentor Neel Matta's son and Dante's best friend—was now legally dead.

He felt a twinge in his chest for exactly one minute.

He'd learned that grief, like regret, was a useless emotion. He'd learned this at the age of thirteen when his father had killed himself instead of facing lifelong incarceration for his Ponzi scheme that had fleeced hundreds of people. He'd learned this when his mother had simply changed her name back to her Sicilian father's and married a man he approved of within a year of his father's death.

Giving in to his emotions would have crushed Dante back then. Vikram was gone; he'd made his peace with it a long time ago.

Quickly, he rifled through the documents, to ensure he hadn't missed anything.

He was almost to the last couple of pages when he stilled.

Voting Shares of the Deceased

The hairs at the back of his neck prickled. His mind instantly rewound back to the conversation he and Vikram had had with Neel when Neel had found he hadn't much time to live.

Neel Matta had started Matta Steel, a small steel manufacturing business, almost forty years ago, but it was Dante who had grown it into the billion-dollar conglomerate it was now. Against his own brother, Nitin's wishes, for the first time in the history of the company, Neel had granted his own voting shares to Dante, an outsider.

He had made Dante a part of his family. And now Matta Steel was the blood in his veins, his mistress, his everything.

Instead of wasting time grieving after Neel's death and Vikram's horrific plane crash, Dante had taken the company from strength to strength, cementing his position as the CEO.

But with Vikram's voting shares being up for grabs now…

His secretary, Izzy, came into the office without knocking. Being another alum of Neel Matta's generosity, Izzy took for granted a certain personal privilege with Dante that he didn't allow anyone else. Neither did he doubt that she'd interrupted him for a good reason.

The redhead's gaze flew to the papers in front of him, clear distress in those green eyes for a moment. But when she met his gaze, she was the consummate professional.

Of course Vikram's death had touched her too, but like him, Izzy was nothing if not practical.

Pushing his chair back, he laced his fingers at the back of his neck and said, "Spill it."

"I heard from Nitin's secretary, Norma, that he's thinking of calling an emergency board meeting with special counsel present."

Neel's brother was so predictable in his greed and deception. "I was expecting that."

"I wasn't sure if you had realized it has to do with Vicky's voting shares being up for grabs now."

"I did." Izzy was both competent and brilliant. And utterly loyal to him. The one quality he knew he couldn't buy even with his billions. "Tell me your thoughts."

She took a seat and opened her notebook. "I pressed a little on Norma and learned that he means to go over the bylaws in front of the board and direct the conclusion that Vikram's shares—" an infinitesimal catch in her throat again "—should go to him, since the bylaws state that the voting shares are to be kept in the family."

"Except when Neel modified them to grant me his shares." They had been a gift when Dante had made a big business win. Neel had been paving his way into retirement, wanting to slow down and let Dante take over. Instead his heart disease had killed him in a matter of months.

"He means to censure that as an aberration on Neel's part due to his ailing health."

Dante smiled. "It's an allegation he's continued to make for nigh on ten years now, even though I have held the controlling stake in the company."

"Also, he's conveniently forgotten Ali."

For the first time in years, Dante found his thoughts in sudden disarray.

His mentor's rebel daughter had always been the one thorn in his rise to success. The one piece of trouble in Neel's life that Dante hadn't solved for the man he'd worshipped. The one element he'd never quite figured out properly.

"No, he hasn't." Alisha's scorn for her father's company wasn't a secret.

He stood up from his seat. London's night was glittering

into life all around them. "Nitin's counting on Ali simply refusing to have anything to do with the company, as always. Which means he can inherit all of Vikram's shares."

"Can't you contest that?"

"I can, but if he gets the board on his side and they rule that the shares go to him, there's not a lot I can do. He'd own the majority. Unless I got…" He trailed off, an idea occurring to him. "Nitin needs to be taught the lesson that I own Matta Steel. Irrevocably."

"I'm assuming you've already come up with a plan for that."

He had. A brilliant one. He hadn't put his heart and blood and soul into Matta Steel just so he'd have to defend it every other year.

Again, that twinge of doubt pulled at his chest. He flicked it away. There was no room for emotions in his decision. The only thing he would never violate was Neel's trust in him—and that meant keeping control of Matta Steel.

Alisha had never wanted to be a part of her papa's legacy. She had turned her back on everything to do with the company and Neel and even Vikram when he'd been alive.

She'd had nothing but resentment for Dante for as long as he could remember. And he would feel no compunction in taking the things he wanted—the things that she scorned anyway—off her hands, forever.

All he needed was leverage.

Everyone had a price and he just needed to find Ali's. "Find out where she's holed up now. She could be anywhere."

Izzy jerked her head up, shock dancing in her green eyes. "Ali?"

There was reluctance, maybe even unwillingness in her stare.

"Yes. Find Alisha," he said, simply dismissing the unasked question in Izzy's eyes. He pulled his jacket on and checked his phone. No reason for him to miss out on his date with the latest Broadway actress touring London.

He reached the door and then turned. "Oh, also, call that PI for me, won't you? I want to have a little chat with him."

"Which one?"

"The one I have on my payroll to keep track of Alisha's movements."

"But you never look at his reports." Izzy's accusation was clear. He'd never given a damn about Alisha except to have someone keep an eye on her, for the purpose of extricating her if she got herself into trouble.

For Neel's sake.

"I didn't need to, until now. She's been safe, mostly, *si*?" It was a miracle in itself, since she traveled through all the hellholes of the world in the name of her little hobby. Izzy didn't need to know he read every single one of those reports. On any given day, he knew how and where Alisha was. "Now, however, I need a little bit more info on her."

"Dante—"

"None of your business, Isabel." He cut her off smoothly and closed the door behind him.

Izzy had been the one constant person in his life for so long, from the moment he had come to live with Neel all those years ago, yes. But it didn't mean he invited her into his private thoughts or that he considered her a personal friend.

Dante Vittori didn't do relationships, of any kind.

"There's someone here to see you, Ali."

Alisha Matta looked up from her crouch on the floor of the Grand Empire Palace restaurant. Her shoulders were tight from supporting the weight of the camera and her thighs burned at her continued position. Ignoring her friend Mak's voice, she kept clicking.

She'd been waiting all morning in the small kitchen of the crowded restaurant, waiting for Kiki to come home.

The pop of the flash of her Nikon sang through her nerves, the few moments of clarity and purpose making the wait of the last three months utterly worth it. "To your right, look into the camera. No, jut your left hip out, you're gorgeous, Kiki," she continued the words of encouragement. She'd managed to learn a little Thai in the last year but her stuttering accent had only made Kiki laugh.

The neon lights and the cheap pink linoleum floors became the perfect background as Kiki shed her jeans and shirt in a move that was both efficient and sensual as hell. Her lithe dancer's body sang for the camera.

But even the perfection of the shot couldn't stop the distraction of Mak hovering.

"If it's John, tell him we're done," she whispered.

"It's an Italian gentleman. In a three-piece Tom Ford suit that I'm pretty sure is custom designed and black handmade Italian loafers. Gucci, I think."

Ali fell back onto her haunches with a soft thud, hanging on to her expensive camera for dear life. Mak was crazy about designer duds. There was only one Italian gentleman she knew. Except, if it was who she thought it was, he shouldn't be called a gentleman. More a ruthless soul in the garb of one.

"Said his name was…"

Ali's heart thudded in tune with the loud blare of the boom box. "What, Mak?"

Mak scrunched his brow. "You know, the guy who wrote about all those circles of hell, that one."

"Dante," Ali whispered the word softly. How appropriate that Mak would mention Dante and hell in the same sentence.

Because that was what her papa's protégé represented to her.

The very devil from hell.

Princesses in glass castles shouldn't throw stones, bella.

Okay, yes, devil was a bit overboard because he hadn't actually ever harmed Ali, but still, Ali hated him.

So what was the devil, whose usual playground was the London social circuit, doing on the other side of the world in Bangkok?

The last time they had laid eyes on each other had been when she'd learned of Vikram's plane crash. She closed her eyes, fighting the memory of the disastrous night, but it came anyway.

She'd been so full of rage, so vulnerable and so vicious toward Dante. For no reason except that he was alive while her brother was gone. Gone before she could reconnect with him.

"He doesn't look like he's happy to be kept waiting," Mak interrupted her trip down a nightmarish memory lane.

Ali pulled herself up.

No, super busy billionaire Dante Vittori wouldn't like waiting in the ramshackle hotel. How impatient he must be to get back to his empire. To his billions.

How dare Ali keep him waiting while each minute of his time could mean another deal he could broker, another billion he could add to his pile, another company he… She smiled wide.

She'd make him wait.

Because Dante being here meant only one thing: he needed something from her.

And she would jump through those nine circles of hell

before she did anything that made his life easier. Or calmer. Or richer.

Slowly, with shaking fingers, she packed up her camera. She pulled the strap of the bag over her shoulder, picked up her other paraphernalia, kissed Kiki's cheek and pushed the back door open.

The late September evening was balmy, noisy and full of delicious smells emanating from all the restaurants that lined up the street.

Her stomach growled. She promised herself some authentic pad thai and a cold can of Coke as soon as she got to her flat. Thwarting Dante and a well-earned dinner suddenly seemed like a highly pleasurable way to spend her day.

Just as she took another step into the busy street, a black chauffeur-driven Mercedes pulled up, blocking her. Ali blinked at her reflection in the polished glass of the window when the door opened. Out stepped Dante.

In his crisp white shirt, which did wonders for his olive complexion, and tailored black pants, he looked like he'd stepped out of a *GQ* magazine cover and casually strolled into the colorful street.

His Patek Philippe watch—a gift from her father when he'd welcomed Dante onto the board of Matta Steel, yet one more thing Papa had given Dante and not her—gleamed on his wrist as he stood leaning carelessly against the door, a silky smile curving that sculpted mouth. "Running away again, Alisha?"

He was the only one who insisted on calling her Alisha. Somehow he managed to fill it with reprimand and contempt.

All thoughts of pad thai were replaced with the cold burn of resentment as that penetrating gaze took in her white spaghetti strap top and forest green shorts and traveled from her feet in flip-flops to her hair bunched into a messy bun on top of her head. It was dismissive and yet so thorough that her skin prickled.

Chin tilted, Ali stared right back. She coated it in defiance but after so long, she was greedy for the sight of him. Shouts from street vendors and the evening bustle faded out.

A careless heat filled her veins as she noted the aristocratic nose—broken in his adolescence and fixed—the dark, stubble-coated line of his jaw and deep-set eyes that always mocked her, the broad reach of his shoulders, the careless arrogance that filled every pore. He exuded that kind of masculine confidence that announced him as the top of the food chain both in the boardroom and out of it.

And his mouth… The upper lip was thin and carved and the lower was fuller and lush, the only hint of softness in that face and body. It was a soft whisper about the sensuality he buried under that ruthlessness.

Her heart was now thundering in her chest, not unlike Mak's boom box. Heat flushed her from within. She jerked her gaze to meet his, saw the slight flare of his nostrils.

Christ, what was she doing? What was she imagining?

Ali moved her tongue around in her dry mouth, and somehow managed to say, "I have nothing to say and I want nothing to do with you."

To do with you…

The words mocked her, mocked the adolescent infatuation she'd nursed for him that she now hated, morphing into something much worse. Everything she despised about him also attracted her to him. If that weren't a red flag…

He halted her dignified exit with his fingers on her wrist, the calloused pads of his fingers playing on her oversensitized skin.

She jerked her arm out of his grip like a scalded cat. His

mouth tightened, but whatever emotion she had incited disappeared behind his controlled mask. "I have a proposal that I'm sure you would like to hear."

God, how she wanted to do or say something that made that mask shatter completely. How she wished she could be the one who brought the arrogant man to his knees. Her sudden bloodthirstiness shocked even her.

She'd always liked coloring outside the lines, yes, but not to the point of self-destruction. And that was what Dante made her do. Always.

At some point, hating him had become more important than trying to build a bridge to her father, than reconnecting with Vikram.

No more.

No playing to his point by doing something he would hate; no trying to stir up that smooth facade and burn her bridges.

You're a necessary nuisance, Alisha. I put up with your mind games for his sake. Only for his.

A calm filled her at her resolution. "What do you want from me?"

A brow rose in the too angular face. There was that tightness to his mouth again. In a parallel universe, Ali would have concluded that that assumption pricked him. In this one where she knew Dante Vittori had no emotions, she didn't.

"Why are you so sure that I want something from you?"

"You're thousands of miles away from your empire. From everything I know, there's no steel plant in this area, nor a lot of demand for it. Unless you're scouting the area to build a new plant with cheap labor, then you're not to check up on me."

"I've always known where you are, Alisha."

She swallowed.

"However much you like to pretend that there are no ties between us, however far you run in pursuit of your little hobby, you are, at the end of the day, his daughter."

His statement put paid to any emotional extrapolation she was still stupid enough to make from his previous one. As if he worried she might read too much—or anything at all—into him keeping tabs on her.

He had always been loyal to her father; would always be loyal to him. Keeping track of her fell somewhere under that umbrella. Nothing at all to do with the woman she was.

Nothing.

"I'm not interested in trading insults with you," she said, unable to stop her voice from cracking. "I'm not... I'm not that impulsive, destructive Ali anymore."

"That would be a nice change of pace for us, *si*? So we'll have dinner and not trade insults tonight."

"I said no insults. That doesn't mean I want to be anywhere near you for more than five minutes." It was her own confused emotions and this...blasted attraction that made her want to avoid him even now.

"Ah..." With a graceful flick of his wrist, he made a big show of checking his watch. "That lasted about thirty seconds." His gaze caught hers. "I'm not and have never been your enemy, Alisha."

And just like that, her attraction to him became a near tangible thing in the air. Her hating him became the only weapon in her armor. "Eating out is a pleasure for me and somehow I don't see that being the primary emotion if we're forced together for too long."

A calculating glint appeared in his eyes. "There's something you want in my grasp. When will you learn to act guided by your goals and not by your emotions?"

She could feel herself shaking. "Not everyone is an am-

bitious, heartless bastard like you are." There went her resolution to be polite. "Just tell me what your proposal is.
Now."

"It has to do with your mother's charity. That's all you'll
get now. My chauffeur will pick you up at six for dinner. And, Alisha, dress appropriately. We won't be eating
hunched over some street vendor's stall in the market. Neither will I appreciate the half-naked, wrapped-around-a-
has-been-rock-star look you sported the last time around
for my benefit."

How she wished she could say it hadn't been for his benefit, but they both knew it had been. Her eighteenth and
his twenty-eighth birthday party would be etched on her
memory forever.

"Arrogant, ruthless, manipulative, controlling, yes, but
I never thought you were a snob," she threw back at him.

"Because I want to have a civilized dinner at a place
where you won't throw things at me?"

Another bad night. Another bad memory.

No, it was time to rewrite how Dante saw her. Time to
stop expecting things from him from some unwritten script
in her own head. "One dinner. No more."

She'd almost walked away.

"Why does it bother you so much to be around me?"

Her face burned and it had nothing to do with the last
of the day's heat. "It doesn't."

"No? Isn't that why you avoid your family home, why
you never come to London? You avoid your extended family, your old friends, you move from place to place like a
nomad."

You took everything that should have been mine, she
wanted to say, like she'd done once. But it wouldn't be
the truth.

Dante hadn't taken anything her father hadn't been more

than happy and willing to give him. Dante hadn't shattered her family. Her father had.

But when it came to him…she was still that morass of anger and attraction and something more that she was terrified to discover. "That mansion, even London, they haven't been home to me in a long time."

That silky, slick smile tugged up the corners of his mouth again. "It's a relief to know then that your life's not revolved around avoiding me then, *si*. See you tonight, Alisha."

He was gone before she could blink, before she could counter the arrogant assumption. As she went home, Ali couldn't shake off the sense of dread that settled in her gut.

She and Dante couldn't stand each other. So why the hell was he insisting on an intimate dinner? And how would she get through it without compromising her dignity?

CHAPTER TWO

OF COURSE THE infuriating man couldn't simply text her the name of the hotel when he'd ordered her to dress appropriately, Ali thought, as the black Mercedes weaved through the heavy traffic, leaving the bustle of the city behind.

But having known Dante since the age of twelve, Ali had made a guess.

Dante was a man who expected, no, *demanded* the best of everything in life. He had a reputation for being a perfectionist with his employees but then no one complained because he rewarded hard work and ambition. God, she'd really gone looking for reasons to hate him back then.

The luxury Mercedes pulled smoothly into the courtyard of the latest on-trend, five-star resort that had been renovated last year to look like it could proudly belong in any posh European city, with the boat-filled canals of the Chao Phraya river offering a lovely view. The seafood at the restaurant was to die for, Mak had informed her, and he'd heard it from one of his many connections in high places.

Okay, so the worst thing that could come of this meeting was that she could walk away having had a delicious dinner at a lovely restaurant. And to prove to Dante that she could fake class and poise with the best of them.

She smoothed her hand over her stomach as she stepped out of the car and was pleased with the light pink sheath dress that she'd chosen to calm the butterflies. In the guise of studying the hotel's striking exterior, she took a moment to study herself in the reflection of the glass facade.

Her long hair, freshly washed and blow-dried to within an inch of its life, fell to her waist like a dark silky curtain, her only jewelry a thin gold chain with a tiny diamond disappearing into the low V-neck of her dress. The linen dress was a cheap knockoff of a designer brand she couldn't afford on her erratic income. But she looked like a million bucks, the fabric clinging to every dip and rise of her toned body as if it were custom designed for her.

The light pink was set off perfectly against her dusky skin and she'd let Kiki do her makeup—smoky eyes, gold bronzer and pale pink lip gloss. Tonight, she would be the sophisticated, poised Ali her mother had raised her to be, even if it killed her.

Another glance at the financial papers of her mother's charity hadn't changed reality. Other than a huge influx of cash, there was nothing anyone could do to save it. So, if Dante had something that could help, Ali would listen. She would treat this as a meeting with a professional.

Her beige pumps click-clacked on the gleaming cream marble floor as she walked up to the entrance to the restaurant. Soft yellow light fell from contemporary chrome fixtures. Beige walls and cream leather chairs gave the restaurant an utterly decadent, romantic atmosphere. Her belly swooped as Ali caught sight of Dante's bent head, the thick jet-black hair glittering in the lights.

Gripping her clutch tighter, Ali looked around. Every other table was empty. She checked her knockoff watch and saw it was only seven in the evening, nowhere near closing time.

The setting was far too intimate, far too private. Just far too much a scene plucked right out of her adolescent fantasies. But before she could turn tail and run out of the restaurant, that jet-black gaze caught her.

The mockery in those eyes made Ali straighten her shoulders and put one foot in front of the other.

He stood up when she reached their booth—a cocoon of privacy in an already silent restaurant. He'd exchanged the white shirt for a slate-gray one that made his eyes pop. With his jaw freshly shaved, thick dark hair slicked back half-wet, he was so…no, handsome was a lukewarm word for Dante's fierce masculinity.

The scent of his aftershave, with an aqua note to it, was subtle, but combined with the warmth of his skin, it sank into Ali's pores. Every cell in her body came alive.

"Where is everybody?"

"Everybody?" he said, standing far too close for her sanity.

Ali sat down with a plop, hand smoothing over her stomach. "Yes, people. Other Homo sapiens. Who might want to partake of the delicious food I've heard they serve here."

There was no mockery now when he looked down at her.

Heat swarming her cheeks, Ali ran her fingers through her hair. "What?"

His gaze swept over her face, her hair, the low V-neckline, but went no farther down. A shiver clamped her spine. "You clean up nice."

"Oh." The one syllable hung in the air, and she looked away, pretending to smooth her dress, putting her clutch down.

He took his sweet time sitting down, not opposite her, but on the side of the table, to her left. Ali shifted her knees away to the far right.

"If you scoot any farther down, you'll fall off the seat. Why are you so jumpy?"

Ali stilled, clasped her restless fingers in her lap. "I'm not."

"*No?* Really?"

His accent got thicker any time he got a little emotional. It was one of the tells Ali had picked up a long time ago. Pulling herself together, she met his gaze. Did he really have no idea what being near him did to her equilibrium? Did he really not feel the charge in the air around them, the pulse of undercurrents in every word, every look…? God, how was it that she was the only one who felt so much?

Not that she wanted Dante to be attracted to her. Her shoulders shook as a shiver of another kind traveled down her spine.

"If you're jumpy around me, it means you've arranged a little something for me. A surprise."

Ah…that was what he attributed it to. She closed her eyes and counted to ten. She couldn't even blame him because back then she'd been a little devil all right.

She'd lit sparklers in his room one Diwali night that had put holes in the new suit her papa had bought him. And that had almost lit the entire house on fire.

She'd taken a hammer to his new cuff links—Vikram's present—and minced them to so much dust.

Oh, and let's not forget the documents for an important merger she'd taken from his room and shredded.

When he'd brought his girlfriend to meet her papa… Ali groaned at the memory. And those weren't the half of all the destructive things she'd done to show how much she hated him.

She cleared her throat. "I told you. I've changed." When he raised a brow, she sighed. "I didn't know where we were dining. How could I arrange anything? I was just surprised to see no other patrons, that's all."

"I had my secretary book the entire restaurant for us." When her mouth fell open, he shrugged. "If you were going to cause a public scene—which given my knowledge of your character seemed like a high probability—I wanted to minimize the public part."

"Fair enough," she replied back with all the sass she could manage. Other people would have been a buffer, other people would have distracted her from this...whatever made her skin prickle with awareness.

Luckily, before her sudden awkwardness could betray her, the maître d' arrived.

"A bottle of your best white wine and the shrimp salad for both of us."

Ali lifted her chin. "I don't want shrimp."

"No?"

His fingers touched her wrist, and again, Ali pulled back as if he were a live current.

His jaw tightened, a flare of heat in his eyes. "Even though it's what this restaurant is famous for and you made that soft moan when your eyes came to that item on the menu?"

Her cheeks aflame, her heart pounding, Ali stared down at the menu. The words blurred, the tension between them winding round and round.

"Madam?" His expression set into a pleasing smile, the maître d' spoke up. "If you don't want the seafood that Mr. Vittori has ordered," he said, "might I suggest something else?"

"No." Ali took a deep breath. It wasn't the poor man's fault that Dante was playing with her. And she had played into his hands like she was still that irrational, impulsive hothead who wanted to hurt him for everything that was wrong in her world. "I'll have the shrimp, thanks."

"Don't," she simply said, once the man left.

Don't manipulate me. Don't rub me the wrong way. Just don't...be in my life.

Dante leaned back, his stare intense. "Don't make it so easy."

Before Ali could launch into another argument, he placed a rectangular velvet case on the table. Ten minutes into the dinner and she felt like she was already emotionally wound up. She fell back against her seat. Of course, he was the master manipulator, playing on weaknesses, while he had remained untouchable.

"What now?"

"Open it."

Just get it over with. Just get it over with. And walk away.

Ali opened the clasp. She caught sight of the tiny, exquisitely cut diamonds set into flowers with such delicate white gold that it always took her breath away, as it glittered under the soft lights. She rubbed the necklace back and forth with the pads of her fingers, compulsively, a balloon of ache in her chest. As if the gentle love of the woman who had worn them might have rubbed off on the stones.

It had taken everything she'd had in her to sell her mother's precious piece.

She pulled the box to her and clasped it so tightly that her knuckles showed white.

First, he had dropped the word about her mother's charity, now the necklace. Dante never did anything without some kind of payoff. He hated her just as much as she did him, and still he had sought her out. The hair on the nape of her neck prickled while her belly went on a swan dive.

"Why do you have this? What do you want, Dante?"

What do you want, Dante?

Dante stared at the tears shimmering in Alisha's large brown eyes, his breath punching into his throat.

It *was* the equivalent of a punch to his gut. He had borne enough of those in Sicily in his teenage years. Boys he'd known all his life had turned against Dante overnight; calling him names, roughing him up.

All thanks to his father's crime.

Those boys' punches had lit a fire in him back then, fueling his ambition to build a name for himself, separate from his father's. They had turned his young heart into a stone that never felt hurt again.

He had craved a fortune and a name all of his own. He had decided never to be weak like that again; never to be at anyone's mercy, least of all be controlled by a woman's love. And he had turned it into reality.

But the candid emotion in Alisha's face as she touched her mother's necklace, the havoc it wreaked on him, was a thousand times worse than any harm that had been inflicted on his teenage self.

When he'd delved into those reports on Alisha, he'd been shocked to find that Alisha had visited London several times over the last five years.

She'd had to go to London to deal with problems concerning her mother's charity. She had even spearheaded a charity gala to raise money. He'd been looking for leverage and he had found it.

He wasn't cheating Alisha out of anything she wanted. He was, in fact, proposing he give her what she wanted out of it, the one thing she held precious in return for what he wanted.

No, what threw him into the kind of emotional turmoil that he'd always avoided like the plague was that he was involving *her* in this play.

Alisha, who was a mass of contradictions, who he'd never quite figured out, who'd been the kind of flighty, selfish, uncaring kind of woman he loathed, was an unknown.

From the moment she'd come to live with her father, Neel, she'd hated Dante with an intensity that he'd first found amusing and then dangerous. Even worse, she'd always incited a reaction in him that no one else provoked.

But all this was before the changes in her the last six years had wrought.

Cristo, the sight of her walking into the back alley a few hours ago—the white spaghetti top plastered to her breasts, her shorts showing off miles and miles of toned legs, the utter sensuality of her movements as she pushed away tendrils of hair falling on her face, the sparkle of the fading sun on her brown skin…

The shock in her face, the greedy, hungry way she'd let those big brown eyes run all over him…even that hadn't made a dent in the need that had pulsed through him.

Dios mio, this was Neel's daughter.

She was forbidden to him. And not just because he was determined to take the last bit of her father's legacy from her. But because, with everything he planned to put into motion, Alisha would be the variable. His attraction to her was a weakness he couldn't indulge, much less act on. There were only two positions for women in his life: colleagues like Izzy and a couple of his business associates, women whose judgment he respected, women he genuinely liked; and then there were women he slept with who knew the score, and didn't want more from him.

Alisha didn't fall into either of those camps.

"Dante? What the hell are you doing with my mother's necklace?"

"I bought it back from the guy you sold it to." He made a vague motion to her tears, more shocked than discomfited by them. He'd never seen her as anything but poised to fight her father, him, Vikram, with all guns blazing. Never in this...fragile light. "Looks like I made the right call in thinking you would like it back. Why did you sell it?"

She took another longing look at the box before pushing it back toward him. "For a pair of Jimmy Choos."

"Don't be flippant, Alisha. I never understood why you were always so determined to be your own worst enemy."

"I have no idea what you're talking about. And really, did you invite me to dinner just to point out my flaws?"

He forced himself to pull his gaze from the way she chewed on her lower lip. Suddenly, everything about her—her mind, her body, *Dio*...everything—felt fascinating. Everything was distracting. "I know your mother's charity is failing. Why didn't you come to me for help?"

"Why didn't I come to you for help?" Some of that natural fight in her crawled back into her shoulders. He liked her better like that. He didn't want a vulnerable Alisha on his hands for the next few months. She laughed. White teeth flashed in that gamine face. "Have you met me? And you?"

Despite himself, Dante smiled.

He'd forgotten how witty Alisha could be, how she'd always laughed in any situation, how even with all her tantrums and drama she'd made the house lively when she'd come to live with Neel after her mother's death. Even with grief painting her eyes sad, she'd been so full of life, so full of character, even at the age of twelve.

He'd never gravitated to her, true, but when she'd blossomed into a teenager, it had seemed as if her hatred for him had grown too. The more he had tried to fix things between her and her father, the more she had resented him.

Her gaze slipped to his mouth for a fraction of a second. Every muscle in him tightened. "I'd starve before I take anything from the company. Or you."

He was far too familiar with that spiel to question it now. "What did you need the money for?"

"If you know I sold it, and to whom, then you know why. Come on, Dante, enough beating around the bush."

The waiter brought their food and she thanked him.

She dug into the food with the same intensity with which she seemed to attack everything in life.

Dante, mostly because of the jet lag, pushed his food around. He watched her as she sipped her wine, her tongue flicking out to lick a drop from her lower lip.

He wanted to lick it with his own.

The thought came out of nowhere, hard and fast. He pushed a hand through his hair and cursed under his breath. *Maledizione!* In all the scenarios he had foreseen for this, he hadn't counted how strikingly gorgeous Alisha had become. Or the intensity of the pull he felt toward her.

Whatever tension had been filling up the air, it now filled his veins. And he realized it was because she wasn't focused on him anymore.

Not so with him. Not even the constant reminder, the ironclad self-discipline that made him a revered name in his business circles, the one that told him this was nothing but a quid pro quo, could distract his gaze from the expanse of smooth brown skin her dress exposed. He took the wine flute in his hands, turned it around and around, watching his fingers leaving marks against the condensation.

He wanted to trace his finger against the slope of her shoulders to see if her skin was as silky as it looked. He wanted to touch the pulse at her throat, to sink his fingers into her silky hair and pull her to him, hold her against his body as he plundered her mouth...

She put her fork and spoon down, and took another sip of her wine. Then she leaned back all the way into her seat, her head thrown back over the top. The deep breath she took sent her chest rising and falling.

Basta! He needed to direct this conversation back to his plan.

"Tell me what you've been up to in the last few years." The words slipped out of his mouth. She looked just as shocked as he felt. "You know, other than living like a hobo and moving around every few months."

She shrugged, and the simple gold chain she wore glimmered against her throat, the pendant dangling between her breasts playing peekaboo with him. "You don't have to pretend an interest, Dante. Not now."

"You're his daughter. I've always been interested in what you do with your life. Until I realized my interest only spurred you toward destruction."

"Water under the bridge." She put her napkin on the table, her expression cycling from wariness to fake cheer. "Thank you for the dinner. That was a treat, even with your company. And on second thought, thanks for buying my mother's necklace back." She took the velvet box from him and put it underneath her clutch on the table. Waggling her brows, she leveled a saccharine smile at him. "You must know me well to give me a present I would so appreciate."

Being on the receiving end of that smile was just so… jarring. "You mean to sell it again, don't you?"

"Yep."

"That will only take care of the payroll for another month. I've seen the financials, Alisha. The charity will be bankrupt in a month."

Her mouth tightened. "I'll find a way. I always do."

"Or you could just ask me for help."

"I told you, I don't want your money. Or the company's or Papa's. I need to do this on my own."

"Does the charity home really mean that much to you?"

"It does. It's where Mama grew up. I spent so much time there with her. Some of the happiest moments of my childhood were there."

"If you really want to save the home, put aside your irrational resentment of me and I will funnel some much needed money into it."

"And what do I have to do in return?"

"Marry me."

CHAPTER THREE

Marry me...

Marry Dante...

Ali's mind went into a loop over that one phrase, like one of those gramophone records her mama had had.

Marry Dante, marry Dante...

Dante, who thought she was selfish and spoiled.

Dante, with whom she reverted back to that lonely girl come to live with a distant father, distracted brother and a resented changeling, after her mama's sudden death.

With Dante she would always be her worst self.

Panic skittled over her skin like a line of fire ants crawling up her legs. She needed to marry Dante like she needed a hole in her head. It would be like all the bad decisions she'd ever made steamrolled into one giant boulder that would chase her for the rest of her life.

A hysterical sound released from her mouth.

"Alisha?"

She brought her gaze to his, stood up from the booth, picked up her clutch and turned. "You've gone mad."

"Alisha, wait."

Nope.

She didn't want to hear more. If she did, he would rope her into it.

As a master strategist, he wouldn't have sought her out across the world, wouldn't have approached her if he hadn't already figured out a way to make her agree. And she needed to flee before that happened. Before their lives were even more tangled. Before she betrayed herself in the worst way possible.

Dear God, when it came to him, all she had left was her pride.

"Alisha, stop!" His arm shot out just as Ali got ready to sprint across the restaurant if necessary.

Long fingers roped around her wrist and because of her desperate forward momentum, her foot jerked to the side. Pain shot up through her ankle and she fell back against him.

The breath punched out of her as he anchored her by throwing his arm around her midriff.

Unstoppable force meets immovable object...

"What happens when they crash, Alisha? Who gets destroyed?"

The world stopped tilting at that silky whisper as she realized she'd spoken out loud. And yet, the explosion his touch evoked continued to rock through her body.

The scent of him was all over her skin, filling each pore, drowning her in masculine heat. His legs were thrown wide, the tensile power of his thighs just grazing the back of hers, his chest pushed up tight against her back. Her chest expanded as she tried to stop the panic. On the exhale, the underside of her breasts fell against his steely arm. A soft hiss of warm air bathed her neck, making it a thousand times worse. Or was that pleasure skittering across her skin?

An onslaught of sensations poured through her, her skin prickling tight, and yet, a strange lethargy crawled through her limbs. She wanted to lean into him completely, until her bottom was resting against his hips. She wanted to feel him from chest to toe against her back, she wanted to rub herself against that hard body until he was as mindlessly aroused as her. Until that iron will of his snapped like a thinly stretched rubber band.

As if he could guess the direction of her thoughts, his fingers tightened around her hip, digging into her slightly to keep her still; to keep her from leaning back and learning his body's reaction to her.

Because, really, in what universe did she imagine Dante would want her back with this same madness?

She groaned—a feral, desperate sound. Why was it that everything she did came back to taunt her a thousand times worse?

"Because you don't think before you do," came the voice at her ear. Ah…perfect! Of course, she'd said that out loud too. "You're impulsive, brash and if I hadn't caught you, you would have fallen flat on your face."

"Kissing the floor sounds like a better alternative," she said, her words throaty and whispery.

"Will you sit down and listen if I let you go?"

As if operating on an instinct that defied rationality, her fingers clenched over his wrist.

She opened her eyes and swallowed hard. Since he'd undone his cuffs earlier, her palm rested against a hair-roughened wrist. She rubbed the skin—the rough texture, the plump veins on the back of his hand—the startlingly sensual contrast between her and him inviting her along further and further.

It was the sharp inhale followed by another curse that pulled her out of the fog.

Her chin flopped down to her chest. "No. I don't want to hear anything you say. I don't want to be near…you in this moment, much less in the future."

The vulnerability she fought every waking minute, the longing for a deeper connection in her past, with anyone related to her past, pervaded her in his presence.

This was what would happen if she agreed: every look, every touch would wind her up; lines between want and hate, reality and fantasy would blur…until she attacked him—claws and all—just to keep herself tethered, to keep herself together. Or until she gave in to this inexplicable yearning she had felt for him for so long.

The stiffness of her posture drained away and she leaned back against his chest. She let herself be weak and vulnerable for five seconds.

Both of his arms wound around her. He held her gently, tenderly and that…that was more than Ali could bear. That uncharacteristic moment between them, the mere thought that he could pity her uncontrollable attraction to him, snapped her out of it.

She wriggled in his embrace and he instantly let her go.

Pushing her hair back, she fought for composure. The glass of cold water down her throat was a much needed burst of reality. When he sat down, when she had her wits together again, she looked back at him. "Tell me why."

"Vikram's been declared legally dead."

Gray gaze drinking her in, he paused. Ali looked away.

That he knew what her brother meant to her, that he had seen firsthand that night her grief, her regrets, it was something she couldn't erase. This nebulous connection between her and Dante—despite the knotted history of it—was the only thing she had of her past. And however far she ran, it seemed she would never be free of it. "And?"

"Your uncle will contest for his voting shares and might win. I'd like to crush his little rebellion with as few resources and as little time as possible. I have a huge merger coming up with a Japanese manufacturing company that I need all my energies focused on. Thousands of jobs and thousands more livelihoods depend on that merger. He's well-known for his ability to create PR damage."

So that was what he'd been counting on—that Ali's loathing of her uncle was greater than her combined loathing of her papa and Dante.

Her uncle had driven a wedge between her parents, though Ali knew it had been her father that had finally broken them apart.

Her father's ambition. Her father's unending hunger for success.

Just like the breathtakingly stunning man sitting across from her.

"I never realized what a true legacy you are of papa. Not Vicky, but you."

"Vicky always blazed his own path."

She nodded, the depth of her grief for her brother a hole in her chest. At least that was one thing she couldn't blame Dante for. Her brother had been a technical genius with no interest in his papa's company.

"If I marry you, I can transfer my shares to you and the eventual fate of Vicky's shares won't really matter. You can continue to be the master of Matta Steel." Even she couldn't dispute the trailblazing new heights that Dante had taken the company to since her father's death.

"*Si.* Your vow not to touch a penny of your father's fortune will not be broken since the voting shares are yours through your mother. Monetarily, they don't have much value, since they can't be sold off, or transferred to anyone outside marriage. So this is a good deal for you."

He had a well-rehearsed answer for every contentious point she could raise. "What do I get in return?"

"Money to throw into the drain that is the Lonely Hearts Foundation."

She refused to bite into that judgmental tone. "As much as I want?"

"A pre-agreed upon amount, *si.*"

"I want a check—from your own personal fortune," she added, determined to wring every drop of blood from him, "for that amount. If I agree."

There was a glint in his eye and a slick smile around his mouth, arrogant confidence dripping from every pore. *"Bene."* A regal nod to her request. "From my personal fortune, *si*?"

And whatever she demanded would be a drop in the ocean for him.

"We can't annul or end the marriage for three years or they will revert back to you. We'll both sign a prenup. At the end of the three years, a substantial amount of money will be settled on you."

"I don't want a settlement, I don't want a penny from you. And I won't—"

"Don't be foolish, Alisha. Throwing away your inheritance when you were eighteen was one thing but—"

"—under any circumstances sign a prenup," she delivered that with all the satisfaction of a well-placed right hook.

Shock etched onto those arrogantly handsome features.

It wasn't wise tweaking the tail of a tiger, especially when he was so royally wound up. But if she expected an outburst, a small glimpse of his infamous Sicilian temper that cowed all his employees, Ali was disappointed. Only a small tic in that granite jaw even betrayed how...thrown he was by her coup de grâce. Since he had dropped the whole thing on her with the sensitivity of a bulldozer, she'd pulled that out pretty fast based on that instinct she'd honed for years to annoy the heck out of him.

But now she realized how much she needed that illusion of control over...this. The only way she could keep the balance in this relationship of theirs was not to give him everything he wanted.

"Why not sign the prenup? All it does is give you money I know you won't touch."

She smiled, thoroughly enjoying herself. "Is that praise I hear for my principles?"

"If you think mucking around through life, running from your own shadow is principled, all power to you. I call it a juvenile need for petty revenge you've yet to outgrow. And I keep waiting for you to wake up from this…protracted dream of yours, for the thud of reality to hit you.

"I know spoiled princesses like you like the back of my hand. There will be a day when you'll crawl back to the luxury of your old life with your tail tucked between your legs. Because, really, what have you achieved in the last six years, except to sell off your mama's jewelry piece by priceless piece?

"Sign the prenup. When that day comes, you'll be thankful to me for giving you that option to fall back on."

Wow, he wasn't pulling his punches. Somehow, Ali kept her smile from sliding off her face.

His matter-of-fact assessment of her stung more than it should. She'd seen that same lack of respect, that same exaggerated patience in her father's eyes on the eve of her eighteenth birthday.

As if dressing like a skank and making out with a former junkie rock star in front of their esteemed guests was all he had expected of Ali. And before she could change his impression of her, before she could apologize for her share of mistakes, he'd been lost to her.

But, if it was the last thing she did, she resolved to change Dante's opinion of her.

Not because she wanted his approval—okay, she did, in some throwback to her angsty, unwise, earlier self—but because she wanted to prove him wrong. She needed to bring that arrogance down more than a peg or two. Really, she was doing a public service on behalf of all the women of the planet.

She needed to find some kind of closure for all the painful history between them. She longed for the day when she could look him in the eye and feel nothing.

No attraction. No wistful ache. No emotional connection whatsoever.

"No. No prenup. Let's not forget I'm doing you a favor. I know you're used to people bending over backward for you but I—"

Dark heat flared in his gray eyes. "Do you really want to threaten me about what I can or can't do with you, Alisha?"

Ali jerked back, the temperature cocoon soaring from arctic cold to desert hot within seconds. Red-hot images of herself doing his bidding, forbidden images of their limbs tangling…the heat between them was a near tangible thing in the air.

Did that mean he felt it too?

Walk away now, Ali. Walk away before you're far too tempted to resist.

But the thought of being able to save the charity that meant so much to her mother, the thought of returning to London, the thoughts of being grounded for a while, the thought of proving to Dante that she wasn't a car crash in the making won out. "I want your word that this agreement is only on paper. That you won't use it to manage me, to manage my life in any way."

His fingers roped over her wrists like a gnarly vine. That accent slipped in through his soft words. "Do not think to play those silly games with me that you did with your father, Alisha. I will not let you drag my name through mud like you did his. No splashing yourself all over the media with some ex-junkie. No sneaking out behind my back with another man. At least not when you're in London."

"If you're not careful with your threats, you're going to sound like a real fiancé, Dante." Whatever his conditions, she knew she'd have no problem keeping them. Like she'd already told him, her days of doing things to wind him up were over.

But she wouldn't let Dante have all the power in this relationship. "Let me get this straight. If I give up men for three years, will you do the same? Will you be celibate for three years?"

"I won't be the reason my name or this agreement of ours gets dragged through the mud."

"That's not really answering the question."

"My name, my reputation…they mean everything to me, Alisha. I built them brick by brick from nothing. Away from the shadow of my father's crime.

"I created a new life from the ground up. I built my fortune, I made my reputation anew after everything I had was destroyed in a matter of days." Ali shivered at the dark intensity of his words, the specter of his past almost a live thing between them. With his ruthless ambition coating every word, it was easy to forget what had brought Dante to her father at all. What had built him up to be this man she saw now.

"You put one toe out of line during any of this and your precious charity won't get a penny."

CHAPTER FOUR

SHE WAS LATE.

Of course she was. It was his own fault for assuming Alisha could ever be a headache-free zone for him. What he should have done was show up at the dingy flat she lived in, insist she pack up and drag her to the airstrip.

Instead, he'd given them both a few days to gain perspective. To make sure he could think, away from the distraction of her...presence. Of her outrageous demands. Like the demand that he forward a sum of ten thousand pounds as the first payment.

Already, his lawyer was freaking out at the massive risk Dante was leaving himself open to by marrying her without a prenup.

And that was before the man found out what a firecracker Alisha was.

But for all the threats and warnings his lawyer had screamed over the transatlantic call, Dante couldn't see her using this marriage to fleece him, to build her own fortune. He couldn't see her dragging him into some kind of court battle—but threatening to sully his reputation in a rage, yes.

That he was more than ready for. In fact, the idea of sparring with Alisha now, the very idea of going toe-to-toe with her sent a shiver of excitement through him. *Cristo*, his life was truly devoid of fun if a battle with Alisha filled him with this much anticipation.

He'd called it her protracted, rebellious phase—he had thought her a spoiled princess but he was beginning to question that. He had had his chauffeur drive him past her flat, he'd seen where she waitressed sometimes. And she'd lived like that for more than five years.

Common sense pointed out that she wasn't going to come after his fortune. Or Matta Steel.

The realization both calmed and unnerved him. Because, for the first time in his life, he had a feeling that reassurance came mostly from a place of emotion, despite the logic of it too. But he was determined to keep control of the situation.

If she thought he was handing over that amount of money without asking questions…if she thought he'd let her play him, play fast and loose in London, if she thought being his wife in name was just the latest weapon she could use against him…

It was time to reacquaint her with her adversary and set the ground rules for this…agreement between them. He refused to call it a marriage, refused to give his suddenly overdeveloped sense of guilt any more material to chew on.

Which was why he was waiting in Bangkok to accompany her back to London in his private jet rather than have his security bring her. He was also determined to accompany her because her return to London would definitely be commented on by the press, and once they announced that they had married, even their planned civil union without pomp and fanfare would still occupy the news cycle for a couple of weeks at least.

Thanks to his father's notoriety during his life and the spectacle of his suicide during his incarceration alongside Dante's swift rise through the ranks of Matta Steel to the position of CEO, there was plenty for the media to chew on. They were always ready to find some chink in his personality, some weak link in his makeup to crow that he was his criminal father's flawed son.

Sometimes they did get their hands on a juicy story from a woman he'd dumped—for the simple reason that she wanted more from the relationship and he didn't. Dante didn't care a hoot about a tabloid feature.

But this…agreement with Alisha would be no small step in the eyes of the media and the world. As such he needed to make her understand the importance of her behavior in the coming months.

The stubborn defiance in her eyes, the stark silence she'd subjected him to through the drive back to her flat hadn't been lost on him.

Alisha didn't respond well to threats.

He remembered the two-day disappearance she'd engineered when, on Neel's instructions, Dante had tried to enroll her in a boarding school in Paris a couple of months after she'd first come to live with her father.

Fighting the near constant hum of his attraction to her had briefly made him forget that.

This was a business deal and he couldn't antagonize Alisha any more than he would lose his temper with a new business partner. There had to be a way to get her to behave, to cooperate without letting the full force of his contempt for her to shine through.

The one thing he knew for certain was that he couldn't punish her for his own attraction to her, for his lack of self-control. And as much as his mind and body were bent on reminding him that she had fancied him once, he refused to go down that road.

No.

After the first hour, he stepped out of his car. The unusually heavy wind roared in his ears and he pushed up his sunglasses even though the sun had yet to make an appearance on the chilly late September morning.

Patience had never been his strong point. And yet he had a feeling that it would be stretched to the limit in the near future. A few months with Alisha was bound to turn him mental in his thirties.

He continued to wait and was just about to call her when a caravan of cars—really, a who's who of colorful vintage cars in different stages of deterioration—pulled up on the long, curving road that led to the airstrip.

Laughter bubbled out of his chest. He sensed his security team giving him sidelong, concerned looks. Well, no one ever made him laugh like Alisha did. Neither had a woman tested his control, or called forth some of his base instincts with a single smile like she did.

How fitting that the drama queen arrived in a ramshackle entourage of her own.

The caravan came to a stop with a lot of screeching noise that confirmed his suspicion that all three cars were on their last legs. But what crawled out of the cars was even more shocking. A surprising number of people clambered out of those small cars, a torrent of English and Thai flowing around. Car trunks were opened and suitcases and bags in different colors and makes pulled out.

Emerging from the third car, dressed again in short shorts that should have been banned, and a chunky sweater that fell to her thighs, almost covering the shorts, was Alisha. Loose and oversize, it fell off one shoulder almost to her bicep, leaving a hot-pink bra strap exposed.

And there was that same black camera bag—heavy from the looks of how the wide strap pulled over one shoulder and between her breasts.

Hair in that messy bun. No jewelry. Combat style boots on her feet.

No makeup that he could see. In fact, in the gray morning light, she looked freshly scrubbed, innocent and so excruciatingly lovely that he felt a tug low in his belly as surely as the sun peeking through the clouds.

Her wide smiles and husky laughter made her eyes twinkle. She stood among the loud group like sun shining on a vast field of sunflowers, every face turned toward her with genuine affection, long limbs grabbing her, hugging her, men and women kissing her cheeks. A sense of disbelief went through him as he spied a sheen of tears as she hugged the man called Mak.

And then she met his eyes.

Current arced between them even across the distance. As one, the group turned their gazes on him. Instead of surprise or curiosity, there was a certain knowledge in the looks leveled at him, knowledge about him. A certain warning in the looks, a subtle crowding around her, as if Alisha had imparted her opinion of him.

Out of the blue, for the first time in their shared history, he wondered what Alisha thought of him. What was behind all that…resentment of him? Did she still believe he'd stolen her legacy?

That hum began again under his skin as she pushed away from the crowd.

His breath suspended in his throat as the subtle scent of her skin teased him. He felt an overwhelming urge to bury his nose in her throat; to see that gorgeous, open smile leveled at him.

"Do you have the money ready?"

"All ten thousand pounds, *si*," he responded, a hint of warning in his tone.

She pulled out a slip from the back pocket of her shorts, the action thrusting her breasts up. He gaped like a teenager until she said, "Please have it transferred to this bank account."

He looked at the slip of paper with a routing number and an account number and raised his brows. "Whose account is it?"

"Kiki and Mak's joint account." She sighed at his silence. "You can't place conditions on how I use the money. No micromanaging my life."

"You're not doing this to piss me off, are you?"

She rolled her eyes. "No. As much as our shared history gives you reason to believe that, I'm not."

He took a step toward her. "Are they blackmailing you? Whatever it is, I'll take care of it. What was it, Alisha? Drugs they hooked you into? Naked pictures?"

"What do you mean, naked pictures?"

Her shock was so genuine that it took Dante a couple of seconds to speak. "Who do you think took care of that junkie rock star before he could sell your pics to every tabloid magazine?"

A frown tied her brow, her gaze staring at him unseeingly. "Richard threatened to sell naked pictures of me? Did you see them?"

"Of course I didn't look at your pictures," he snapped. "He gave us enough proof to show it was you."

He pushed a hand through his hair, the very prospect of that idiot taking advantage of a young Ali turning him inside out even now. It was the one time in his adult life that Dante had lost his temper and given in to the urge to punch the man's pretty face.

Vikram had had to restrain him physically.

"So did you pay him?" Ali asked softly.

"I don't respond well to threats, just like you. He gave me the flash drive with the pics on it and I smashed it with a paperweight."

She laughed, the sound full of a caustic bitterness. "Wow, you really don't think much of me, do you?" Her mouth trembled. "Mak and Kiki are the last people who would blackmail anyone. For the first year, when I moved here, I didn't pay for anything. Board or food. Whatever I pay them, believe me, it's very little in return for what they did for me."

Would the woman never develop a sense of self-preservation? "It's not a hardship to be kind to an heiress, Alisha. A payoff is usually expected at some point."

Hurt painted her small smile, her eyes widening, even as she bravely tilted her chin.

He had hurt her. The realization sat tightly on his chest.

"They don't know who I am, Dante. When you showed up at the restaurant a week ago, it was the first time I told either of them who I was."

"Alisha, I don't—"

"And if you say some stupid thing like I haven't earned it to give it away, believe me I did. Mama earned each and every one of those voting shares. She lost Papa to the blasted company. And all she got were those in return. So, yes, she paid for them. And y'know what? I paid for them too because I should've grown up with my father and brother and Mama in the same house. I shouldn't have had to wonder why Papa barely visited me. Vicky shouldn't have had to wonder how Mama could have so easily given him up. I shouldn't have had to wonder why it took Mama's death for him to be in my life.

"I shouldn't have to wonder what I lacked that meant he chose…" Her chest rose and fell, a haunting light in her eyes. "I paid for those shares, Dante. And I want some good to come out of what I'm signing up for with you. Something to ground me when you drive me up the wall over the next few months. That money will be a nice deposit for the business Mak and Kiki want to begin." She swallowed and met his gaze. "They welcomed me with open arms when I desperately needed friends, when I needed to be loved."

The vulnerability in her words struck him like a punch to his solar plexus, bringing in its wake a cold helplessness.

I'm not that impulsive, destructive Ali anymore.

Her words from a week ago haunted Dante as he watched her climb the steps to the aircraft. Maybe she wasn't that same old Alisha anymore. But as far as he knew, people didn't really change.

A reckless Alisha wouldn't have visited London three times and tried to patch up her mother's favorite charity.

A spoiled Alisha wouldn't have lived in anonymity when she could have simply used her father's name to live in luxury.

So maybe he hadn't known Alisha at all.

Maybe he didn't know the woman he was marrying after all.

CHAPTER FIVE

ALI STARED MINDLESSLY as she stepped onto the flight and elegant luxury met her eyes. Every moment she spent with Dante, the past relentlessly pulled at her. Along with all the moronic decisions she'd made in anger, in hurt, coming back to take a chunk out of her ass.

From the moment she'd stepped out of the car, she'd been aware of his eyes on her every second. His silent scrutiny, the way his gaze devoured her expression made her skin feel stretched tight. Any hope she had indulged that that pulse of attraction at the restaurant was just a heightened reaction because she was seeing him for the first time in six years died a quick death.

Even with her friends surrounding her—she still couldn't believe how many of them had showed up—she'd been aware of him.

It was as if, overnight, she'd developed an extra sense. A sixth sense that evolved to keep her in tune with Dante's every move, his every look, his every breath. And now they had twelve hours of flight in the enclosed space together, and the fact that the interior of the aircraft was much more expansive and luxurious than a commercial flight made no difference whatsoever.

Feeling hot and agitated, she tugged at the hem of her sweater and pulled it up in one quick move.

Like her, Dante also shed his jacket with a flick of those powerful shoulders.

Trying to look away was like the earth trying to pull out from its orbit around the sun. The cabin shrunk around them, and her breaths became shallow. Even before take-off, oxygen was in short supply.

Instead of his formal attire, which was second skin to him, today he wore a sky blue polo T-shirt that made his gray eyes pop.

If virility needed a picture in the dictionary, Dante would be perfect.

For virility see Dante Vittori.

Just the sight of his biceps and thick arms with a dusting of dark hair was enough to send her belly swooping. The blue denim clung to his tapering hips and powerful thighs. Ali sighed and pulled in a long breath. God, this was going to be a long flight. She couldn't take this much of him—the proximity, the constant awareness, the constant tugging in her belly urging her to look at him, to breathe him in.

And she craved more.

It wasn't just the physical attraction.

When she'd first moved in with her father after her mama's death, Dante had made quite the impression on her.

He'd been serious, brooding, off the charts handsome, and the worst of all: so close to her father—something she'd desperately needed but hadn't had. Her papa's eyes had been so full of pride for his protégé's achievements, his single-minded focus, his ambition.

At thirteen, she'd been hormonal, lost and he had been a hero, the golden son who had gotten everything she'd coveted. The one man who seemed more confident, more powerful, more handsome than any she'd known. She'd left London five years before because she'd been lost, grieving, sick of the imbalance in the dynamic between them.

Yet, it seemed nothing had changed.

Would he always be like this to her—this magnetic, confident embodiment of the perfect man? She looked up and found his gaze on her. Clearly disapproving. "What? Why are you giving me the stink eye?"

"The stink eye? What are we, six?"

"I could be six. You're what…a hundred and thirty now?"

The soft material of his T-shirt stretched taut across his wide chest and hard abdomen, mocking her words. "I'm old because I don't engage in childish behavior and language? Because I show up on time?"

"No, you're old because you…" Her words veered off as he walked closer, the very air filled with his dark masculinity. "You were probably born old with no sense of humor and an exaggerated sense of your own importance."

He raised a brow.

Heat rushed up her neck. "Okay, fine. I was two hours late, but I'm not really sorry. I told you I couldn't make a seven a.m. flight. You went ahead anyway. We planned Kiki's birthday party four months ago and it had to be this morning."

"You couldn't have had it last night?"

"She works nights. So it's your own fault if you waited for two hours. I told you, Dante, this whole thing…isn't going to be all by your rules. You're going to have to treat me like an adult."

"*Bene*. As long as you conduct yourself like one."

"Fine."

"Now that we have gotten that out of the way, I have some things I would like to discuss."

Ali folded her arms and tilted her chin up. "*Fine*. But first you have to feed me. I haven't had anything to eat since yesterday afternoon."

"No wonder you look like a bag of bones."

"I'm sorry I'm not curvy enough to fit your standards." He sighed.

Ali scrunched her nose. "Hunger makes me cranky."

His mouth twitched. "Is that an apology?"

"Of sorts."

He nodded and like magic, the flight attendant arrived with a tray.

Ali dug into the bowl of creamy penne pasta with a delicate white wine sauce. The soft clink of the silver utensils filled the silence, which had an almost comfortable quality to it. It was only when he looked at her, as if he meant to see into her soul, as if she was endlessly fascinating, that she got flustered. Great, all she had to do to keep her sanity was avoid looking at him. "Okay, talk."

Dante seated himself in the opposite seat from Alisha and stretched his legs the other way. He'd stared earlier, his thoughts going in an altogether wicked direction when she'd removed the sweater and it had made her nervous. Which in turn had made her flippant. How was it that it had taken him that long to figure out that that was Alisha's default when she was unsure of herself?

"A team is airing out Matta Mansion as we speak. It's quite a drive from my flat in central London but it should work. You'll make it your home base for the near future and I can visit you there. There'll be a certain amount of media coverage on this so Matta Mansion will provide the perfect cover. My PR team's drafting a statement to announce our engagement."

"I don't want to live there."

Dante gritted his teeth, determined not to lose his temper. "Alisha, you just promised that you wouldn't fight me on every single thing."

"And you said you wouldn't railroad me. I can't…" Distress filled her eyes and his retort died on his lips. "I won't go back there. Not without Vikram and Papa. Not to an empty house…" She looked away, her profile lovely as she swallowed.

Dante sat back in his seat, fighting the urge to pull her into his arms and soothe her. *Cristo*, living with Alisha would be like riding a never-ending roller coaster. One moment he wanted to throttle her, one moment kiss her senseless and the next hold her tight.

He wanted her where he could keep an eye on her. Especially because of the media storm she didn't understand would hit them. "That only leaves my flat."

The devilish imp was back in her eyes when she turned to him. "I never thought I'd see the ruthless Dante Vittori scared."

Again, that overwhelming sense of relief poured through him. The vulnerability in her eyes sometimes made him feel like that adolescent youth again—powerless and all too aware of his own needs. And in its wake came the most overwhelming urge to hold her and kiss her until it was gone from her eyes.

Pure lust, he could handle. This…dangerous urge to play her hero—no!

"Scared?" he asked.

"The idea of me in your flat terrifies you to your hardened soul."

He laughed and the sound of it was a shock to his own ears. She dug her teeth into her lower lip, but couldn't quite arrest her smile either. "Fine, the flat it is. But—"

"I'll respect the rules of your domain. I'll control the

urge to have orgies every night. I'll be mindful of your pristine reputation and the shadow I could cast over it as your wife. How was that?"

He was still smiling. "That sounds like you drafted it."

"All night," she retorted, the irreverent minx. "Anything I missed?"

He shook his head, all the threats and conditions he meant to impose on her disappearing from his mind. She was a live wire, he didn't forget that for one second. Nor could he think. Because of the manifesto she'd read him, his ordered and peaceful life would remain that. And yet, he couldn't muster a sense of dread over it. He couldn't bring the words to his lips to kill that wide smile. He couldn't contain the little flare of excitement in his blood every time she leveled those eyes on him, every time she fought with him, every time she looked away but not before he saw the interest she couldn't hide in her eyes.

This was a dangerous high he was chasing, and *Dios mio*, where was his sense of self-preservation? So when he said, "What about you?" his voice was harsh.

She raised a brow. "What about me?"

"Any demands or expectations?"

"Not really. I'm…excited to put your money into the charity. I have some contacts I would like to network—"

"For what?"

"For my photography," she said, her smile dimming. "I'm going to see if I can sell them in the market for a penny a piece." Shift to sarcasm. It was like watching a panorama of emotions. "Oh, I also need a studio—a darkroom essentially." Back to a practical survival instinct he couldn't help but admire. "All in all, I'm looking forward to being back in London."

"You develop your own prints?"

"Yes."

"I'll arrange it."

"Thank you. Between the charity and the darkroom, you won't see me. Your perfectly ordered life will remain just the same."

Put like that, she sounded so sensible that Dante wanted to believe it. He not only had to believe it, he had to keep it like that. There was no feasible route his fascination with her could take.

No other outcome was possible between them. No other.

Ali had no idea if it was the unusually long-lasting peace on the flight or being back in London under the same roof, but the moment Dante showed her into the guest room, she made the connection she'd missed earlier.

What he'd said had been eating at her.

Richard had tried to blackmail Dante for those pics... great judgment call, Ali!

She finished her shower in a hurry, and pulled on the first pair of panties, shorts and T-shirt she could find in her bag. Hair wet and dripping down her back, she barefooted it to Dante's door.

He opened on the first knock, his hands pulling his T-shirt from those jeans. The slab of abdominal muscles she spied before she jerked her gaze to his almost made her forget why she sought him out. Almost.

She stepped back as he closed the door behind him.

"Alisha? What is it?"

"You said 'us'. You told Papa about the pictures Richard claimed he had, didn't you?"

It had been exactly around that time that she'd been summoned into her father's study and while her father had sat silently in the corner—his disappointment a noxious cloud in the air—Dante had informed her that she wouldn't be going away as apprentice to a world-renowned photographer as planned. Or at least, the exorbitant fee she'd needed to pay wouldn't be coming from her father's bank account.

Vikram, as usual, had been absent, working in his lab, and her father had refused to talk to her that evening, even as she'd pleaded with him to rethink his decision. That was the last time she'd talked to her father.

Dread coursed through her that she was once again locking herself in that bubble with Dante, her mind and body constantly battling it out.

Dante stilled. "What?"

"That's why he…cut me off. Refused to pay the fee for that apprenticeship. You told him and I lost a chance at the one thing I wanted to do most in the world. Being accepted into that program…it was the one thing that got me through so much. Through Mama's death, through being thrust into living with you three strangers…and because of you, I lost the opportunity to learn, to see if I could follow my passion.

"Did you hate me so much, Dante? Yes, I made impulsive, rash decisions, but you know what the worst part of it was? Papa died thinking I was determined to shame him in front of the world."

Tears filled her eyes. She swiped at them angrily. Regrets were useless. The past was done.

His fingers on her arm turned her, his grip a vise. Ali couldn't look up, everything in her cringing that he saw her like this. The last thing she wanted was his pity.

"Alisha, look at me. Alisha!" His growl filled the space between them. "I didn't tell Neel, okay? I just dealt with Richard. Vicky told your father."

She blinked. "What? Why?"

"Vicky loved you and…he was worried for you. He felt guilty for neglecting you for so long, for being preoccupied with his lab. He convinced Neel that separating you from the heiress label would cut off all the hangers-on and leeches. Maybe ground you a little. Give you a chance to see the reality of your friends. I..."

"What, Dante?"

"I tried to persuade Neel not to do that."

"I don't believe you."

He flinched. Just a tremble of that upper lip, but it was there. "I told you, I'm not your enemy. You reminded me of someone I despised for so long. You were spoiled and immature and rebellious, but I didn't hate you.

"I knew photography meant everything to you, how *not*...miserable or angry or rebellious you were when you walked around clicking away on that old camera. I tried to convince Neel that he could pay the fee and still cut you off from the rest of your trust fund. He wouldn't listen. I think he felt you'd pushed him too far that time."

Ali nodded, her chest so tight that it took all her wits to keep breathing. Dante had supported her. Dante had intervened on her behalf. "That's funny, isn't it? All the tantrums I threw for his attention, all the really bad decisions I made because I was so lost...and he punished me for the one thing I didn't do by taking away the most important thing to me. I beat myself up every day that I didn't take the chance to get to know him, that I ruined our relationship. But he didn't even try to get to know me."

"I think you reminded him too much of Shanti. He never got over the fact that she left him."

"That's not my fault. I was a child, and so was Vicky."

Something dawned in those jet-black eyes. He ran a hand over his face, exhaling a long breath. "He was a good man, but not perfect." Suddenly, his head jerked up, his gaze pinning Ali to the spot. "What do you mean he punished you for something you didn't do?"

"I don't know what Richard showed you but I never

posed for any pictures naked. And even if I had, even if I had made bad choices, I didn't deserve to be punished by Papa and Vicky and you for it. You three had each other. Who did I have?"

He jerked back, a whiteness around his mouth.

She'd shocked him—with the truth or with her tears, she had no idea. But for once, it didn't feel good to shock Dante. How could she think anything but hurt and destruction could result from this stupid agreement?

Ali was almost out of his sight when she stilled.

I knew photography meant everything to you.

No, no, no.

He couldn't have, could he?

She didn't want to ask, she didn't want to know. But the question would eat her up.

Dante reached for her, his fingers drawing circles over her wrist. "Alisha, what?"

Just weeks after that scene with her father, mere days after she'd moved out of the mansion once and for all, she'd received the camera. One of the costliest professional cameras on the market—almost forty thousand pounds even five years ago, it had arrived by a special courier.

With no message.

It was not the most expensive thing she'd received in her life, thanks to her father's birthday gifts every year. But it had been the most thoughtful present anyone had bought her, the present that had brought her more joy, more peace than anything else.

She'd simply assumed at the time that it was Vicky's gift. She'd even texted him thanks but had never received anything back. She'd attributed it to her brother's usual neglect of any communications.

"My Nikon XFD45…"

He didn't quite shy away his gaze from her but Dante

released her instantly. "There's nothing to be achieved by raking over the past." He patted the pad of his thumb under her eyes, a quick, feathery stroke, something dark flashing in his eyes. "You're tired. Go to bed."

Ali pushed into his personal space, heart racing. "Dante, who bought that camera for me? Who sent it to me?" And when he opened his mouth to blurt out some nontruth, she covered his mouth with her palm. "Please, Dante, the truth."

He pushed away her hand from his mouth. His nostrils flared, emotion glinting in his eyes.

"I did. I saw how you cried that night. I argued with Neel to no avail. And when I went to your bedroom and found it empty, I knew you weren't coming back. Days later, it wouldn't leave me alone so I ordered the camera."

Words of gratitude hovered on her lips. She'd always viewed him as the enemy, had hated him on principle, but this one gift…it didn't negate all the barbed history they shared. And yet, suddenly, Ali felt like the ground had been stolen from under her.

"Why didn't you—?"

"I felt guilty that evening. Powerless to right what I thought was a needlessly harsh action against you." His mouth took on that forbidding slant she knew well. "Of course, you pushed and pushed and pushed me…yes. But after I realized you were…" It was as if he couldn't put into words what he felt. "Buying that camera for you relieved my guilt. Don't read too much into it, Alisha."

For once, Ali didn't balk at his dismissal. She was more than ready to leave behind the cutting awareness of being near him, of the seesaw of her own emotions.

But as she dried her hair and crawled into bed exhausted, her heart refused to believe the perfectly rational explanation Dante offered.

He'd asked Papa not to take away the photography program from her.

He'd checked on her, even if it had been out of guilt.

He'd bought her that camera, knowing how much it would mean to her.

Maybe he had cared about her a little. Maybe Dante wasn't...

That sent a sharp spike of fear through her rambling mind, had her sitting up in the bed even as her eyes burned for sleep.

This whole idea of a platonic marriage between them, her very sanity, hinged on the fact that Dante was an unfeeling, ambitious man.

If that fell apart, what else was left to protect her heart from the intimacy of the next few years, from her foolish attraction, from her own endlessly naive heart?

CHAPTER SIX

THUD. THUD.

"Alisha?"

Thud. Soft *thud.* Followed by a curse in Italian.

"Alisha, fifteen minutes or I break down this door."

They were tight, softly spoken words, and yet filled with that controlled fury they made Ali jump. She stepped out of the hot shower that she'd been standing under for far too long. She shivered and grabbed two towels—one for her hair, and one for her body. Her cell phone chirped and she glanced at the time and grimaced.

She glanced at the date and grimaced a little more. Any more grimacing and her face was going to be permanently frozen into a...grimace.

Today was the morning of her wedding. To Dante.

She was marrying Dante today.

Or Dante was marrying her?

Ten days of repeating that to herself hadn't made it any easier to face today.

She hurriedly toweled down her body, threw on panties, tugged on denim shorts and a loose T-shirt, just as the knock came again.

Toweling her hair with one hand, she opened the door.

Dante pushed inside.

The towel fell from her hands while her heart thudded against her rib cage. Ali rubbed at her chest and stared at him, a prickle of heat flushing all over her and pooling between her legs.

She groaned and closed her eyes. But nothing could erase the sight of him from her mind. Strikingly handsome didn't do him justice at all.

Black jacket that defined his powerful shoulders; white dress shirt that stretched against his broad chest; black pants that molded to his powerful thighs; jet-black hair slicked back, gleaming with wetness. A smooth shave of that sharp, defined jawline that she wanted to run her tongue along; dark eyes—penetrating and gorgeous, glimmering with interest and intensity.

He was too much.

This was far too much for anyone to bear. If she'd known all her bad decisions and all the pain she'd caused her papa and her brother and Dante could come back to her in this form… Karma was indeed a bitch.

Ten days of being back in London, ten days of seeing Dante every morning, impeccably dressed in a three-piece suit—sometimes he was ready to leave for the day when she was getting ready to crawl into bed after hours spent in the darkroom—had taken a toll on her mental health.

It was too much Dante to stomach on any given day.

Furthermore, he'd been determined to oversee a wardrobe upgrade for her because no, he still didn't trust her not to play some cheap trick to embarrass him. They'd also been forced together while he explained in detail the legalities of transferring her voting shares that he insisted she understand, and because of her ill-thought-out idea of coming to him with some financial questions regarding her mom's charity—the only time she sought him of her own accord. Yes, they had spent far too much time, far too close to each other.

In the blink of an eye, she could now recall a hundred different expressions he wore.

With one breath, she could remember the scent of him.

At the drop of a hat, in the middle of the night or day, whether she was at the Lonely Hearts HQ or in her darkroom, she could conjure the curve of his mouth when he smiled, the laconic glint in his eyes when she was flippant, the way his nostrils flared and his jaw tightened when she annoyed him.

It was as though her mind was happily compiling a database of Dante-related details to draw upon whenever and wherever it wanted.

As a teenager, it had been an inexplicable obsession, a weird love-hate relationship, a mild form of nauseating hero worship. Within a few days of returning to London she'd learned that she knew nothing of the real man beneath the insufferable arrogance and ruthless ambition. It was only after she'd burst the bubble of illusion had she realized the safety there had been in it.

Now she saw a complex and interesting man. She saw that beneath the ruthless ambition, there was integrity and a moral compass that no one could shake. Beneath the rigid discipline and control, there was a man who knew every single employee by name and their family conditions. There was a man who saw more than profit margin, much as he coated it with what he called simple business tactics. This was the man her father had nurtured and loved.

Where had all the animosity she'd nursed and tended to with such care for almost ten years gone? Was she so pathetically deprived for affection that the stupid camera incident had changed the entire dynamic between them?

It was now replaced by an awkwardness filled with anticipation, tension and lot of tongue-tied staring on her behalf. Like now.

She opened her eyes and caught him doing a leisurely perusal of her T-shirt sticking to her still damp body. Her meager breasts looked round and high, her nipples clearly distended with wetness. Jerkily, she tugged the shirt away.

His jaw tightened, that infinitesimal flare of his nostrils freezing her midaction.

He was just as aware of her as she was of him. Was that possible?

His ankles crossed, he was a picture of masculine arrogance and yet there was tension around that mouth, a wave of something radiating from him, filling the air around them.

Awareness pounded into her, stronger and sharper than an IV of caffeine. He did notice her. He wasn't immune to her. He was...attracted to her?

She swayed on her feet and he was instantly there, anchoring her, a warm marble slab to her touch, his heartbeat a thunder under her skin. She snatched her arm away just as he raised his own.

"You're not ready." Gravelly and husky, he sounded unlike himself.

The moment stretched as they stared at each other, the world outside held at bay. Her skin pulsed, her breasts falling up and down as if she were running.

She wanted to reach out again and touch him. She wanted to run her fingers over that defined jawline, press her tongue against the hollow of his throat, unbutton his shirt just a little and slip her fingers inside until she could feel the sparse hair that dotted his chest—she'd snuck a peek when he'd come in from a run one morning. She wanted to check for herself if his heart was thundering like hers was, run her hands down, down, down until she could trace his hard abdomen, down into his trousers until she could see if he was—

The sound of his curse, gritted out with near-violence sent a blast of heat up Ali's chest and cheeks. "I'm ready, okay? Just…" She rubbed a hand over her forehead, lowering her tone to normal. "As ready as I'll ever be for this. So let's get this over with, please."

He pushed a hand through his slicked-back hair, making it flop forward. "What you're wearing is not…appropriate. Only you can make an old T-shirt look like it should come with a red-hot warning."

The words fell from his mouth fast, totally unlike him. By the skin of her teeth, she somehow, somehow, managed to ignore the rough texture of his tone.

"Not this again, please." She pushed her hand through her hair, realizing it was dripping wet. "All we'll do is sign papers in front of two witnesses. The registrar will make us repeat those vows—which I've learned by heart, okay? I'll sign my name, you'll sign yours. *It will be over.* Nothing changes between us. Everything remains the same." It had been her mantra since she'd woken up at five in the morning.

When he stared back at her with infinite patience, she let her anxiety seep into her tone. "Don't make it harder than it has to be, Dante."

"There'll be press waiting outside the registrar's office."

Ali sank back. "What? Who could have leaked it?"

His hands smoothed over his jacket and he almost seemed reluctant to speak. "I invited them."

"Why?"

"Have you seen the headlines since we returned?"

"Yes."

Just as he'd predicted, there was far too much interest in his every move.

The rebel Matta heiress engaged to her father's protégé and confirmed billionaire bachelor Dante Vittori was far too juicy a story. All her previous transgressions had already been dragged into the spotlight again to contrast her record with Dante's pristine reputation.

There was no doubt in anyone's mind that she was the lesser one, the one found wanting in their coupledom.

A half laugh, half bark tore out of her chest as she remembered the headline that had described Dante on an online gossip site that Ali should've known better than to click. Consequently, she'd fallen into the internet hole of Dante's love life over the past ten years.

Models, actresses, there had even been one popular daytime talk show host. When she'd dug herself out of the hole, like everything related to gossip sites on the net, Alisha had felt like a pervy spectator with ringside seats to his love life.

What was worse was that old feeling of inadequacy, the sense of not being good enough, that had plagued her all her adolescent life and driven her to make horrible choices. Really, it was mind-boggling how she could believe she wasn't enough of a woman for a fake marriage to the perfect male specimen that was Dante Vittori.

Fake marriage, people!

"Isn't it bad enough that my reputation precedes me? Bad enough that every stupid online magazine is speculating that you're somehow saving me by marrying me. Old friends are calling me with all kinds of questions."

He frowned. "Why didn't you tell me? Have they been harassing you?"

"Mrs. Puri, our old housekeeper, called the other day and asked me if I was pregnant. And then blessed you in Hindi for two whole minutes for your loyalty and refused to stop giving me tips on how to be a good Indian bride.

"When I pointed out that you were Sicilian, she went off about how Sicilian men, like their Indian counterparts, expect a traditional, biddable wife. She had the gall to tell me that I was lucky to have caught a handsome, loyal man like you despite all my flaws. I wouldn't have been surprised if there'd been smoke coming out of my ears."

Of all the reactions she'd expected from him, it wasn't the hearty laugh that shot out of his mouth. His eyes lit up as if there was a light behind them, and his teeth flashed white in his olive face. Her fingers itched for her camera. She wanted to capture him in that moment forever. Like a hundred other moments. "I adored Mrs. Puri. How is she?"

Ali glared at him even as parts of her down south melted at how gorgeous he looked. How carefree and approachable and affectionate. "She's happy and cozy in Cambridge with the huge pension you settled on her. Why didn't you tell me you did that for all of Mama and Papa's old staff?"

An uncommunicative shrug. "What else did she say?"

He was still smiling and it felt like the sun was peeking through the gloomy October morning.

"I'm glad you think my life is funny. They think you're coming to my rescue. That my life went off the rails again because of something I'd done, and you, for the sake of Papa, are sacrificing your demigod-like virility on the altar of my thoughtless recklessness. I don't want to give them more—"

A feral smile playing around his mouth, he threaded his hand through her hair and tugged her forward. Mouth dry, heart palpitating, Ali went, like a bow flexing in the hands of a master archer. "Sacrificing my demigod-like virility at the altar of your thoughtless recklessness? Only you can come up with such outrageous descriptions."

She licked her lips and his gaze arrested there. "The legion of your female admirers saddened by our engagement give complete credence to my statement."

He traced his knuckles against her cheek, a thoughtful curiosity in his eyes. It was barely a touch and yet all of her being pulsed beneath that patch of skin. Slowly, he released her hair and the progressive loss of his addictive scent and his warmth made her want to weep.

"Just the idea of our engagement did that. There's no way to stop the press from following this story like rabid dogs when it comes out that we've married so quickly. They will hound me, but I'm used to it. They'll make your life hell. This way, we give them what we want. We control the narrative. A quick statement from us and a couple of orchestrated shots means the story doesn't take off in a hundred different ways."

"I don't want to pretend anything."

"It'll just be a photographer and one journalist from a reputed online website. They won't even be allowed inside where we sign the papers. Dress like you mean it. Turn the world on its head. Think of it as armor, Alisha. Dazzle them so much that they don't wonder the why of this anymore. Surprise them with all the changes you've made."

"The changes I've made?"

"Haven't you made changes? I barely see you during the day and you're at that studio most nights. Be smart about the publicity you'll garner over the next few months. Use this opportunity. Use me."

Her gaze drifted to his broad shoulders. "Use you?" she whispered, a veritable cornucopia of forbidden, erotic messages downloading into her brain for using him.

"*Si.*" An unusual smile curved his lips. "Being my wife will automatically give you unwanted attention. People who want to get to me will clamor for your attention first. Invitations for lavish dinners and charity events will flow. Make connections. Use these people to build up the charity. You can either hide over the next few months or you can use the time to achieve your goals. It all depends on how you choose to look at the situation."

Put like that, it made so much sense to her.

He was right. It was inevitable that his reputation, his high connections would overshadow her life for a long while. So why not make use of it all for a good cause?

A bright energy infused her veins. For the first time in her life, there was someone who understood her, who encouraged her. On an impulse, she threw herself at him. Arms wrapped around his neck, she pressed a hard kiss to his cheek. It lasted only a few seconds, half a minute at the most.

And yet, she couldn't forget the steely cage of his arms around her waist, the rough smoothness of his cheek, or the way everything in her body felt loose and heavy at the same time.

Pulling away, she refused to look at him.

In her wardrobe, she pulled out a cream, knee-length, silk sleeveless dress, one of the classiest creations she'd ever seen.

The dress slithered over her skin with a soft whisper. But she couldn't get the back zipper all the way. Fake it 'til you mean it. That was what she was going to do. With the world and with Dante.

Face frozen into an unaffected smile, she walked back out and presented her back to him. "Zip me up."

An eon seemed to pass before he tugged the zipper up, and another eternity when the pads of his fingers lingered on the nape of her neck. While he watched, she finished putting the final touches on her face. A dab of eyeshadow, the perfect shade of red lipstick and then hands on his arm, she pushed her feet into three-inch stilettos.

"Do I look good enough to be Mrs. Vittori now?"

A fire licked into his eyes. His arm rose toward her

face, slowly, his features tight. But it fell away before it reached her mouth.

She saw the bob of his Adam's apple, the controlled tremor that seemed to shake his powerful body. "Forget all the rubbish the media writes about my affairs, the compare and contrasts, *si*? You're beautiful, and talented, and you could take any one of those women singlehandedly."

Any other day, she'd have preened under his praise. But today, it served as a much needed reminder. The research into his love life was a reminder.

He'd never even had a girlfriend for longer than three months.

But for those voting shares, for the sake of the blasted company, he would sign his name next to hers on a piece of paper without even a prenup.

That was like a tiger willingly walking into a cage.

Until she had arrived back in London, until she had heard all the hoopla about his billions, until she had read about his rigid but straightforward tactics when it came to the company, she hadn't appreciated what a big thing that was.

He had billions, an empire he had built piece by piece over the last two decades and he was leaving it open to attack, making it vulnerable by marrying her without the prenup.

Like an eager puppy that returns again and again for affection, Ali couldn't help but think that it was because he trusted her not to come after his fortune.

Maybe just a little bit.

Being the one woman that ruthless Dante Vittori trusted beyond anyone or anything was bound to go to the head of even the most sensible woman between sixteen and sixty, any woman who had a working vagina, any woman who could appreciate having a little glimpse into a powerful and striking man like Dante.

And Ali had never been rational or sensible when it came to Dante.

For a quiet, civil ceremony, there were too many people waiting in the registrar's office. Somehow, Ali had made it without hyperventilating through the ride.

Izzy's gaze sought hers but Ali didn't meet it. There was only so much acting she could do and quiet Izzy would know in a second how this affected her. She and Marco, Dante's head of security, were to be the two witnesses.

Three men stood in the outer office, a lot of paperwork in front of them, and Ali realized they were lawyers. A tall woman and two men stood behind her—the gossip columnist and her team.

"Come," Dante whispered at her ear and Ali followed him inside.

Somehow, she made it through, smiling, shaking the kind registrar's hand. She even laughed vacuously at some thin joke.

And then it was time for the vows.

When the man asked her if she wanted to add anything personal to the preexisting set of vows, Ali wanted to run away. This was wrong. All wrong.

She felt the warmth of Dante's body by her side before he turned her toward him. And slowly, the declaratory words came, more easily than she had thought they would, his gaze holding hers, anchoring her, his broad shoulders her entire world.

"I do solemnly declare that I know not of any lawful impediment why I, Alisha Rajeswari Matta, may not be joined in matrimony to Dante Stefano Vittori."

Steady and clear, she finished her vows.

When Dante spoke, with no inflection or tone, his gaze fixed, each word swept through her with the force of a thunderstorm. Ali trembled all over.

And then he was finishing… "I call upon these persons here present, to witness that I, Dante Stefano Vittori, do take thee, Alisha Rajeswari Matta, to be my lawful wedded wife."

My lawful wedded wife… The words clung to her skin, as if tattooed there.

She took the pen from the waiting registrar and scribbled her name in a flourish.

A second time.

A third time.

By the fifth time, her fingers shook. Sweat beaded on her upper lip. Ali had no idea how she kept it together when, with each scribble of her name, it felt as if she was twining her fate with his.

Okay, yes, she'd never really given much thought to families and weddings in the last few years.

A wedding had always been some future affair, a loving marriage a dream she had put on the back burner while she figured out the hard path she'd chosen for herself. While she figured out how to save her mother's charity. While she made something of herself that would have made her mama and papa, and maybe even Dante proud.

Which was also why it had been so easy to say yes to this blasted arrangement.

But now her breaths rushed in and out, fast and shallow. She focused on them, willing herself to calm down. It didn't help. Her hands trembled. The next few months would be hard enough without lying to herself.

Being Dante's wife—even in name only, even temporarily—meant something to her. Because he was the one man she'd always…what? Admired? Wanted? Lusted over?

What was it that she felt toward him?

Dante went next.

Despite the misgivings in her tummy, she watched mesmerized as he signed his name with a flourish. No shaking fingers for him.

Because this whole thing meant nothing to him.

Except the company, Dante cared about nothing and no one. That had to be her mantra for every waking minute and disturbingly dream-filled nights. She walked as if in a trance as the registrar wished them well and they walked out into the lounge. With people, waiting and watching them.

"Izzy, give me the rings."

Her mouth fell open. "You didn't..."

His big palms landed on her hip, and pulled her up toward him with the slightest pressure. Heat from his hands burned through the silk of her dress, stunning her, stealing her breath. Her hands were trapped between their bodies, on his chest.

His nose was buried in her hair as he whispered, "Stop looking as if you were trapped in a nightmare." A thread of impatience and something else colored his words. He shifted her hair away from her neck. She knew he was using the thick curtain of her hair to hide his words but still she trembled all over. His breath was warm over her bare neck, sending silky ripples down her spine. "Do a better job unless you want to confirm *I'm* sacrificing myself."

He tugged her fingers up and slipped two rings onto her left ring finger, as casually and as intimately as if he were buttoning her shirt.

The camera went click, click, click, in tune to her thundering heart.

The solitaire diamond in its princess setting winked

at her, the accompanying platinum band beautiful in its simplicity. The rings felt like a vow, a bond tying her to him.

Tears filled her eyes and she hurriedly blinked them back.

God forbid that camera had caught those tears. They would say she'd cried and gone down on her knees at his feet out of gratitude or some such.

He opened her palm and dropped another ring there. Fingers shaking, Ali somehow managed to hold the ring in two fingers. He extended his hand to her. For the life of her, she couldn't come up with something casual to say, to shrug off the moment.

She looked down at his hand. Blunt, square-tipped nails on elegantly long fingers. Such a small detail. Such an intimate detail.

The Dante database in her brain pinged. God, she was going mental with this. Holding his fingers, she slipped the ring on.

"Now, if we can get a couple of shots of you two kissing," the beige pantsuit said with a smile, "our readers are desperate for more about you two. It would be icing on the cake."

The rest of the reporter's words drifted away into nothingness as Ali's gaze jerked to Dante's.

Shock pulsed through her. Jet-black eyes held hers, curiously devoid of anything. No mockery, no warning. Just waiting for her to follow his lead.

He had known this was coming, had known what the reporter would ask. He'd probably planned it out in his diary the day he'd proposed this arrangement. And yet, he'd left her in the dark.

If he kissed her, if he even touched her, there was no way to hide her desire for him. To hide this madness he stirred up in her. And the thought of rejection in his eyes, or even worse, pity…

But he didn't give her a chance to protest.

Or to think.

Hands on her hips tugged her forward. Dark, fathomless eyes held hers as he bent his head toward her.

Ali could feel herself falling into those eyes, drowning in their intensity. Swimming in the dark depths. Terrified that she'd betray her own longing, she closed her eyes.

Every other sense magnified a thousand times. The world around them—the reporters, the witnesses, the dingy old walls, everything melted away.

Only Dante remained.

"Put your arms around my neck." He sounded needy, husky, hanging on the edge of desperation. She refused, or couldn't curb, her overactive imagination. Her hands crept around his neck.

He smelled like heat and masculine need and dark desires. His hands patted her back, as if to soothe her continuous tremors, up and down until suddenly they were digging into her hips.

His breath hit her mouth in soft strokes, the knot in her belly winding and whirling upon itself.

And then his lips touched hers in a soft, silken glide. Just there and gone, before she could pull a breath. Ali jerked at the contact, nerve endings flaring into life. She tried to jerk away from his hold.

His curse filled her ears. "Shh…*bella mia.*"

One hand settled at the base of her neck, holding her still and he pressed another of those featherlight kisses.

Tease and torment.

An infinitesimal moment after an eternity of longing.

It wasn't enough. A feral groan rippled up through her body as he pressed another kiss. Ali opened her mouth.

And the careful swipe of his tongue against his own lips became something else.

Acting on an instinct as old as time and space itself, she slid her tongue against his lush lower lip then dug the tips of her teeth into it.

The tenor of the kiss changed from one breath to the next. Rough hands moved from her hips to her buttocks, cupping, kneading, pressing her close. The sound that tore out of his mouth was growly, hungry, and it lit a spark of hunger in her body.

Ali pressed herself into him and trembled all over again.

He was aroused. He was aroused. Dear God, he was aroused.

His erection was a brand against her belly, his hard thighs cradling hers. His hands crept into her hair, pulled at it until her head was tilted at the perfect angle. Until her mouth was open for his assault.

Dante's mouth. On hers.

Feral. Hungry. Ravenous.

Hot. Hard. Wild.

It wasn't how she'd imagined it would feel. It was a million times better.

He plunged his tongue into her mouth, sliding it against hers, licking, nipping, biting. And then he did it all over again. Again and again.

There was no sense of that self-control, the self-possession that he was known for in his kiss. A torrent of Italian fell from his mouth, gliding over her sensitive skin. Her breasts were heavy, her nipples peaking at the constant rub against his chest.

Her hands clutched his biceps when his tongue swooped in, licking, stroking, nipping and repeating the sensual torture all over again. His hands roamed all over her, kneading, stroking, kindling the spark into an unquenchable fire.

He didn't let her gasp for air. His mouth rubbed up over hers again and again.

Until she was trembling like a leaf against him. Until there was wetness against the soft folds of her sex. Until she splayed her leg around his lean hips and sank into him. That contact was like a jolt of electricity. Liquid fire in her veins.

Until a cough and a whistle and a "Hot damn, they're really into each other" punctured the moment.

Dante wrenched his mouth away from hers, his hands on her shoulders firmly setting her back from him. His breath was harsh, his mouth swollen and dark pink.

Ali had no idea what he barked at Izzy and the rest of them. Had no idea what was up, what was down. Had no idea if she was walking or floating.

She went where he took her.

The hard slam of the door woke her up and she looked out at her surroundings. They were back in his chauffeured limo, cut off from the world. He sat opposite her.

Color burned in those high cheekbones. "It shouldn't have gone that far."

The cutting coldness in his tone pushed Ali out of the sensual fog. She licked her lips and tasted him there. And liked it far too much.

She knew how he felt. She even agreed with him. No good could come out of this attraction. This mutual attraction. This red-hot attraction that wasn't all in her head.

Dante wanted her. Her mind was stuck in that loop.

"If you blame me for it, I'll sink my nails into your pretty face." Good, she sounded steady. Like her knees weren't still quaking. "You orchestrated that whole thing there, so don't you dare blame me if it went off your precious script."

Something dawned in his eyes. For the life of her, Ali didn't know what. Even his remoteness now, as if that kiss hadn't made even a dent in his self-control, couldn't douse the feral satisfaction that ran through her.

The dynamic between them shifted and swirled in the luxurious interior of his car.

"One kiss doesn't mean anything, Alisha."

She fell back down to earth with a vicious thud even as she told herself the same thing. "No, it doesn't."

But it meant everything.

The taste of him lingered on her lips, the press of his fingers on her hips a burn.

It meant Dante saw her as a woman.

It meant Dante wanted her desperately.

It meant Dante and his self-control could go on a hike when she was near.

It meant for the first time in her life, the power in their relationship was fluid.

She wasn't foolish enough to pursue this thing, but man, it felt good to have it. She let a sassy smile curve her mouth, determined to come out on top. No matter that she would relive that kiss a million times from here to the end of eternity.

No matter when she went to bed tonight, her wedding night as it turned out, she was going to play that in her head while she got herself off. In the twisted world that they were inhabiting right now, she actually had the right to him, didn't she?

Lawful wedded husband and wife and all that...

"What are you thinking?" he asked, that something flashing in his eyes again. And this time, Ali recognized it for what it was.

Dante's desire for her, despite his self-control.

"That after my X-rated dreams about you for so long,

this time, I have real material to work with tonight. Conveniently, my wedding night," she said, brazening it out.

The curse that fell from his mouth was filthy and long and ricocheted around the leather interior. It was music to her ears.

Ali laughed, the power that rocked through her washing away the sense of inadequacy that had haunted her for so long.

Color bled into his high cheekbones, his eyes filled with dark desire as he held hers. He was imagining what she'd said, he knew that, she knew that.

Ali refused to look away.

"Alisha, if you—"

"What's in my mind is not in your control, Dante. Let it go."

Another short, pithy curse this time. "You really thrive on it, don't you? You have to control everything around you."

He nodded and looked away. "*Si.* It's… I can't undo it now. This is a marriage on paper, Alisha."

Warning reverberated in his words and hit her right in the solar plexus. But nothing could take away the high she was riding. "You said to control the narrative, *si*? So, I've got it. You fell in love with me on one of your visits while trying to pin me down all these years. Desperately. I led you on a merry chase all around the world and finally, I let you catch me.

"That kiss says that perfectly. I want to be the star of this story. I want to be the woman who brought Dante Vittori to his knees in love. And when this is over, I will be the one who walked away. Capisce?"

She stared at him defiantly, daring him to contradict her. Seconds felt like eons. Whatever vulnerability she had felt earlier, whatever emotion had gripped her, lifted as she wrested control of the situation.

She would be the one to walk away, she'd make sure of that. And in the meantime, she was going to have a hell of a lot of fun poking the sexy, gruff bear.

His gaze searched her, as if he was seeing her for the first time. As if she'd morphed into something he didn't understand right in front of his eyes.

And it was a power trip for her.

CHAPTER SEVEN

THE TASTE OF Alisha's mouth—so potently sweet, so addictively warm—clung to Dante's lips even a fortnight later. Through meetings with the Japanese team over negotiating a multibillion-dollar contract supplying steel spread over ten years, through board meetings that he and Ali attended together to present a united front to Nitin and the rest of the board members, through endless evenings when Dante caught her in the sitting room of his flat before she disappeared into the darkroom on the lower floor.

She'd been so dainty, so fragile, trembling like a leaf when he'd clasped his arm around her waist, when he'd pressed his palm into her slender back to pull her closer... but her passion had been voracious, honest, a force of its own.

He'd just meant to touch his lips to hers in a quick press. He'd meant to keep it platonic.

But thinking Alisha would behave when she could wreak mischief on the whole situation, when she could use the moment to challenge him, to pay him back for surprising her with the press, had been his first mistake.

Imagining that the attraction between them would wither away if he continued to ignore it, his second.

Just as Dante had predicted, the media and the world exploded at the shots he'd had his PR team release.

The Kiss, as it was being referred to by the entire world, had taken the media by storm.

Except the kiss hadn't turned out to be the perfectly set up shot he'd planned. No, it was a minute-long clip that had gone viral already on a million websites, as one of the most candidly romantic shots.

Especially because he looked ravenously hungry for her, because in his adult life, he'd never once lost himself in a woman like that. Ali had gotten what she wanted. The whole world believed she'd brought him to his knees.

Dante couldn't even blame the press for sensationalizing the story. The defiant tilt of Ali's chin as she pressed herself to his body brazenly, the hunger and passion in that moment… His lower body tightened every time he watched it—like a teenager watching his first porn video.

One glance at the clip and he had an erection.

Dios mio, it consumed him night and day. It came to him when he saw her lithe body in those skimpy clothes she paraded around in in the flat. It came to him when they were forced into physical intimacy at any public outing they had to attend as a couple.

It came to him when he simply looked at her mouth.

His entire adult life, he'd thrived on control in every aspect of his life and that meant his libido too. The women he'd chosen to take to his bed—he'd never let lust drive those choices. His affairs—even the short-term ones—hadn't involved wanting one woman so badly.

They had been more of a quest for release.

Wanting Alisha of course fell into none of the principles he lived by. If it had been just a physical attraction to her—if it was a matter of an itch needing to be scratched because of their history, because, in his entire life, Alisha was the one woman who never seemed to be cowed by him, who challenged his control, who with delicious defiance came toe-to-toe with him—it would have been different.

If she had continued to tease and torment him, if she had used the knowledge of his desire for her as some kind of weapon—damn it, it almost seemed like he half expected and half wanted her to do it—then it would have been another matter altogether.

No, the equally ferocious depth of her desire for him had been a one-off.

In a strange role reversal, she seemed to be the one conducting herself perfectly, a charming socialite wife, a smart charity hostess in the public eye and a polite, courteous stranger under his roof.

The charity was growing from strength to strength now that she had thrown herself into it. She had used the news of their engagement to raise its profile, make connections. Her photography she still held pretty close to her chest. He was getting more and more curious about it, he'd even told her he wouldn't comment on or mock something that was simply a hobby, but she refused to let him see even a single portrait.

An empty attraction to a woman he didn't quite admire or even like was an easy matter. But the more days that passed by, the more he saw a different side to Alisha.

The way she'd thrown herself into it over the past couple of weeks was eye-opening.

He'd even dropped in one afternoon, with a valid reason in hand—more papers to sign confirming that she was releasing the voting shares to him—at the office space she'd rented. Alisha had been deep in conversation with the new accounts manager she'd hired, looking at a presentation he knew she'd slaved over for the last week about expansion plans she wanted to take up in the next two years with the new infusion of cash—a dream that her mother, Shanti, had put on hold after she'd left Neel.

He'd found himself smiling when he dropped by in the middle of the day sometimes and found her at the piano, playing old Hindi melodies that he'd heard Neel play many years ago. And when she wasn't working on the charity, she escaped into her darkroom. He'd been tempted, more than once, to ask her if she was hiding from him. From them.

But asking her meant acknowledging what they were both trying to deny. It meant asking himself a question he didn't want to probe within himself.

Restlessness plaguing him, he walked to the portrait that hung on the wall in his office. He and Neel had been interviewed for a *Business Week* article and had posed for the picture.

He looked at the man who'd given him the chance to make something of himself. The man who'd taken him at his word, the man who'd seen and nurtured his work ethic and not the dark shadow of his father's crime. Neel had given him a chance at a second life, a better life, a new path.

Alisha was Neel's daughter.

And so Alisha would always be forbidden to Dante, especially for the sort of relationships he had with women.

He had easily bartered for her voting shares because those shares would be used to drive the best interests of the company, but kissing her, touching her, thinking these thoughts of her…

There was a spike in his heartbeat when his phone rang and Alisha's face lit up the screen. He let it go to voice mail.

Two minutes later, a series of pings came through. An almost juvenile thrill went through him at the thought of those waiting texts.

Spending tonight @ MM

He frowned. MM meant Matta Mansion. The house where she'd refused to stay just a few weeks ago.

The next text was a series of emojis with cake and wine bottles and champagne glasses.

FYI Getting drunk. Won't return tonight. Don't freak out. Send Marco tmrw morn. Good night, Dante.

And then a kiss emoji.

He smiled, her irreverence coming through in her texts.

But he didn't know whether it was simply an FYI as she claimed, or a red herring to hide what she was really up to. He hadn't missed the fact that she'd been unusually subdued yesterday night too.

He noticed the missed calls from his mother. She called him only a few times a year.

Hurriedly, he looked at the date. He left the office, even as reams of paperwork awaited him, without second thought.

He couldn't leave her alone, tonight of all nights.

With its white marble facade and once beautifully maintained grounds, Matta Mansion greeted Dante like an old friend. *Dios mio*, he shouldn't have let the house fall into such a state of neglect.

Even though Shanti had already been gone for years with Ali in tow, he knew Neel had kept it in great condition with the hope that she'd come back to him.

Dante had moved out after Vikram had died in that crash and Ali had left London. Neel had treated him as another son, but it hadn't felt right to be there without them.

A lot of good things had happened in his life here. He'd found solid ground to stand upon, belief in himself after his life crashed and burned, all thanks to Neel's generosity.

But Alisha... For the first time since she had walked into the mansion—a thirteen-year-old girl with a haunting ache in her eyes and a defiant distrust of her father, her brother and himself—he saw it from her point of view.

How scared and lost she must have been. How, lost in his own grief, every action Neel had taken regarding her had been neglectful and alienating and sometimes downright cruel.

Neel had never hugged his daughter. He'd never reassured her that he wanted her in his life. And when she'd started acting out, he'd cut communications, he'd had Dante implement his decisions for Alisha.

Dante had been blind to it all.

His wife, Shanti's, death had hit his mentor hard. Dante had never pried into why she'd walked out on Neel with her daughter in tow. He had automatically assumed that it had been somehow Shanti's fault.

God, even then, he'd been a distrusting cynic.

You three had each other. Who did I have?

They were there for me when I was lost and alone.

Those words haunted Dante as he slid his Mercedes through the electronic gates and into the courtyard.

She had no good memories of this place. And yet, she was here tonight.

For once, Dante wanted to be what Alisha needed. He wanted to care for her.

What he felt in his chest didn't feel like some misguided sense of loyalty. The knot of anticipation as he walked in through the foyer and took the stairs up the winding staircase didn't feel like responsibility.

The thrill that coursed through his blood, the swift punch of desire tightening every muscle as he opened the door to her old bedroom and found Alisha on the floor, leaning against her white princess bed, her head bowed, her knees pulled up to her chest, didn't feel like pity for a girl he should have tried to understand better back then.

She'd turned on the lamp on the side table next to her and the soft pink walls created a glow around her leaving the rest dark. A bottle of Scotch and a couple of glasses lay in front of her. In her hand was a framed photograph of her mother, more on the floor.

Of Neel with Dante and Vikram.

Of Neel with her, both of them stiff and unbending.

Of Dante and her, at one of the parties that Neel had insisted on throwing.

She looked so painfully alone that a wave of tenderness swept through him. But even that couldn't arrest the swift rush of desire.

A pale pink spaghetti strap top and shorts, her usual attire, bared her shoulders. In the glow of the lamp, contrasted by the surrounding darkness, her skin, silky and smooth, beckoned his touch. Her hair rippled every time she took a long breath.

Unwilling to disturb her, he looked around the room he hadn't entered in years.

A room of her own, built with a domed ceiling and fairy lights, handcrafted furniture custom ordered for her, couture clothes and jewelry, antiques, priceless Indian pieces acquired at royal auctions, modern, light pieces that Shanti herself had favored—Neel had given Ali everything a princess would expect.

But not what she'd so desperately needed.

Affection. Understanding. Love.

Suddenly, in this room she'd perceived as a cage, Dante saw Ali for who she truly was.

The glimpses of vulnerability beneath the brazen facade, the reason she was slaving to save her mother's charity, the very reason she'd accepted his proposal… Ali lived and breathed emotion as much as he scorned and avoided it.

But even that didn't send him running.

She looked up at him, and her eyes grew wide. The long line of her throat was bare, the pulse jumping rapidly. "What are you doing here?"

"I wanted to see—"

"If I was dragging your good name through mud and dirt, emboldened by my father's Scotch? Throwing a wild party with a lot of naked people gyrating on the floor?"

Once those taunting words would have riled him no end. Now, all he saw was the vulnerability she hid under the affected defiance. He removed his jacket, draped it on the bed and joined her on the floor.

She stared at his feet and then up, her gaze touching every inch of his body. *Cristo*, had she any idea what she was doing to him?

"You remembered to take off your shoes and socks?"

Something mundane. To fill the silence. "Of course. This was my home for years."

"I…want to be alone. Now that you have confirmed that I won't cause any bad PR, you can leave."

He undid his cuffs and rested his hands on his knees. Her eyes followed his every move, her disbelief and something else coloring the silence. "I thought I should join the celebration. How many did we celebrate together?"

"Seven, eight?" Her fingers were tightly furled in her lap. She crisscrossed her legs, giving him a view of her toned thighs. Feeling like a Peeping Tom, he looked away. "I hated each and every one of them, just so you know. That first year, I thought at least for my birthday, he would be mine, just mine. Instead he forced me to share it with you."

"Neel held me up as an ideal, demanded that you treat

me like the demigod I am and so you hated me on principle."

She made a sound that was half snort and half laugh.

He liked that sound. He liked when she was her flippant, brazen self.

The moment made the thick mass of her hair hit his neck and his shoulders. The side of her grazed him and he tightened every muscle in his body to minimize the contact. He tensed against the pleasure barreling through him.

Still, he didn't leave.

"It wasn't all just on principle, Dante. You…you made it—"

He took her hand and squeezed, guilt sitting on his chest like an anvil. He'd been the recipient of a self-indulgent parent's neglect and yet he hadn't seen the same in her plight. "I'm sorry for not seeing how alienated and alone you felt in your own home, thanks to me."

The stillness that came over her was like a seismic shift. Except she didn't explode. He saw the sheen of tears in her eyes and turned away. She wouldn't want him to see her like that.

A strange, unbidden, unwanted sentimentality swirled through him tonight and he didn't want to feed it any more fuel. Seeing Ali in pain, he was sure, would qualify as fuel.

"I… It wasn't all you," she whispered. "You just made an easy target. I despised you because you were so close to him and I took every chance I could to show you. And him."

"Your father was a man with a great vision. But he wasn't perfect. I've been blind to that."

Another stretch of silence.

"I'm sorry I was so horrible to you. That I burned your Armani suit with those Diwali sparklers, and for shredding important contracts."

"What about the terror you unleashed on my girlfriend? Melissa? Melody?"

"Meredith," she corrected with a smirk. "She deserved it. She was horribly snooty." When he looked at her, she turned her face away. "I had the most humongous crush on you, which is really twisted given how much I hated you."

"I'm not sure if I guessed that or not. You were...hard to understand."

Her shoulders shook as she laughed and buried her face in her hands.

"Pour me a glass, *si*?"

Her fingers trembled as she lifted the decanter and poured him a drink. He took the tumbler from her hands before it slipped to the carpet and turned so that he could better see her.

Her skin glowed golden, the thin bridge of her nose flaring. Her mouth...just the sight of her lips sent desire crashing through him. *When had want become need?*

He raised his glass. "Happy birthday, Ali. What are you, eighteen now?"

"I'm twenty-six," she said, bumping him with her shoulder. "You, on the other hand, are what, a hundred and twenty?" When he didn't answer, she clinked her glass against his. "Happy birthday, Dante."

He took a sip of the Scotch.

They stayed like that for he didn't know how long. That current of awareness still pervaded the air, but there was also something else. A comfortable silence. All that shared history finally untangled enough to realize that there was a bond between them.

A new beginning, maybe. A fragile connection.

Something he hadn't known weighed on his chest for so long seemed to lift. She was her papa's legacy even if she desperately denied it. And she'd always been his responsibility, even before he'd made her take his name.

The Scotch was both fiery and smooth as it went down her throat and settled into a warm fire in Ali's veins. It seemed to open up her senses even more, as if the awareness of Dante sitting next to her, his thighs grazing hers slightly, the masculine scent of him—sweat and cologne and him an irresistible combination—wasn't enough.

The last thing she'd expected when she'd texted him was to see him here. All day she'd been in a melancholy mood that she hadn't been able to shake. The charity gala her team was putting together to raise more funds or even the meeting with an agent she desperately wanted to sign— nothing could hold her interest. In the end, she'd called in sick to both, and drifted from place to place all over London, ending up at a quaint coffee shop she used to visit when she'd shared a flat nearby with two girls.

She liked to think of it as her grounding year.

She'd moved away from Matta Mansion, walked away from her father and Vicky and Dante. It had been the hardest thing she'd ever done but also the most liberating.

But even the coffee shop that was like a warm, old friend hadn't been able to chase away the blues.

She was lonely.

She'd been lonely for a long time now, ever since her mother's death. The last few years had been better. She'd surrounded herself with friends who cared about her. She'd filled her days with meaningful charity work wherever she lived, in those lulls between her photography stints, but being back in London was unsettling.

No, it wasn't London.

It wasn't even this house that her father had built for

her mother when they'd been newly married, where painful memories dwelled.

No, this ache in her chest, this constant thrum under her skin, was because of the man next to her. But she couldn't take a step toward him, she couldn't bear it if he rejected her, even if this time she wanted to be with him for all the right reasons. She wanted to be with him as a woman who understood herself and her desires and her own shortcomings.

She liked him. A lot.

She liked her father's protégé who was ten years older than she was and knew all her flaws and vulnerabilities.

She liked the man she'd had a crush on for years.

She liked the man she was married to. If it weren't so tragic, it would be comic.

Her thoughts swirled, her senses stirred. It was exhausting to feel like this all the time. She couldn't—

"Are you going to tell me what brought you here tonight?"

She whirled the glass in her hand, watching light reflect and refract through the golden liquid. "Do you really want to know?"

"Yes, Alisha. When I ask you a question, usually it's because I want to know the answer."

"I don't... I was feeling melancholy. So I took the bus around most of London today, just...reminiscing. I ended up at this coffee shop I used to go to with friends after I left...to live on my own. I ran into my ex there."

He didn't move or even bat an eyelid. But she sensed the stillness that came over him as surely as if a cold frost had blown into the room. "Jai?"

He didn't remember his own girlfriend's name but he remembered Jai? "Yes."

"Ah…you're pining over him." Was there an edge to those words that she could detect beneath the control?

"It was a shock to see him, yes. But out of all the decisions I made then, Jai was… He was a good influence on me. He made me see that just because I didn't do that apprenticeship didn't mean I had to give up photography. When he saw me today, he gave me a quick hug, all open smiles. Talked about his start-up, congratulated me on my news—"

"Your news? Did that agent sign you on? Why didn't you tell me?"

Putting her glass away, Ali stood up, scooted onto the bed and leaned against the headboard. Dante stood up in a lithe move, a tic in his tight jaw as he looked at her.

"What? I'm getting a crick in my neck turning to see your face and my bottom is falling asleep on the floor." She patted the place next to her on the bed and smiled, faking a brazenness she didn't feel. "I won't bite, Dante."

He said nothing. Just stared at her for a few more seconds, then sat down near her feet.

"I haven't heard from the agent. I actually haven't sent him my portfolio yet."

"Why not? You've been in your darkroom for hours and hours this week." He took her hand in his. "You are scared of being rejected."

She shrugged. Yes, she was. "No one's ever seen my work."

"And you'll never know where you stand unless you send it." He looked at her hand in his, his voice husky, his head bent down. Her fingers itched to sink into his hair. "What was Jai congratulating you about then?"

"Our wedding. He was congratulating me on…" She compulsively turned the ring on her finger. "This." Jai had been genuinely happy for her, that she'd finally achieved her heart's desire, he'd said.

When she'd looked at him blankly, he had smiled understandingly.

You think I didn't know? I liked you, Ali, really. But even for the few months we were together you had too much baggage. Too much... You were fixated on him. On Dante. He was all you talked about. His personal life, his relationship with your father, his relationship with you. It was clear that Dante would always be the primary man in your life. You were half in love with him, as much as you continuously claimed that you hated him.

She'd always wondered why Jai had ended their relationship. But she'd moved on easily. She'd wanted to travel, she'd wanted to focus on photography. Today, his answer had shaken her.

She'd been fixated on Dante back then, yes, but that wasn't love. What the hell did she know about love anyway?

For the rest of the day, Jai's words had haunted her. Now she saw it.

The melancholy that had gripped her, it was an ache to be with Dante.

To spend time with him in comfortable silence like now, or trading snappy comebacks, to discuss stoicism and pop culture—three guesses who was into which—to laugh with him, to understand what drove that razor-sharp mind and fueled that ambition, to touch him, to have the freedom to run her hand over his cheek whenever she wanted, to sink her fingers into his thick hair, to press her mouth to his in a quick kiss every time he got that brooding look in his eyes...

To be just a woman with him. A woman he liked and respected and wanted. Their lives were intricately twined now, for the first time seeing each other clearly and her feelings consumed her.

She pressed the heels of her palms to her eyes. "You were right. I... I think I'll move back here. There's just more room here and once the novelty of our announcement dies down, it's not like the media can see if we're spending our nights together in one room. I mean, in the same house. We both work insane hours anyway."

In the dim light of the lamp, his scowl was downright ferocious. "What?"

"As big as your flat is, it's...like living in each other's pockets. This way, we'll have more freedom, more...space."

"More space to do what, precisely? See your ex again? Should we expect him to come knocking on the door any moment now? Is that why you wanted me to leave?"

She jumped off the bed, fury burning away that achy longing. "That's unfair. The last thing I'd do is have a secret affair while the whole world is crowing about our wedding as the most romantic thing in the decade. Not that you deserve my...fidelity. I just can't do this anymore."

She turned to leave the room, to leave his unfair comments to himself, but he grabbed her arm.

Ali ended up against him, his legs straddling her hips, her hands on his chest. He rubbed her back gently, his breath feathering over her forehead. The scent of him made her skin tight. The incredible warmth of his body made hers hum.

She wanted to stay like that the entire night. An entire lifetime.

His hands were gentle as he clasped her cheek, a slumbering warmth in his eyes. "If it's the agent, I'll make some calls. If it's the charity that worries you, don't. And if it's the media scrutiny that's bothering you, it will die down soon.

"You're...you're so much his daughter, Alisha. Driven

and grounded. I was wrong to think you were a spoiled princess. Whatever the problem is, I'll fix it. I owe it to Neel to do right by you."

Just like that, he tramped all over Ali's budding feelings. She didn't want his loyalty or his sympathy because she was her father's daughter. She wanted him to see her. Alisha. "It's you." The words tumbled out of her mouth. "You make this all strange and wrong and hard. I feel like I signed away more than those blasted voting shares."

Shock filled his eyes. Slowly he pulled his hand away. "I would never harm you, Ali."

She nodded. He didn't get it. He would never get it. Ambition and goals and reputations, those things he understood. Matters of the heart were a different matter.

She was terrified that slowly, irrevocably Dante was stealing hers. And if she didn't stop it, if she didn't steel herself against him, if she was foolish enough to offer it to him, he would crush it into a thousand pieces.

Still, she asked. "Are you happy to pretend that kiss didn't change anything between us?"

After a long time, he blinked slowly, tension pulling at his mouth. "Yes."

She fisted her hands. "I don't have your self-control, nor do I want to suppress every little thing I feel when I genuinely like you. I can't live with you and pretend as if I don't want to do this."

"Do what?"

"This."

She pressed her mouth to his, every breath in her bracing for him to push her away. His lips were soft and firm. Scooting closer on her knees, hands on his shoulders, she tasted the skin just under his ear, felt the shudder that moved through his hard body.

He tasted like heat, like heaven, like homecoming.

When he gripped her hands to push her away, she trailed her tongue up to his jaw, alternating with nips and bites until she reached the sexy hollow of his throat. She pressed her tongue against that hollow, feeling his pulse inside her. Feeling the power of his body inside her. "Tell me the truth just once. Tell me you don't want me and I'll do whatever you ask. I'll never talk about this again."

Without waiting for an answer, she nipped his skin, hard, long, with her teeth. He growled, a drawn-out erotic sound. The tips of her breasts grazed his chest and she let his hard body take even more of her weight. Tipsy, drunk, delirious, she felt a buzz at his harsh breaths. She pushed her hand down his broad chest, over the hard ridge of his abdomen to his belt and below. His breath was like the bellows of a forge in her ears.

Her hand found the waistband of his trousers and then the zipper. Belly clenching, she traced the hard ridge pressing up beneath the fabric. Up and down, just with one finger, until he grew harder and longer beneath her touch. Nerves tight, she covered him with her palm. His shaft twitched against her hand, making her mouth dry.

God, an incredibly unbearable erotic rush filled her very veins. He was that hard for her. She could have died and gone to heaven, just for that.

He gripped her wrist like a tight manacle, stilling her. But he didn't push her away. And Ali pushed her advantage.

Sinking her fingers into his hair, straddling his hard thighs, she pressed shamelessly closer. Their mingled groans rent the air as his hardness pressed against her sex at just the right spot.

Rough hands tugged her by her hair and then he was kissing her with a ferocious hunger that matched her own. Teeth banged as he plunged his tongue inside her mouth and dueled with hers. His tongue thrust and withdrew from her mouth, making her sex clench. Whorls of sensation built in her lower belly. The kiss whipped her senses into a frenzy.

Mouth open, he left damp patches on her throat. His lips soothed while his teeth bit, and soon Ali was sobbing for more. She pulled his hands from her hips to her breasts, the tips aching for his touch. "Please, Dante...more."

She didn't care that she was begging. That she was raw and vulnerable and all the things she'd promised herself she wouldn't be with him. But whatever madness had her in its grip seemed to hold him too.

Still holding her gaze, he brought his mouth down to her neck, to the upper curve of her breasts. "Pull your T-shirt up."

Fingers trembling, Ali did it. He traced the seam of the white lace with his tongue, a dark fire in his eyes. Transfixed, Ali watched as his rough mouth found the peak jutting up lewdly against the thin silk fabric.

His fingers were so unbearably gentle when he pulled the lace cup down. Her breast popped out, jutted up by the tight wire of her bra, the peak tight and begging for his attention.

Breath hung in her throat as he closed those sinuous lips around it. She jerked her hips against his when he pressed his tongue against her nipple and grazed his teeth over its surface.

She moaned, and twisted her hips in mindless abandon when he sucked her nipple and the curve of her breast into his mouth. The pulls of his mouth, the thrust of his hips, the press of him against her core...sensation upon sensation built in her lower belly. She was moaning, she was panting. He used his teeth against the plump tip and Ali felt like she was lifting out of her body.

She thrust against him, shameless in her pursuit for release, her thighs in a death grip around his hips, her fingers holding his mouth to her chest, her heart beating like a fluttering bird against its cage.

Relentless waves of pleasure beat down over her, drenching her sex in wetness. Her throat felt hoarse from all the screaming. She hid her face in his shoulder, a strange joy fluttering through her veins.

A torrent of curses ripped from Dante, puncturing the deafening silence around them with a contained violence. He dislodged her onto the bed.

He ran a hand through his hair, standing against the door, his chest heaving, a sheen of perspiration on his forehead. His hair was sticking out at all angles because she'd pulled and tugged at it to her heart's content while he'd made her body sing.

"*Cristo*, this is your childhood bedroom, in his house!"

The aftershocks of her orgasm unfurled through her pelvis even as tears filled her eyes.

No, damn it, she wasn't going to cry. She'd wanted what had happened, she wanted a lot more. But neither was she going to enter into a cycle of self-pity. She wasn't going to beg him to give this thing between them a chance.

She'd shown him, told him what she wanted. Now, it was up to him. She had far too much self-respect to beg a man to act on what he clearly felt for her.

Ali pulled herself up on the bed.

His head jerked up at that moment, the shadow of his hunger for her still in his eyes.

Dark color slashed his razor-sharp cheekbones as that hot gaze drifted down to her breasts. Her nipples were swollen and tight from his fingers, from his mouth. His evening shadow had left a mark on the upper slopes.

Chin tilted, Ali faced him. Her insides were a gooey, painful knot, while her hands shook. Holding his gaze, she hooked her bra together and pulled the straps into place, adjusting the cups at the front. It was a push-up bra, designed to create cleavage.

And still, he stared. She looked around for her T-shirt and pulled it on. Then she raked her hands through her hair, hair he'd tangled by pulling it while he plundered her mouth.

There wasn't a part of her body on which he hadn't left an impression. Just the memory of his erection rocking into her was enough to send a sweet ache between her legs.

"Ali—"

"It happened. I'm not sorry it did. With all the pheromones running wild in my system right now, I think it's impossible to regret that." She held his gaze, for the first time since she'd seen him as a thirteen-year-old, hiding nothing from him. "It was the most amazing experience of my life with a man I like, I respect and I want. Don't cheapen it, don't tell me why it's wrong. Don't take this away from me."

He walked toward her with each of her words. Ali flinched when he clasped her cheek reverently, when he rubbed his thumb over her lower lip. "Do you know, that's the first time in a long while that I've forgotten what I stand for? Seeing you come apart like that…" Naked desire filled his eyes. "I've never lost my mind like that. I've never wanted a woman so much that it's messing with my work, never. The passion in your kiss, the honest desire in your eyes, the sounds you make when you climax…they will haunt me for the rest of my life. For all my fortune, you're the one thing I can't afford."

Ali braced herself, like a leaf in a cool autumn wind. Whatever emotion she'd spied in his eyes drained away, leaving that cool, unflappable mask. "You and me, this can't go anywhere. I don't do relationships and doing this with you, when I know I can't give you anything else… that will just make me the kind of man I spent my whole life trying not to be."

"What kind of a man would that be? A man who feels emotion, a man who clearly cares for those around him, a man capable of far more than he lets himself give?" Ali demanded. Her own strength surprised her. But then, Dante had always been capable of pushing her.

His eyes flared, something almost like fear in them. God, she was being delusional. What could a man like Dante fear?

"I deserve at least an explanation after that orgasm you gave me."

This time it wasn't fear, but self-disgust. "If I take you tonight, just because I want you, because you want me, knowing that all I can give you is a cheap, torrid affair under the guise of this marriage, it's a betrayal of all the trust your dad gave me."

"Papa has nothing to do with this."

"Neel will always have everything to do with me and you, Ali," he shouted the words at her. Self-disgust painted his features harsh. "If I screw you against the wall, here in his house, it makes me the same selfish bastard as my father was."

"Jesus, Dante, your father fleeced thousands of euros from innocents. How can you say you're the same?"

"I'll be the same because you're innocent and I'll have given in to my basest desires. And all I'll do is take what you give and then discard you when I tire of you. What I want from you—the only thing I want from you—are those voting shares. And you've already given them to me."

The cruel finality of his words pierced Ali like nothing else she'd ever experienced. How could it hurt so much when it was what she'd expected?

When she didn't really know what she wanted from him?

It felt like giving up but she nodded anyway. Survival instinct took over.

She stiffened when he took her hands in his and pulled her into his arms. The tenderness of his embrace stole her breath. Earlier, it had been the way he'd played her body, made her mindless, and now this side of him...

Who knew there was so much depth to the hard man he showed the world? Who knew that even his rejection would only make her like him even more?

She felt his mouth at her temple, the long breath he drew in her hair, the slight vibrations that seemed to shake his shoulders. Her arms went around his waist loosely, for he was the safest place she'd found in a long time. "I understand why you want to leave the flat. But for now, for tonight, will you please come home with me, Alisha? I can't... It would eat me up to leave you here. Do this for me. *Por favor, bella mia.*"

Ali laughed into his neck, even as her tears seeped out and soaked into his skin. Raw vulnerability cloaked her and still, it seemed what had happened, what he said couldn't happen, couldn't puncture the bond that had formed between them.

"What?"

Tilting her head back, she looked at him. Stared into his eyes. Her chest ached at the concern she saw in them. How had she ever thought him uncaring? "I didn't think you knew that word."

He smiled back at her, lines at his eyes, teeth flashing. "I know it." His gaze swept over her face, as if he couldn't help himself. "I just didn't think there would come a day when I would say it to you."

Still smiling, Alisha withdrew from his hold. Shying her gaze away, she packed up her things into her tote bag. "Just for that, I'll make sure you say it again and again to me. In fact, I'll make sure, somehow, I make you beg, Dante."

She walked out of her teenage bedroom without looking back, feeling as if she'd grown a thousand years in just one evening, wishing Vikram was here to hug her, wishing Papa was here to hold her in her confusion, wishing she weren't falling for Dante.

Wishing, once again, in the very same house like she'd done all those years ago, that she could change Dante's mind, that she was enough, wishing he cared about her more than he did.

CHAPTER EIGHT

It seemed to Dante that the universe or some karmic superpower was conspiring against him.

What he'd done with Ali, to Ali, in her bedroom, of all places… The memory of her flushed face, the image of her lush breasts in his hand, the sensation of those brown tips so hard on his tongue, the wildness of her body as she rocked into him and found her pleasure… *Dios mio*, it haunted him in the fortnight he'd spent in Tokyo on business.

Even in his dreams, Ali was there, taunting him, teasing him, the trusting smile on her lips, the raw desire in those eyes just as arousing as the invitation of her naked limbs.

Until he'd driven her to his flat that night, and bid her good-night at her bedroom door, he'd been terrified that she would refuse him. That he had crossed a line he never should have, that she wouldn't forgive him for his seesawing behavior.

No trip had ever felt so long. Because he'd never had anything to come home to before.

When he'd returned late at midnight, she'd already been in her bedroom. Somehow, he'd buried the urge to knock, to check that she was really in there. Even though his security team had assured him that she was.

This morning, he had another important meeting with the shareholders. He canceled it.

There was a ruckus involving the Japanese firm and some

miscommunication about production schedule and delivery dates between his team and their team. A ten-billion-dollar contract and thousands of new jobs hinged on the deal he had negotiated.

Instead of the usual urgency to smooth out the knots, all he felt was a strange tiredness for his job. *Cristo*, he'd been working nonstop for almost twenty years and this morning he wanted to damn it all to hell.

It had taken Izzy a few tries—at the end of which she'd remarked on his distracted mood—to tell him that all of his management team was sitting on tenterhooks, waiting for his wrath for such a major communications blunder. They were right, he didn't tolerate sloppiness or inefficiency in himself, or his teams. They went through rigorous training and usually his employee base, especially the upper management team, were people who'd been with him for years. And if a mistake of this proportion had been made, the person responsible would have informed him of it immediately and taken corrective steps.

In the end, Dante had figured it out.

It was all Nitin's doing. His petty little revenge was causing havoc. He had been attending meetings he hadn't been invited to behind Dante's back, promising to take the lead on communications and then dropping the ball, leaving some unsuspecting newcomer to take the fire all the while their Japanese client waited for an important communication. It was exactly the kind of games that had made Neel distrust his brother wholly, that had made him try to keep Nitin's corporate decision-making ability severely limited.

That Dante had unequivocally taken a controlling stake in Matta Steel after acquiring Ali's voting shares was a bitter pill for Nitin to swallow.

It had taken Dante longer than it would normally have taken him to figure it out, and to come up with a strategy for how to react appropriately. That morning he'd skipped his usual run, poured himself coffee—coffee he'd automatically made to Ali's liking—and sat at the breakfast bar waiting for her to show up.

Izzy's shock had been palpable on the video call when he'd informed her he intended to work from home that day. Especially with the situation being what it was at work.

But for the first time in his life, he couldn't focus on work. He couldn't think of anything other than facing Ali this morning. Of how to make her stay. He didn't want her at the big, empty mansion with all the sad memories dragging her down. He wouldn't have a moment's rest thinking of her there alone. The loneliness in her eyes—it was the same thing he'd spied in his own eyes before he'd come to live with Neel. But where he had channeled all the powerlessness and the rage he'd felt back then into ambition, into freezing his emotions, Ali was the opposite.

She lived bravely. Everywhere she went, she spread her love and generosity around.

The protectiveness he felt toward her was so new and so intense that he felt a restless urgency in his veins. The idea of her leaving this flat, of leaving London while he'd been gone had consumed him.

The sound of her bedroom door opening jerked his head up. Instead of the shorts and sleeveless T-shirts he'd come to expect from her, she was dressed formally in a fitted dress shirt that hugged her high breasts, a lovely contrast against her brown skin, and black trousers that showcased her long legs. Pink stilettos added a pop of color—that signature Alisha layer to her serious outfit. Her hair fell like a silky curtain to the middle of her back, light gold tints in it catching the weak sun filtering through the high bay window.

Those strands had felt like pure raw silk in his hands that night and he had to fist his hands to fight that urge now.

He watched silently as she placed her jacket and a portfolio bag on the sofa in the living room. There wasn't even a token protest in his mind that he was obsessed with her. Then she checked her cell phone and slid it back into her bag.

She pulled out her left hand and stared at her fingers. She fiddled with the two rings, the princess-cut diamond glittering at him even across the distance. Every muscle in his body knotted as he forced himself to stay quiet.

She pressed a hand to her nape, giving him the lovely lines of her profile. With a soft sigh, she took both the rings off her finger, stared at them a little longer and then slipped them into her handbag.

A roar of denial built through him. He wanted to demand she put those rings back on, he wanted to sink his fingers into her hair and hold her for his kiss, he wanted to throw her over his shoulder and claim his right over her mind, body and soul...

The force of those urges left him stunned.

In just a matter of seconds, he saw his whole life—the life he'd methodically created for himself, the future he'd always envisioned—fall apart like a stack of cards.

He wanted Alisha with a depth of desire he couldn't understand.

He wanted his rings on her finger.

He was already obsessed with the way she leveled those beautiful eyes at him—sometimes in fury, sometimes with laughter, sometimes with such naked, honest desire that it felled him at the knees.

He didn't want her running away again from the charity, from London.

He didn't want her alone in some corner of the world.

He didn't want her running away from him.

And the only way he could have her, was if she was truly his wife.

* * *

Ali walked into the kitchen and stilled at the sight of Dante sitting at the gleaming quartz breakfast bar. Usually he left for work at the alarmingly inhumane hour of six thirty having finished his run, his breakfast and his shower.

She devoured him openly, like soil deprived of water, unable to tear her gaze away since he'd been gone for a fortnight. Dark shadows hung under his slate-gray eyes. He'd obviously showered because his hair gleamed with raven-black wetness but strangely, he hadn't shaved yet. She knew he shaved twice a day and judging by the thick bristle covering his jaw, he'd missed more than once.

His lovely mouth was hidden and yet Ali liked him like this. He looked gruff and approachable and sexy. She could go on a discovery path, trailing her mouth over that bristle looking for the mouth that kissed so well. That tasted like heaven and heat.

His pale gray shirt was untucked and a couple of buttons were undone. When he stood up, she saw that he was wearing dark jeans and the denim molded enticingly to his hard thighs. Her mouth dried, and every promise she'd made to herself that she wouldn't moon over him like a lovesick teenager died an instant death.

"*Buongiorno*, Alisha."

Deep and husky, the sound of his voice was so good to hear. She'd desperately missed it and him. But seeing him when she couldn't touch him was just as bad an ache.

"I don't think I've ever seen you without a close shave," she said, her voice barely rising above a whisper. "Although the lumbersexual look works too."

Only when his brows raised and his eyes came alive with a fiery glint did she realize what she said. Heat filled her cheeks. "You surprised me. Izzy said you wouldn't be back until Sunday."

"I cut the trip short. I tried not to wake you last night."

"I heard you though, so—"

"So it's not really a surprise to see me this morning then, is it?" He had her there. "You look tired. Lovely but tired."

"I haven't been sleeping well. Been working a lot. How was Tokyo?"

"Same old stuff. Lots of meetings from dawn to dusk, then dinner, then more work. And few hours later, this morning, the same old fires again."

She'd never heard him sound so...dismissive of work before. Never seen him looking anything but perfectly put together in his Armani three-piece suits. Almost as if the power was a cloak he wore to hide the complex man beneath.

She frowned, even as she greedily swept her gaze over the way the tight denim clung to his thighs. She knew the power in those thighs, remembered how they'd clenched rock hard when she dug her nails in. "You're wearing jeans. And you didn't shave. It's nine thirty and you're still here. Your laptop is not even open." She rattled off one thing after the other, trying to arrest the pure longing coursing through her. "I know because I checked the time before I came out. I've been awake since five thirty and I took extra long in the shower because I know you don't leave until six thirty and I made sure that..."

"Made sure that you didn't come out until I left?"

His gaze held hers and all the air left her lungs. She licked her lips and a fierce fire awakened in his eyes. The memory of what had happened between them that night charged the air. Her breasts ached for his hands, and wetness pooled between her thighs.

"Yes. I have a big day."

His elegantly long fingers stilled in the process of pouring coffee from the French press in his hands. The slosh of the liquid made him look down. He shook his fingers and pushed them under the tap. Ali didn't move even as she wanted to go to him. She would beg again, and she'd promised herself she wouldn't.

"There's burn cream under the sink," she offered.

He turned the tap off and looked sideways at her, his mouth twitching. "Are you not going to move from that spot?"

"I have to leave."

"Without your coffee first?" The teasing tone of his words, the way he was looking at her, Ali was terrified and ready to run. This was pure torment on so many levels.

"Where are you off to?"

She checked the platinum wristwatch—her mother's old watch that he'd found in her father's things and had had fixed for her. So many small things he had done for her. The camera, the studio, this watch…and yet he denied her with his words. "I'm meeting with that agent this afternoon."

He smiled and it lit up the entire room. "Good. That's good. Give me fifteen minutes to deal with something and I'll drive you."

Alarm bells went off in her head. And her body. The last thing she needed was continued exposure to him. He was her kryptonite, he always would be. And wasn't that just pathetic?

"Why?"

"For moral support."

She glared at him. "Because you think my work is so bad that he'll automatically reject me?"

He raised his hands, palms up in an "I surrender" gesture. "Are you always going to twist my words and fight me for the rest of our lives?"

The rest of their lives…it was like a punch to her midriff. There was no rest of their lives, not if she wanted to be sane. Once she saw this agent, she would know what to focus on next. Her career at least would always provide an escape from London. And from him.

"You think you're not good enough—for your papa, for the charity, for the agent. For the world. Not me. You made that decision all by yourself."

"That's not true," she offered as a token protest, the depth of his perception stealing her breath.

He was right. Despite her mama's best efforts, she'd always wondered why her papa had given her up. Why Vikram had simply abandoned her.

Why her papa had never loved her like he did Vicky and Dante.

Why, why, why, why had she so easily assumed it was she that lacked something?

Not good enough for Dante either.

That was what she had thought that night at the mansion.

Why assume that Dante didn't want to be with her because she was not good enough?

Was that why she was ready to run away again instead of standing and fighting for the most real relationship she'd ever had in her life?

The questions came at her like missiles while he simply watched.

"Why do you want to come with me?" she said, going on the defensive. It was her one remaining coping mechanism. "When just a few weeks ago, you called it my fun hobby?"

"*Mia dispiace*, Ali. I was wrong about you on a lot of levels. I've seen you slog in the darkroom for hours on end. And I'm assuming at least some of it wasn't just to avoid me. *Si?*"

"*Si.* I've been working on this collection for a long time now and it's finally coming together. I develop my own prints and it's time-consuming."

Tenderness she'd never thought him capable of shone in his face. "Will you forgive me for mocking your passion? For—?"

"For being an arrogant jackass for as long as I've known you?" she added with a smile of her own.

His chin hit his chest in a mockery of remorse, his palm went to his breastbone and he glanced up at her through those long lashes that should have made him look feminine and instead made him stunningly gorgeous. She laughed out loud.

Who knew the man could be just as dramatic as her?

"*Si*, I forgive you. I... We were both wrong on many things. I didn't realize how many things we even have in common."

Like their ambition to prove themselves to the world, their loyalty and their love for her father and...

"Yeah? Like what?"

She blinked at the sudden intensity of his question. "Like our love of cheese. I mean, come on, that's a solid basis for a lifelong relationship." Her words drifted away onto a whisper as she realized what she was saying.

He didn't want a relationship with her.

Only her voting shares—no one could blame Dante for mind games at least. "It's not necessary. I've been doing things alone for a long time."

"I don't want that to be the case anymore. I want to come with you because I remember how nervous I was the first time Neel asked me to handle a client all on my own. I was—" he scrunched his brow and she wanted to kiss the line he got between his eyebrows when he did that "—twenty-three, twenty-four...and I was so determined to make a good impression that I almost sent out contracts with the wrong dates on them. I'd like to be there for you, Alisha."

"Because you owe it to Papa?" She folded her hands, hurt splintering through her. "This sympathy thing is getting old fast."

She got out nothing else for he covered the distance between them. The scent of him had her swaying toward him. She wanted to bury her face in his neck, she wanted to breathe him in until he was the only one in her world. "No. I'm not doing this for Neel. Or for the company. Or any*one* or any*thing*. I want to do it for you."

"Don't you have to work?" she said, his words weaving magic into her soul.

"I thought I'd take the day off. After your meeting, we can go out for lunch."

"Lunch? Dante, I told you, I don't want to—"

He bent and kissed her cheek and every molecule in Ali's body stilled. The contact was soft, tender, his beard a rough rasp in contrast. Her knees shook beneath her and she had no choice but to anchor her hands over his shoulders.

She felt the tremble that went through him as he wrapped his fingers around the nape of her neck. "I promise you, *bella mia*. Tonight we'll talk and if you still want to leave the flat, we'll discuss our options. But you can't just leave London." The emotion in his eyes was a hot burn against her skin, stealing away her protest. "I would never hurt you, Ali, you know that, *si*?"

Ali hid her face in his chest and nodded. Even knowing that, it wasn't in his hands. For all his good intentions, he would hurt her. Because he was becoming more and more important to her, no, *essential* to her and she had no way to stop that.

She was just about to pull away from him when the front door to the penthouse opened. They turned like that together, surprised, since security hadn't even called to announce the arrival of any visitors.

An older woman and a younger woman—the former clearly Dante's mother from the strong resemblance between them—walked in. The security guard placed a collection of designer luggage discreetly behind them and left with a nod at Dante.

Both women stared at the way she was half leaning into Dante, her body pressed into his side with his fingers around the nape of her neck. As if walking in on a married couple in an intimate embrace was a shocking sight.

For all they knew, she and Dante could have been having sex on the living room sofa or at the breakfast bar, or standing up against the back wall, or...

Coloring at how quickly her thoughts had gone in that direction, Ali tried to move away from Dante but his arm held her rigidly, his fingers digging into her hips. He relented a little when she gasped, but his arm stayed around her waist, pressing their sides together. He seemed oblivious to her discomfort as he stared at the woman standing behind his mother.

"*Buongiorno*, Dante," the striking beauty said, tilting her chin up in a silent challenge. A torrent of rapid-fire Italian fell from her mouth.

There was a thread of something, a possessiveness, an intimacy, that brought Ali's spine straight. She glanced between the woman who had to be Dante's age and Dante, who still looked at her as if he was seeing a ghost.

The woman had exquisite features, was dressed in the height of haute couture in a beige-colored pantsuit that clung to her voluptuous curves and looked as if she had just walked off the pages of a fashion magazine instead of a long flight.

A surge of something unpleasant rose in Ali's chest. Without thought, she covered Dante's fingers with her own. To pull him back to the present, she told herself.

The words rang hollow, even inside her own head. Good Lord, the last thing she was going to do was fight over him when he'd been clear about what he didn't want from her.

And it didn't look like he was even going to introduce her to his guests. Neither of the women so much as looked in her direction.

She went on her toes and said, "I'm going to leave while you…deal with them. Enjoy your day off." And since her mama had taught her manners, she smiled at the two women. "I'll see you later."

His fingers fanned around over her hip as he pulled her even closer. The press of his chest against hers made her breathless. "I told you I'd drive you to the meeting." He bent and rubbed his nose against hers. "Don't run away, Alisha."

Her heart beat double time, a whisper of hope and joy threading through her.

The other woman spoke again, in Italian, something to the effect of she'd been looking forward to seeing Dante or spending time with Dante. Ali frowned. "Are you doing this for…her sake?"

He scowled. "What?"

"Did you take the day off for them?"

"I had no idea my mother was on a flight to London." When that melodious voice piped up again, he cut her short with one look. "Ali doesn't understand Italian. Please speak in English, Francesca."

Francesca's smile dimmed at the edges as she nodded at Ali, as if she were the bloody queen of England granting a peasant a great honor. "Hello, Alisha."

"Hi, Francesca."

"Aren't you going to welcome us, Dante?" Sylvia Ferramo asked.

Ali knew very little about his mother, even for all the sensational coverage of his father's crime all those years ago.

Sylvia looked no older than forty-five at the most. There was a delicacy to her expression, a fragility to the bones of her face as if she would break at the lightest whiff of air.

Finally, Dante addressed his mother. "Since you decided to take the trip *without* informing me, Mama," he stressed and the woman colored, and the tight grip on Ali's heart released, "I'm sure you do not require me to invite you in. You can breakfast with us and shower if you'd like. I'll ask my assistant to book you a suite at Four Seasons."

"No," Sylvia said, walking in and reaching for his hands. "I'm seeing my son after a long time, *si*?" One arm still around Ali's waist, Dante bent only after she tugged at him so that she could kiss his cheeks. He offered no embrace and even worse, he radiated a brooding tension that clearly discouraged her from coming closer. "Francesca and I will not mind sharing a room here. Our visit is short and I, especially, want to see more of you than I would at some luxury hotel."

He still said nothing. Ali had never seen him so shocked, or so intentionally rude. Hoping to cover up the protracted silence, she offered her hand to Sylvia. "Hello, Mrs. Ferramo. Please, stay for as long as you like. I'm gone for most of the day anyway and in fact, if it gets too tight here, I can just bunk out on the sofa in my studio on the forty-eighth floor."

"You're not going anywhere," Dante commanded, just as Sylvia shook her hand.

Though there was no warmth in her eyes, her smile was polite and open. She examined Ali as if she were a foreign insect. As if she could weigh just from one look whether Ali was good enough for her son. "I was quite surprised to read about your wedding in the news. I have no idea why my son chose to hide his bride from me. Or why it all happened so quickly."

This time, there was no mistaking the implied innuendo in her words. "Mama, if you want to spend time with my wife and me, without being invited in the first place, then you will at least be civil. You'll keep your numerous innuendos and suggestions and caustic remarks to yourself. Alisha is mine to protect and I will not tolerate the kind of poison you're so good at spreading here, capisce?"

Mine to protect. Her heart crawled into her throat.

Her cheeks paling, Sylvia nodded.

"Now let me show you to your rooms."

Feeling like a fourth wheel who didn't understand the undercurrents, Ali picked up her handbag and portfolio from the sitting lounge. The coffee would be cold now anyway. She didn't miss the longing, doe-eyed look Francesca cast Dante either. The woman had come with the express purpose of renewing a friendship, even knowing that Dante had a wife of barely a month.

Maybe because Dante had told her how it was between them?

She came out into the foyer and pressed the button to call the elevator. This was good. Francesca and his mother were exactly what she needed until she figured out her next step.

"Where are you going?" Dante said right behind her, and before she could respond, he took her portfolio from her. "I told you I'd take you to the meeting. And before you ask again, for God's sake, I didn't invite my mother, or Francesca."

"So, is she the blast from your past?"

"What?"

Very much not the question she needed to ask. "Never mind. It's not my business."

Holding her gaze, he put her portfolio down with the utmost care and then advanced on her. Like a frightened rabbit, Ali stepped back until her bottom hit the back wall.

Leaning forward, he caged her on all sides. He was all over her and yet he wasn't touching her at all. "Ask me, Ali. Anything."

She wanted to ask him why he was so cold toward his mother, or why he never mentioned her. Or why she'd not been a part of his life for all these years. Why a man who'd been so devoted to her father, who'd grieved Vikram and who cared about Ali, didn't care about his own family.

Instead, she asked the question she knew would devour her for the rest of the day. "Who is she?"

"The girl I wanted to marry a long time ago. She broke it off and, with hindsight, I'm glad she did. And she's firmly in the past."

"So that…thing between me and you back there was petty revenge?"

"Nessuno." The foyer rang with his denial. "I would never, never use you like that."

"Then what was it?" She closed her eyes. Their relationship was like a minefield—so many unexploded and untouchable subjects. But one touch and the passion between them ignited. One step and their bodies would connect and it would be heaven and she was shaking for the effort it took to hold herself back. "Don't play games with me, Dante. I'm not as strong as you think."

"I think you're the strongest, bravest, the most beautiful woman I've ever known." His breath caressed her cheek, sending sparks swooping down her skin. "Ali?"

"Hmm?"

"Don't you want to wait until tonight to know?"

She opened her eyes and as she saw her reflection in his gray eyes, Ali knew. It was too late for her. "Know what?"

With each word, he moved closer, until his nose was buried in her neck. Until she felt the tension swathing his powerful frame. Until he was everything, her entire world.

"I want this…us to be real." He lifted her left hand and stared at her bare finger. "I…want you never to take off your rings again. I want to take you to bed and stay there for a month. I want your loyalty and your fidelity. I want you to be my true wife."

"And what do I get?" she whispered automatically, mesmerized by the intensity of his expression, unable to kill the hope fluttering in her chest.

To belong to Dante, to be his in every way…

He smiled then and it was a thing of wicked beauty. "I never intended to marry, you know. After the thing between Francesca and me. Never. But you… I don't think I can go another day without making you mine. You will have everything I have to give. My fortune at your feet, my body and my fidelity. It'll be my privilege to call you my wife, my privilege to take care of you, my privilege to give you all the pleasure you could ever want."

Not love. Everything but love.

She knew him well and she knew that he hadn't left the word out on purpose. For a man who'd never meant to marry, for a man who had a long-standing mistress in Matta Steel, of course, love wasn't a priority.

Love wasn't even in his thoughts.

He hadn't said he wouldn't love her either. God, was she clutching at straws?

He touched his forehead to hers and let out a long exhale. "Say yes, Alisha, and you'll never be alone again. You'll never want for anything."

Before those words could sink in, before her world could tilt back to its right axis, he pulled away. His gorgeous eyes shimmered with desire, his hands tucked into his trouser pockets pulled at the front, calling her gaze to his arousal.

A soft sound fell from her mouth as desire hit her hard and fast. She fisted her hands, fighting the urge to trace the shape of him, the urge to beg him to take her here, in the foyer, while his mother was in the next room.

"*No.* Don't take another step. Be my wife and I'm all yours."

Ali cursed as even now he denied himself and her.

"This is the only way this is going to happen." He ran his palm over his jaw, devouring her with his gaze, his shoulders tight. "In fact, I'm shocked at how long it took me to realize how perfect you and I will be. I'd like to think even Neel would have approved. I want you and I like you and I want to protect you. We know each other. The fire we have…is no common thing. Together, we can build a good marriage based on respect and a bond that will never break. Together, we'll be his legacy."

She spoke through panic, from the same desire running fierce in her veins. "If you say marrying me is paying his debt to you, I'll never look at you again."

"No, *cara mia.* It's not a debt. But I'm a man with principles and as much as I want to be inside you right now, it won't happen. You are not any woman. You'll never be just any woman to me. Be my wife, Alisha, give me your vows truly. Promise me your commitment. There will be no cheap, dirty affair so that you can scratch an itch and run away when it suits you. Or when it gets hard. Or when it gets old.

"For once in your life, have the courage to stay.

"It has to be all the way between us, *tesoro.* All or nothing."

CHAPTER NINE

Come to me, Alisha.

DANTE'S TEXT FROM two hours ago drummed in her head as Ali finally rode the elevator to the penthouse. It wasn't lost on her that he hadn't explained his disappearance for most of the evening, with Francesca in tow, after stealing the ground from under her with his announcement.

He didn't say please.

He didn't cajole or persuade even.

He just commanded her as if she were his to command. As if there was no doubt she'd accept this. As if she was so desperate to be with him that she would simply breeze into being his wife.

And this was how their relationship would be too, she had no doubt. He might as well have said *Give me your heart and soul* outside the elevator earlier in the day.

Oh, but she desperately wanted to belong to him. Not because she'd spent her whole life looking for a place to belong. But because he was what she'd been searching for.

Because he was right, she was tired of running away. Of being scared.

She wanted to stay and fight for him, for this, for them.

But incensed by his arrogance, she'd texted back.

Say plz.

His silence for almost a half hour had killed her. She'd just stared at her phone waiting, watching, desperately yearning.

Sitting in the quiet blackness of her darkroom, the *ping-ping-ping* of her cell phone had set her heart thundering in her ears. Her fingers shaking, she'd looked at the texts.

Just "please", cara mia? Come to me and I'll go down on my knees for you.

You're mine, Alisha. So stop playing games.

Take one step toward me and I'll give you heaven.

The possessiveness, the promise, the passion… She had trembled at the picture he painted, laughed at how, even in his texts, he was so… *Dante.*

Because what he did give was absolute. It was in his actions, it was in the way he gave everything to her father's legacy and it was in the way he cared about his employees. In the way he'd gotten to the core of her in mere weeks. In the way he'd prodded and pushed her into being her best.

She could tour the world another decade and she'd never find a man like Dante.

So there she was, standing outside his bedroom door while her future waited on the other side. The rectangle of light peeking from under the door made her pulse dizzy. It was half past one in the night and finally, thankfully, the flat was silent.

Of course, Ali could never forget the fact that Sylvia and Francesca were just a few doors down, after refusing again his offer that they'd be more comfortable at the Four Seasons. For her part, Sylvia seemed desperate to make a connection with Dante and Ali couldn't begrudge her that.

She'd give anything to see her papa or Vikram just one more time and say sorry for all the hurtful things she'd done. But Dante's ex was another matter altogether.

Ali had ended up going alone to the meeting with the agent. Because something had blown up with the Japanese merger and Dante had had to leave. She hadn't pinned her hopes on him coming and yet she'd been disappointed.

She'd been waiting on tenterhooks most of the evening for Dante and Francesca to return from some urgent meeting. During dinner, Sylvia having grilled Ali enough to last a lifetime, about Papa and Vikram and their wedding, he hadn't offered any more info on the big secret meeting.

Now here she was, outside his door, her heart battering against her rib cage. But if she didn't go in, she'd never forgive herself for chickening out, for not even giving them a chance.

Gathering a long breath, she twisted the knob, walked in and closed the door behind her.

He was sitting at his desk, the lamp playing with the planes and hollows of his face. He was still in his white dress shirt, unbuttoned all the way now, and black trousers. His hair stood out at all angles, making even more of his high forehead and the slashes of his cheekbones.

The air around him thrummed with palpable tension, and Ali saw there was nothing in front of him on the desk except the phone.

She hadn't texted back after his messages, which had been a half hour ago. And as he stared at her, she saw in his face the same desperation she felt, the taut need, the uncertainty in the tight line of his mouth.

His gaze swept over her from top to bottom—from her hair in that messy topknot to the tight stretchy sweater dress.

She leaned against the door, digging her nails into the wood grain. "Did you think I wouldn't come?"

He shrugged and the action parted his shirt wider, giving her a peek of his defined pectorals with flat brown nipples and tight abdominal muscles. She licked her lips, imagining running her tongue against that rock-hard band.

He made a low, growling sound that went straight to her sex.

"Tell me."

"I wasn't sure you'd come." He ran his hand through his hair as if the admission cost him.

She thought it would make her feel better, less vulnerable to see that he hadn't been sure of her. She didn't. Suddenly, she wasn't interested in power games with him. Not anymore. "Why didn't you come to me then? Why this mindplay?" A raw vulnerability filled her, coating her throat with tears. She wanted him so much. She ached to be held by him, she longed to belong to him.

"Isn't it enough that I've been yours for the taking from that first evening in Bangkok? Enough that I came back to the flat against every rational instinct? Enough that I waited all evening, after you disappeared for the evening with your ex?

"What do I have to do—crawl to you on my knees to make you understand that this isn't just an itch? That this is not a phase or a stopgap or a…"

He pushed off from the desk, reaching her before she could blink. His hand went around her neck, pulling her to him. His mouth took hers in such a roughly erotic kiss that her throat dried, her breath stuttered, her belly swooped. She gasped and he swooped into her mouth with a mastery that made her sex clench and throb.

"It had to be your choice, Alisha. Do you not see, *bella mia*? This is far too important to me. This is…" he whispered against her mouth, his gaze so intense that she felt stripped to the bone. "This can't be some boardroom deal where I use your weakness against you to make you surrender. This can't be a taking. I needed you to come to me, to choose this on those conditions."

He clasped her cheeks and peppered kisses all over her face, a desperate intensity in his words. "This is the first time in my life I've waited, and wanted, not knowing what the outcome would be. But now that you're here, *cara mia*, you'll never have to take that step again.

"I'll forever cherish what you give me. You've undone me, *tesoro*."

His teeth bit, his tongue stroked, his body pressed her against the wall until every inch of his hard body was plastered against hers. His unrelenting chest crushed her breasts. His lips—God, his lips—nipped and rubbed until Ali was nothing but a quivering mass of sensations. Until hunger for more consumed her.

His deep groan soothed and excited at the same time. And then his tongue was inside her mouth again, laving at her with rough, long strokes. She stroked hers against his and then sucked on it. His arms around her tightened, one hard thigh wedging between hers.

Hardness and heat, he was hers. Tremors swept through her.

His mouth moved to her jaw. He licked her earlobe before his teeth bit down on the tender flesh. Ali jerked and rubbed her core against his thigh.

"Wait," he said, jolting his lower body away from her, his glorious chest falling and rising. "Francesca...her ex pumped all her money into some get-rich scheme and she came here for my help."

"She came here for more than that, believe me."

"We spent all evening with my team of lawyers and PIs to figure out how to help her. And I did it tonight because I want her out of here as soon as possible. Whatever she and Mama thought about coming here, I have no interest in her." He took her hand up to his mouth and kissed her palm. "You're my wife and tell me you believe me that I'll never look at another woman like that again. My word means everything to me."

Ali nodded, feeling a catch in her throat.

He gathered her into his arms, his forehead brushing hers. And sighed. "Tonight is your lucky night, *cara mia*."

"Why just me?" She dug her teeth into his chin and he jerked. "I'm a good lay too, you know. If you want proof—"

He tugged at her hair roughly, thrusting his tongue in, murmuring something in Italian that she was pretty sure meant her mouth was going to get her into a lot of trouble. Or that he was going to shut her up the only way he knew.

He was hot, rough, thrusting in and out with his tongue. His hands moved compulsively over her back, her waist, coming to rest on her buttocks. In a rough movement that betrayed his lack of control, he pulled her up until his erection pressed up against the V of her legs. Their groans rent the air, the hard ridge of his shaft a perfect fit against her soft core. "I forgot to buy condoms." His hands snuck under her top and her belly clenched at the rough contact of his palm. "So, it's all you tonight."

Ali shivered at the wickedness in his tone. "As exciting as that sounds, why do you not have condoms here?"

"I don't bring lovers here. You're the first woman who's lived in this flat, who's come into my room and who's going to share my bed."

"That makes me feel special," she said flippantly. Because flippancy had always been her default response when she was protecting herself from hurt.

"You think I do this lightly?"

Ali shook her head. The one thing she'd never doubt

was Dante's word, his commitment once he gave it. "Two lovers. I'm clean and I'm on the pill."

His eyes took on a thunderous look, as if he didn't like hearing that. He rubbed his jaw, and studied her. "Five. I'm clean."

That unpleasant feeling gripped her and she tried to chase it away. He was hers now. "Five? Maybe you forgot how to count because I can recount off the top—"

"Rumors and gossip? I took Matta Steel to a net worth of five billion dollars in ten years. I don't have time to have as many affairs as the media hints."

"Is... Francesca one of those five?"

The shutters that fell down in his eyes were instant. He let her go and Ali missed his warmth like a limb. "Let it go."

"How would you feel if Jai was in the flat, two doors down?"

"I'd throw him out by the scruff of his collar."

"Even though I repeatedly told you he was out of my life?"

He rubbed his face again. "This will never work if we don't trust each other."

"I do trust you. It's just that...you know everything about me. All my weaknesses. I know nothing about you."

"You haven't let me see your work."

"So earn that right, Dante."

"Francesca's parents broke off our association the minute the news of my father's crime came out. We'd been together for most of our lives. When I asked her about her parents' decision, she said she was abiding by it. She didn't want to marry a man whose father's crime would always cling to him. Who owed millions to people, who could never leave that infamy behind."

"She broke your heart."

He looked up and shook his head. "*No*. Funnily enough, by that time, I'd been dealt much worse."

Maybe Francesca hadn't broken his heart but she'd made him close himself off. Ali went to him, hating the distance he put between them. "I'm glad then that she has such a fickle heart. Because now you're mine.

"One woman's discard is another woman's hero."

A white smile flashed in his dark face, lust turning his eyes impossibly darker. "I'm no hero, Ali. Heroes don't exist, *cara mia*. Only men with weaknesses and men without."

She didn't like the gravity of his tone. The shadow of his father's dark past was in his eyes. Twining her arms around his neck, she rubbed herself against him shamelessly. His erection was a brand against her belly. "Fine, you're no hero. You're the perfect man with the perfect hard-on and I can't wait—"

He tucked a swath of hair behind her ear. "I need to learn what turns you on. I need to make you scream. I need to lick every inch of you. Then, if you're still willing, then I will be inside you, *cara mia*."

Heat scoured her cheeks and Ali tugged her gaze down to his neck. "Oh, God, you're going to be all methodical and in control, aren't you?"

His laughter surrounded her even as his words wound anticipation tighter and tighter inside her. She snuck her fingers into his hair, pushing away the thick lock that fell onto his forehead. He looked down at her and smiled and in that smile, Ali found the entire world. The thing that she'd been searching for through the years and continents—a place to belong. A place to call her own.

This man was worth staying still for. Worth fighting for. It felt as if she'd been waiting her whole life for this moment. With this man. Every choice she'd made had led her here. To tonight.

To Dante.

Dante moved away from Ali. Every muscle in him curled tight with a hunger he couldn't deny anymore.

It felt right. All the way to his bones.

Her soft voice, full of vulnerability tugged at him. Reaching for the wall behind him, he turned on the overhead ceiling lights and the room was instantly ablaze. And in the middle of the room, leaning against his king bed, stood Alisha.

The cashmere dress she wore hugged every swell and dip of her body, the peach tone setting off her dusky skin. The dress ended inches above her knees, while her legs were clad in knee-high brown boots, leaving miles of toned thighs on display. Her breasts jutted up high and firm and he knew, just knew, that she wasn't wearing a bra.

After years of self-discipline and having sex for the simple release it provided, tonight he wanted to gorge on her.

Now that she was here, he wanted to take his time. He wanted her limp and damp and blown apart. He wanted to drown her in so much pleasure that she'd forget any other man's name. He never wanted her to feel as if she'd made a compromise with him. She would never want for anything as his wife. Not for riches, not for security and not for pleasure.

He ran a hand over his jaw, feeling the scratch of his stubble. "Stay there while I shave. I won't be long."

"No, don't." The tip of her tongue swept over her lush lower lip and he felt that hesitant stroke lower on his body. The very thought of her hands on his shaft, that tongue wrapped around his hardness sent him to the very edge he'd talked himself away from just now.

"No?" he said, raising a brow. Silky, hoarse, his voice sounded so unlike him. "Tell me why not."

"I... I like your stubble."

He had no idea how he managed to stay still, all the way across the room. How he managed to hang on to the last thread of his control when all he wanted was to splay her legs wide and pound into her. "Why?"

She tucked her hand into the cowl-neck of her sweater dress, as if she found her very skin restless. As if she couldn't wait to shed it all. "I want to feel it against my skin."

Desire slammed into him anew, a fever in his blood. "Where, Ali?"

She lifted her chin, his equal every step of the way. "Here." She rubbed her cheek. "Here." Her pink-tipped fingers rubbed the nipple poking against the dress. "Here." Her palm swooped down over her belly. "And here." Now her palm was between her thighs.

His mouth dried out. "Pull your hair down."

Hands raised into that mass, she pulled at the clip and it all came tumbling down in glorious, silky brown waves that framed her lovely face. And then she shook her head in that classic feminine gesture that drew his balls tight. He wanted to feel that hair on his belly and lower, he was going to fist his hands in that heavy mass and hold her still for him while he thrust into her wet heat.

Cristo, there were a thousand things he wanted to do to her. Inside her. With her. An eternity wouldn't be enough for all of it. "You'll feel it, *tesoro*, against your skin." He let his gaze rest on the jut of her breasts, her flat belly, to her thighs. "Everywhere."

Brown eyes widened into deep pools, and a soft mewl fell from her mouth. "Any other requests from my sexy wife?"

"Take your shirt off," she commanded him, in a tone that thrummed over his skin.

He shrugged it off his shoulders. It fluttered to the floor in a whisper. Her gaze moved over him hungrily, from his throat to his shoulders to his nipples, to the light sprinkling of hair on his chest, and then to the line of it that disappeared into his jeans.

And then strayed over the bulge in his pants.

Again, her tongue came out and licked her lower lip. His shaft lengthened, almost painfully hard now.

"Take that dress off," he said, struggling and failing to remove the rough need in his words. "Leave your boots on."

Her gaze gleamed. His breath hung on a jagged edge when she picked up the hem and pulled it over her head. Lust slammed into him like the side of a mountain. A growl escaped his throat—half pain, half pleasure at the breathtaking sensuality of her body.

She wasn't wearing a bra. Her breasts were small and high and round, the brown nipples puckered into tight knots. His mouth watered. Miles of smooth brown skin shimmered flawlessly under the bright lights. Silky hair fluttered over one side of her shoulder, beckoning his touch.

Her chest curved sharply into a narrow waist, small enough for him to wrap his hands around and flared into wide hips, followed by long, shapely thighs and legs, legs he wanted wrapped around him while he plunged into her.

Dios mio, she was a red-blooded male's wet dream. And she was his.

Only his, forever. This night and all the nights to come.

"Now the panties." His command rolled out of a dry mouth.

He thought she would refuse him, on principle. She'd always hated that he ordered her around, that he knew what was best for her.

"No arguments?" he said, goading her, wanting her to fight him. Needing something to fracture that utter surrender in her eyes. In her body.

"I've no problem following your commands when I know you have my best interests at heart."

A shudder went through him at the arrogant confidence in her voice, the husky timbre of it. Chin tilted up defiantly, gaze burning bright, she tucked her fingers into the thin seam of her panties and rolled them down.

She had to lean back against the bed to pull them over her boots and her hair fell forward like a silky curtain, covering her breasts from his view.

Skin clammy with need, he took her in, as she threw the panties at him, a wicked smile curving her mouth. The fabric fell to the ground as he moistened his lips.

His gaze went from her flat belly to the V of her pelvis, down to the black curls hiding her sex from him. She was gloriously sexy.

He shook with the need to just take her right there, standing like that, her eyes wide and swimming in desire. But not tonight. He would do that another night. He would take her without preamble, he would reach for her one night, kiss her awake slowly and she would welcome him and he would be inside her while they were laughing with each other, in the kitchen, in the living room, in the shower.

But tonight, he intended to take it slow if it killed him. He sat down on the leather recliner. "Come here to me," he growled out, patting his lap.

And she did, her hips swinging with each step, her breasts swaying up and down, her mouth curved in a teasing light. She came over to him with such naked want in her eyes that his erection pushed against his trousers. When she stilled in front of him, her knees hitting the recliner, he leaned forward. His hands filled with her buttocks, he pressed her forward into his face. The scent of her arousal seeped into him like a drug. He shook from the force of his desire. He licked around her navel, breathing her in.

He left his trousers zipped, for he needed every ounce of control he had to bring her to climax first. For the first time in his life, Dante had nothing left because Ali had undone him.

Simply by giving him everything she had with such trust. Such open affection. Such...

It was a gift, he knew, and he promised himself he'd cherish it even if he couldn't return it in full measure.

"Climb into my lap. And straddle me."

Ali barely heard, much less understood Dante's words beneath the rushing in her ears. Knees shaking like Jell-O, she climbed up onto the recliner, while his hands traveled over every inch of her bare skin.

Cupping her buttocks, smoothing over her hips, tracing her rib cage, palming her breasts, then sweeping between her inner thighs without really touching her where she needed to be touched. Next they were at her back, pushing her down and forward. She sank into his lap and the feel of his hard shaft against her sex was like electricity in her veins.

Instantly, mindlessly, she moved over him and his growl ripped through the air. Rough hands gripped her hips, staying her. "Don't move, not yet. I want to come inside you."

"Yes. Please," she whispered on a dry mouth.

He tongued her nipple. A wet lash. Her back arched into the hot caress. Murmuring in Italian, he repeated the soft flicks of his tongue over and over again, until she was panting. Sobbing. Shaking. She dug her fingers into his thick hair and held his head to her breast, demanding more. Needing more. His teeth nipped before he closed his lips over the peak. "Every night after that time, I dreamed of this." He rolled her nipple in his mouth, pressed his tongue against it again and again before he sucked on it.

Fire burst through her belly.

Sensations poured over her like warm honey, beating on her, sending arrows of shooting pleasure down to her lower belly. And just when she was at the edge of mindless ecstasy, when she could taste the pleasure on her tongue like bottled lightning, he stopped.

Made her come down from the edge.

He repeated the torment again and again, until her skin was clammy with sweat. Her thigh muscles were trembling. And she was shaking with need. She looked down into his dark eyes. "You want me to beg, don't you? This is payback for all the trouble I caused you all these years?"

Rough hands stroked her bare back, down the line of her spine to her buttocks, up and down soothing her. He pressed a fierce kiss to her mouth, tongue and teeth whipping her into a frenzy again. His hand shook as he pushed back damp hair from her forehead, desire and something else in his eyes. "I like seeing you like that. Desperate for me. My name on your lips like a chant. Your eyes hazy and clouded. Your body so achingly gorgeous and mine to play with. It's like a drug, *cara mia*. Building you up, seeing you crave me like that… You give of yourself so boldly, so completely, so…generously. I promised myself I would have you limp and screaming my name for hours." Huskiness filled his words.

She rocked into him, craving his hardness at the apex of her thighs, delirious with need. Mindless for his possession. "Inside me, Dante, now, please."

He lifted her onto her knees. The rasp of his zipper, the sliding whisper of his jeans were havoc on her skin. His erection released up toward his belly, thick and long with veins she wanted to trace with her tongue. She licked her dry lips, and he growled. "Not tonight, *cara mia.*"

Ali shook with violent need when he took himself in hand. "Lower yourself, slowly."

She lowered her hips and he rubbed the length of him against her wet folds. Pleasure knotted in her pelvis and she jerked at the overwhelming sensation.

His dark gaze stayed where he could see their bodies straining to join. "Do it again," he commanded and she did.

Once more, again and again, she pressed the plump head against her clit. And the next time she did it, he thrust his hips and he was inside her.

Ali gasped at how embedded he was inside her like this, stretching her to the hilt.

Sweat beaded on his forehead, the thick corded muscles of his neck standing out in stark relief. "*Maledizione,* you're so tight."

"It's been a long time. And now I know why I didn't even miss it. I was waiting for you, Dante."

A stillness came over him. "Ali, I don't deserve—"

"Shh…" she whispered and took his mouth in a soft kiss.

Stiff at first, slowly he melted into it as she tangled with his tongue just the way he liked. She ran her hands all over his warm, damp skin, loving the tight clench of his shoulders, the taut skin stretched over his chest. "You know, Jai was right. I didn't realize it for so long."

He scowled and cursed.

She wrapped her arms around him, loving the warmth and hardness of him surrounding her. "I've always had a thing for you. I've always weighed every man I meet against you. I don't even know when…"

His hands in her hair jerked her head back roughly. His nostrils flared and he rotated and thrust his hips at the same time. His thumb found her clit and pressed. On and on he worked her, with his shaft inside her, his fingers on her clit, as if he meant to make her mindless. And without warning, Ali came, liquid lightning splintering through her belly and lower.

His dark gaze devouring her, he kept thrusting, and the waves came and came, drowning her, dragging her.

She fell onto him, moaning, chasing the high still. "When what, Alisha?" he demanded, a craven starkness in his voice. "When what?"

"I don't know when it happened. Or maybe it was already there and it's only that I just see it now."

He stood up with their bodies still joined, his hands on her buttocks and he brought them to his bed. Pleasure began fluttering through her pelvis again when he kept her at the edge of the bed and started moving inside her.

There was an angry glint in his eyes, color burning beneath those cheekbones. The tenor of his thrusts quickened, his fingers painfully digging into her hips. She loved it, she loved that he was selfishly chasing his climax, that he wasn't clad in that cloak of control.

Ali pulled herself up on her elbows and met his mouth. "For years, it was easy to hide behind my hate." She dug her teeth into his lower lip and pulled. And in reward, his hips flexed and rotated.

Feral want painted his features with a harshness. His shoulders stood out in stark relief, a tremor in his skin when she claimed every part of him.

His nostrils flared as he dragged her even closer, pushing her thighs indecently wide with his shoulders.

He was glorious and she was the only one who could give him what he needed. She locked her legs at his buttocks and gave herself over to his rhythm.

Sweat beaded on his throat and then he pistoned once, twice, thrice, with a jerking motion. A growl fell from his mouth as he came—an uncontrolled, raw sound. She licked the sweat at his neck and bit his shoulder hard. "I love the sound you make when you come undone. I love how you know me so well. I love you, Dante. I'll always love you."

Smiling, Ali fell back against the sheets, her pelvis sore from the pounding, from the way he'd used her, her thighs trembling and aching. Her heart was so overflowingly full. He'd lost control there at the end because of what she'd said. And she reveled in it even as he remained silent. Even if every second of that silence pierced her.

She closed her eyes and turned her head away.

But not before she saw the shock in his eyes. And the stillness that came over him. And the way his entire body shuddered, his chin jerking as if she'd somehow dealt him a lethal blow.

For once, she didn't care what he was going through.

She was in love with him and there was a certain freedom in admitting that. In saying that out loud. In flinging her heart wide open and embracing what she felt.

In lying, satiated, next to the man she loved.

CHAPTER TEN

PINK DAWN WAS sweeping its fingers through the sky outside his bedroom, the world, the city pulsing into life as Dante came awake. For the first time in his life, he felt no rush to meet it. No urgent meeting, no PR emergency could wrench him away from the warm bed, the haven of his room, from Ali.

Two short weeks into his relationship with Ali, their true beginning, and it seemed like it had been two lifetimes. The first couple of days, he'd braced himself for some… flash of reality maybe, something to make him pay for the out-of-body experience he'd had with her that first night.

He kept expecting her to demand something, anything, in return for the declaration she'd made so boldly, so brazenly, so unflinchingly.

After all, he had countless memories of his mother declaring her love for his father, and then demanding a gift. A more expensive car, a diamond bracelet, a better flat… as if her love was a transaction. As if no word or deed was ever enough.

And his father, falling deeper and deeper, had never realized that whatever he did would never be enough for her.

A knot formed in his stomach every time Ali kissed him, or laughed at him, or just plain looked at him. An expectant bracing to see what she would ask of him. Of what she'd demand that he couldn't give in the name of love.

It would be an awkward conversation, a hurtful one, but he'd been prepared to have it. She also seemed to have no expectation of hearing him return her declaration.

Because he couldn't love her. There was no force on earth that could propel him to open himself up to that kind of vulnerability, that kind of weakness, no way he would give her that power over him.

But she asked nothing of him, except his body. She was insatiable, just as much as he was and every night she came to him with that same naked desire in her eyes. She explored his body as if he was a sumptuous buffet she intended to gorge on, with her mouth, tongue, fingers.

She demanded her pleasure from him and took such effervescent delight in his pleasure, in seeking and discovering new ways to break his control, to bring him to his knees.

She asked nothing of him except his laughter, his company, his opinions. She didn't seem to have a plan beyond giving herself to him and simply expecting him to enjoy being with her. It was as if she'd reached through the fortress he'd built around his emotions and he found himself opening up.

This wasn't a transaction to her. Her love, or even her admission of it didn't demand a price.

She just gave. It just was.

I love you, Dante.

He couldn't tell himself it was from the sexual high she was floating on for he had never seen such clarity in her eyes. Such courage.

It had been like looking at the sun. He'd never thought giving could be as powerful as taking. And yet Ali managed to do just that, with him.

No, she had gazed into his eyes, both vulnerability and boldness in the tilt of her chin, her body thrusting up toward him, matching his hunger with hers, milking his shaft with her heat, her mouth against his chest, his heart thundering away under her touch, aching endlessly, craving more and more. She whispered those words like a benediction. Like a promise.

Just the memory of her was enough to send blood pooling in his groin, for that thrum to fill his blood. The sheet tented in front of him and he reached out a hand for her.

Cold, empty sheets greeted his hand. He frowned just as he heard the continuous *click-click* of a high-speed camera. With a curse, he sat up in the bed.

Dressed in a sleeveless T-shirt that stuck to her breasts and pink panties with cute bows on the sides, she was switching on the overhead lights. Dante blinked as bright light pierced his eyes. "Turn off the lights, *cara mia*. And come to bed."

She didn't answer. The sound of the shots she took pinged over his skin.

"Sit up for me, won't you, Dante? Please."

He sat up, almost unconsciously, the command in her voice driving his movements. She sounded nothing like the Ali he knew. "Push your hand through your hair."

Again, he found himself doing it before muttering, "I'm no model, Ali."

She dug her teeth into her lower lip, a frown on her face. "You're the sexiest man I've ever photographed and believe me, I've shot attractive men before."

"Naked?" he asked, possessiveness and something much baser filling his chest.

"*Si*, naked. Raise your arm, *por favor, caro mio*. I want the birthmark under your bicep in the shot. It's the only imperfection I've found so far in your body."

He smiled, the cajoling tone of her washing away anything else, the heat of the memory when she'd traced that and the small mole on his right thigh with her tongue filling his veins. "Make me a deal I can't refuse."

Warmth flushed her cheeks as she lowered the camera for the first time since he'd woken up. A wicked smile curved her lips. "I'll go down on you."

His erection twitched under the sheets and she licked her lips. He groaned.

"Altro," he said, knowing there was nothing in the world he would refuse her.

"You always ask for more," she pouted. "I'll let you go down on me."

As bold as she'd been the first night, it seemed there were depths to Alisha he would never learn. Hiding her face in his chest, she'd confided one night that her experiences had been few and not really of the adventurous type.

He let his gaze run down her belly to the V of her thighs, the pink silk barely covering her mound. His mouth watered at the very prospect of latching his lips over her sex, of thrusting his tongue into her tightness while she screamed his name. Of holding her down while she writhed under his mouth.

She clutched her thighs close as if she could hear his thoughts and he laughed. *"Altro."*

"I will let you see my work," she said softly. "But you have to promise me that you won't…that you will not… It's my heart and soul, Dante."

Warmth unlike anything he'd ever known spread through his chest. "It would be my honor to see your work. And my privilege to pose for you," he added and saw her smile widen, reach her eyes, and just like that, another layer of ice around his heart seemed to thaw.

That tension faded from his body. They would have the marriage he wanted. They would have everything together without the emotional transaction of love coloring every exchange.

"Okay, now, raise both your hands for me, please," she commanded and he happily played along.

A week later, Ali waved at Izzy as she passed her desk and without knocking, pushed open the door to Dante's office on the top floor of Matta Towers.

Standing against the far wall, with his back to her, he didn't hear her arrival. Ali took the time to study him, her heart pounding away. She'd never visited Matta Towers, even when her papa had been alive, on principle.

Vikram had invited her, several times. She even remembered Dante inviting her once, going as far as saying that Neel would be happy to see her there. She, intent on cutting off her nose to spite her face, had refused. Because she'd been waiting for her papa to invite her.

Now, she would wait forever.

And she didn't want to let him make the same mistake.

His suite was vast with a stunning view of the London skyline, a dark mahogany desk, as imposing as the man himself, taking center stage. Creamy leather sofas sat in the small sitting area to the left, and to her right was another door through which she knew was his personal suite. Where he had probably been sleeping for the last three nights, because he certainly hadn't come home.

When she had called his cell phone and asked after the first night, he'd informed her, almost politely it had seemed, that the Japanese merger was taking all his time. Having heard of the passive-aggressive communication misfire her scheming uncle had taken part in, almost bringing the deal to a halt, she knew that he was telling her the truth. Not that she thought Dante would lie to her. If he was bored with her, or if that initial frenzy of desire they had both been drowning in receded, he would tell her.

She had a feeling it was to do with the frequent bouts of his mother's crying in the evenings, in the confrontations she seemed determined to have, regardless of the fact that it embarrassed Ali and infuriated Dante. Thank goodness Francesca had left after the first few days.

But the wretchedness in Sylvia's eyes tore at Ali and she couldn't just watch anymore.

"Dante?" she whispered, bracing herself for that consuming gaze.

He turned and just like that, pure longing filled her. He looked sharp and arrogant as usual, but there were dark shadows under his slate-gray eyes. Warmth flicked into life in his tired eyes and her heart ached.

She thought he might ask her to come to him. Or he would come to her, take her in his arms and kiss her senseless. After all, it had been three days since he'd touched her or kissed her or even held her. She missed him like there was an ache in her chest.

But he did no such thing. The warmth of that smile dimmed as he pushed his hands into his trouser pockets and leaned back against that wall.

In that moment, Ali realized something. He never touched her outside the context of sex. As insatiable as his passion was when he wanted her, he wasn't the demonstrative kind in public. But his stance clearly said that she was interrupting. He confirmed it when he said, "I have a meeting in fifteen minutes. Why didn't you tell me you were coming all the way over? I would've told you I was busy."

She swallowed, refusing to take his words as the complete dismissal they were. He wasn't going to get out of it that easily. This wasn't even about her, she reminded herself. It was about him.

And his mother and his past.

Brazening it out with a wide smile, she covered the distance between them. Before he could push her away, she went on tiptoes and kissed his mouth softly. Slowly. Pouring all the love in her heart into the kiss. For all the hardness of his body, she was amazed how soft his lips were, and for all his dismissive words, how he let her do what she wanted.

She traced the sharp angles of his face with her mouth— the blade of his nose, the high planes of his cheekbones, the hollows of his cheeks, his tight brow. Sinking her fingers into his crisp hair, she tugged and pulled. He came to her, willingly, giving in. She traced her way down to his neck, licked his pulse, pressed her tongue into the hollow of his neck. The familiar taste of skin, the scent of him calmed the furor in her blood. "Didn't anyone ever teach you that was the proper way to greet your wife after not seeing her for three days?"

After what seemed an eternity, the stiffness left his shoulders. A familiar shudder went through him. He pushed off from the wall with a soft growl, his hands sinking into her hair. "No, this is how I would greet my wife," he said, and bit hard into her lower lip. When she gasped at the pain-pleasure, he licked the hurt away. He took over the kiss with utter possession that sent currents arrowing toward her sex.

Wet, warm and wanton, she clung to him for breath, clinging to him for everything he could give. Hands around his shoulders, Ali rubbed herself against him mindlessly desperate for more. His hands were at her buttocks again, his mouth at her neck. "I'll ask Izzy to postpone the meeting for another half hour. I need to be inside you, now."

She had no idea how she found the strength to say no; to pull away when all she wanted was to feel him inside her to feel the closeness he allowed only during sex, to feel as if everything in her world was right again. "No, Dante, I didn't come here to have sex."

He released her so fast that she'd have fallen back if not for his swift reflex. His chest rose and fell, his mouth narrowed. Eyes glittering, he rubbed the back of his hand over his mouth. As if he wanted to wipe her taste away. "Then what was the point of the kiss, *cara mia*? To prove that you can fell me to my knees in a matter of a few minutes?"

She flinched at the soft cruelty of his words.

"I wasn't aware that we're supposed to keep track of who breaks whom. I never… I kissed you because I missed you. And that turned into something else, because it always does when we kiss. Or have you been sleepwalking through the last few weeks?"

Color washed over his cheeks. "I… I don't have time for this. Go home, Alisha."

He never called her Alisha like that anymore, the very word dripping with contempt and exaggerated patience. As if she was being purposely troublesome.

Which in itself was a clear sign that he wasn't all right. A month ago, she was sure he wouldn't have lost his temper like that with her. But neither was she going to think of his nasty words as some sort of progress between them.

She folded her hands, the hurt cycling to anger. "But you have time to have a quickie with me against the wall? And after? You'll make me clean myself up in the bathroom and send me home with a pat and some cash?"

The curse that fell from his mouth sounded downright filthy. He bent toward her, fingers coiling in her hair, his breath coating her face. "Don't cheapen it. It's never like that between us."

"You're the one cheapening it."

"Ali…" He sounded distressed, at the end of his rope.

"Please leave. I... I'm not in a place where I can handle this in the right way. I don't want to hurt you, *cara mia*."

"Then don't hurt me. Don't dismiss me as if I'm a nuisance. The whole reason I risked the rush-hour traffic is to see you. You're upset about something. I get it. But being nasty to me is unfair. Maybe you're not used to relationships with give-and-take. But you don't get to order me around like I'm some disposable member of staff.

"You don't get to make me do all the emotional work, always. And just because I love you doesn't mean I'll let you walk all over me."

The effect of her ultimatum was ruined when tears filled her eyes. Pushing away from him, she angrily swiped at her cheeks. God, did he have any idea that he could destroy her with one harsh word?

She had almost reached the door when she heard him say, "Don't leave, Ali. Don't let me chase you away."

Hand on the knob, Ali stilled. Loving him did make her vulnerable, but not weak. She felt him at her back and the entirety of her being wanted to lean into his waiting arms, to take the only comfort he offered in his touch, to lose herself in the fire between them. "Don't. Touch me."

The sharp inhale of his breath, the stillness, conveyed his shock.

"*Mia dispiace*, Ali. It seems I'm always saying sorry to you. Turn around and look at me. Please."

She turned but couldn't manage to look at him. Instead, she made her way to the sitting area, took a bottle of water from the small refrigerator and gulped the cold water down. She found him sitting at the two-seater and chose a sofa opposite him. His mouth narrowed but he didn't say anything.

"Do you accept my apology?"

"I don't know," she said with a shrug. "I came because she's leaving, Dante, your mother's leaving in a few hours."

Any tenderness that had returned to his expression faded. His face became that stony mask again. "I know."

"I feel sorry for her. She seems so desperate to make a connection with you. I'd give anything to see Papa again, to tell him how sorry I am, to tell him that all I ever wanted was to love him, and to have his love in return. Can't you forgive her for whatever she's done? For yourself, at least? It's clear it hurts you to see her."

He didn't say anything for so long that Ali braced herself for another cutting remark. His gaze grew distant, tight lines fanning out from his face. *"Nessuno."* The refusal rang around the silence like a pistol shot. "I don't think it's even a matter of forgiving her because I don't feel anything for her. Even before my father was incarcerated for his crime, she cut all ties with him. Took her maiden name again. Within months, she had married her second husband. She urged me to change my last name too."

The utter lack of emotion in his eyes terrified Ali. It seemed that he really wasn't acting from a place of anger but nothingness.

Forgetting all her vows to herself, she went on her knees in front of him and took his hands in hers. He was cold, as if the past hadn't quite left him. "It makes her weak, yes, but not a monster, Dante."

"But he did it all for her. He was so in love with her, he so desperately wanted to please her that he cooked the books, embezzled from hundreds of innocents."

Ali fell back onto her haunches. "What?"

"She's from a wealthy Sicilian family with old ties to Mafia. He was a humble accountant. My mother…on the outside, she's a delicate flower but on the inside, she's spoiled, privileged. She is insidious with her demands, with what she thinks is her due. She was in a rebellious phase when she met him and he fell hard for her.

"Soon, I came and then reality descended on her. There were no cars, no villas, no jewelry, nothing exciting about being a mother at twenty-two. She grew up like royalty. Her discontent was like cancer and he...for her, he was determined to do anything. Which he did. Our wealth grew exponentially over a few years. Cars, mansions, a jet-setting lifestyle, he lay everything at her feet, her utter slave.

"I'm not justifying the number of innocent lives he ruined but *dios mio*, even at the end, he didn't regret it."

"You can't blame her for what he did. They were both weak." Fury filled her for between them they had distorted his view of love. And for that, she didn't want to forgive either of them.

He looked down at Ali, frowning. "You're right. It was his lack of a moral compass. But every time I see her, I can't forget that after everything, she didn't even have compassion for him, much less love. He rotted in that jail cell and when she refused to even visit him... When he heard that she'd married again, he hanged himself."

He rubbed his forehead with his fingers, and Ali's heart ached for him.

"When I see her, I remember his face. He was such a fool in love. To this day, I can't understand how a sensible man could lose himself like that. His love for her was his biggest weakness. It led to the destruction of countless others and himself. It's poison..." he said in a voice that was so full of bitterness that Ali thought she might choke on it.

Dante thought love was poison. A weakness. She felt as if someone had dropped a huge boulder on her chest, crushing the very breath out of her.

She had known he didn't believe in love. But to think of it as poison...

When he pulled her up, Ali went into his embrace and buried her face in his chest. "She doesn't deserve your tears, Ali. Or your sympathy." He seemed to hesitate, his mouth buried in her hair. "You were right. I don't do well with emotions. I will learn, *tesoro*, to be a good husband, to communicate with you. Never to hurt you like that again. We'll have a good marriage based on mutual respect and passion. When the time is right, we'll have a big family, if that's what you want. But you should know..." A tremor coated his words. "I will never allow myself to feel like that, never put my faith, my life in the hands of love. I can't change for you. I can't be anything other than what you see. Don't ask it of me."

Having dealt her that soft but final statement, he left her standing alone in what used to be her papa's office, her heart breaking softly.

For the young man who'd never had the chance to believe that love wasn't always a poison, or cancer. For a young man who didn't understand that even as he wreaked immense hurt on her, she still loved him with every molecule of her being.

That she could no more stop loving him, that she couldn't stop hurting for him any more than she could stop breathing.

Dante returned home that night, feeling like the lowest of the low.

His feet automatically took him to the guest room. His mother had left then. He stood in the center of it, the faint scent of gardenias filling his nostrils. For as long as he could remember she'd worn that scent. For as long as he could remember, she'd been a fragile beauty with no spine, letting the world sway her back and forth.

And to think he'd once assumed Ali was a spoiled princess like her and Francesca. He'd called her a pampered princess, once he'd even called her a waste of space.

No, his wife was a lioness with a heart of gold. And he'd hurt her tonight.

Unable and unwilling to face her reaction to his blunt words, he had left her alone in his office.

Dios mio, he couldn't bear to hurt her any more than he could love her. And the warring instincts constantly ate away at him.

She had come to offer comfort and he'd crushed her heart. But seeing his mother these past few weeks, dealing with the guilt in her eyes, reliving the worst years of his life all over again...he felt as powerless as that sixteen-year-old.

Left with the legacy of his father's crime and his death.

Left with discovering how, through the weakness they called love, they had fractured their family, his faith in them, his faith in everyone and everything.

For all the billions he'd amassed, for all the stains he'd removed from his reputation, Dante felt like a jerk, a weak man unable to stop wreaking hurt on the one woman who thought him worthy of her adoration, who refused to stop looking at him as if he were a hero.

He'd had Izzy schedule the meeting on a different floor, hiding away like a coward. Not that he'd been able to focus on a single word.

Maledizione! Enough was enough. He didn't intend to let the past rot his future with its poisonous fingers. He and Ali, against all odds, had made a fresh start and he intended to have a full life with her.

He would spend his life earning that adoration in her eyes. He meant for them to be consumed by the fire between them, again and again. For it was the one place where he could give of himself completely.

A sudden desperation gripping him, he checked the room she'd occupied when she'd moved in. There was no way he was going to let her spend the night in a differen bed. She belonged with him. He switched on the lights in that room and found the bed neatly made, bare of any of her things.

Panic like he'd never known unfurled in his belly. Had she left him? Had he broken her heart? By the time he walked to his bedroom, his heart was thudding against his rib cage.

The bedroom door swung open wide and there she was in the middle of his bed, illuminated by a pool of light. Tenderness and relief and desire, a knot of emotions crowded in his throat. There was a rational voice crowing too but he couldn't even hear it.

She lay on her tummy, her leg splayed, her round buttocks thrust up, her face to the side, taking up most of the bed, as she always did. Moving to her side, he pushed the silky strands from her back and placed his palm on there. Just touching her calmed the wild need inside him. Just breathing in the scent of her, of seeing her in his bed night after night…desire crawled through him, sinuous and hard, as it always did.

He stripped and crawled into bed. Fear beat a tattoo in his head that he was far too deep already. But it didn't stop him from kissing the smooth skin of her back.

From shifting the thick curtain of her hair to the side until he could kiss the shadows under her eyes. Shadows he knew he had put there.

From inhaling the scent of her deep into his lungs until she was a part of him.

From drawing a wet trail of kisses down to the round globes of her buttocks.

From turning her lithe body to the side until her back was resting against his chest.

From slipping one arm under her heated flesh until he reached the round fullness of her breast.

From rubbing his cheek against hers, against her shoulder, every inch of her he could reach like a starving man.

From whispering a torrent of mindless Italian at her ear, from threats to promises to pleading.

From smiling when she woke up with a soft mewl and when her sleep-mussed eyes alighted on his.

From saying "I'm sorry" a hundred times.

From the hardness in his chest melting when her mouth curved into a soft, welcoming smile.

From rubbing her plump nipple back and forth between his fingers.

From growling when she pressed herself into his touch wantonly.

From kissing the graceful curve of her neck.

From digging his teeth into the soft muscle of her shoulder.

From growling like a Neanderthal when she pressed her bottom into his groin, rubbing against him, until he was rock hard again.

From peeling her panties away from her legs like a man possessed.

From the utterly masculine grunt that escaped his throat when her wetness coated his fingers.

From nudging her upper leg up and away, from opening her wide for him, from pushing into her wet heat and lazily thrusting up into her until the restless beast in him calmed again.

From trailing his other hand down her silky body until it reached her clit.

From whispering, "Yes, again, *cara mia*," like a man possessed when she pleaded with him that her sensitive flesh couldn't clench and fracture again after her first release.

From the desperate need that crawled through his legs toward his spine when she turned and looked into his eyes, and said against his plundering mouth, "You can be self-ish, Dante. You can take me once without thinking of my release. I'm more than happy for you to use me for your pleasure. As you want it, whenever, wherever."

From his chest cracking wide open.

From the cold sweat that claimed his skin as he worked his fingers and himself in tandem, determined that she would fly with him again.

And when she came with his name on her lips, and her muscles clenching and releasing around him like a silken glove, he couldn't stop himself from pushing her facedown onto the bed, from pulling her up onto all fours and thrusting into her from behind.

He couldn't stop his heart from aching, his body from shuddering again and again when she turned toward him, an impish smile around her mouth and said, "Harder, Dante. Deeper, please. I want to come again. With you."

He had no idea how he managed to bring her to climax again. All he knew was that she fell apart and he lost even the semblance of control. For the first time in his life, nothing mattered but his own release. Nothing mattered but the burn riding up his thighs and pooling in his balls.

Nothing mattered except losing himself inside her. Hands fisted in her hair, teeth sinking into her shoulder, he drove in and out of her, working himself to the edge.

His climax when it came was the most powerful thing he'd ever experienced. The most raw, honest, revelatory moment in all his life. The most he had ever shared of himself, the most he had ever taken of someone.

He flopped onto her body, resting his weight on his elbows, his harsh breaths making her hair fly under him, their sweat-slicked bodies gliding and sliding against each other. Still, he wasn't satisfied. She was so fragile, so delicate beneath him. "Ali, look at me."

Hoarse. Raw. Uncivilized. Each word of his felt different. Felt new. He felt different. Somehow less, not enough for her.

She turned, her chin resting against the white sheets. Her hair flew away from her face as she blew at it, and then, after the spine-tingling experience they had just had, after the rough way he had used her, somehow she managed to smile at him. A gloriously warm smile that made her eyes shine and her mouth wide. "Hi."

A single, weightless word that lit up an incandescent joy in his chest.

When he finally noticed the uneven rhythm of her breath, he tried to move off her.

She shook her head.

"I'll crush you," he whispered, undone by the smile, by the warmth. By her.

"Not just yet."

"I'm sorry for earlier. For…leaving you like that."

"As long as you find your way back to me, we're okay, *si*?"

"*Si.*"

And then she tugged his head down to her and took his mouth in a wet, open, raw kiss that made him semi-hard between their bodies again. Her smile was pure wickedness. "That was fantastic, mind-blowing. You give good sex, babe. You're always worth the wait."

Like a teenage boy, he could feel himself blushing. He rubbed his thumb over her lip. "I didn't hurt you?"

"No, but it's your turn to compliment me. I know how fabulous I am but a girl needs compliments now and then."

He knew she was teasing but he couldn't laugh. He couldn't imagine life without her now. He rubbed his fingers over her shoulder and placed a reverent kiss to her damp skin. Emotion was hard for him, and words to express what he felt, even harder. "I'm glad I blackmailed you."

She flipped herself onto her back under him, and the rasp of her breasts against his chest made them both groan. And then her hands clasped his cheeks, her eyes shining. "I'm glad I caved."

With that simple statement, she rolled over to her side, pulled his arm over to kiss his palm and nestled into him as if she belonged there.

His wife was the bravest woman he'd ever met. And he, a powerful, arrogant thirty-six-year-old who ruled his life with precise ruthlessness, was terrified of what else she would unleash on him.

Of what else she would ask of him that he couldn't, wouldn't be able to give. Of what he'd do the day she realized that finding his way back to her simply wasn't enough.

CHAPTER ELEVEN

ALISHA STARED AT her reflection in the mirror, her eyes wide at the outrageously sexy outfit she'd chosen for the party tonight.

And this dress she'd had specially commissioned from an up-and-coming British-Indian designer was it. It was an extravaganza for a woman who'd lived in jeans and T-shirts for a decade but Ali wanted to make her parents proud tonight.

She wanted the world to know of her happiness.

She wanted to share it with these people who'd been part of Matta Steel for generations.

She wanted to embrace her part in her papa's legacy.

She wanted Dante to be proud to call her his wife.

The wide, ruffled skirt of her mauve *lehenga* had layers upon layers of ruffles, giving her the fairy-tale princess look that was all the vogue on the runway this year. But the true genius of the outfit was in the *choli* and the *dupatta*.

When the designer, Maya, had showed the sketch to Ali, her first impulse had been a resounding no. It bared too much, it was too risqué. As far as she knew, a traditional *choli lehenga* was a wide, full skirt with a blouse that bared her midriff, yes, but covered everything up front with a silky *dupatta* to trail from her shoulder.

But since Ali had asked for a modern take on it, for something that was traditional and yet looked sensual,

Maya insisted she give it a chance. And when Ali had tried it on, it had looked simply stunning.

The blouse was strapless with gossamer mauve sleeves hanging low on her arms leaving her entire neck and shoulders bare. But the silky blouse cupped her breasts from beneath, like a lover's hands, leaving the upper curves bare. Since she didn't have big boobs, it wasn't so much the cleavage that was outrageous but the way it covered only the lower half.

The *dupatta*, which was a silky shawl in the same mauve, shimmered with intricate silver thread work, hung from one shoulder.

At Ali's insistence, Maya had hitched it across her chest and pinned it to the skirt. So the effect was the mirage of the *dupatta* covering her torso on one side while her breasts played peekaboo on the other.

Big chandelier earrings hung from her ears while she left her hair down to show off the new haircut. She had made her eyes up into a subtly smoky kohl look and had dusted dark blush onto her cheeks. A light pink shimmering gloss on her lips and she was done.

She was ready to meet the world.

And she was ready to meet her husband whom she hadn't seen in three weeks.

She had so much news to share with him, so many plans to make, so many things to look forward to that she felt as if she was bubbling over with happiness.

Ali had wanted to shock and surprise Dante but she was the one who got the surprise of the century as she stepped out of the chauffeured Mercedes that evening.

Matta Mansion glittered like a new bride on the night of the Diwali party, decorated with hanging lights everywhere. Focus lights from the grounds made the white marble facade glitter like an Indian palace of old. The gardens beyond had been decorated with fairy lights, every brass and copper artwork that had been the highlight of her mom's art collection polished to a sheen.

Ali walked into the ballroom and gasped. Thousands of red, earthenware *diyas* with cotton wicks had already been lit and cast shadows on walls. She had no idea how Dante's staff had managed to lay their hands on so many of them. No idea how he'd found out all the lovely Hindu traditions that surrounded the festival of Diwali and had them implemented. Especially when he'd been in Tokyo for three weeks.

A small trio of players were seated on a divan behind the main dais, decorated with flowing silks, playing *shehnai* and *tabla*. The scent of fresh flowers filled every nook and cranny. Just the delicious aroma of all the sweets the chefs had laid out on the massive buffet table had her mouth watering.

Ali stood on the second-floor balcony and looked out over the gardens. In another hour, every inch of space would be crammed with guests Dante had insisted they invite. Dusk was just an hour away. Once everyone was here, Dante would welcome them all.

They would light some sparklers and then there would be a feast.

Tears filled her eyes as unbidden, a memory came to her, drowning her.

Of her mama decorating the house just like this when Ali had been maybe four. Of throwing open the doors to every member of staff and employee of Matta Mansion. Of dressing Ali and Vikram in traditional clothes while she herself had worn a bright red sari and the diamond necklace that Alisha now owned. Of her papa picking her up and then kissing her mama on the forehead.

"Ali?"

Ali turned so fast that she almost tripped on the hem of her *lehenga*.

Dressed in a conservative black suit with a white shirt underneath, Dante looked suave and powerful and utterly masculine. Air left her lungs in a hurried rush. The platinum cuff links she had left for him on his study table glimmered at his cuffs. That unruly hair was combed back, highlighting the harsh features, rendering him absolutely magnificent.

"You look…incredible."

The husky, rough tone of his words made butterflies flutter in her belly. Suddenly, she was glad she'd gone with Maya's outrageous creation.

His hands landed on her shoulders, the rough pads of them slithering against her bare skin. Dark eyes studied her with lingering intensity. His gaze moved from her hair to her shoulders, lingering for just a few seconds on the way the *choli* cupped her breasts. Her nipples tightened, her blood thick as honey in her veins.

"I should have believed you when you said I'd be floored, Alisha." The way he said her full name made her smile. Exasperation coated his words. "Asking me to foot the bill for that dress is tricking me. It bares too much, Ali."

"It's called a *lehenga*," she said swishing the wide skirt in her hands with a brazen smile. "I told the designer to make it the most spectacularly sexy outfit London has seen in a while. I told her it should befit the wife of a gorgeous, arrogant, wonderful husband. I told her the world should remember the night when Alisha Matta—"

"Vittori."

She blinked. "What?"

"Alisha Vittori. You're Alisha Vittori. Not Matta anymore."

Alisha Vittori.

It was just a name, and yet her heart thudded against her rib cage.

She scrunched her nose and his jaw tightened. "Nobody really changes their name these days."

"Mrs. Puri, in all her omniscience, it seems, was right. I find I'm a traditionalist at heart. I want my wife to take my name. I want the entire world to know that, while you have me wrapped around your finger, I have a claim on you too. I never want there to be a doubt about why I want you as my wife."

The voices downstairs floated away leaving Dante and her alone in their own world. His finger rubbed her collarbone, relentless heat spewing from the small touch.

With a groan, he covered her mouth with his. Completely. Utterly. The kiss was tenderness itself. Soft. Inviting. Opening up the whole world and putting it at her feet.

It seemed as if it was the very essence of the man he was—full of depth beneath the isolation he set upon himself, full of emotion and passion that he was determined to deny. A heart so big and that gave generously while remaining closed off to receiving anything in return.

He venerated her with those soft lips, his eyes shining because she'd given him everything. He knew it, she knew it. The words didn't need to be said. It was as she'd guessed—the only way into Dante's heart, the only way to carve a small place for herself in there, was to surrender everything. To lay everything open at his feet.

She felt as if she was stripped to flesh and bone, all her armor falling away. As if his kiss was what she was made for.

He deepened the kiss, his fingers in her hair, his hold on her heart tightening.

It spoke of things he would never say. It showed her that

she had a place in his heart too, however small. It told her that this arrogant, powerful man was no more in control of the bond between them than she was.

He kissed her as if she were the most precious thing he had ever held. He extracted a tiny velvet box from his jacket and her heart raced.

Every inch of her trembled as he pulled out a delicate-looking necklace. Three diamonds glittered in the middle of the thin chain, while tiny black beads lined up on either side. Ali stood, stunned, as he pushed her hair back and hooked the delicate chain behind her neck. It was a *mangalsutra*, the chain a husband put on his wife in the Hindu tradition.

His fingers lingered at her nape, his chin resting on her head.

She kept her head bowed, fighting the tears prickling behind her eyes. Fighting for breath. Struggling to stay still while the ground rocked from under her.

As if he understood, he wrapped his arms around her and held her tight. Her breasts pressed against his chest, her trembling legs held by the cradle of his powerful thighs.

"Mrs. Puri told me that I wasn't being fair. That your father would have demanded that I do right by you. That I was doing everything by my family's traditions, leaving yours out."

"She called you and took you to task?" Ali demanded. "She worships the ground you walk on."

The few seconds he waited resonated with his reluctance. "I called her and asked her to explain how things had been done with your parents. And she walked me through them. Ali, if you want a Hindu wedding or a reception, or a *mehendi* night or a bachelorette party, whatever you want, I want you to have it. I don't want you to resent me ten years down the line because I cheated you out of some tradition or custom. I don't want you to tell me in thirty years that

I didn't give you a bride's trousseau as custom demands. I want you to have everything you desire, *cara mia*."

He had the whole mansion looking like it had during her childhood. Like a beautiful bride waiting for her groom.

He had decided that they would resurrect the tradition of the Diwali party, which had been her mother's yearly extravaganza. He'd invited so many of the old staff, Matta employees, charity workers, even Jai.

He had asked Mrs. Puri so that he could do right by her family's traditions.

And he claimed, again and again, that he had no heart to give. That he wasn't a romantic. That he didn't do relationships. That he didn't do love. Her heart seemed to have crawled into her throat and lodged there. Making even breathing difficult.

"Look at me, Alisha," he said in that commanding tone of his.

Chin quivering, Ali did. If he kissed her, she would melt into him. He was everything she had ever wanted and she felt as if she were in some fairyland where all her wishes were being granted. Terror filled her when she thought of that midnight stroke that would return everything back to reality, to a world without him.

"Will you be my wife, Ali?"

She took his hands in hers, tears running down her cheeks, and brought his hand to her cheek. "I don't need ceremonies to define this thing between us. The first time I walked into your bedroom, I became your wife, Dante. You're making me cry and I look like something the cat dragged in when I cry…and—oh, no, my makeup," she wailed.

Laughing, he produced a handkerchief and carefully blotted her cheeks. "You're always beautiful and it will drive me insane the whole evening that other men will see you in that outfit."

"Did Mrs. Puri tell you that according to Hindu traditions, you're stuck with me for seven lifetimes?"

He nodded and there was such tenderness in his eyes
that it stole her breath. "I'm hoping that this is the first one.
Shall we go down?"

"It's not fair," she whined.

He frowned. "What's not fair?"

"It's been three weeks and I'm dying to get you into bed,
or against the wall, and there are all these people waiting
for us…"

He pressed a chaste kiss to her temple as if to tease her
even more. "Patience, *tesoro*. Remember, good things come
to those who wait."

And he was worth the wait.

By the time they had seen the last guest off and were riding the elevator toward Dante's penthouse, it was past one
in the morning.

Ali was so tired she felt like she could fall asleep standing up.

His arm around her shoulders, Dante pulled her to his side
until all her weight was against him. His mouth was soft at
her temple. And then he nuzzled her throat, the gesture less
sexual and more tender. "Bed for you, I think. I've been waiting all evening to get you out of your…*lehenga*," he said gin-
gerly, trying out the word, "but I'll do it to put you to bed."

Ali smiled so widely that she thought her mouth would
crack. "No, no, no. I have a million things to tell you, plans
to make for us and it's been killing me to wait."

His gaze lingered on the shadows under her eyes. "Ali,
we can do it tomorrow morning. I'm not going anywhere."

"Please, Dante."

He laughed and pressed a swift kiss to her mouth. "Well,
if you ask nicely like that, *si*."

Excitement replacing the exhaustion, Ali hit the number for the floor to her studio. "First thing on the agenda for tonight—do you want to see my work?"

The anticipation and the pure joy that filled his eyes made him look breathtakingly beautiful. "*Si*, please."

She took his hand and dragged him with her. Just as they reached the door to the studio, she halted. "Actually, that's not the first item."

"Ali, I hate that I've made you so insecure with my cruel words, but please, *cara mia*."

"No. It's not that. I... I just... I came up with this during the party."

His smile disappeared. "No, you can't be friends with Jai. I had Izzy invite him because you said he was looking for capital for his start-up and it would be good for him to network and meet some of the shareholders. It's not that I don't trust you, it's just that your ex in your life is not something I can tolerate. Please don't—"

She wanted to argue just for the heck of it. But Dante was taking tentative steps toward communicating his feelings with her and really, she didn't even want Jai in her life. They had nothing in common anymore. Instead she said, "Okay. I won't."

He looked so shocked by her easy acceptance that she laughed out loud.

"Just like that?"

Going on her toes, she whispered, "Today's your lucky day, mister." She swiped her tongue over his lower lip until he opened for her. "I hope you take complete advantage of it. Of me." His answer was to kiss the hell out of her, until she forgot her own name.

He was panting when he pulled away, lust etched on every inch of his face. "If you want me to listen to all the items on your agenda, you had better keep your hands to yourself, *cara mia*."

Out of breath herself, Ali nodded.

It took her several minutes to retrace their conversation. "So, the first thing is that today, I... Having the party at the mansion, it made me realize... I want to live there. I mean, us, I want us to live there. To make our home there, make it a happy place again, fill it with good memories and laughter and..." She swallowed the word *love* at the last second.

"I think it would have made both Mama and Papa and even Vikram happy, don't you think? We can—" heat swarmed her cheeks at the intensity of his gaze "—like you said, when we're ready, we... I do want a big family and the grounds and the house would be perfect to raise an army of kids."

"An army?" he said in such a low voice that she laughed again.

"*Si.*"

"Okay. We'll live at Matta Mansion."

She took his hand and rubbed the palm against her cheek. Her heart was in danger of exploding out of her chest. "Just like that?" she said, trying to breathe over the lump in her throat.

"Today's your lucky day. I hope you take advantage of that, *bella mia*."

I love you so much. The words flitted to her lips but Ali swallowed them away. She didn't want to bring awkwardness to such a beautiful day and she didn't want to make him uncomfortable.

Instead, she just nodded, took his hand and pulled him into her studio.

Dante had no idea what to expect. His disparaging comments before still shamed him. So he had forced himself to keep an open mind, to support and encourage her when she needed it, to catch her if she faced disappointment. Not because he thought she would fail but because art was such a subjective world and he just...he wanted to be there for her.

As Ali turned on the huge industrial-strength lights he'd had the workmen install when he had purchased two flats and had them converted into a large open studio for her, he told himself that whatever she showed him, he would praise her, he would encourage her effort. He would—

A number of blown-up framed photographs stood leaning against the walls all around him.

He found himself at an utter loss for words.

Each print was a candid shot—a starkly beautiful life moment captured in time. One was a naked woman in the kitchen of that restaurant in Bangkok—no hint of vulnerability in her face as she met the camera head-on. One was a woman feeding her child—utter bliss on her face. One was a man on his knees in front of a woman with his mouth on her sex, one of a woman covered in bruises from fingerprints on her neck to the impression of shoes on her belly and it went on and on and on.

Every single one of them was hauntingly beautiful, tender and yet real at the same time—life in all its glory and indignity—and each one spoke volumes of the extraordinary talent and perspective of the woman who had captured them.

Shame and pride warred within him, and still he had no words to say.

"Dante?" she whispered, no tentativeness or need for validation in her words.

Standing amid her black-and-white and color prints, she was a goddess.

He went to her, took her hands, kissed her knuckles. Searched his mind for the right words. *Cristo*, what could he say that would tell her how humbled he felt that she had shared them with him.

"I don't know why you did it, but thank you for buying me that camera all those years ago."

He shook his head, emotion clogging his throat. "Don't… lay this at my feet, *bella*. If I hadn't, you'd have found another way to make it happen. You're…your work is…" he laughed. "Your papa…he would have been so proud, Ali. He would have been elated to see how extraordinary you are."

Tears overflowed in her eyes and fell down onto her cheeks. She came to him like lightning and fire and he caught her in his embrace. Held her while she cried. Glad that for once in his life, he'd found the right words to say to her.

Hoping that every time she came to him for something like this, he had enough to give her what she needed.

Hoping that, for the first time in his life, his past hadn't robbed him completely of his ability to give affection, to receive the love she gave him.

Ali had no idea how long she stayed in Dante's arms like that. All she knew was that life couldn't get more beautiful. Or more giving. He was so solid and real and wonderful in her arms that she never wanted to let go. The moment was so tender and loving and complete she almost changed her mind. Almost.

But she didn't want to start their new life hiding something so important from him. She didn't want to make this decision on her own. She shouldn't have to. Especially since it affected them both. And she was sure, whether he agreed with her or not, he would want to know.

So, as much as she wanted to stay in his arms and beg him to take her to bed, she took a long breath, filled her lungs with the essence of him and pulled back slightly. "Do I look all grungy then?" she said, still trying to find the right words. "I have too much makeup on to be crying every other second."

He didn't smile. A little line appeared between his brows, as if he knew she was delaying. But then, he did know her very well.

"What is the third thing on your agenda?"

She stepped out of his embrace completely and faced him. "My agent wants me to do an exhibit, as soon as possible, actually. Her team is trying to decide which gallery will display it best. And she told me that they're all trying to get it to theirs. It will start in London, and based on the reception, it might…go to other cities, like New York, Beijing. We're still talking about the details.

"It's all happening so fast. I've hired an employment agency and put out ads for employees for the charity too."

"That's fantastic news. The world should see your talent. And it looks like you're doing the best thing for the charity. You can still be involved at a higher level. Are you worried about the travel?"

Ali shook her head and swallowed the misgivings in her throat. "No, no… That's not it. It's just that something else has come up too. Do you remember that photography apprenticeship I had wanted to go on but that never happened?"

He didn't completely withdraw, but his mouth tightened. *"Si."*

Ali looked down at her laced fingers. Christ, why was this so hard? Why did it suddenly feel like there was an ocean between them already? "My agent showed some of my work to this American entrepreneur/philanthropist who puts together teams to work in some of the remotest areas of the world, like Tibet, Bosnia, Haiti. You know, sometimes they're war zones, sometimes it's just a rebuilding effort to clean up after natural disasters.

"Anyway, he got in touch with me a week ago, out of the blue. No introductions. Not his agent reaching out to mine. Just called me one afternoon when I was here and asked me if I could meet him in a couple of hours because he was leaving London that night.

"Two minutes into the meeting, he asked me to join his team on the next expedition. Apparently, he always hires a world-renowned photographer to capture the expedition, sort of to bring those things to the world's notice. My agent told me he's never asked anyone as young as me before, but apparently, when she forwarded some of my work to him, he instantly decided that he wanted me. I've been reading up all about his teams and the trips they take, and I realized what an honor it is to be chosen."

Dante covered the distance between them and hugged her tightly. "I'm not surprised."

Some of her tension dissolved. When he held her like that, it felt as if there wasn't anything she couldn't conquer. "Yeah?"

He tipped her chin up. "You didn't say yes?"

"No. I… First, I was just so stunned. It took me a while to realize what a big compliment it was to my work. Not until I Googled the hell out of him. And then that night, my agent asked me what I was waiting for. I told her I'd have to talk to you. I mean, it's a decision that affects both of us, our life together and I… It didn't feel right to just say yes and then tell you about it afterward. I wanted to talk to you about it. It's been so hard to just sit on it while you were in Tokyo."

Once again, Dante had no words. He kept thinking he had the measure of her and she kept surprising him. His chest felt tight, as if his heart was too big for it. "Ali…"

His hands shook as he gathered her to him. "I'm glad you waited to discuss it with me although it's not necessary. This is your career and I want it to go from height to height until the whole world takes pleasure in your work."

She nodded but her anxiety was like a cloak around her. He hated to see her smile dim. He pushed the hair back from her shoulder and covered the silky bare skin. "What is worrying you? Is there a fee you have to pay? Don't worry about finances or the charity."

"No, there isn't. Of course, I don't get paid either because it's a privilege to join his team."

"So what's the problem?"

"The next trip that he wants me to go on...will leave in a month."

"And?"

"I'll be gone for at least eighteen months. Might be more. If I agree and sign the contract, I'm bound by it. I can't just up and leave if I don't like it. Of course, there will be scheduled breaks but I'm told they won't be long."

It was like a punch to his stomach. He couldn't imagine not seeing her for eighteen months. *Cristo*, he felt like a teenager saying goodbye to his first crush. It felt like a lifetime. "I see," he said, just to give himself time to gather his fragmented thoughts.

Ali hid her face in his chest, as if afraid of his reaction. The graceful line of her profile, the small tremors he could feel in her shoulders... This was the opportunity of a lifetime.

He couldn't be selfish. Her commitment to their marriage, to him, it was more than he'd ever expected to have in life. She was more than he'd ever expected to have. "There's nothing to it but that you go. *Si*, it will be hard not to see each other for that long but I... I'm going nowhere. Our life together is going nowhere.

"Just don't…fall in love with some guy on this expedition." The words fell away before he could prevent them. He cringed at how pathetic and insecure he sounded. But there was no arresting that chain of thought. He pulled her left hand up, the diamond winking at him. "Remember that you belong to me, *cara mia*."

Brown eyes glared at him through thick lashes. "It's not funny, Dante. Do you really not trust me?"

He rubbed his thumb over her cheek, compulsively. "Of course I trust you. You're just…" He blew out a big breath. Damn it, he'd always been strong and he needed to be strong for her in this. He couldn't use her affection for him to sway her. She would come to hate him for it and he couldn't bear that.

"Eighteen months is a long time!" He slammed his head back. That was the exact opposite of what he meant to say.

"Exactemente!" Instead of looking upset, she nodded her head fiercely. "I was hoping you'd say that. I don't think I can go that long without seeing you. No, I know I can't. These two-and three-week trips to Tokyo have been bad enough." She nuzzled into his neck, and he felt the flick of her tongue at his throat. The bite of her teeth at his pulse. He hardened instantly against the soft curve of her bottom and she groaned. "I…was hoping you'd come with me."

Dios mio, when she moved like that, all he could think of was to be inside her. Eighteen months was a long time, his brain repeated the thing on a loop. It took him a couple of minutes to process her last sentence. "What?"

She pulled back so that she could look into his eyes. "You know, like a long honeymoon. Except instead of luxury hotels as you're used to, it will be tents or huts or whatever accommodation they give us. We wouldn't have to be apart at all. I checked with my agent and his team and they said spouses are welcome. Of course they'll expect you to pitch in, but I don't see that as a problem. That way eighteen months will just be a breeze and then we can return—"

"Stop, Alisha! Just…stop talking." He felt as if she'd knocked him down.

She turned those big eyes on him. Expectant. Wide. Full of hope and happiness.

But nothing could stop his answer. "I can't just take eighteen months off. I run a billion-dollar company."

"I know. I mean I'm sure you can stay in contact with your teams even in the remotest areas. The voting shares have been officially transferred so you don't have to worry about a coup or any such thing. Izzy told me how Uncle Nitin tried to sabotage the Japanese deal and how that forced you to finally put him on a leash. So he's not a worry anymore either."

Dante stiffened. "What Nitin almost got away with proves that I need to be at the helm. I can't just walk away."

She leaped out of his arms, as if being near him was unbearable. Shaking her head, clutching her midriff. As if he was supposed to agree instantly to her madcap idea. "No one's asking you to quit Matta Steel. I don't think what you do is easy or small. I know that thousands of livelihoods depend on the company. If you're willing to at least give this thought, I'm sure it'll be a matter of snapping your fingers to have the technology to support it ready."

Dante paced the floor, feeling as if there was some dark force coming at him but he couldn't do anything to avoid it. As if he was losing her, but there was nothing he could do to hold on to her.

What she was suggesting was…unthinkable. The company was everything to him. "I can't go away for eighteen months, Ali. I just can't. What you're suggesting is childish and… I understand you're excited and got carried away but it's not that simple."

"Ask me not to go then. This is a great opportunity to build my career, to bring exposure to my work, yes. But at the end of the day, it is only one way. Ask me to give it up for you, for us, for our marriage and I'll do it. I'll happily stay, Dante. Please, just ask me. Demand it of me."

"*No!* Don't do that, not for me. I don't deserve it. Damn it, Ali... I can't give you anything in return for such a sacrifice." The words piled out of his mouth, a strange tightening in his throat. It felt as if she was cutting his very breath off. Felling him at every turn. Like his heart was in her hand and she was fisting it tight.

"It's not a sacrifice, Dante. That's what you don't seem to understand. I love you. I want to spend my life with you. I want to make our marriage a priority. I just... Don't cut me down at every turn. Please, Dante."

He didn't want her sacrifice. It would choke him for the rest of their lives. "I can't ask you to set your career aside for me. For us."

Hurt made her stomach so tight that Ali felt as if she couldn't breathe. He wasn't even going to consider any option she presented. He refused to take a step toward her, and he forbade her from taking one toward him. She pulled at her hair, fear beating a tattoo in her veins. "So how does this work then? What if, after this trip, I go on another one? How will this marriage work then?"

"You're asking me hypothetical questions to which I have no answers. Matta Steel is my lifeblood. I can't shirk my responsibilities. I can't risk something I have given decades to."

"Won't or can't, Dante?" she said, anger coming to her rescue. "What's the point of being a bloody billionaire if you can't even be your own boss? What's the point of this marriage if we are together when it's convenient for your career and mine? When you won't let me give myself to it completely and neither will you? You would have us live in this strange…limbo just because you fear love?"

A cold frost filled his eyes, turning his gray eyes unbearably distant. Even cruel. He was a stranger again. A man she hated. A man who had not an ounce of tenderness in him. A man who cared about nothing but the company. "Don't make this small thing between us into a transaction, Alisha. Don't twist this into some sort of big, romantic gesture that I'm supposed to do for you to prove what you mean to me.

"You don't get to dictate how this marriage works. Now or in the future. I can't just step away from the company I've given everything to, from the role for which I married you in the first place. I'm not my father. I never will be."

She nodded, suddenly everything so clear to her naively wishful heart. "But I'm not asking you to make a big, romantic gesture. I'm not asking you to give up Matta Steel. I'm just…"

It wasn't that he wasn't even giving her idea a chance. It was the rigidity with which he did it. He'd always draw careful, clear lines between them. Always be a little out of her reach. Always decide what their relationship would be and would not be. Push him a little and he trampled her. Demand a little more than he wanted to give and he would crush her heart.

God, she'd been so stupid. She'd imagined them in some tent under the stars in some remote location, weaving an even stronger bond for life. She'd imagined having him all to herself. She'd built so many castles in the air.

The idea of walking away from their life together before it had even begun made her chest ache. "No. You won't even give this thing between us a chance. God, Dante, you don't even know how to take that I'm happy and what I'm willing to give. You're so terrified that I'll demand some price for not going. For simply loving you. What do I have to do to prove that I won't? How long will I have to worry what I say or do will make you think I'm asking something you can't give. That I'm asking too much of you. It will always be me reaching out. Always be me waiting for you to love me, maybe just a little."

"I can't… I won't be manipulated in this relationship, Alisha."

"Then there's nothing more to be said except goodbye."

"Ali—"

"I'm going back to the mansion. Don't come after me, please. Not tonight. I… I'll leave soon and it will provide you with the perfect excuse to tell your precious media. And don't worry, your reputation will be pristine, just like always. I won't tell the world I fell in love with a man who truly doesn't know the meaning of the word."

Every instinct in her clamored to wait for him. To let him catch her, to let him hold her, to let him chase away the pain in her heart. But he was the one breaking it. He was the one throwing it away, the one who didn't realize what her love truly meant. He would always measure it like a transaction, always think of it as a weakness.

She had put her world, her heart, at his feet. And he had simply kicked it away.

So she held her head high and went back to the elevator.

She'd lived alone before, she'd somehow made it through, and she would do it this time too. Even if it felt like the pieces of her were too many ever to mend again.

CHAPTER TWELVE

SHE WAS GONE.

She'd been gone for over a month.

First, she left the flat, bunking down one floor below him, in the studio he had had built for her. Because he'd been worried about what trouble she would get herself into, and he wanted to keep an eye on her. Because he'd thought Alisha was a liability he was taking on. And he would need to do damage control.

The first couple of days in the flat without her had been his first glimpse of hell. Memories of her seemed to have been absorbed into the very walls, the very fabric of his home.

He'd lived alone for countless years and yet the silence now had a different, haunting quality. So Dante had taken to sleeping at his suite at work.

Then she'd walked up to the flat one evening when he'd returned for a change of clothes.

Clad in that off-the-shoulder loose sweater and some kind of leggings, she'd looked so excruciatingly lovely that it had been a kick to his gut. "You cut your hair," he'd said, unable or unwilling to keep a possessive tone out of his voice.

She hadn't even called him on it. Fingering the wispy ends that framed her delicate face and highlighted those sharp cheekbones, she'd simply said, "It will be easier this way. I won't have time to wash and blow-dry."

you want. We'll never return to London again. Never buy a home. We'll do it all your way."

Ali sank to her knees and burrowed into him. "No. All I wanted was for you to take a step toward me. To let me love you like I want to. To love me back just a little."

"I love you a lot," he said and utter joy spread through her.

"I will make my home with you, wherever you are, Dante. You're my home, don't you see? Always, you've been the place I can land, the person I can love. You're everything to me."

Dante picked his wife up in his arms, his heart bursting with love for his wife.

* * * * *

COMING SOON!

We really hope you enjoyed reading this book. If you're looking for more romance, be sure to head to the shops when new books are available on

Thursday 15th November

To see which titles are coming soon, please visit
millsandboon.co.uk

MILLS & BOON

MILLS & BOON

Coming next month

MARRIED FOR HIS ONE-NIGHT HEIR
Jennifer Hayward

'What were you going to tell Leo when the time came? The truth? Or were you going to tell him that his father was a high-priced thug?'

She flinched. Lifted a fluttering hand to her throat. 'I hadn't thought that far ahead,' she admitted. 'We've been too busy trying to survive. Making a life for ourselves. Leo's welfare has been my top priority.'

Which he believed. It was the only reason he wasn't going to take his child and walk. Do to her exactly what she'd done to him. Because as angry as he was, as unforgivable as what she had done had been, he had to take the situation she'd been in into account. It had taken guts for her to walk away from her life. Courage. She'd put Leo first, something his own mother hadn't done. And she had been young and scared. All things he couldn't ignore.

Gia set her gaze on his, apprehension flaring in her eyes. 'I can't change the past, Santo, the decisions I made. But I can make this right. Clearly,' she acknowledged, 'you are going to want to be a part of Leo's life. I was thinking about solutions last night. I thought you could visit us here... Get Leo used to the idea of having you around, and then, when he is older, more able to understand the situation, we can tell him the truth.'

A slow curl of heat unraveled inside of him, firing the blood in his veins to dangerously combustible levels. 'And what do you propose we tell him when I visit? That I am that *friend* you referred to the other night? How many *friends* do you have, Gia?'

Her face froze. 'I have been building a *life* here. Establishing a career. There has been no time for dating. All I do is work and spend time with Leo, who is a handful as you can imagine, as all three-year-olds tend to be.'

The defensively issued words lodged themselves in his throat. 'I can't actually imagine,' he said softly, 'because you've deprived me of the right to know that, Gia. You have deprived me of *everything*.'

She blanched. He set down his glass on the bar. 'I am his *father*. I have missed three years of his life. You think a *weekend pass* is going to suffice? A few dips in the sea as he learns to swim?' He shook his head. 'I want *every day* with him. I want to wake up with him bouncing on the bed. I want to take him to the park and throw a ball around. I want to hear about his day when I tuck him into bed. I want it *all*.'

'What else can we do?' she queried helplessly. 'You live in New York and I live here. Leo is settled and happy. A limited custody arrangement is the only realistic solution for us.'

'It is *not* a viable proposition.' His low growl made her jump. 'That's not how this is going to work, Gia.'

She eyed him warily. 'Which part?'

'All of it. I have a proposal for you. It's the only one on the table. Nonnegotiable on all points. Take it or leave it.'

The wariness written across her face intensified. 'Which is?'

'We do what's in the best interests of our child. You marry me, we create a life together in New York and give Leo the family he deserves.'

Continue reading
MARRIED FOR HIS ONE-NIGHT HEIR
Jennifer Hayward

www.millsandboon.co.uk

LET'S TALK
Romance

For exclusive extracts, competitions
and special offers, find us online:

- **f** facebook.com/millsandboon
- **🐦** @MillsandBoon
- **📷** @MillsandBoonUK

Get in touch on 01413 063232

For all the latest titles coming soon, visit
millsandboon.co.uk/nextmonth